Candy Canes & Sweet Dreams

Mistletoe Falls Series, Book #4

Tara Baisden

Sterling Ridge Press LLC

Copyright

Published by: Sterling Ridge Press, LLC www.sterlingridgepress.com

ISBN: 978-1-966093-39-8 Printed in the United States of America

First Edition: October 2025

For permissions, contact: tara@tarabaisden.com or visit www.tarabaisden.com

Dedication

To every woman who has packed her life into boxes and driven toward
hope—
To the small towns that welcome strangers like family—
To the patient hearts who love us while we learn to love ourselves—
And to the Aunt Phyllises in the world, who see something special in us
long before we see it in ourselves.
This one's for you.
Sweet dreams and sweeter tomorrows,
Tara

Contents

Chapter 1

The eviction notice taped to the apartment door was just the perfect ending to what had already been a terrible Tuesday in Megan Caldwell's life.

She stared at the bright orange paper fluttering in the November wind, reading the words "FINAL NOTICE" in bold black letters that seemed to mock her with their certainty. Behind the door, she could hear her roommates engaged in what sounded like an argument.

Megan closed her eyes and counted to ten. Then twenty. Then gave up on the counting entirely because no number was high enough to make this day better.

The promotion she'd been promised at her job at the copy center had gone to Brandon, a twenty-two-year-old who still lived with his parents and whose biggest qualification seemed to be his ability to smile and flirt with female customers. Her manager had delivered the news with all the sensitivity of someone canceling a dentist appointment, suggesting that maybe Megan should "work on her enthusiasm" if she wanted to be considered for future opportunities.

Future opportunities. Right. Because six months of showing up on time, never calling in sick, and covering everyone else's shifts clearly hadn't demonstrated enough enthusiasm.

She pushed open the apartment door to find Taylor and Stephanie in a heated discussion about whose video game system was taking up too much space in the living room. Brittany sat cross-legged on the couch, painting her toenails a blinding shade of purple. And somewhere in the back bedroom, Jenna's music thudded through the thin walls with a bass line that made Megan's teeth ache.

Nobody looked up when she entered. Nobody asked about her day. Nobody noticed the way her shoulders slumped or how she had to step over three pairs of shoes and a pizza box to reach the hallway that led to her room.

Her twin bed took up most of the space, with just enough room for a dresser she'd found at a thrift store and a milk crate that served as her nightstand. Her clothes hung on a tension rod she'd mounted herself because the "closet" didn't have one.

This was what twenty-eight looked like when everything had gone wrong so far in your life and you were stuck in an endless rut that kept cycling round and round with no exit.

Megan sank onto her bed and pulled out her phone, scrolling through her bank account with the kind of resignation that came from already knowing the news would be bad. Rent was due in five days. After she covered her portion of the rent, she had a little over two hundred dollars left to live on until her next paycheck. And if that eviction notice was real—which, given her luck, it probably was—she'd need first and last month's rent for a new place.

A new place that she couldn't afford on her own.

A new place that would most likely be just as terrible as this one.

Her phone buzzed with a text from her mother in Florida: *Rick and I are headed to the Keys for a week. Just wanted you to know.*

Rick. Her mother's new husband, the reason Sandra Caldwell had moved to Tampa and left Megan behind in Kentucky with a cheerful wave and promises to visit that hadn't materialized yet. Not that Megan blamed her mother for wanting a fresh start. Sandra had earned that after years of working double shifts as a nurse and raising Megan alone after the divorce.

After her father left.

Megan closed the text without responding. She wasn't doing well, but her mother didn't need to know that.

She grabbed a package of ramen noodles from the box where she kept her food stash hidden from roommates who treated anything in the kitchen as communal property, regardless of who'd actually paid for it. As she was opening her bedroom door, her phone rang.

Unknown number. Tennessee area code.

Probably a spam call. Or a credit card company trying to get her to apply for a line of credit. Or someone trying to sell her an extended warranty on her car.

She almost didn't answer. But something made her thumb hit the green button—some tiny spark of curiosity or maybe just the need to hear another human voice, even if it was a recording.

"Hello?"

"Hello, is this Megan Caldwell?" The voice was male, warm but professional, with a hint of a Southern accent that softened the consonants.

"This is she." Megan sat up straighter on the bed.

"Ms. Caldwell, my name is Kyle Porter. I'm an attorney in Mistletoe Falls, Tennessee." He paused, and something in that pause made

Megan's heart start to beat faster. "I'm deeply sorry to be the one to tell you this, but your aunt, Phyllis Caldwell, passed away last week."

The words didn't make sense at first. Aunt Phyllis. The name conjured images of a cozy candy shop, the smell of chocolate and peppermint, and a kind woman with a smile that lit up the room and drew a person in. But those memories were old, dusty things from childhood visits that had stopped when Megan was thirteen.

When her father left.

"I... I didn't know," Megan managed, her voice sounding strange even to her own ears. "I mean, we lost touch years ago. After my parents divorced."

"I understand. Your aunt's passing was sudden—a heart attack. She went peacefully, if that provides any comfort."

"It does. Thank you." Megan pressed her fingers against her eyes, fighting back the sting of tears for a woman she barely remembered but had never stopped missing. Those childhood visits to Mistletoe Falls had been the bright spots in her early years, the place where everything felt magical and right. Where someone had seemed genuinely happy to see her and made her feel loved and wanted.

"Ms. Caldwell, the reason I'm calling is that your aunt left a will, and you're named as the primary beneficiary. The inheritance includes some significant assets that we need to discuss. I know this is a lot to process right now, but I'd like to arrange a time for you to come to Mistletoe Falls so we can go over everything in detail."

Megan's brain stuttered over the words. Inheritance. Assets. Beneficiary.

"I'm sorry, could you say that again?"

She heard papers rustling on the other end of the line. "Your aunt left you her business and property in Mistletoe Falls. The details are extensive, which is why I'd prefer to discuss them in person rather than over the phone. Would it be possible for you to come to Tennessee? Anytime that works for you, though sooner would be better for settling the estate."

"Her business." Megan's voice sounded hollow. "The candy shop?"

"Yes, Sugar & Spice Candy Shop. Along with the building it's housed in and the apartment. Your aunt thought very highly of you, Ms. Caldwell. She spoke of you often."

The tears Megan had been fighting spilled over. "She did?"

"She did. Phyllis and I were friends, and she talked about you often—always with such warmth. I remember her saying once, 'There's something about little Meggie... she's something special for sure.' She believed in you, Ms. Caldwell. That much is clear through her wishes in her will."

The words hit Megan like a physical force. Believed in you. When was the last time anyone had said that to her? When was the last time anyone had believed she was capable of anything?

"I can come." The words came out before she'd fully thought them through. "I can leave tomorrow. I just need the address."

"That's wonderful." She could hear the smile in Kyle Porter's voice. "My office is at 665 Hollyberry Lane—we can meet there to go over everything. Does sometime in the afternoon work for you? The drive from Bowling Green is probably about five hours."

Megan grabbed a pen and scribbled the address on the back of a receipt. Hollyberry Lane. Of course, an attorney's office in a place called Mistletoe Falls would be on a street called Hollyberry Lane. The image made her want to laugh and cry at the same time.

"Afternoon is perfect. Thank you, Mr. Porter."

"Kyle, please. And Ms. Caldwell?" He paused, and when he spoke again, his voice carried a warmth that made her chest ache. "I'm looking forward to meeting you, and safe travels."

After they said goodbye, Megan sat on her bed staring at the address she'd written down, her phone still clutched in her hand. Outside her door, the argument about video game systems had escalated into a debate about whose turn it was to clean the bathroom.

She looked around her closet-sized room, at the life she had that wasn't really a life at all, just an endless series of temporary solutions and compromises that had somehow become permanent.

An inheritance. A business. An apartment.

A chance.

A gift.

At this point in her life, what did she have to lose?

Megan pulled her suitcase from under the bed and started packing. She didn't have much, and everything she owned could fit easily in her Honda Civic with room to spare.

That realization should have been depressing, but instead it felt like freedom.

By the time she'd sorted through her belongings, separating what she'd keep from what she'd donate, it was past ten o'clock. Megan's entire life sat stacked against the wall of her bedroom in seven cardboard boxes and a suitcase that had seen better days.

It was pathetic, really. Twenty-eight years of living, reduced to something that could fit in the trunk and back seat of her eight-year-old car. But it also made things simple.

The apartment had finally quieted, her roommates asleep or at least pretending to be. Megan stood in the kitchen, making a cup of instant coffee with hot water from the tap because the coffee maker had broken weeks ago.

She thought about her father, about the day he'd left when she was thirteen. He'd waited until her mother was at work, then packed his car while Megan watched from the porch. "Sometimes people need a fresh start," he'd said, his eyes not quite meeting hers. "You understand, right, kiddo?"

She hadn't understood then. She'd spent years not understanding, wondering what she'd done wrong, what had made her not worth staying for.

But maybe this was her fresh start.

Maybe Aunt Phyllis, who'd sent birthday and Christmas cards every year, who'd remembered her even when her own father hadn't, was giving her the chance to make something of herself. A fresh start.

Megan washed the coffee cup and left it on the dish drainer. She'd tell her roommates in the morning that she was leaving. She'd text her manager at the copy center that she wouldn't be coming back. She'd call her mother from the road and try to explain what she was doing, even though she didn't fully understand it herself.

***

The November morning was cold and gray as she pulled away from the apartment complex.

Her phone's GPS directed her toward Interstate 65 South, the calm voice promising arrival in Mistletoe Falls, Tennessee, in four hours and forty-three minutes. Megan merged into early morning traffic, the Honda's engine rattling in a way that it had been doing for months but that she'd learned to ignore.

The road stretched ahead, and somewhere in the Tennessee mountains, a place called Mistletoe Falls was waiting. A candy shop was waiting. An inheritance she didn't understand was waiting.

And Kyle Porter, with his warm voice and genuine kindness, was waiting.

Megan pressed the gas pedal and drove toward the unknown, toward possibility, toward a future that terrified and thrilled her in equal measure.

She wondered what Aunt Phyllis had been thinking, leaving everything to a niece she hadn't seen in years. She wondered what kind of business she was about to inherit, what kind of place Mistletoe Falls had become, and whether her memories of magic and safety had been real or just the rose-tinted recollections of childhood.

Furthermore, she wondered if Kyle Porter looked anything like his voice sounded.

The highway signs blurred past, counting down the miles to Tennessee. Megan turned on the radio, found a station playing something upbeat and hopeful, and settled in for the drive. Her hands were steady on the wheel, her jaw set with a determination that felt both familiar and new.

Behind her, Bowling Green and all its disappointments faded into nothing. Ahead, somewhere past the state line and the mountains and the winding roads, a new chapter was beginning.

Chapter 2

The GPS had to be wrong—no place could actually look this much like a Christmas card and still be real.

Megan slowed her Honda to a crawl as she approached the Snow-bell Covered Bridge, her breath catching in her throat. The old timber bridge stretched across Mistletoe Creek, draped in evergreen garland and twinkling lights that glowed softly in the afternoon sun. Through the bridge's opening, she could see the town beyond, and the view made her wonder if she'd somehow driven onto a holiday movie set.

She eased the car onto the wooden planks; the tires hummed a different tune as pavement gave way to timber. The bridge's roof created a tunnel of soft shadows and filtered light, and for a moment, Megan felt suspended between the world she'd left behind and the one waiting ahead.

Then she emerged on the other side, and Mistletoe Falls opened before her like a memory coming to life.

The covered bridge fed directly onto Hollyberry Lane, and as Megan drove deeper into town, her childhood memories collided with the present. She remembered this place—or pieces of it, anyway. The Victorian buildings with their gingerbread trim. The way the street curved gently around what had to be the town square. But the town had grown, expanded, and become more than her thirteen-year-old mind had been able to hold.

Every building wore Christmas like a second skin. Twinkling lights outlined rooflines and wrapped around porch posts, even though it was only early November and the sun still hung in the afternoon sky. Window boxes overflowed with evergreen arrangements dotted with red berries and pinecones. Wreaths hung on every door, each one different but somehow harmonious with its neighbors.

This wasn't a town that decorated for Christmas. This was a town that was Christmas all year round.

Gas lamp-style streetlights marched down both sides of Hollyberry Lane, their posts wrapped in garland that looked fresh enough to smell. Wide brick sidewalks invited strolling, and wooden benches appeared at regular intervals, positioned perfectly for watching the world go by. A few people walked past shop windows, bundled in coats against the November chill, their breath visible in small clouds.

The mountains rose in the distance, their peaks dusted with snow that caught the afternoon light. Closer in, the town nestled in its valley like something protected, something treasured.

Megan's GPS announced her destination was ahead on the right, and she scanned the buildings. She'd expected a professional building, maybe brick, with a brass nameplate and frosted glass windows. Something serious and adult, where important business happened.

Instead, her GPS directed her to a building that looked like it had been designed by someone who believed in the magic of Christmas.

The building at 665 Hollyberry Lane occupied a corner lot; its cedar siding was painted a warm cream color with red trim. Two large display windows flanked a red front door, and every inch of those windows showcased elaborate Christmas scenes—a miniature village in one, a forest of decorated trees in the other. Above the door, a hand-painted sign declared "The Christmas Shop" in elegant script, with "Since 1982" in smaller letters below.

Twinkling lights framed the windows and wrapped around the porch columns. A wooden bench sat to one side of the door, and even it had a festive cushion tied to its seat.

This was where Attorney Kyle Porter worked?

Megan pulled into a parking spot across the street, turned off her engine, and sat staring at the building. Maybe she'd written down the address wrong. Maybe her GPS had made a mistake. Maybe Kyle Porter was playing some kind of an elaborate joke on her.

But her GPS insisted she'd arrived at her destination, and the address on the building matched the receipt she'd scribbled on yesterday. This was the place.

She climbed out of her car, stretching cramped muscles, and looked down at herself. Jeans, an old college sweatshirt, and sneakers that had seen better days. She'd been driving for hours, probably had coffee breath, and definitely had highway hair from the wind through her slightly open window.

Not exactly the professional image she should probably try for.

Oh well, nothing I can do about it now, she thought.

Megan crossed the street, climbed the three steps to the porch, and pushed open the red door. A bell chimed overhead—not the electronic buzz of a commercial door chime, but an actual brass bell that rang with a clear, pure note.

The shop interior hit her like stepping into a different world.

Every surface sparkled with Christmas magic. To her left, a section labeled "The North Pole Workshop" displayed toy soldiers, dancing elves, and collectible Santa figurines arranged on shelves that climbed toward a pressed tin ceiling. Straight ahead, a doorway led to another room where she could see the silver-and-white glitter of a winter wonderland theme. To her right, a cozy display featured rustic cabin decor—wooden signs, flannel stockings, and ornaments made from natural materials.

Instrumental carol music drifted through the air, soft enough to be pleasant without being overwhelming. The scent of cinnamon and pine wrapped around her like a hug. Soft lighting made everything glow, and thousands of ornaments caught that light and threw it back in tiny sparkles.

A woman of about Megan's age stood behind a counter near the back, arranging something in a display case. She looked up with a professional smile. "Welcome to The Christmas Shop! Let me know if you need any help finding something."

"I'm actually looking for Kyle Porter?" Megan's voice came out more uncertain than she'd intended. "The attorney? I have an appointment, but I think maybe—"

"You're in the right place!" The woman's smile widened, becoming genuinely warm. "Let me grab him for you." She disappeared through a doorway marked "Employees Only," calling, "Kyle! Your appointment's here!"

Megan stood awkwardly in the middle of the shop, staring at everything around her. A Christmas shop. An attorney worked at a Christmas shop. She was meeting with an attorney about a significant inheritance in a store that smelled like a gingerbread house and played "Silent Night" through hidden speakers.

Movement caught her eye, and she turned to see a man.

Megan's brain stuttered to a complete stop.

He was tall—easily over six feet—with broad shoulders that filled out his flannel shirt in a way that suggested actual physical work, a physique not earned from a gym membership. Dark hair that was just a little too long curled slightly at his collar. He had what could only be described as a workingman's build—strong, solid, and capable. Work boots and jeans completed the picture of someone who'd be more at home fixing a roof than filing legal paperwork.

And he was walking toward her with a smile that did something unfortunate to her ability to think clearly.

"May I help you?" His voice matched the one from yesterday's phone call—warm, with that soft Southern accent that turned the words into something almost musical.

Megan's mouth opened. Closed. Opened again. "I'm looking for Kyle Porter? The attorney? I'm supposed to meet him to discuss Phyliss Caldwell's will."

The man's smile widened. "That would be me."

"You're…" Megan blinked, her brain trying to reconcile the flannel-wearing, ruggedly handsome man in front of her with her mental image of the attorney she'd spoken to yesterday. "You're Kyle Porter. The attorney."

"I am." He extended his hand toward her. "And you must be Megan Caldwell. I'm so glad you made it safely."

"I just—" She gestured vaguely at the surrounding store, her hand still in his, her thoughts scrambling. "I've never heard of an attorney working out of a Christmas store."

Kyle's laugh was genuine, and he released her hand. "It's definitely not traditional. But my sister Leslie and I own this place, and it made sense to put my law office in the back for convenience. Most of my work is estate planning, contract review, and that kind of thing. Nothing that requires a downtown law office with my name on the door."

"Your sister." Megan latched onto that detail, grateful for something concrete to focus on that wasn't his forearms or the way his flannel shirt was rolled up to his elbows. "The woman at the counter?"

"That's Leslie. She runs the shop—the creative vision, customer service, all of that." His smile turned a little self-deprecating. "I handle the boring stuff. Bookkeeping, ordering, vendor contracts, legal paperwork, and anything else that needs attention around here. I practice law on the side."

"On the side," Megan repeated, still trying to wrap her head around this. "So this store—" She gestured at the sparkling wonderland around them. "This is your main job?"

"My passion," Kyle corrected gently. "The law practice... well, that's what I went to college for, and I enjoy it, but this?" His expression softened as he looked around the shop. "This makes people happy. This shop makes me happy."

Something about the way he said it made Megan's chest ache. When was the last time she'd felt passionate about anything?

"An attorney with an office in the back of a Christmas store." She shook her head, a surprised laugh escaping. "Are you for real?"

"Very real. I get that reaction a lot. Usually from people who've only ever dealt with attorneys in suits and high-rises."

"That's undoubtedly what I expected," Megan admitted. "This is... unexpected."

"Good unexpected or bad unexpected?"

The question was casual, but something in his tone suggested her answer mattered. Megan looked around the shop again—at the twinkling lights, the carefully arranged displays, and the obvious care that had gone into creating something beautiful and joyful. She thought about the sterile office building she'd imagined and the cold professionalism of attorneys in expensive suits.

"Good," she said finally. "Definitely good."

Kyle's answering smile did something warm and dangerous to her stomach.

Leslie appeared at Kyle's elbow, and Megan saw the family resemblance immediately—the same hazel eyes, the same warm smile, though Leslie's dark hair was longer and pulled back in a ponytail.

"I'm Leslie Porter, Kyle's sister and co-owner of this place," she said, extending her hand.

Megan shook her hand, grateful for the distraction from Kyle's presence. "It's nice to meet you. This store is incredible."

"Thank you! It's been in our family for years." Leslie glanced at her brother with an expression Megan couldn't quite read—fondness mixed with something that looked like gentle teasing. "Kyle, why don't you take Ms. Caldwell back to your office? I'm sure she'd like to discuss the estate matters somewhere more private than the middle of our sales floor."

"Right. Of course." Kyle gestured toward the "Employees Only" door. "My office is this way. It's nothing fancy, but it's quiet and private."

As Megan followed him through the door, she caught Leslie watching them with an expression of open curiosity. Great. She'd been in town for all of five minutes, and already the locals were forming opinions.

The back hallway was more utilitarian than the shop floor—plain walls, fluorescent lighting, and a few storage boxes stacked neatly against one wall. Kyle led her past what looked like a break room and a storage closet, then stopped at a door marked with a small brass nameplate: "Kyle Porter, Attorney at Law."

He opened the door and gestured for her to enter first. "Welcome to my office."

The room was small but surprisingly professional. A sturdy wooden desk occupied most of the space, its surface organized with neat stacks of files and a laptop. Bookshelves lined one wall, filled with legal volumes and what looked like local history books. Two comfortable chairs faced the desk, and a small window overlooked what appeared to be a courtyard garden behind the building.

The only concession to the Christmas shop outside was a small pine tree in the corner, decorated with simple white lights.

"Have a seat." Kyle moved around to the other side of the desk, pulling a file from his drawer. "Can I get you anything? Water, coffee? I think Leslie just made a fresh pot."

"I'm fine, thank you." Megan settled into one of the chairs, her hands gripping her purse a little too tightly. Now that they were alone in a professional setting, the reality of why she was here came rushing back. Aunt Phyllis was gone. She'd been mentioned in her will. And this man—this impossibly attractive, flannel-wearing man who owned a Christmas shop—was about to tell her more about this unexpected gift.

Kyle sat down across from her, and his expression shifted from friendly to gentle, professional concern. "Before we get into the legal details, I want to say again how sorry I am about Phyllis. She was a remarkable woman."

"You knew her well?"

"Yes." His smile turned nostalgic. "Phyllis and I served on the town's business council together. She had strong opinions about preserving Mistletoe Falls' character while still welcoming growth. And she made the best peppermint fudge I've ever tasted. She'd bring it to every council meeting."

The detail was so specific, so real, that Megan felt tears prick her eyes. "I remember her peppermint fudge. She used to make it for me when I visited as a kid."

"She talked about those visits." Kyle's voice was soft. "She mentioned you often—always with such warmth."

Megan swallowed hard against the lump in her throat. "I don't understand why she left me anything. We hadn't seen each other in years. After my parents divorced, well... my life just changed, and I lost touch with her."

"Sometimes the people who believe in us the most are the ones who see us clearly even from a distance." Kyle opened the file on his desk. "And Phyllis was very clear about what she wanted. She asked me to revise this will last year, and you were her only heir."

"Only?" Megan's voice came out barely above a whisper. "But surely there was someone else—someone who knew her better, who deserved—"

"She chose you," Kyle said firmly but kindly. "For her own reasons, she chose you."

Chapter 3

"I have to warn you," Kyle said, adjusting his position in the leather chair across from her, "your aunt Phyllis was full of surprises, and this inheritance will probably be full of them for you."

Megan tried to smile, but her hands were shaking slightly as she gripped her purse. "I'm not sure if I can handle any more surprises. Between this unexpected inheritance and finding out the attorney handling my aunt's will works out of an office in the back of a Christmas shop, I think I've exhausted my surprise quota for the day."

Kyle's answering smile was warm and genuine. "Fair enough. But I think you'll want to hear these particular surprises." He opened the file folder and pulled out several documents, arranging them on the desk between them. "Let's start with the most straightforward part—the property itself."

He pulled out what looked like a deed and turned it so Megan could see. "Sugar & Spice Candy Shop occupies the first floor of a three-story Victorian building at 136 Mistletoe Lane. The building also includes a two-bedroom apartment on the second floor and storage space on the third floor. Phyllis owned the entire building outright, and now... it's yours."

"The whole building." Megan's voice sounded hollow in her own ears. "Not just the shop, but the building."

"The whole building," Kyle confirmed. "No mortgage, no liens. It's yours, free and clear."

Megan stared at the deed, at her name typed neatly on the line that used to hold Phyllis's name. Property owner. She'd never owned anything more valuable than her eight-year-old Honda Civic.

"The apartment above the shop," Kyle continued, his voice gentle, "has been vacant for about two years. Phyllis had been renting it out in the past, but after the last tenant, she decided not to rent it out until she could hire someone to update the place. According to the property inspection I requested, the apartment needs some work, but it's structurally sound. I'm guessing with some work, it could be a comfortable home."

A home. Not a cramped room in a shared apartment, but an actual space of her own. Space to breathe.

"Now, the business itself." Kyle pulled out another document. "Sugar & Spice Candy Shop has been operating continuously since 1998. It's well-established, profitable, and beloved by both locals and tourists. The shop currently employs five people, most of whom have worked there for years. In fact, Phyllis specifically requested in her will that you retain all current employees if possible—she believed they were essential to the shop's success and wanted them to teach you the business."

"Teach me." Megan looked up from the documents, panic rising in her chest. "Kyle, I don't know anything about making candy. I can barely make toast without burning it."

"That's exactly why Phyllis wanted the staff to stay," he said, his tone reassuring. "A couple of the employees were her closest friends, and they are knowledgeable about this business. She wasn't expecting you to walk in as an expert. She was giving you a team of people who already knew everything there is to know about running the shop. Kay Sinclair, the general manager, has been with Phyllis for over twenty years. Linda Foster, the lead candy maker, trained under Phyllis herself. They're not just employees—they're the heart of the business."

He paused, studying her face with an expression that was part professional concern, part something warmer. "Phyllis thought about this very carefully. She wasn't setting you up to fail. She was giving you the tools you'd need to succeed."

Megan pressed her fingers against her eyes, fighting back the tears that threatened. "Why? Why would she do all this for me?"

"I can't answer that in all honesty." Kyle's voice was soft but certain. "I do know she believed in you. When she had me update her will last year, she was quite certain and determined about the specifics of this will. Phyllis had just been diagnosed with congestive heart failure, and though I don't know the specifics of that diagnosis, I got the feeling at that time that she needed to make sure that if anything happened to her... everything she had built here would go to someone she believed could continue the business but not only that, deserved it. That someone is you."

He let that sit for a moment before continuing. "Now, let's talk about the financial aspects, because this is where things get even more interesting."

Kyle pulled out several bank statements and organized them in front of Megan. "Phyllis maintained three accounts at Mistletoe Falls Community Bank. The business checking account currently has approximately forty-two thousand dollars in it—that's the operating capital for the shop, covering payroll, inventory, utilities, and other business expenses."

Megan's eyes widened. Forty-two thousand dollars. That was more money than she'd ever seen in one place.

"The business generates consistent revenue," Kyle explained. "The shop has steady year-round sales. Based on the last few years of financial records, the shop typically profits between eighty and ninety thousand dollars annually after all expenses. Not a fortune, but a solid, comfortable living."

Eighty thousand dollars. A comfortable living. Megan had never earned more than twenty-two thousand in her best year.

"Then there's Phyllis's personal savings account." Kyle slid another statement across the desk. "She was quite frugal and saved diligently. The account currently holds one hundred and fifteen thousand dollars."

The number didn't even register at first. Megan stared at the statement, at the balance that had so many zeros it looked like a mistake.

"One hundred and fifteen thousand," she repeated numbly.

"Yes. Then, her personal checking account balance is two thousand four hundred dollars and some change. And there's also the life insurance policy." Kyle pulled out another document. "Phyllis had a policy worth fifty thousand dollars. After the costs of her cremation—which was her explicit wish, which included no memorial service—there's approximately forty-six thousand remaining. That money will be transferred to you once all the estate paperwork is finalized."

Megan couldn't breathe. The numbers swirled in her head, refusing to make sense. Yesterday she'd had two hundred dollars to her name. Today she was... what? Rich? Comfortable? She didn't even know what to call it.

"I know it's a lot to process," Kyle said gently. "Take your time."

"That's... that's over two hundred thousand dollars." Megan's voice cracked. "Plus a business. Plus a building. Plus an apartment. I don't... Kyle, I don't understand. How could she just give all this to someone who—"

"Who she loved," Kyle interrupted firmly. "Who she remembered and thought about and believed in? This is family taking care of family. This is a gift."

The tears came then, hot and fast, and Megan didn't even try to stop them. Kyle silently pushed a box of tissues across the desk, his expression patient and kind.

"I'm sorry," Megan managed, wiping her eyes. "This is so unprofessional."

"This is perfectly normal," Kyle countered. "You just found out that someone changed your entire life. You're allowed to have feelings about that."

Megan grabbed another tissue, trying to compose herself. "Is there more?"

"A bit, yes." Kyle's smile was gentle. "Phyllis also left you some personal items. Her family photo albums—she wanted you to know where you came from and to see the family history. Her china tea set, which was her grandmother's. And her vintage Christmas ornament collection, which is actually quite valuable. She started collecting ornaments when she first opened the candy shop, and some of them are worth hundreds of dollars each."

"She collected Christmas ornaments," Megan said, a surprised laugh escaping through her tears. "Of course she did."

"She also left you something that might be the most valuable part of this inheritance of all." Kyle pulled out a worn leather journal and a recipe box covered in faded floral fabric. "These contain all of Phyllis's candy recipes. Every single one she ever perfected. The peppermint fudge, the hand-pulled taffy, the caramels, the chocolate truffles—all of it. She documented everything in meticulous detail. Measurements, techniques, timing, and temperature. She wanted you to have the foundation to continue her legacy."

Megan reached for the recipe box with trembling hands. The box was heavy. She lifted the lid and saw dozens of recipes on index cards, each one carefully labeled and dated. Some cards had notes in the margins—"adjust vanilla," "customers love this one," "perfect for Christmas."

"She really did think of everything," Megan whispered.

"She did." Kyle's lips quirked into an amused smile. "There's something else I should mention. Phyllis had a cat."

"A cat?"

"Her name is Hazel." Kyle pulled out a photograph from the file and slid it across the desk. The image showed a plump, imperious-looking gray tabby with green eyes, lounging on a velvet cushion. "Hazel is four years old, has very particular opinions about everything, and, according to Phyllis's instructions, 'believes herself to be the rightful queen of any residence she inhabits.'"

Despite everything, Megan laughed. "She left me her cat."

"She did. Along with very specific care instructions about Hazel's preferred food, her favorite sleeping spots, and a warning that Hazel does not appreciate closed doors inside a home or being told what to do." Kyle's smile widened. "I've been taking care of her at my cabin since Phyllis passed. She's... adapting. Mostly by ignoring me and yet at the same time making her imperial presence known."

"Your cabin?"

"I live in a log cabin on my parents' resort property. Hazel has made herself quite comfortable there, though she's made it clear she's merely tolerating the accommodations. Once you're settled in the apartment, I'll bring her to you. Fair warning—she's used to being in charge."

Megan looked at the photograph of the round, dignified cat and felt something warm expand in her chest. Phyllis had thought of everything, right down to making sure her beloved pet would have a home.

"I've never had a cat before."

"Hazel will teach you everything you need to know. Mostly that she's in charge and you're the help." Kyle's expression softened. "But she's actually quite sweet once you earn her approval. And Phyllis loved her dearly."

"Then I'll love her too," Megan said.

"Good. Now, there is one more thing." Kyle pulled out another document. "Phyllis owned a Victorian home on Jingle Bell Lane—the house where she lived for most of her adult life. It's a beautiful historic property, one of the original homes from when Mistletoe Falls was founded."

Megan looked up. "Is that mine too?"

"No. She left that home to the city of Mistletoe Falls, with the intention that it be preserved as a historic landmark." Kyle's expression softened. "But she made a very specific request. She wanted you to serve as one of the curators—to help preserve its history, share stories about the house and the family who lived there, and be part of maintaining its significance to this town. She wanted you to have a role in keeping that history alive."

"She wanted me to be part of the town's history," Megan said slowly, the realization settling over her. "Not just inherit her business, but belong here... make a home here."

"Exactly." Kyle set down the document and leaned back in his chair. "That's what all of this is really about if you think about it. Phyllis wasn't just leaving you money and property. She was inviting you home."

The silence in the office stretched, broken only by the soft ticking of a clock on the bookshelf and the distant sound of Christmas music from the shop beyond the door. Megan looked at the documents spread across the desk and tried to understand what had just happened to her life.

"I don't deserve this," she said finally.

"Why not?"

The question was so simple, so direct, that Megan didn't have an answer ready. "I... I haven't done anything to earn it."

"Love isn't something you earn," Kyle said quietly. "It's something you receive. And Phyllis loved you. That's all the reason she needed."

Megan pressed her hand against her chest, where something tight and painful was starting to unravel. "I don't know how to do any of this. Run a business, make candy, manage money, be a curator of a historic house. Holy cow... and I have to be a cat mom. I don't know the first thing about any of it."

"You don't have to know right now." Kyle's voice was steady, grounding. "You have time to learn. You have people who will teach you. And a community that loved Phyllis and will welcome you because you were important to her."

"What if I fail? What if I ruin everything she built?"

"What if you don't? What if you take this gift she's given you and build something even better? What if you surprise yourself?"

Megan wanted to argue, to list all the reasons why this was impossible, why she wasn't capable, and why this couldn't possibly work. But the words wouldn't come. Instead, she looked down at the recipe box in her lap and thought about birthday and Christmas cards that arrived every year without fail. About someone who remembered her even when everyone else forgot.

"I have so many questions," she said finally.

"I'd be worried if you didn't." Kyle smiled. "Ask me anything. That's what I'm here for."

"The employees—Kay and Linda and the others. Do they know about me? That Phyllis left everything to someone they've never met?"

"They know. I met with them last week, right after Phyllis passed, to let them know what the will specified. They were surprised, certainly, but not upset. Kay actually said she was relieved that Phyllis had someone to leave the shop to. They'd been worried about what would happen to the business."

"Were they angry? That some stranger was inheriting their workplace?"

"Not angry. Curious. A little nervous about change, which is natural. But mostly they seemed hopeful. They loved Phyllis, and they love that shop. They want it to succeed." He paused. "I think they'll welcome you."

Megan nodded slowly, trying to picture these people she'd be working with, depending on, and learning from. "And the apartment—you said it needs work?"

"Yes. The basics are fine from my understanding. But it hasn't been lived in for two years, so I imagine it needs cleaning, painting, and maybe some other minor things."

"How much work are we talking about, do you think? Weeks? Months?"

Kyle considered. "I haven't personally seen the apartment, but I'd be happy to show it to you. And you can decide if it's move-in ready or maybe consider another option until it meets your standards."

"Well... my standards are low and... I don't have anywhere else to stay."

Megan looked down at the documents again, at the tangible proof that her life had completely changed. "What do I do first? Where do I even start?"

"How about we start simple?" Kyle stood, gathering the documents into a neat stack. "The shop is open right now; the staff kept it running after Phyllis passed because she would have wanted that. It's on Mistletoe Lane, maybe a five-minute walk from here. Would you like to see it? Meet the people who'll be working with you."

The suggestion was so reasonable, so practical, but Megan's heart started racing at the thought. Meet the employees. See the shop. Start becoming the owner of a business she didn't know how to run.

"I look terrible," she protested weakly. "I've been driving all day, and I'm wearing jeans and an old sweatshirt, and—"

"You look like someone who just drove five hours to start a new life," Kyle said gently. "Besides, there's no dress code for visiting a candy shop. Trust me."

Megan looked at him—at his flannel shirt and work boots, at his patient smile, and at the obvious confidence he had in her ability to handle this.

"Okay," she said, standing on shaky legs. "Let's go see the candy shop."

Kyle's smile brightened, and he gestured toward the door. "After you, Ms. Caldwell. Your inheritance awaits."

Chapter 4

Megan stood on the brick sidewalk, staring up at the building that was apparently hers, and couldn't make her feet move forward.

The Sugar & Spice Candy Shop occupied the first floor of a three-story Victorian building painted a soft cream color with burgundy trim. Large display windows flanked a burgundy door, and even from outside, Megan could see the vintage charm of the interior—polished wood, gleaming glass cases, and rows of colorful candies arranged like jewels. A hand-painted sign above the door declared "Sugar & Spice Candy Shop" in elegant script, with "Est. 1998" in smaller letters below.

It was beautiful. It was perfect. It was completely terrifying.

"Take your time," Kyle said from beside her, his voice quiet and patient. He'd walked her here from The Christmas Shop, carrying the file folder with all her inheritance documents while she'd clutched the recipe box like a lifeline.

"This is really mine," she said, more to herself than to Kyle.

"It really is."

Megan looked at him—at the way his flannel shirt brought out the green flecks in his hazel eyes, at the patient set of his shoulders, at the small encouraging smile that made her think maybe, possibly, she could do this. He'd been so steady through everything in his office, so kind when she'd cried, and so matter-of-fact about life-changing information that had left her reeling.

"What if the employees hate me? What if they think I'm just some stranger who wants to swoop in and take their workplace?"

"They won't hate you. They're not like that. They loved Phyllis. And if you were important to Phyllis. That matters to them."

Megan nodded, trying to draw courage from his certainty. She straightened her shoulders, adjusted her grip on the recipe box, and reached for the door handle.

A brass bell chimed overhead as they entered, and the scent hit her immediately—warm vanilla, rich chocolate, sweet peppermint, and underneath it all, the buttery smell of caramel. It was the smell of childhood, of safety, and of Aunt Phyllis's hugs and laughter.

The shop itself looked like it had been frozen in time. Original hardwood floors, worn smooth by decades of foot traffic, stretched toward a long marble-topped counter that dominated the back wall. Behind the counter, shelves rose toward a pressed tin ceiling, displaying vintage candy jars filled with colorful sweets. Glass display cases lined both sides of the shop, their contents arranged with obvious care—truffles here, caramels there, hand-pulled taffy in a rainbow of colors.

To the left, a section was dedicated to chocolate-covered treats—pretzels, strawberries, and graham crackers, each one looking almost too perfect to eat. To the right, shelves held gift boxes and baskets in various sizes, some already assembled, others waiting to be customized.

And everywhere, the warm glow of vintage light fixtures cast everything in soft golden tones that made the whole space feel like stepping into a memory.

"Oh," Megan breathed, her eyes stinging with sudden tears. "I remember this. I remember all of this."

Kyle's hand touched her elbow briefly, steadying her. "Are you okay?"

She nodded, not trusting her voice. She'd been so young the last time she'd stood in this shop, but the bones of it were the same. The marble counter. The tin ceiling. The way the afternoon light came through the front windows and made everything glow.

Movement behind the counter drew her attention, and Megan saw a woman emerge from the kitchen area. She was in her early fifties, with dark hair pulled back in a ponytail and an apron that read "Sugar & Spice and Everything Nice." Her expression was professionally friendly until she saw Kyle, and then her smile widened with genuine warmth.

"Kyle! What brings you by today?" Then her gaze shifted to Megan, and something in her face changed—understanding, maybe, or recognition of who this stranger must be.

"Kay, this is Megan Caldwell," Kyle said. "Phyllis's niece."

Kay came around the counter, wiping her hands on her apron. She was a few inches shorter than Megan, with kind brown eyes and the sort of capable presence that suggested she could handle any crisis that came her way. "Ms. Caldwell. It's good to finally meet you."

"Please call me Megan." She shifted the recipe box to offer her hand, and Kay shook it firmly.

"I'm Kay Sinclair, the general manager here. I've been working with Phyllis for over twenty years." Kay's smile was warm but tinged with sadness. "She talked about you often. It's wonderful to have you here, though I wish the circumstances were different."

"Thank you. I'm sorry for your loss. I know she meant a lot to you."

"She meant everything to me and this place." Kay glanced around the shop with obvious affection. "We all loved her very much. She wasn't just our boss—she was family."

The word hung in the air between them, and Megan felt the weight of it. Family. These people had been Phyllis's family. They'd seen her every day, worked beside her, and shared her joys and struggles. And now Megan was supposed to step into that space.

As if reading her thoughts, Kay's expression softened. "Why don't I introduce you to everyone? We're all here this afternoon."

She turned and called toward the back. "Linda! Tonya! Beth! Savannah! Can you come out front for a minute?"

One by one, they emerged from the kitchen area. Linda Foster appeared first—a woman in her mid-fifties with silver-streaked hair in a long braid. Her hands were strong and work-worn, and she had the calm demeanor of someone who'd spent decades perfecting her craft.

"Linda's our head candy maker," Kay explained. "She trained under Phyllis herself. If you want to know how to make anything in this shop, Linda's your person."

"Nice to meet you, honey," Linda said, her voice soft and kind. "Welcome home."

The words made Megan's throat tight. Welcome home. As if this had always been waiting for her.

Tonya Wright bounded out next, energy radiating from her every movement. She was around Megan's age, with dark curls barely contained by a bright red bandana and a smile that could light up a room.

"Oh my gosh, you're Megan! Phyllis showed me pictures of when you were a little girl. You look just like your dad's side of the family."

"Tonya's our candy assistant," Kay said with obvious fondness. "Her grandfather taught Phyllis how to pull taffy. She's a third-generation confectioner."

"And I'll teach you everything I know," Tonya said enthusiastically. "Though fair warning—taffy pulling is an arm workout. You'll feel muscles you didn't know you had."

Despite her nervousness, Megan laughed. "I'll keep that in mind."

Beth Carson emerged more quietly, carrying a clipboard and wearing an apron over sensible khakis. She was in her mid-thirties with a warm, open face and the sort of unflappable presence that suggested she could handle twelve customers at once without breaking a sweat. "Welcome, Megan. I'm Beth, senior sales associate and office manager. If you need to know anything about customers, orders, or how Phyllis liked things run out front, I'm your girl."

"Thank you. I appreciate that."

The last young woman was probably in her early twenties, with straight dark hair and sharp, intelligent eyes behind trendy glasses. She had the look of someone who was most likely in college, and she carried herself with the confidence of youth combined with genuine capability.

"Savannah Tillman," she introduced herself, shaking Megan's hand firmly. "Junior sales associate and resident computer nerd. I handle the website and all the social media. I've been bugging Phyllis—" She stopped, her expression flickering with pain. "I was trying to convince Phyllis to let me freshen up the look of our current website. Maybe you'd be interested in that?"

"Maybe," Megan said, feeling overwhelmed by the barrage of names and roles and skills she didn't have. "I'm still trying to wrap my head around all of this."

"Of course you are," Kay said kindly. "Would you like a tour? See where everything is, how things work?"

"Yes," Megan said, squaring her shoulders. "A tour would be great."

Kay led them through the shop with obvious pride, pointing out the various display cases and explaining what each one held. The truffle case featured flavors from classic dark chocolate to adventurous combinations like lavender honey and bourbon maple. The caramel section offered everything from plain vanilla to salted chocolate to apple cider.

"Phyllis believed in quality over quantity," Kay explained as they walked. "Every piece of candy in this shop is made by hand, in small batches, using recipes she perfected over decades. No shortcuts, no artificial flavors. That's why people drive from all over to shop here."

They moved behind the counter, and Kay pushed open a swinging door that led to the kitchen. "This is where the magic happens."

The kitchen was larger than Megan had imagined. Copper pots hung from ceiling hooks. A marble slab—for tempering chocolate, Kay explained—dominated one workstation. Industrial mixers sat beside vintage candy thermometers. Everything gleamed, obviously well-maintained and loved.

"Linda, Tonya, and I do most of the candy making," Kay said. "We usually start early in the morning, get batches going for whatever's running low or whatever seasonal flavors we're featuring. Phyllis had a schedule—certain days for certain candies—but she was also flexible based on what customers wanted."

Linda spoke up from where she was stirring something in a copper pot. "Don't worry about learning it all at once, honey. We'll teach you step by step. Candy making is part chemistry, part art, and mostly patience."

"And arm strength," Tonya added with a grin. "Seriously, so much arm strength."

Kay led them past the kitchen to an office tucked in the corner. "This was Phyllis's office."

The office was cozy and cluttered. A wooden desk held a computer that looked at least a decade old. Filing cabinets lined one wall. But what caught Megan's attention were the photographs covering every available surface—pictures of the shop at various stages, of staff members, of satisfied customers, and of Phyllis herself smiling and holding up various candies.

And there, on the desk, was a photograph in a silver frame—young Megan, maybe seven or eight years old, standing in the shop and holding up a giant lollipop, her face split in a grin.

Megan picked up the frame. She didn't remember this moment specifically, but she remembered the feeling of it—safe, happy, and loved.

"She always kept that photo right there on her desk," Kay said quietly. "She'd look at it sometimes and smile. She loved you very much."

Megan couldn't speak. She just held the frame and tried not to cry again.

After a moment, Megan set the frame back down and turned to Kay. "What else should I see?"

They toured the large storage area at the back of the shop—shelves upon shelves of ingredients, supplies, boxes, ribbon, everything needed to keep the business running. Kay explained the inventory system, the ordering schedule, and the suppliers Phyllis had worked with for years.

"It probably seems like a lot," Kay said, watching Megan's face. "And it is. But you don't have to know everything right away. We're all here right behind you. We know the routine and what works and what doesn't. Not only that, but we want this place to succeed. Phyllis loved you and trusted you with her legacy, and we trust her judgment."

"But you don't even know me," Megan protested. "How can you trust me when I don't know the first thing about running this business?"

"Because Phyllis chose you," Linda said, appearing in the storage room doorway. "That woman had excellent instincts about people. If she believed you could do this, then you can."

"No worries, dear, we've got your back," Beth added, joining them.

Tonya peeked over Beth's shoulder and smiled. "Plus... you seem nice. And you didn't waltz in here acting like you own the place—even though you literally do own the place."

Despite everything, Megan laughed. The sound felt foreign after the emotional whiplash of the day, but also necessary. "I definitely don't feel like I own anything. I feel like I'm playing dress-up in someone else's life."

"Well, given the circumstances, that's to be expected," Kay assured her. "Change is hard, even good change. But you'll grow into this. We'll make sure of it."

Megan looked around at these women—these strangers who were welcoming her, offering to teach her, and promising to support her. She thought about Phyllis choosing her, believing in her enough to leave her entire legacy in Megan's uncertain hands.

"Thank you," she said, her voice rough with emotion. "Thank you for keeping this place running after Phyllis passed. Thank you for being willing to work with me. Thank you for not..." She stopped, not sure how to finish.

Kay smiled. "I can only imagine how overwhelmed you are. Take your time and get used to everything that has been dropped in your lap, and just know, we're all glad you came to join our happy family."

Kyle had been quiet during most of the tour, staying back and letting the staff take the lead. But now he stepped forward slightly, his presence drawing Megan's attention. "If you're ready, we could take a look at the apartment. Get a sense of what needs to be done there."

Megan looked at him—at his patient expression, at the folder he still carried, at the way he seemed to anticipate what she needed before she knew herself. She was exhausted, overwhelmed, and emotionally wrung out. But she also needed to see the apartment and had to understand the full scope of where she'd be living.

"Okay," she said. "Let's see the apartment."

Kay pointed toward a door at the back of the storage area. "That leads to the alley behind the shop. There's an exterior staircase that goes up to the apartment entrance. Fair warning—the stairs are a bit steep, and they might be slippery if there's any frost."

"I'll be careful," Megan promised.

Kyle moved toward the door, then paused and looked back at her. "Ready?"

Megan took a breath, clutched the recipe box a little tighter, and nodded.

She wasn't sure she'd ever be ready for any of this. But standing in the shop, surrounded by people who wanted her to succeed, with Kyle waiting to show her what came next, she thought maybe ready didn't matter as much as willing.

And she was willing. Terrified, but willing.

"Let's go," she said, and followed him toward the door.

Chapter 5

Kyle had seen many neglected properties in his legal practice, but the apartment above Sugar & Spice made him wonder if Phyllis had forgotten she even owned it.

The exterior staircase was steep, the metal treads showing rust in places and flexing slightly under their weight. He kept one hand on the railing and stayed close behind Megan, ready to steady her if she slipped.

"Careful," he said. "These stairs weren't exactly built with modern safety codes in mind."

She glanced back at him with a nervous smile that did something uncomfortable to his chest. "I'm good. I've got this."

At the top of the stairs, Kyle pulled the key ring out of his pocket. Three different keys for three different locks, which suggested the door had been retrofitted multiple times over the years. The deadbolt stuck, and he had to jiggle the key while applying pressure to get it to turn.

"That's promising," Megan said, her tone attempting lightness that didn't quite land.

Kyle pushed the door open, and the smell hit them immediately—musty, stale air mixed with the faint scent of mildew and dust. Not overwhelming, but enough to make it clear no one had lived here in a long time.

The door opened directly into what should have been a living area. Gray afternoon light filtered through dirty windows, illuminating a space that was... empty. Completely, utterly empty except for dust bunnies.

Kyle stepped inside first, his boots echoing on the bare floor. The apartment was freezing; it felt colder inside than it had been in the alley. He could see his breath.

"The heat's not on," he said, moving toward what he assumed was the thermostat on the far wall. He flipped it up, and somewhere in the building, ancient radiators clanked to life.

Megan walked around the space slowly, still clutching the recipe box like a lifeline. Kyle watched her face as she took in the apartment—the water-stained ceiling, the peeling paint in the corner, the windows that were clearly single-pane and doing nothing to keep out the cold.

"It's... bigger than I expected," she said finally.

Kyle looked around the space, mentally cataloging everything that needed attention. The windows rattled in their frames from the wind outside. The walls needed more than paint—there were visible cracks in the plaster. The hardwood floor was decent but needed refinishing.

"Let's see the rest of it," he said, trying to keep his voice neutral.

They moved through the apartment together. The kitchen was small, tucked into an alcove off the main living space. A wobbly wooden table sat in the center, its surface scarred. The cabinets looked original to the building—beautiful craftsmanship, but the doors hung at odd angles, some with broken hinges. Where a refrigerator should have been, there was only an empty space with old linoleum curling at the edges. The stove was a tiny two-burner apparatus that looked like it belonged in a camper, not a permanent residence.

Kyle opened the cabinet under the sink and found exactly what he'd feared—water damage, warped wood, and the telltale signs of an old leak.

"There are a few things that need some attention," he said, more to himself than to Megan.

She was running her hand along the counter, her expression unreadable. "It has character," she offered.

Down a short hallway, they found two bedrooms. The first was decent-sized, with a window that overlooked the alley. The second was smaller, and Kyle's heart sank as he saw the window—a spiderweb of cracks spreading across the glass, with actual gaps where cold air whistled through.

"That'll need to be replaced immediately," he said, moving closer to inspect the damage. "You can't live here with that window like this."

"Maybe I could tape it or something," Megan suggested. "Just temporarily."

Kyle turned to look at her. She was still smiling, but he could see the disappointment she was working so hard to hide. Her shoulders had the same defensive hunch he'd noticed when she'd first entered The Christmas Shop, like she was trying to make herself smaller, less of an imposition.

"Megan—"

"Let's see the bathroom," she interrupted, moving past him with false brightness.

The bathroom was the only room that showed any real promise. The fixtures were old, but the clawfoot tub was beautiful—white porcelain with brass feet that had seen better days but could be restored. Kyle turned on the faucet, and water trickled out in a weak, stuttering stream.

"The water pressure's terrible in here," he said, watching the pathetic flow.

Megan stood in the doorway, hugging herself against the cold that permeated every room.

"It's not that bad," she said finally. "I can make it work. Really. I just need to... clean it up. Maybe get a space heater for the bedroom. Tape that window until it can be repaired. It'll be fine."

Kyle turned off the faucet and faced her fully. She was shivering slightly, though whether from cold or emotion, he couldn't tell. Her determination was admirable, but it was also breaking his heart a little.

"Do you have furniture being shipped?" he asked. "Belongings coming from Kentucky?"

The question made her stiffen. "No. I... everything I have is in my car."

Kyle absorbed that information, working to keep his expression neutral even as surprise and concern warred inside him. Everything she owned fit in a car.

"Okay," he said simply, not pressing for details he could sense she didn't want to share. "That makes moving easier, at least."

She gave him a grateful look, but her jaw was set with stubborn pride. "I can sleep on the floor for a few nights. Maybe get an air mattress from somewhere. And I don't need much—"

"Megan." Kyle kept his voice gentle but firm. "You can't stay here. Not tonight. Not until this place has been properly repaired and made livable."

"I don't have anywhere else to go," she said, and the admission clearly cost her. "I can't afford a hotel... well, I guess now I can, but—"

She stopped, pressing her lips together as if physically preventing more words from escaping.

Kyle's protective instincts kicked into overdrive. He pulled out his phone before he could second-guess the impulse.

"What are you doing?" Megan asked.

"Calling my parents. They own the Snowflake Mountain Resort, just outside town. They have A-frame cabins, and I know for a fact they're not fully booked right now."

"Kyle, no. I can't—"

"You're new in town," he interrupted. "You need a place to stay while this apartment gets fixed. This is what we do here. We help each other."

"But I'm not—I'm just—" She struggled with the words. "I don't want to be a burden. Or take charity."

The phone was ringing. Kyle held up a finger, asking her to wait. His mother answered on the second ring.

"Kyle! How are you, honey?"

"Hi, Mom. I'm good. Listen, I need a favor." He watched Megan's face as he spoke and saw her worrying her bottom lip with her teeth. "I'm with Megan Caldwell—Phyllis's niece, the one who inherited the candy shop. The apartment above the shop isn't livable right now. Do you have any cabins available? She needs a place to stay while we get some repairs done."

"Oh, of course! We have several cabins open. When does she need it?"

"Now, if possible."

"Absolutely. Bring her by. We'll get her all settled in. The Evergreen cabin just opened up this morning—it's one of our nicer ones. And Kyle? Tell her it's on the house, no charge. Phyllis was a dear friend. Consider it our welcome gift."

Kyle smiled. His mother's generosity was legendary. "Thanks, Mom. We'll be there in about an hour."

"Perfect. I'll get everything ready. I can't wait to meet her."

"Love you."

"Love you too, honey."

Kyle ended the call and looked at Megan, who was shaking her head before he could even speak.

"Kyle, I can't. I should just stay here and—"

"And what? Freeze? Sleep on a floor in a building that's barely heated with a broken window?" He kept his voice gentle but didn't back down. "Megan, you can't stay here. Not tonight. The apartment needs work—real work. My dad does contracting, and I'm going to ask him to look at this place tomorrow and give you a realistic timeline for repairs. But tonight, you need somewhere warm and safe to sleep."

She looked torn, pride warring with practical need. Kyle could see the exact moment practicality won, even as it clearly pained her.

"I'll pay your parents back," she said firmly. "Whatever the cabin costs, I'll pay them. This isn't charity."

"You can discuss that with them later," Kyle said, choosing not to mention that his mother had already made her intentions clear. "The important thing is getting you somewhere comfortable for the night."

Megan nodded slowly, then looked around the apartment one more time. Something in her expression made Kyle's chest tighten—disappointment and determination mixed with exhaustion that went deeper than one day's travel.

"I really thought I'd be sleeping here tonight," she said quietly. "In my own place. Starting my new life."

"You will," Kyle said. "Just not tonight. The business can run fine without you living directly above it."

She managed a small smile. "You're very insistent about this."

"I've been told I can be stubborn when I think I'm right." He gestured toward the door. "Come on. Let's head back to The Christmas Shop so you can get your car. You can follow me to the resort, and we'll get you settled in."

"Kyle." Megan's voice stopped him as he reached for the door. "Thank you. For... for all of this. For not making me feel pathetic for not being able to handle this on my own."

He turned back to her, surprised by the vulnerability in her voice. "You're not pathetic. You're practical. There's a difference."

She didn't look convinced, but she followed him out of the apartment. Kyle locked the door behind them, already mentally composing a list of repairs that needed to happen before Megan could safely live here.

As they descended the steep stairs, Kyle stayed close again, hyperaware of her presence just ahead of him. He noticed things he shouldn't be noticing—the way her hair caught the fading afternoon light, the determined set of her shoulders even in defeat, and the way she clutched that recipe box like it contained all her hopes.

He barely knew this woman. She'd been in town for a handful of hours. But something about her pulled at him in a way that felt both natural and terrifying. The urge to protect her, to solve her problems, to make sure she didn't have to face any of this alone—it was stronger than professional courtesy dictated.

He needed to be careful. She was his client technically. She was vulnerable, newly arrived, and overwhelmed by circumstances. The last thing she needed was her attorney developing feelings that crossed professional lines.

But as they reached the bottom of the stairs and she turned to thank him again, her green eyes bright with unshed tears and stubborn pride,

Kyle had the sinking feeling that being careful might already be a lost cause.

"Ready?" he asked, keeping his voice steady even as his mind raced with everything he needed to arrange for her.

"As I'll ever be," she replied.

Chapter 6

Megan followed Kyle's black F-150 out of downtown Mistletoe Falls, and for the first time since arriving, she had a moment to simply breathe.

The road climbed gradually into the mountains, winding through forests where bare trees mixed with evergreens, their branches outlined against the darkening sky. The further they drove from town, the more the landscape opened up—rolling hills gave way to dramatic peaks, and the valley spread below them like something out of a painting. The snow appeared deeper at the higher elevations, catching the last light of day and turning everything golden-pink.

It was beautiful. Overwhelmingly, impossibly beautiful.

Megan gripped the steering wheel and tried to process everything that had happened in the last 24 hours. Yesterday she was living in a cramped apartment with four people she tolerated in Bowling Green, Kentucky, with a couple hundred dollars to her name, an eviction notice, and no prospects. Now she owned a business, had over two hundred thousand dollars, and was following a ruggedly handsome attorney to his parents' resort because the apartment she'd inherited was uninhabitable.

Her life had become similar to one of those cutesy movies she'd watched on television in the past, complete with a small Christmas town and a man who kept swooping in to help her.

Except this wasn't a movie. This was real. The inheritance was real. The apartment was real. And Kyle Porter—with his patient smile and gentle voice and the way his flannel shirt stretched across his shoulders when he'd reached up to turn on the apartment's heat—was very, very real.

She shouldn't be noticing things like that. She shouldn't be thinking about the way he'd stayed close on those steep stairs. She shouldn't be replaying the moment when he'd looked at her in that freezing apartment and said she wasn't pathetic; she was practical.

But she was thinking about all of it anyway.

Ahead, Kyle's truck signaled a turn, and Megan followed onto a narrower road marked by a carved wooden sign: "Snowflake Mountain Resort." The road curved through more forest before opening into a clearing, and Megan's breath caught.

The resort stretched across gentle slopes, its main lodge built from massive timber and native stone that made it look like it had grown naturally from the mountainside. Warm light glowed from floor-to-ceiling windows, and smoke drifted from multiple chimneys. The parking area was well-maintained, with decorative light posts that were already coming on as dusk settled.

But what really caught Megan's attention were the A-frame cabins scattered across the property like a village of tiny mountain chalets. Their distinctive triangular shapes and cedar siding made each one look like something from a storybook, connected by winding paths lit by lanterns. Some had smoke curling from chimneys. Others had lights glowing warmly in their windows.

Kyle pulled into a spot near one of the cabins and got out, waiting while Megan parked beside him. When she climbed out of her car, the mountain air hit her—cold and clean, scented with pine and wood smoke.

"This is incredible," she said, turning in a slow circle to take it all in.

Kyle smiled, and the pride in his expression made her chest warm. "My parents built most of these A-frames themselves." He gestured toward the cabins. "The A-frames are their signature feature here at the resort. Guests come back year after year just to stay in them."

"I can see why." Megan followed his gaze to the nearest cabin—the distinctive triangular shape, the warm cedar siding, and the small porch with its rocking chairs. "They're like little alpine cottages."

"That's exactly what my mom was going for. Your cabin is this way. It's called Evergreen."

They walked along a lit path that wound between several cabins, each one marked with a hand-carved wooden sign. Snowberry. Pinecone. Mistletoe. And finally, Evergreen, tucked slightly away from the others with a view that looked out toward the mountains.

Kyle climbed the three steps to the small porch and tried the door. It opened easily, and he gestured for Megan to enter first. "Mom said she'd leave the key inside."

Megan stepped into the cabin and stopped, taking it all in.

The interior was exactly as charming as the exterior promised. The ceiling soared overhead, exposed beams creating dramatic lines that drew the eye upward. A stone fireplace dominated one wall, already laid with logs and kindling, ready to be lit. The open-concept living area featured a comfortable-looking sofa and chairs arranged around a pine coffee table, with soft lighting from table lamps casting everything in warm tones.

To the right, a small but well-equipped kitchenette held a fridge, microwave, cooktop, and a coffeemaker that looked brand new. Everything was clean and welcoming, from the quilted throw blanket draped over the sofa to the potted plant on the windowsill.

A sleeping loft was visible above, accessed by a sturdy wooden ladder, and Megan could see the edge of what looked like a comfortable bed with white linens.

"The bathroom's through there," Kyle said, pointing to a door tucked under the loft. "And the loft has a full-size bed. Mom always puts good mattresses in the cabins—she says nobody sleeps well on a cheap mattress, no matter how pretty the view is."

On the kitchen counter, a key ring sat next to a folded note. Kyle picked up the note and handed it to Megan.

The handwriting was neat and welcoming:

Welcome to the Snowflake Mountain Resort, Megan! The cabin is yours for as long as you need it. I stocked the fridge with some basics to get you through tonight and tomorrow. We're so glad you're here. Please come by the main lodge whenever you'd like. -Ann

Megan read the note twice, her throat tightening. "Your mother seems very kind."

"She is. Sometimes too kind, according to my dad's accounting spreadsheets. But she says some things matter more than profit margins."

Before Megan could respond, the cabin door opened again, and a couple entered—clearly Kyle's parents based on the family resemblance. The man was tall and solid, with silver threading through dark hair and the weathered hands of someone who worked outdoors. The woman was petite and energetic, with warm eyes and a smile that reached out and wrapped around you.

"Megan!" Ann Porter moved forward immediately, pulling Megan into a hug. "Oh, honey, welcome. I'm Ann, and this is my husband, Mitch. We're so glad you're here, though I'm sorry about the apartment situation."

"Thank you for letting me stay here," Megan managed, slightly overwhelmed by the instant warmth. "I promise I'll pay—"

"Nonsense." Ann waved a hand dismissively. "Phyllis was a dear friend. This is the least we can do."

Mitch extended his hand, his grip firm but gentle. "Nice to meet you, Megan. Kyle mentioned the apartment needs some work."

"That's putting it mildly," Kyle said and proceeded to describe the broken window, the weak water pressure, the cabinet doors, and the lack of appliances.

Mitch listened with the focused attention of someone mentally cataloging repairs. "Doesn't sound like anything too major. Mostly cosmetic and a few fixtures. The window's the priority—can't have that cracked glass letting in cold air. I could start on it tomorrow if you'd like, Megan. Kyle, if you're free to help, we could probably knock out most of it in a few weeks."

"I would appreciate your help if it's not a problem," Megan said.

"I can help," Kyle said immediately.

"Good." Mitch nodded, already planning. "I'll run by the apartment in the morning and then get materials ordered. Meanwhile, Megan, you just settle in here."

Ann was unpacking a grocery bag she had brought with her, arranging items in one of the cabinets. "I brought extra coffee, creamer, sugar, and filters. There are extra blankets in the chest by the sofa if you get cold. Firewood is stacked on the porch, and matches are on the mantel. Oh, and breakfast is served in the main lodge from seven to nine if you want a hot meal instead of fixing something here. Just come on over—no reservations needed."

"Thank you," Megan said, feeling overwhelmed by their generosity. "This is all so much. I don't know how to—"

"You don't have to do anything except rest and settle in," Ann said firmly, patting Megan's arm. "You've had a long day. Tomorrow's soon enough to start figuring everything out."

"If you need anything—anything at all—you just call the main lodge. The number's on the notepad by the phone. We're here, and we're happy to help." Ann gave Megan another quick hug.

And then they were gone, their warm presence lingering even after the door closed behind them.

Megan stood in the middle of the cabin, trying to process what had just happened. "Your parents are…"

"A lot?" Kyle said with a smile.

"Wonderful," Megan corrected. "I was going to say wonderful."

Kyle's expression softened. "They are pretty great."

Megan turned away, pretending to examine the kitchenette. "So, your dad thinks a few weeks for the repairs?"

"It sounds like it." Kyle moved to the fireplace, crouching to arrange the logs. "Want me to start a fire before I go? It'll warm the place up quickly."

"That would be nice, thank you."

She watched him work, and within minutes, flames were crackling, casting dancing shadows across the cabin walls.

Kyle stood, brushing off his hands. "That should do it. The damper's open, so you're all set. Just add logs as it burns down."

"Okay." Megan wrapped her arms around herself, suddenly aware that once Kyle left, she'd be alone in this beautiful cabin with nothing but her thoughts.

"I should get going," Kyle said, but he didn't move toward the door. "Let you settle in. It's been a long day."

"The longest," Megan agreed. "But also kind of amazing? Is that weird? I feel more hopeful than I have in years?"

"It's not weird." Kyle's voice was soft. "It's honest."

They stood there, the fire crackling between them, neither quite ready to end the day. Megan noticed the way the firelight caught the green in his hazel eyes, the way his expression held both warmth and something that looked like reluctance.

"Thank you," she said. "For everything today. For being patient with me, for helping with the apartment, and for bringing me here. You didn't have to do any of that."

"I wanted to," Kyle said simply. "Just remember, you've got people here who want to help if you need it."

"People I barely know."

"For now," he said, and smiled. "Give it time. Mistletoe Falls has a way of making people feel like family."

He moved toward the door then, and Megan followed. On the porch, he paused, looking out at the darkened mountains.

"Get some rest. I imagine tomorrow will be a busy day for you. But tonight, just... breathe. Let everything settle."

"I will," Megan promised.

"Goodnight, Megan."

"Goodnight, Kyle."

She watched him walk down the path toward his truck, his form disappearing into the darkness between lanterns. Megan stepped back inside and closed the door.

The cabin was warm, and the fire was crackling cheerfully. The coffeemaker gleamed on the counter. Fresh groceries filled the small fridge. A comfortable bed waited in the loft above.

Megan slid down the door until she was sitting on the floor, her back against the wood. Exhaustion crashed over her—the drive, the emotions, and the overwhelming generosity of strangers who were quickly becoming something more.

Twenty-four hours ago, she'd been a nobody from nowhere, with nothing to look forward to except more of the same.

Now she was... what? A business owner. A property owner. Someone people believed in enough to help without asking for anything in return.

Megan closed her eyes and let herself imagine, just for a moment, what her life might look like if she actually succeeded here. If she learned to make candy and run a business and become part of this town, that seemed too good to be true. If she let herself trust and lean on others.

The possibilities terrified and thrilled her in equal measure.

Megan let herself feel something she hadn't allowed in years.

Hope.

Chapter 7

Megan had lived in plenty of temporary places, but none had ever felt like a haven until she woke up in the A-frame cabin with early morning light streaming through the tall windows.

She lay still for a moment, disoriented by the unfamiliar ceiling—those dramatic exposed beams soaring overhead, the soft glow of early morning sun filtering through glass that wasn't grimy or covered by cheap blinds. The bed beneath her was actually comfortable, the blankets warm without being suffocating, and the air smelled clean instead of like old carpet and other people's cooking.

It took her a moment to remember where she was. Why she was here.

Then it all came rushing back—the inheritance, Kyle Porter with his flannel shirts and patient kindness, the apartment that wasn't livable, and his parents' immediate generosity. The recipe box sitting on the kitchenette counter. The staff at Sugar & Spice who'd welcomed her like she belonged there.

Megan sat up slowly, her body protesting.

She'd slept. Really slept. No roommates arguing through thin walls, no police sirens wailing past on city streets, and no anxiety or dread about what the next day would bring.

The cabin was cool but not cold, the fire from last night reduced to gray ashes in the stone fireplace. Megan climbed down from the loft and grabbed the quilt on the back of the couch—a beautiful patchwork thing in shades of green, blue, and cream.

She wrapped it around her shoulders and padded to the kitchenette. The process of making coffee felt almost ceremonial—measuring grounds, pouring water, and watching the dark liquid drip into the carafe while the machine hissed and gurgled.

When it was ready, she poured herself a cup and added cream. The first sip was perfect—hot and rich and exactly what she needed.

Through the tall front windows, the sky was shifting from gray to pink, dawn breaking over the mountains in shades that looked painted. Megan slipped on her shoes, unlocked the cabin door, and stepped out onto the small porch, the quilt pulled tight around her shoulders against the November chill.

The view stole her breath.

Mountains rose in every direction, their peaks catching the first light of day. Closer in, the resort's other A-frame cabins dotted the landscape like a village from a storybook, smoke curling from a few chimneys where early risers had started their fires. The main lodge sat beyond, its timber and stone construction looking solid and permanent in the morning light.

Megan sank into one of the rocking chairs, cradling her coffee cup in both hands. The wood was cold against her back even through the quilt, but she didn't care. She just sat there, watching the sun climb higher, the shadows shift and change, and the world wake up around her.

This was a luxury. Not the cabin itself—though it was nicer than anywhere she'd lived in years—but this moment. This quiet. This view. The space to simply sit and breathe without someone needing something from her, without worrying about the next crisis, and without counting pennies and calculating whether she could afford both groceries and gas.

How had Aunt Phyllis known? How had she understood that what Megan needed most wasn't just money or property, but this—a chance to stop, catch her breath, and imagine a future that looked like something other than survival?

The thought made her throat tight. She took another sip of coffee and let herself feel it—the gratitude, the grief for a woman she'd loved and lost touch with, and the overwhelming sense that her entire life had pivoted on its axis in the span of twenty-four hours.

When the sun had fully risen, and the coffee cup was empty, Megan went back inside. The cabin felt warmer now, the heat from the rising sun and the automatic thermostat combining to chase away the morning chill. She refilled her coffee cup and sat at the small kitchen table, staring at the blank notepad Ann had left beside the phone.

She needed a plan. Some kind of strategy for how to approach this new life she'd inherited. But where did she even start?

Megan pulled the notepad toward her and uncapped the pen, tapping it against her lip while she thought. After a moment, she started writing:

<u>Things I Need to Do</u>

The list came slowly at first, then faster as her brain started organizing the chaos:

- Learn candy making (start with basics?)
- Understand business finances (I really need help with this)

<ul>
<li>Meet with Mitch about apartment repairs</li>
<li>Get furniture eventually (where?)</li>
<li>Learn staff routines (and fit into them, not change them).</li>
<li>Figure out the inventory system</li>
<li>Understand customer base</li>
<li>Learn seasonal products</li>
<li>Study Phyllis's recipes</li>
<li>Meet more of the community</li>
<li>Get Hazel the cat (when the apartment is ready or now?).</li>
</ul>

She stared at the list, feeling simultaneously motivated and overwhelmed. It was so much. How did people just step into running a business they knew nothing about? How did you go from making copies at a print shop to managing employees and making candy and balancing books?

The rational part of her brain knew the answer—one step at a time, with help from people who already knew what they were doing. But the scared part, the part that had learned early that stability was an illusion and people left without warning, had her wondering if she was setting herself up for spectacular failure.

What if she couldn't learn fast enough? What if the staff realized she was incompetent and quit? What if the business started losing money under her inexperienced management? What if she let everyone down?

Megan pressed her palms against her eyes, trying to quiet the spiral of worry. She'd survived her father leaving. She'd survived her mother's emotional distance and workaholic tendencies and then sudden change of life, second marriage, and her moving off to Florida, leaving her behind. She'd survived living with various roommates and terrible jobs, overdrawn checking accounts and surviving on very little, and more eviction notices than she cared to count. She could survive learning to make candy.

She had to.

The question was where to begin. The apartment repairs were in Mitch and Kyle's hands—she couldn't do anything about that except stay out of their way. The business finances could wait until she understood what she was even looking at; she didn't even want to touch that money until she understood how everything worked. The recipes were important, but they wouldn't make sense until she knew the basics of candy making.

Which meant the logical first step was the candy shop. Immersing herself in the daily routine, watching Kay and Linda and the others work, and learning by doing rather than overthinking.

She was adding "go to Sugar & Spice and ask to shadow someone" to her list when a knock sounded at the cabin door.

Megan jumped. She obviously wasn't expecting anyone.

She opened the door to find Kyle standing on the porch, looking somehow more rugged and handsome in the morning light and holding two to-go cups in his hands.

"Morning," he said, his smile easy and genuine. "Thought you might enjoy a cup of the best coffee in town. No offense to my parents's hospitality, but the basic coffee grounds they stock in the cabins aren't known for quality."

"I actually thought the coffee was pretty good."

"Then this will blow your mind." He held up one of the cups. "This is from The Cozy Cup. I got you a vanilla latte. If you don't like vanilla, I can drink it and you can have my black coffee, but fair warning, I take mine strong enough to strip paint."

She took the offered cup, her fingers brushing his. "A vanilla latte... never had one, but I'm willing to try it. Thank you."

"Mind if I come in?"

Megan stepped back, suddenly very aware that she was still in the clothes she'd slept in—an old t-shirt and yoga pants that had seen better days. Her hair probably looked like a disaster, and she definitely hadn't bothered with makeup.

Kyle didn't seem to notice or care. He walked to the small table where her list sat and raised an eyebrow. "Making plans?"

"Trying to." Megan closed the door and joined him, pulling the quilt around her shoulders. "There's just so much I don't know where to start."

Kyle studied her list, his expression thoughtful. "This is good. Organized. But maybe a little overwhelming for day one?"

"Everything's overwhelming," Megan admitted. She took a sip of the latte and had to suppress a sound of appreciation.

"Good?" Kyle asked, watching her face.

"Really good. Dangerously good. This is the kind of coffee that ruins you for normal coffee."

His smile widened. "That's the goal. The Cozy Cup is one of the few businesses in town that isn't completely Christmas-themed. The owner says there are limits even in Mistletoe Falls. She offers various blends from normal to exotic to Christmas-themed flavors and everything in between."

Megan laughed, surprised by how natural it felt. "Smart business decision."

Kyle pulled out the other chair and sat, his long legs stretched out in front of him. "So. Your list. Want to talk through priorities?"

"I was thinking I should just go to the shop. Start learning by doing instead of planning myself into paralysis."

"That's probably smart." Kyle tapped her notepad. "But before you do, my dad wanted me to ask if you could be at the apartment around ten. He wants to walk through everything with you and get your input on what's a priority versus what can wait."

"My input?" Megan blinked. "I don't know anything about construction or repairs."

"But you know how you want to live. What your budget looks like for the work." He paused. "Unless you want Dad and me to just make those decisions for you?"

The way he said it—gentle, without judgment—made Megan realize he was testing her. Seeing if she wanted to be involved or if she preferred to hand everything off to someone else.

She thought about the list in front of her, about Phyllis's faith in her, and about the staff waiting at Sugar & Spice. About the fact that she'd driven five hours on a leap of faith toward something that terrified and excited her in equal measure.

"I want to be there," she said firmly. "I want to understand what needs to happen and be part of the decisions."

Kyle's smile was approving. "Good. That's what I told him you'd say."

"You did?"

"You don't strike me as someone who wants other people running her life." He took a sip of his coffee. "So. Ten o'clock at the apartment?"

Megan nodded. "Ten o'clock... I can do that."

"And tonight, if you're up for it, my sister Leslie wanted to know if you'd like to have dinner. Nothing fancy, just pizza at her place above The Christmas Shop."

The invitation surprised her. "She doesn't have to do that."

"She wants to." Kyle's expression turned slightly amused. "Fair warning—she's going to ask you a thousand questions. She's curious by nature, and you're the most interesting thing to happen in Mistletoe Falls in months."

"I'm not that interesting."

"You inherited a candy shop and drove across state lines with everything you own in your car to start over in a town you barely remembered. That's pretty interesting."

Megan felt heat creep into her cheeks. "When you put it like that."

"Just being honest," he said as he stood up. "I should let you get ready. I've got to open the shop at nine, and Leslie will have my head if I'm late again."

"Again?" Megan asked, walking him to the door.

"I have a terrible habit of losing track of time. Last week she got hit with a massive rush of customers, and I was knee-deep in a contract review for a client. I simply forgot to check on her and got lost in the world of law." He grimaced. "She threatened to lock me out of my own office." Kyle paused at the door, looking down at her with an expression that made Megan's pulse skip. "You doing okay? Really? Yesterday was a lot."

"I'm terrified and hopeful and completely overwhelmed and also kind of excited?"

"Sounds about right for someone whose whole life just changed." His voice was soft. "For what it's worth, I think you're going to do great."

"You don't know me well enough to think that."

"Maybe not. But I knew Phyllis, and if she believed in you this much, I'm inclined to trust her judgment."

Megan's throat went tight again. "Thanks for checking on me. And for the coffee. And for just being—" She stopped, not sure how to finish that sentence.

"Being what?" Kyle prompted, his hazel eyes curious.

"Kind," she said finally. "For being kind when you didn't have to be."

"Kindness isn't something you have to earn, Megan. It's just how people should treat each other."

He said it as if he meant it, like it was obvious. Megan wanted to believe him.

Kyle stepped out onto the porch, turning back with a small wave. "See you at ten. And Megan? Don't overthink things. Just take the next step, then the one after that. That's all any of us can do."

She watched him walk down the path. The morning sun caught in his dark hair, and she noticed the confident set of his shoulders, the easy way he moved through the world like someone who knew exactly where he belonged.

Megan closed the door and leaned against it, the vanilla latte warm in her hands.

She had two hours. Two hours to shower, dress, and mentally prepare for whatever came next. Two hours to transform from Megan-who-simply-existed, to Megan-who-owned-a-business-and-had-a-future.

The list on the table caught her eye, all those tasks waiting to be tackled. But underneath the worry and the uncertainty, there was something else—a kernel of determination that had been growing since yesterday's phone call.

Phyllis had believed in her. Kyle's parents had welcomed her unquestionably. The staff at Sugar & Spice had offered to help her.

She had been given a gift. Even if she wasn't sure what to do with it yet, exactly, she'd figure it out one way or another.

Megan pushed away from the door and headed for the shower.

Chapter 8

Megan stood in the middle of the empty living room in the apartment, notepad in hand, trying to see past the water stains, cracked walls, and peeling paint to whatever potential might be hiding underneath.

She'd arrived at nine-thirty, giving herself time to walk through the space alone before Mitch and Kyle arrived. The steep exterior stairs had been slippery with morning frost, and she'd gripped the rusted railing tighter than necessary, half-convinced the entire structure would collapse beneath her weight.

But she'd made it. And now she stood in what would one day become her home.

Megan uncapped her pen and started a new list:

<u>**Things That Need to Be Fixed/Done**</u>
- Fix outside stairs (Replace? Is that possible?)
- Cracked bedroom window (URGENT)
- Water damage under the kitchen sink

- Kitchen cabinet doors (broken hinges)
- Need refrigerator
- Better stove (current one is tiny)
- Peeling paint (everywhere)
- Wallpaper in bedrooms (gotta go)
- Water-stained ceiling
- Weak water pressure in the bathroom
- Heat works, but the radiators are loud/old
- Windows drafty (all of them?)

She stared at the list, then started another one on a fresh page:

<u>Things I Need to Buy</u>
- Bed
- Mattress
- Bedding (sheets, blankets, pillows)
- Sofa or couch
- Kitchen table and chairs (can do without at first)
- Dishes, glasses, silverware
- Pots and pans
- Coffee maker
- Towels
- Shower curtain
- Lamps
- Curtains or blinds
- Cleaning supplies
- Everything else???

The second list was overwhelming in a different way. Each item represented money she'd have to spend and decisions she'd have to make. New or used? Cheap or quality? Essential or can-it-wait?

She added a note at the bottom: Where to buy furniture in Mistletoe Falls?

Then another: Should I buy new or used? Used is cheaper, but will it last? New is expensive, but might be worth it? How do people make these decisions? What can I live without for now and get later?

Megan walked into the kitchen, her footsteps echoing on the bare floor. The space where a refrigerator should be mocked her with its emptiness. The wobbly table sat off-center, and the two-burner camp stove looked even more pathetic today.

How did you furnish an entire apartment when you'd never had to do it before? When you'd always lived in places that came with at least the basics or shared spaces where other people's furniture filled the gaps?

She had money now, sitting in bank accounts she still couldn't quite believe belonged to her. But that money represented security, possibility, and Phyllis's life savings. The thought of spending it carelessly made her stomach hurt.

Megan was staring at the empty refrigerator space, trying to calculate whether a used fridge would save enough money to be worth the risk of it breaking down, when heavy footsteps sounded on the exterior stairs.

"Megan?" Mitch Porter's voice carried through the open door. "You up here?"

"In the kitchen," she called back, quickly closing her notepad like she'd been caught doing something wrong.

Mitch appeared in the doorway, tool belt already strapped around his waist, followed by Kyle carrying a clipboard and measuring tape.

Both men had the easy confidence of people comfortable in work clothes and planning projects.

"Morning," Mitch said, his smile warm. "You beat us here."

"I wanted to look around first. I'm trying to figure out what needs attention first and what I can live with and tackle later." She gestured vaguely at the apartment. "There's a lot that needs attention."

"There usually is with places that have sat empty for a while." Mitch moved into the kitchen, immediately crouching to inspect the cabinet under the sink. "Kyle mentioned water damage under here?"

Mitch opened the cabinet door—which swung crookedly on its broken hinge—and peered inside with a small flashlight. After a moment, he grunted. "Warped wood, old leak. We'll need to replace this whole bottom section. The good news is the leak itself is old—the pipe's been fixed already, probably years ago."

Kyle was walking the perimeter of the kitchen, making notes. "What about appliances? You'll need a full-size refrigerator and a real stove."

"I know," Megan said. "I made a list." She opened her notepad, suddenly self-conscious about her scribbled notes and questions.

Kyle moved closer to read over her shoulder, and she was acutely aware of his presence—the smell of his cologne and the warmth radiating from his flannel shirt. "That's a pretty good start."

"It's overwhelming," Megan corrected.

"That too. But it's a good start. Mind if we walk through the entire place together? Get your input on priorities?"

Megan nodded, following as Mitch and Kyle moved through each room. They pointed out things she hadn't noticed—a loose floorboard that needed securing, outlets that should be replaced and brought up to code, and the way the bathroom door didn't quite close all the way because the frame had settled over the years.

In the bedroom with the cracked window, Mitch pulled out his measuring tape. "This requires immediate replacement. Can't have you living here with cold air pouring in. I can get a new window ordered today and have it installed by early next week."

"How much will that cost?" Megan asked.

Mitch glanced at Kyle, then back at her. "A few hundred dollars for the window. Megan, it needs to be replaced; there is no other way."

"I know. I just..." She trailed off, not sure how to explain the anxiety that came with spending money, even necessary money. "I need to be careful."

"You also need to be warm," Kyle said gently. "There's a difference between being careful and making yourself miserable trying to save money you actually have."

Megan knew he was right. But knowing and feeling were two different things.

They returned to the living room, and Mitch pulled out a notebook of his own. "Okay. Let's talk priorities. What matters most to you about this space?"

The question was so direct, so practical, that Megan almost laughed. "I don't know. I've never had to think about it before."

"Well, what did you like about the places you've lived?" Kyle prompted.

"I've never lived anywhere I liked," Megan admitted. Then, hearing how that sounded, she tried to soften it. "I mean, they were fine. Temporary. Shared. I had a room, not a place. I haven't really liked any place I've lived since I lived with my mom years ago."

Both men were quiet for a moment. Then Mitch said, "So what do you want this place to feel like?"

The question landed differently. Megan looked around the empty apartment, trying to imagine it not as it was but as it could be.

"Home," she said finally. "I want it to feel warm. Safe. Like a place I would rather not leave."

"That's a good start," Mitch said, making notes. "Warm means functioning heat, good windows, and no drafts. Safe means a solid structure, working locks, and good lighting. You want the basics done right—not fancy, just right... to feel like home. That what you're saying?"

"Yes," Megan said, relieved that someone understood. "Exactly that. I want a home."

"Then that's what we'll do." Mitch tucked his notebook away. "New window, fix the cabinet damage, get your appliances installed, patch the ceiling, fix and paint the walls, refinish the floors, and make sure heat and water work properly. Fix any other drafty windows, which, just to warn you, the windows in this apartment are old, and you may be better off replacing more than just the window with the broken glass. But just talking about the basics... two weeks, maybe three. Nothing fancy, but it'll be livable. Comfortable. Yours."

The way he said "yours" made Megan's throat tight. "That's what I want. Livable. Thank you."

"Where do I buy furniture?" She continued. "I mean, is there somewhere in town, or..."

"Holly & Hearth on Hollyberry Lane has good quality furniture," Kyle said. "A little pricey, but they use local craftsmen, and everything's built to last."

"There's also a home goods store in Pigeon Forge," Mitch added. "About an hour northwest. More selection, lower prices."

Megan bit her lip. "Is there a thrift store? Or somewhere that sells used furniture?"

The two men exchanged glances. "Not in Mistletoe Falls," Kyle said carefully. "Nearest one would be in Pigeon Forge as well. I could take you if you want."

"I don't know what I want," Megan burst out, frustration bleeding into her voice. "I don't know whether I should buy nice furniture that'll last for a while or just get whatever's cheap and figure it out later. I don't know if I should spend money or save money or—" She stopped, pressing her hand against her forehead. "I'm sorry. I'm acting like a child... I need to get a grip."

"You're not acting like a child," Kyle said firmly. "You inherited a lot of money very suddenly. It's scary."

"I don't want to waste it," Megan said quietly. "Phyllis earned and saved that money. I can't just throw it away on things I might not need. I think I may need help trying to figure all the financials out... I just don't want to do anything wrong or mess up."

"You need a bed," Mitch pointed out practically. "And a way to keep food cold. Those aren't luxuries."

"I know, but—" Megan gestured helplessly at her notepad. "How do I know what's worth spending money on? How do I know if I'm being smart or stupid about this?"

Kyle's expression shifted to something gentle and understanding. "Have you ever handled large amounts of money before?"

"No." The admission felt shameful. "The most I've ever had saved was twenty-two hundred dollars, and that was before I had to use it for car repairs."

"Then it makes sense that you're scared to spend," Kyle said. "But Megan, you can't live in an empty apartment eating takeout while sitting on the floor. You're going to have to make some decisions."

Megan looked up at him.

"Listen... the apartment repairs will take a couple of weeks minimum," he continued. "You're comfortable at the resort, right? So what if you just set the furniture and money questions aside for a few days? Work at the shop, get to know the staff and the business, and let yourself settle in. Then make a few decisions from a less overwhelmed place."

Megan looked at Mitch, who nodded. "Makes sense to me. Kyle and I will get started here in the apartment. You go get to know your new employees. Deal?"

It felt too simple. But it also felt like the only manageable path forward. "Okay," Megan said. "Okay. That's... I can do that."

"Good." Mitch smiled. "Then that's settled. Now, about the financial stuff—you said you might need help with that?"

"I don't know anything about managing money," Megan admitted. "I mean, I know how to budget when there's nothing to budget, but this is different. I don't want to do something stupid."

"Then don't do anything at all right now," Kyle suggested. "The money's safe in the bank. It's not going anywhere. When you're ready to think about it—investments, savings accounts, whatever—I'll introduce you to someone who actually knows what they're doing, or I can help you myself, whatever you're comfortable with."

"You'd help me with that?" Megan asked.

"Of course." Kyle said it as if it were obvious. "That's what friends do."

Friends. The word settled over her strangely. She barely knew these people, but they kept showing up, kept offering help, and kept treating her like she mattered.

"Thank you," she said. "Both of you. For not making me feel silly about this."

"First off, you're practical and cautious," Mitch said firmly. "Which are good things when you're making big decisions. Don't let anyone tell you differently."

Megan felt something ease in her chest. "So you'll just... start on the repairs here in the apartment? You don't need me for anything here... right? I can just go to the shop and do whatever there?"

"That's the plan," Kyle confirmed. "Unless you want to help us rip out the bottom of that cabinet? Fair warning, it's dusty work."

Despite everything, Megan laughed. "I think I'll pass."

"Smart choice." Kyle said with a smile. "Go get to know your employees. Enjoy your day. We'll handle this."

"What do I owe you?" Megan asked Mitch. "For the work, I mean. What's your rate?"

Mitch waved a hand dismissively. "We'll settle up when everything's done. No rush."

"But—"

"Megan." Mitch's voice was kind but firm. "I'm not worried about you paying me right now. Go on. Get out of here before we put you to work."

She wanted to argue. But the truth was, she was overwhelmed and grateful and maybe just a little bit relieved to let someone else carry part of this new burden in her life.

"Okay. Thank you."

Kyle walked her to the door, following her out onto the exterior landing.

"You doing okay?" Kyle asked quietly.

"I think so? Maybe?" Megan managed a smile. "I'm trying."

"That's all you need to do." He paused, looking like he was considering something. "Hey, what about tonight?"

"Tonight?"

"Leslie invited you over for pizza; remember me mentioning it this morning?"

"She did," Megan said, then felt her face flush. "I completely forgot about that. With everything this morning, it just—"

"It's fine," Kyle assured her. "I was actually going to ask if you'd mind if I joined you two. I don't want to intrude, but—"

"No, I'd like that," Megan interrupted. "I mean, I don't know, Leslie... really, I don't even know you. But having you there would be nice."

His smile widened. "Yeah?"

"Yeah."

"Then it's a plan. Meet here around five? We can walk over together."

"That works." Megan clutched her notepad. "I should probably head to the shop now."

"Go." Kyle made a shooing motion. "Go meet your new employees, learn secret candy recipes, and have some fun. Become a confectionery master. Live your best life."

Megan laughed, surprised by how good it felt. "I'll try."

She descended the stairs carefully, aware of Kyle watching to make sure she made it down safely. At the bottom, she turned back to wave, and he was still there, leaning against the railing with that easy confidence that made him seem like he belonged everywhere he went.

"Kyle," she called up to him. "Can you ask your dad if there's a way to fix those stairs or even replace them? They scare the daylights out of me."

Kyle grinned. "Congratulations, Megan Caldwell, you just made your first new-home decision. You're doing just fine... you've got this."

Chapter 9

Megan pushed open the back door to Sugar & Spice and stepped inside, letting it close softly behind her.

The storage area spread before her—shelves lined with industrial-sized containers of sugar, flour, cocoa powder, and ingredients she couldn't even name. Two large walk-in coolers hummed against the far wall, their doors marked with temperature gauges and handwritten notes about what was stored inside. To her right, the door to the kitchen stood open, and she could hear voices, the clatter of pans, and the low hum of machinery.

She stood there, notepad still clutched in one hand, suddenly unsure what to do with herself.

This was hers. All of it. The ingredients, the equipment, the business humming along without her. But it didn't feel like hers. It felt like she was trespassing, like any moment someone would notice she didn't belong here and ask her to leave.

Megan took a breath and moved toward the kitchen door.

The scene inside was organized chaos. Kay stood at the marble slab, her hands working methodically as she spread something across the surface. Linda was at the stove, stirring a copper pot with the focus of someone conducting a symphony. Tonya moved between them, carrying trays and checking temperatures, her energy somehow both frenetic and perfectly controlled.

The air smelled like butter and sugar and something warm and soothing that Megan couldn't quite identify but that made her mouth water.

"Morning," Megan said, her voice tentative.

All three women looked up. Kay's face broke into a welcoming smile. "Megan! Good morning. We wondered when you'd make it in."

"I had to meet with Mitch about the apartment repairs." Megan stepped further into the kitchen, trying to stay out of the way. "It took longer than I expected."

"How'd that go?" Linda asked, not pausing in her stirring.

"Overwhelming. But manageable, I think." Megan watched Kay's hands working what looked like caramel, fascinated by the practiced ease of the motion. "What can I do? I mean, how can I help?"

Kay straightened, wiping her hands on her apron. "What would you like to start with? You shadow any of us to get a feel for different parts of the business."

"I don't know," Megan admitted. "I've never done anything like this before. I don't even know where to begin."

"Well, there's plenty to learn," Tonya said cheerfully, setting down a tray. "Candy making, packaging, inventory, customer service, bookkeeping—take your pick."

The list only made Megan feel more lost. "Maybe I should just watch for a while? See how everything works?"

"That's not a bad start," Kay agreed. "Though—"

"Hold on just a second." Beth's voice came from down the hall, followed by the sound of a chair rolling back. She appeared in the kitchen doorway, reading glasses perched on her nose. "Before we get Megan started on anything, I should probably get her set up properly."

"Set up?" Megan asked.

"On the payroll system." Beth gestured for Megan to follow her. "Come on back to my office. It'll just take a few minutes."

Megan glanced at Kay, who nodded encouragingly. "Go ahead. We'll still be here when you're done."

Beth's office was small but organized, with filing cabinets lining one wall and a desk that held a computer that looked much newer than Phyllis's.

"Have a seat," Beth said, settling into her chair and pulling up something on the computer. "This won't take long. I just need some basic information from you—social security number, address, that sort of thing. Then we'll get you added as an employee so you can start drawing a salary."

"A salary?" Megan sat in the chair across from Beth's desk. "I own the business. Do I need a salary?"

"Well, you need to pay yourself somehow," Beth said with a grin. "Phyllis paid herself a regular salary just like the rest of us. We can set you up at the same rate she was taking, if that works for you."

"I have no idea what would work for me," Megan confessed. "What was she paying herself?"

Beth clicked a few keys and turned the monitor so Megan could see. "She was making forty-eight thousand a year, paid biweekly. That's after we upgraded her salary last year when the shop's profits increased. Then, at the end of every year, she was paid a bonus, all of which depended on the end-of-year profits."

Forty-eight thousand. More than Megan had ever made in her life. "That seems like a lot."

"It's fair for managing a business," Beth said. "You're going to be working here full-time, right? Learning the operation and eventually taking on more responsibility? You deserve to be compensated for that."

The word "deserve" stuck in Megan's throat. "I guess so. Yes. That would be fine."

"Great." Beth pulled out some forms. "I'll need you to fill these out—W-4, direct deposit information if you want it, and emergency contact. Just standard employment paperwork."

Megan took the forms, staring at the blank lines. Direct deposit. Emergency contact. It all felt so official, so permanent. Like she was really doing this, really staying, really building a life here instead of just visiting for a while.

She picked up a pen and started filling in the information. After a few minutes, she looked up. "Can I ask you something?"

"Of course."

"Are you okay with this? With my just showing up and inheriting everything? I mean, you've been here for years. You know how to run this place. And I'm just... I don't know anything."

Beth set down her pen and gave Megan her full attention. "Am I okay with it? Honestly?"

"Honestly."

"I was worried at first," Beth admitted. "Not because I wanted the business for myself—I never expected that. But because I wasn't sure what kind of person would be inheriting it. What if you wanted to sell? What if you wanted to change everything? What if you didn't care about the shop the way Phyllis did?"

"And now?" Megan asked quietly.

"Now I've met you." Beth's smile was genuine. "You care. That's obvious. You're overwhelmed and uncertain, and that's perfectly fine, but you care. You haven't given me the impression that you plan to take advantage of anything or make a quick profit. You seem willing to learn, and I respect that."

Megan felt her eyes sting. "I don't want to mess this up. I don't want to let anyone down."

"Then let us help you." Beth leaned forward. "Here's the thing, Megan. This shop runs because everyone has a role. Kay manages the kitchen and coordinates candy production. Linda's the master candy maker and can make any recipe... and so can Kay, for that matter. Tonya handles candy making; her specialty is taffy and detailed work... Our specialty items are where she shines, but just like Kay and Linda, she can make anything. Savannah works the front and handles our online presence; that is her main focus, but she makes candy as well when she has time. I manage the business side—payroll, inventory, ordering supplies, bookkeeping, and... if you haven't already guessed, I make candy as well. We're all just one happy family here. We each have distinct jobs, but at the same time we all love the candy-making process; that's what makes this business work and run smoothly."

"And Phyllis?"

"Phyllis did a little bit of everything. She managed overall, yes, but her real love was making candy, testing new recipes, and taking care of customers. Those were her three favorite things. That's why she hired competent people to handle everything else—so she could focus on what she loved."

Megan absorbed this. "So what am I supposed to do?"

"Whatever you want," Beth said simply. "If you love working the front of the store, talking to customers, and building relationships—do that. If you fall in love with candy making and want to work in the kitchen all day—do that. If you want to do a little of everything, moving around wherever you're needed—do that. There's no wrong answer here."

"But surely there's something I should be doing. Some role I should fill."

"Your role right now is to learn and have fun doing it," Beth said. "Figure out what you enjoy. Don't try to force yourself into a role that might not fit. Figure out what you're good at. Where you fit naturally. The shop's running fine. We've got the systems in place. You have time to find your place; there is no rush."

The relief that washed over Megan was almost too much. "You're sure? You don't mind running things while I figure it all out?"

"I'm sure." Beth's voice was firm. "I'm happy to do it. This is what I'm good at. And honestly? It's easier for me to keep doing what I do best while you learn, rather than try to suddenly train you on everything at once and throw you into a management role you're not ready for or that you might not even want."

"That makes sense," Megan said slowly.

"Besides," Beth added with a smile, "you'll naturally start taking on more as you get comfortable. One day you'll realize you're making decisions without thinking about it, and that'll be when you know you've found your footing."

Megan finished filling out the forms and handed them back to Beth. "Thank you. For being patient with me. And for being honest."

"That's what we do here." Beth filed the paperwork. "We're a team. We support each other. That includes you now."

Megan nodded, not trusting her voice. In less than forty-eight hours, she'd gone from having no one to having an entire team of people willing to help her succeed. The shift was dizzying.

"So," Beth said, turning back to her computer. "I'll get this processed today. You should see your first paycheck next Friday. Meanwhile, go have fun, shadow whoever you want, ask as many questions as you need, and generally just absorb how things work around here."

"Okay." Megan stood, then hesitated. "Beth? What did Phyllis usually do on a typical day?"

Beth considered. "She'd come in early, check on what was being made that day, and usually help with making candy. Then she'd spend time in the front, talking to customers, ringing up sales, and making recommendations. She'd handle any special orders personally; she absolutely loved making up gift baskets and adding her own little touches for any special orders that came in. She would check inventory, approve supply orders, and solve whatever problems came up. And she'd always spend the last hour before closing in the kitchen, cleaning up and prepping for the next day."

"She did all that?"

"Most days, yes. But she'd been doing it for years... so it was her habit and her comfort. She was a person who liked to fill her days doing what she loved. She knew every inch of this place. You'll get there too. Just give yourself time; you'll figure out what works best for you."

Megan nodded again, feeling slightly less overwhelmed. Not completely calm, but slightly less like she was drowning.

She was about to head back to the kitchen when Kay appeared in Beth's doorway, her apron dusted with what looked like powdered sugar.

"Sorry to interrupt," Kay said. "But Megan, if you're done with the paperwork, I'm about to start a batch of maple fudge. Thought you might like to watch, if you're interested."

Maple fudge. Megan remembered that from childhood visits—the smooth, sweet taste that wasn't quite like anything else. "I'd love to."

"Great." Kay's smile widened. "Fair warning—it's going to smell spectacular, and you'll want to eat half the batch. I can't promise I'll stop you."

Megan laughed, surprised at how good it felt. "Lead the way."

Chapter 10

Megan followed Kay back into the kitchen. Linda was now working at a different station, pouring what looked like molten caramel into rectangular molds with the steady hands of a surgeon. Tonya had moved to the marble slab, stretching something pale and glossy between her hands with a rhythmic pull-and-fold motion that looked almost hypnotic.

And at the sink, Savannah was washing her hands with the thoroughness of someone preparing for surgery, her dark hair pulled back in a tight ponytail.

"Savannah!" Kay called. "Taking a candy break from the register?"

"It's Beth's turn to cover the front for an hour," Savannah said, drying her hands. "Thought I'd help Linda with the caramel apples before the afternoon rush hits."

Kay turned to Megan with a smile. "First things first. Let's get you started off on the right foot."

"I really just want to watch," Megan protested.

"You can watch with clean hands and an apron," Kay said, already pulling a fresh apron from a hook by the door. "Here you go."

Megan tied on the apron—white with "Sugar & Spice" embroidered across the chest in burgundy thread—and moved to the sink. The soap smelled like lemons and something antiseptic, and she scrubbed her hands the way Kay demonstrated, paying attention to every detail.

"Good," Kay approved. "Now, come stand here by me. You can see everything I'm doing without being in the way."

Megan positioned herself at Kay's elbow, notepad abandoned on a nearby counter. She'd write things down later. Right now, she wanted to just absorb everything.

Kay pulled out a heavy copper pot—one that looked like it had been used for decades—and set it on the industrial stove. "Maple fudge," she began, her voice taking on the tone of a teacher who loved her subject, "is all about the maple syrup. Real maple syrup, not the fake stuff. We use Grade A Dark Amber from a supplier in Vermont."

"Why that grade specifically?" Megan asked.

"Because it has the strongest maple flavor. Grade A Golden is too delicate for candy—the flavor gets lost when you cook it down." Kay reached for a large container and began measuring syrup into the pot. "See how thick it is? That's what we want."

Linda's voice carried from her station. "Kay's maple fudge is the best you'll ever taste."

"Linda's biased," Kay said, but she looked pleased.

"Linda's honest," Tonya corrected, still working her taffy with that mesmerizing rhythm. "I've tasted fudge from fancy shops in Gatlinburg and Nashville. Nothing beats Kay's."

Megan watched as Kay added butter to the pot, then sugar, then cream. Each ingredient was measured with practiced precision, and

Kay explained every step—why the butter went in before the sugar, how to tell when the cream was the right temperature, and why the pot had to be copper instead of stainless steel.

"Copper conducts heat more evenly," Kay explained. "With candy, consistent temperature is everything. Too hot, and it burns. Too cool, and it doesn't set properly."

"How do you know when it's right?" Megan asked.

"Experience mostly. But we also use these." Kay tapped a candy thermometer clipped to the side of the pot. "For fudge, you want to hit exactly 234 degrees. That's called the soft-ball stage."

"Soft-ball stage?" The term sounded almost comical.

"It means that if you drop a bit of the mixture into cold water, it forms a soft ball that flattens when you take it out." Kay stirred the mixture with a wooden spoon, her movements slow and deliberate. "Every candy has a different stage. Soft-ball, hard-ball, soft crack, and hard crack — each corresponds to a specific temperature and texture."

Savannah spoke up from where she was dipping apples in caramel. "I burned through three batches of toffee before I figured out the difference between soft-crack and hard-crack."

"We all have learning disasters," Linda said kindly. "I once made peanut brittle so hard it cracked one of Phyllis's teeth."

"You did not!" Megan looked at Linda in surprise.

"I absolutely did. She was very gracious about it, but we had to throw away the whole batch," Linda said while smiling.

The kitchen filled with the smell of maple and butter as Kay's mixture began to bubble. She adjusted the heat slightly, watching the thermometer with the focus of someone who'd done this thousands of times but still treated each batch as important.

"So, Megan," Tonya said, her hands never stopping their pull-and-fold motion with the taffy. "What made you decide to come here other than Phyllis's will?"

The question was casual, but Megan felt all eyes shift to her. She could deflect, make a joke, or give some vague answer about fresh starts. But these women were being honest with her, sharing their mistakes and their stories.

"That's a tough question to answer. I didn't really decide... well, I mean I guess I did make the decision to come here... but I really felt it was the right time in my life, and I felt out of options," Megan admitted. "I didn't get the position at my former job that I felt I deserved. I got a final eviction notice for the apartment I shared with a few roommates. The building owners were going to turn the building into condo units. That same day, Kyle called about the inheritance. I realized I had nothing tying me to Bowling Green except a job I hated and roommates I barely tolerated. So really... the decision was made for me. What did I have to lose?"

"What kind of work were you doing?" Savannah asked.

"Most recently? Working at a copy center. Before that, various retail jobs. Before that, restaurant hostess. Before that, a waitress. Before that..." Megan shrugged. "Dead-end jobs. That's what I'm good at, apparently. Finding jobs that go nowhere and pay just enough to keep you trapped in this endless cycle of survival."

The honesty felt exposing but also freeing. These women could judge her for being a failure at twenty-eight, for having no career and no prospects. Or they could understand.

"I worked in fast food for three years," Savannah said. "I hated every minute. The only reason I'm in college part-time now is because Phyllis convinced me I was smart enough to try."

"I cleaned houses for a decade," Linda added quietly. "Didn't start candy making until I was thirty-five. Never too late to find what you love."

Kay kept stirring, but her voice was warm. "I bounced around too when I was younger. I worked in a factory, then a grocery store, and then a nursing home kitchen. I didn't discover candy making until I was about twenty-five years old. Sometimes the path in life isn't straight, but I think eventually most people get to where they're meant to be."

Megan felt her throat tighten. "Did you all know right away? That this was what you wanted to do?"

"Goodness, no," Tonya laughed. "I thought I wanted to be a graphic designer. I spent two years at a community college for that. Then I came home for summer break and saw a help-wanted sign Phyllis had put in the front window. After one week of working here and I was hooked."

"I needed a job, and Phyllis was hiring," Kay said simply. "I didn't realize I'd fallen in love with it until a month in, when I made my first perfect batch of fudge and felt like I'd accomplished something real."

"That's exactly it," Linda said, nodding. "It's real. Physical. You take ingredients and turn them into something people enjoy. There's satisfaction in that."

The thermometer was climbing—230 degrees, 232, 234. Kay removed the pot from the heat with practiced efficiency and began stirring more vigorously. "This is the critical part. Cooling it down while keeping it smooth. If you stir too much, it crystallizes wrong. Too little, and it won't set creamy."

Megan watched, fascinated, as the mixture transformed under Kay's spoon. What had been thin and bubbling became thicker, glossier, taking on a texture that looked almost like satin.

"See how it's starting to lose its shine?" Kay pointed with her free hand. "That's when you know it's ready to pour."

She moved to a buttered pan and poured the fudge in a smooth stream, tilting the pan to spread it evenly. The smell was incredible—rich maple and sweet butter that made Megan's mouth water.

"Now it has to cool," Kay said, setting the pan aside. "That's the hard part. Waiting."

"How long?" Megan asked.

"Couple hours at room temperature. Then we cut it into squares, wrap it, and it's ready to sell." Kay wiped her hands on her apron. "Want to try one from yesterday's batch?"

"Yes, please."

Kay retrieved a small square from a nearby container and handed it to Megan. The fudge was firm but not hard, and when Megan bit into it, the flavor exploded—intensely maple, creamy smooth, with just enough sweetness to balance the richness.

"Oh my gosh," Megan said through her mouthful. "This is incredible."

"Told you," Linda said smugly.

"How do you not eat this all day?" Megan asked, savoring another bite.

All four women burst into laughter.

"Seriously," Savannah said, "you learn to pace yourself. Otherwise you end up with a sugar headache and a stomachache."

The afternoon continued in that pattern—work and conversation flowing together naturally. Linda explained how she tempered chocolate, showing Megan the precise temperature ranges and how to test if it was ready. Tonya demonstrated taffy pulling, her hands moving in that rhythmic pattern that looked exhausting but that she claimed was meditative once you got the hang of it.

Savannah finished her caramel apples—perfect red orbs dipped in golden caramel and rolled in chopped pecans—and excused herself to return to the front counter. But not before asking Megan questions about Bowling Green, about what kind of movies she liked, and about whether she enjoyed outdoor winter activities.

"I've never been much of a cold weather fan," Megan admitted. "And the way my life has been, I never had time for hardly any outdoor activities, let alone in the winter."

"We have plenty of fun things to do around here. There's skiing, tobogganing, hiking the trails, ice skating... just all sorts of outdoor stuff," Savannah said. "We should plan a day and go as a group and show you some fun things to do around here."

"I wouldn't mind that. Let me get settled in a little more, and we'll plan something. For now, let me at least figure out if I can make a batch of candy successfully."

"Are you up for trying right now? Just a simple batch, with our help?"

"I thought I'd just watch today."

"You've been watching for two hours," Kay pointed out. "At some point, you have to just jump in and get your feet wet."

Megan looked at the copper pots, the marble slab, the thermometers, and the molds and tools that these women wielded with such confidence. Then she looked at their faces—encouraging, patient, ready to help her succeed rather than waiting for her to fail.

"Okay," she said. "What should I try?"

"Fudge is a good start," Kay said. "Classic chocolate fudge. Hard to mess up, and even if you do, it still tastes delicious."

"Hard to mess up?" Megan raised an eyebrow. "That sounds like a challenge."

"Oh honey," Tonya laughed. "You have no idea. Linda, remember when Savannah—"

"We don't talk about the peppermint incident," Linda interrupted, but she was smiling.

"The what incident?" Megan demanded.

"Another time," Kay said, pulling out a fresh pot. "Right now, we're going to teach you the fundamentals of chocolate fudge. Ready?"

Megan took a deep breath, nerves and excitement warring in her chest. "Ready."

Kay moved beside her at the stove, close enough to guide but not so close that Megan felt crowded. "First, we measure. Everything in candy making is precise..."

Chapter 11

Kyle stood in the alley behind Sugar & Spice at five o'clock sharp, hands in his jacket pockets, leaning against the brick wall near the back door. The November evening had the crispness of early winter.

The back door opened, and Megan emerged, pulling a cardigan tighter around herself. She'd changed out of the apron but still had that slightly dazed look of someone who'd spent hours absorbed in something new.

"Hey," Kyle said, straightening. "How was day one?"

"Overwhelming. Educational. Possibly life-changing?" She laughed, and the sound did something to his chest. "I made chocolate fudge."

"How'd it turn out?"

"Edible, barely." Megan fell into step beside him as they started walking toward The Christmas Shop. "Kay said it was perfectly fine for a first attempt, but I think she was being generous. It's definitely not going to win any awards."

Kyle smiled at her self-deprecating tone. She did that—made jokes at her own expense in a way that suggested she genuinely didn't take herself too seriously. It was refreshing after years of dealing with legal clients who couldn't admit when they didn't know something.

"Everyone starts somewhere," he said. "I burned three batches of cookies the first time I tried baking for a Christmas Shop promotion. Leslie still mentions it."

"Only three batches?" Megan's eyes sparkled with amusement. "I'm already planning to beat that record."

They walked down Mistletoe Lane, their breath visible in the chilly air. The streetlights were just starting to come on—those gas lamp-style fixtures that made downtown Mistletoe Falls look like something from another century. Most of the shops were closing for the evening.

"Is it always this quiet?" Megan asked, looking around.

"Weeknights this time of year, yeah. But things will really change after Thanksgiving; most shops extend their hours and stay open later because our tourist traffic in town quadruples from then until after the New Year. Wait until you see it when the Christmas season really starts. You can barely move with all the tourists."

"I like it here," Megan said. "It feels... safe and welcoming."

Something about the way she said it made Kyle glance at her. There was a wistfulness in her expression, like she was testing the words to see if they fit. He wondered what her life in Bowling Green had been like, beyond the dead-end jobs and cramped apartment she'd mentioned. What made someone feel unsafe enough that a quiet Thursday evening in a small-town felt noteworthy?

"The walk feels good after being inside all day," Megan added, breaking the moment.

"I agree. Dad and I took measurements for your new staircase to-day," Kyle said. "We ordered the framework. Should arrive next week."

Megan stopped walking. "That fast?"

"Sure, Dad knows a local contractor that specializes in metalwork. He had time to fit you into his schedule." Kyle started walking again, and Megan hurried to catch up. "Your new stairs will be sturdy. Nothing fancy, but safe."

"Safe is exactly what I need."

There it was again—that emphasis on the word safe, like it meant more than just structural integrity.

They reached The Christmas Shop, its windows dark except for the security lighting that made the ornament displays glow softly. Kyle led Megan around to the back of the building, where a set of wooden stairs led up to the second floor.

"These are more like what I think my apartment needs," Megan said. "Solid. Not terrifying."

"Leslie made Dad reinforce these twice," Kyle said, climbing ahead of her.

At the top, Kyle opened the door without knocking—Leslie never locked it when she was expecting him—and called out, "We're here."

"Finally!" Leslie's voice came from deeper in the apartment. "I'm starving."

Kyle held the door for Megan, watching her face as she stepped inside.

The living room stretched before them, painted in a warm tan color, with deep burgundy accents in the throw pillows and curtains. A plush sofa faced a gas fireplace, and bookshelves lined one wall, crammed with everything from classics to romance novels to reference books about Christmas traditions. A few candles were lit, their flickering glow making everything feel cozy despite the overhead lighting.

"This is beautiful," Megan said.

"Thank you!" Leslie emerged from the kitchen area, wiping her hands on a dish towel. She wore jeans and an oversized sweater, her dark hair loose around her shoulders. "I've been working on it for years. My mom calls it 'organized chaos,' but I prefer 'eclectic cozy.'"

"It's perfect," Megan said, moving further into the room. "This is exactly what I want my apartment to feel like. Warm and inviting and... like somewhere you actually want to be."

Leslie beamed. "Well, I'm happy to help you decorate once your apartment's ready. Fair warning—I have strong opinions about throw pillows."

"I don't even own any... I don't even know what throw pillows are for, really," Megan admitted with a laugh.

"That's what friends are for." Leslie gestured toward the dining table that dominated one end of the open-concept space. "Come on, the pizza's getting cold."

Two large pizza boxes sat on the table, along with paper plates, napkins, and various drinks.

They settled around the table—Leslie at the head, Kyle and Megan on either side. Leslie opened the pizza boxes with a flourish. "We've got one supreme and one pepperoni. I figured variety was safest."

"Both look wonderful," Megan said, reaching for a slice of pepperoni. "I haven't had decent pizza in forever. The place near my old apartment was terrible."

"Define terrible," Leslie said, serving herself a slice of supreme.

"The kind where you're not sure if what you're eating is actually cheese or some kind of cheese-adjacent substance." Megan took a bite and made a sound of appreciation. "This is so good."

Kyle helped himself to pizza, content to let the women talk.

"So," Leslie said, settling into her chair. "How's the candy shop? Is everything going okay? It must be overwhelming."

"That's an understatement." Megan dabbed at her mouth with a napkin. "Two days ago, I was working at a copy center in Bowling Green, and today, I'm working in a candy shop that I now own. It doesn't feel real."

"That's a massive change," Leslie agreed. "Are you planning to stay? Or is this more of a temporary thing while you figure out what to do?"

Kyle held his breath, waiting for Megan's answer. Something about Megan made him want her to stay, to give Mistletoe Falls a chance.

"I'm staying," Megan said. "At least for now. I don't have anywhere else to go, and honestly? This might be the best opportunity I've ever had. I'd be stupid to run from it."

"I can understand that," Leslie said. "How are the employees doing at the shop?"

"They are incredible. Kay, Linda, Tonya, Beth, and Savannah—they've all been so welcoming. I was worried they'd resent me a little maybe, but they seem genuinely happy I'm here."

"They are all good people," Leslie said.

They fell into a simple rhythm after that—eating, talking, the conversation flowing from topic to topic without awkward silences. Leslie told embarrassing stories about Kyle's teenage years, and Kyle retaliated with stories about Leslie's early years in high school. Megan laughed more than Kyle had heard her laugh before, and he watched her face, cataloging the way her eyes crinkled when she was genuinely amused and how she ducked her head slightly when she was embarrassed.

"How did you two end up owning The Christmas Shop?" Megan asked eventually. "Kyle mentioned your parents used to run it?"

"They did," Leslie said. "Mom and Dad bought it back in the early nineties, right after they got married. It was their first big investment, and they poured everything into making it successful."

"They were good at it too," Kyle added. "Mom handled the creative side—displays, inventory, and seasonal themes. Dad managed the business end. They complemented each other well."

"Then Snowflake Mountain Resort came up for sale a few years ago," Leslie continued. "The previous owners were retiring, and it needed someone who really understood mountain hospitality. Mom and Dad had always loved that property—Dad actually worked there as a teenager—so when the opportunity came up, they jumped on it."

"They sold us The Christmas Shop," Kyle said, "figuring we'd already been helping run it for years, anyway. It just made sense to keep it in the family."

"And you wanted to run a Christmas shop?" Megan asked, directing the question at Kyle. "I mean, you're a lawyer."

Kyle set down his pizza, considering how to answer. "I went to law school because I thought it was what I wanted to do for the rest of my life. Stable career, good income, and a respected profession. I moved back here after graduation and set up a small practice on the edge of town—mostly estate planning, contracts, that kind of thing."

"He was miserable," Leslie said bluntly.

"I wasn't miserable," Kyle protested. "Just... unfulfilled, maybe."

"You were miserable," Leslie repeated. "You'd come home and complain about how boring your day was, how every client wanted the same thing, and how you felt like you were just going through the motions."

Kyle shot his sister a look. "You're not helping."

"I'm being honest." Leslie turned to Megan. "He tried to convince himself he was fine for almost two years. Then Mom and Dad offered us The Christmas Shop, and suddenly he came alive again. Started talking about inventory systems and display strategies like they were the most exciting things in the world."

"They are interesting," Kyle said defensively. "There's a lot of psychology involved in retail merchandising."

"See?" Leslie gestured at him. "This is what I mean. He loves it."

Kyle felt his face heat slightly. "The point is, I realized I didn't have to choose. I could practice law part-time, handle the legal work for the shop, and offer my services to the community on my terms, and spend the rest of my time doing something I actually enjoyed. It's not traditional, but it works."

"That's actually smart," Megan said. "If you think about it, you have a creative outlet and something physical to do, and both jobs fulfill the technical side of your mind... at least that's the way I see it."

"What about you?" Kyle asked, genuinely curious. "Did you ever go to college?"

Megan was quiet for a moment, pushing a piece of pepperoni around her plate. "I never wanted to go to college. Everyone acts like that's this terrible thing, like you're dooming yourself to failure if you don't get a degree. But I was never interested in sitting in classrooms. I've been working since I was sixteen—retail, food service, whatever would hire me. I kept thinking I'd eventually find something I loved, some career that would click into place." She paused. "It never happened."

"Maybe you just haven't found the right thing yet," Leslie suggested.

"Possibly." Megan looked up, and Kyle saw uncertainty in her green eyes. "Or maybe I'm just not cut out for having a career, you know? Maybe I'm meant to bounce between jobs forever."

"You inherited a business," Kyle pointed out. "That's not bouncing—that's landing."

"Landing somewhere I don't know how to navigate," Megan countered. "I made fudge today, and it barely turned out edible. I don't know how to run a retail store. I don't know how to manage employees or handle bookkeeping or any of the things Phyllis did. I'm completely out of my depth."

"Everyone's out of their depth at first," Leslie said. "I have a journalism degree, but that didn't teach me how to run a Christmas shop. I learned by doing, by making mistakes, and by asking questions. You'll do the same."

"The staff already likes you," Kyle added. "That's huge. They could have made this difficult, but instead they're supporting you. That's more than half the battle."

Megan's expression softened slightly. "They were really great today. Patient and funny and willing to teach me. Kay let me watch her make maple fudge and explained every step. Linda showed me how to temper chocolate. Tonya demonstrated taffy pulling—which looks way harder than it seems, by the way."

"It is," Leslie confirmed. "I tried it once and nearly dislocated my shoulder."

"How does that even happen?" Kyle asked.

"I don't know, but I managed it." Leslie refilled her drink. "So what's your plan for tomorrow? More candy making?"

"Maybe. Or I might spend time in the retail area and learn how the front of the store works. Beth mentioned I should probably go through everything in Phyllis's office at some point—there are files and records I should familiarize myself with." Megan sighed. "There's so much to learn. I wonder if I'll ever feel like I actually know what I'm doing."

"You will," Kyle said with more certainty than he felt. "It just takes time."

They talked more as they finished the pizza—about Mistletoe Falls, about the upcoming Christmas season, and about the quirks of small-town life that Megan would need to adjust to. Leslie asked about Megan's mother, and Megan admitted they weren't particularly close, that Sandra had remarried and moved to Florida and seemed happy with her new life.

"She's supportive in theory," Megan said. "But we've never been... close, I guess. Not since my dad filed for a divorce and left. She was a changed person after that, not the mother I knew before. She worked a lot from that point on and put herself through nursing school. I basically raised myself from the age of thirteen on. I was a latchkey kid."

Kyle heard the loneliness in that admission and wanted to say something reassuring, but what could he say? That it would get better? That found family could fill those gaps? It felt presumptuous to make a promise about her future.

"Well, you've got a whole town of people here now," Leslie said, her voice warm. "Whether you want them or not. That's small-town life—everyone knows your business, but they also show up when you need them."

"Like jumping in to fix up my apartment?" Megan said with a small smile in Kyle's direction.

"Exactly like that," Leslie confirmed. "Get used to it."

The conversation continued late into the evening, flowing from lighthearted to serious and back again. Kyle found himself talking more than he usually did, drawn out by Megan's genuine interest and the easy dynamic between the three of them. Megan had the rare quality of being comfortable without trying too hard and of laughing at herself while still taking things seriously when it mattered.

Around eight-thirty, Megan stifled a yawn. "I'm sorry. I am so tired."

"First days are exhausting," Leslie said sympathetically. "Especially when you're learning entirely new skills."

"I should probably head back." Megan stood, helping clear plates despite Leslie's protests. "I'm parked behind Sugar & Spice, and I need to drive out to the resort before I fall asleep standing up."

"I'll walk you back," Kyle said, standing as well. "My truck's still there too."

They said their goodbyes to Leslie, who hugged Megan and made her promise to come over again soon. Then, Kyle and Megan descended the stairs into the November night, which had grown noticeably colder in the hours they'd been inside.

"That was really nice," Megan said as they started walking. "Your sister is great."

"She is." Kyle watched their breath cloud in the air. "I'm lucky to have a good sister."

They walked in comfortable silence for a bit, their footsteps echoing on the empty sidewalk. All the shops were dark now, and the streetlights created pools of golden light that they passed through one by one.

"Oh!" Megan stopped suddenly. "I completely forgot about Hazel."

Kyle turned back to face her.

"Your cat. Well, my cat now, I guess." Megan pressed her hand to her forehead. "I'm supposed to take her, right? But the apartment isn't ready, and I don't know if the cabin allows pets, and—"

"Megan, breathe." Kyle moved closer, resisting the urge to take her hand. "Hazel's fine at my place for now. But yeah, you should probably eventually take her."

"This weekend, maybe?" Megan suggested. "Would Saturday work?"

"Saturday's perfect." Kyle pulled out his phone. "Here, let me get your number. That way I can text you when I'm heading over with her."

They exchanged numbers, Kyle trying not to notice how her fingers trembled slightly—from cold or nerves, he wasn't sure. When they finished, they continued walking until they reached the alley behind Sugar & Spice, where both of their vehicles were parked.

Megan unlocked her Honda and then turned back to Kyle. "Thank you. For walking me back. And for dinner. And for, I don't know, just being so helpful with everything."

"It's not a problem at all," Kyle said, and meant it.

"Still. Thank you." She climbed into her car and started the engine.

Kyle stood in the alley, hands in his pockets, watching her taillights disappear around the corner. His truck sat a few feet away, but he didn't move yet.

He was in trouble. The kind of trouble that came from spending an evening with someone and realizing you wanted to spend many more evenings just like it. The kind of trouble that made you volunteer to fix staircases and apartments and deliver cats.

Kyle had been careful with his heart since moving back to Mistletoe Falls. Small-town dating was complicated—everyone knew everyone, and breakups became community knowledge. He'd convinced himself that being single was simpler, that focusing on work and family was enough.

But watching Megan drive away, Kyle knew his careful plans were already unraveling.

Chapter 12

The newspaper clipping was yellowed with age, the edges brittle enough that Megan handled it carefully as she smoothed it flat on Phyllis's desk.

Grand Opening: Sugar & Spice Candy Shop Sweetens Downtown Mistletoe Falls

The photograph showed a younger Phyllis standing in front of the shop with scissors poised above a red ribbon. Her smile was luminous, the kind that reached all the way to her eyes and made everyone around her want to smile too. The article was dated October 15, 1998.

Megan had been four years old.

She set that clipping aside and reached for the next one in the stack. March 2003—a feature story about Phyllis's hand-pulled taffy winning first place at the Tennessee State Fair. Then in September 2007, Sugar & Spice was named "Best Candy Shop in East Tennessee" by a regional tourism magazine. December 2012—a holiday spread showcasing Phyllis's peppermint bark recipe and her philosophy that "every piece of candy should be made with love."

There were dozens of them, carefully preserved in a file folder labeled "Press" in Phyllis's neat handwriting. Each one told a piece of the story—awards won, community events hosted, and milestones celebrated. The shop's tenth anniversary. It's fifteenth. The twentieth, with a photo of Phyllis surrounded by Kay, Linda, and the rest of the staff, everyone laughing like family.

She picked up another clipping, this one more recent—just two years old. The headline read: *Local Business Owner Phyllis Caldwell Receives Chamber of Commerce Lifetime Achievement Award.*

The photograph showed Phyllis accepting a plaque, older but still radiant. The article quoted her: *"This shop has been my life's work and my greatest joy. Every customer who walks through my door, every piece of candy we make—it all matters. Because we're not just selling sweets. We're creating moments people will remember."*

Megan's vision blurred. She set the clipping down and pressed her fingers against her eyes, trying to hold back tears that came anyway.

Phyllis had devoted everything to this place. Had built it from nothing into something that touched people's lives, that employed loyal staff, and that had become part of the town's identity. And she'd left it all to a niece she hadn't seen in fifteen years.

Why?

Megan pulled open another drawer, finding it stuffed with file folders—financial records, supplier contracts, and employee documents. But tucked in the very back, she found something else. Three leather-bound journals, their covers worn soft with handling.

She pulled out the first one and opened it to a random page. The date at the top read June 12, 1998—four months before the shop opened.

The inspectors came today. Everything passed! I can hardly believe it—after months of renovations and planning and second-guessing every decision, I'm actually going to do this. Some people think I'm crazy for being so nervous, but opening your own business is terrifying. What if nobody comes? What if the candy isn't good enough? What if I've made a terrible mistake?

But then I remember what Mama used to say: "Fear is just excitement that hasn't found its courage yet." So, I'm choosing to be excited. Scared out of my mind, but excited.

Megan smiled through her tears. She flipped forward several pages.

October 20, 1998—We've been open five days, and I think we're going to make it. People keep coming back! Mrs. Hoffman bought three pounds of fudge yesterday and said it was the best she'd ever tasted. Mr. Clark special-ordered caramels for his wife's birthday. And today, a little girl came in with her piggy bank and counted out exact change for a package of gumdrops, then told me, "This candy is the prettiest in the whole world."

This is why I'm doing this—for moments like that. For the joy on a child's face. For the way candy can make an ordinary Tuesday feel special.

Megan set that journal aside and reached for another—this one more recent, the leather still supple. She opened to a random entry dated March 2019.

Kay asked me today if I ever regretted not having children of my own. The question caught me off guard—we were making caramels and talking about nothing in particular when she just asked it outright. I had to stop working because my hands were shaking.

The honest answer is yes. Of course, I have regrets. The childhood illness that left me unable to bear children took away a choice I didn't even know I had yet. I was only nine years old when the fever came, and by the time it passed, the doctors had delivered news I was too young to fully understand. It wasn't until I was older, watching friends get married and start families, that the weight of it really settled in.

I never found my person—the man I could imagine building a life with. And I sometimes wonder if that's because I was too afraid to let anyone get close enough to hurt me. What man would want a woman who couldn't give him children? I convinced myself it was better not to try, better to build a life that didn't require someone else to make it complete.

But the truth? I've always wondered what it would have been like. To be someone's mother. To be a wife. To tuck my child into bed at night, to watch them grow, to love someone that completely. I thought about adoption over the years—thought about it seriously more than once. But I never took the leap. Fear, maybe. Or the worry that I'd waited too long, that I'd be too old to keep up with a young child's energy. Or perhaps just the knowledge that doing it alone, without a partner, felt too overwhelming.

So yes, I have regrets. Deep ones that ache in the quiet moments when I see mothers with their children, when I attend baby showers for my staff, and when I think about growing old with no one to leave my legacy to except one niece I barely know.

But my life is also full—fuller than I could have imagined when I was young and thought I knew what happiness looked like. I have this shop. I have people I love who love me back. I have purpose and community and more blessings than I probably deserve. It's not the life I dreamed of as a girl, but it's a good life. A meaningful one.

I told Kay a version of this—the gentler version, the one that doesn't expose quite so much of the raw hurt underneath. She squeezed my hand and said, "You've been a mother to all of us here, whether you know it or not." The kindness nearly broke me.

Maybe she's right. Maybe there are different ways to love, different ways to leave your mark. Maybe being someone's aunt, someone's mentor, someone's safe harbor—maybe that counts for something too.

I hope sweet Meggie knows she was loved like a daughter, even if I could never claim that title.

I have this shop. I have my staff, who feel like family. I have this community that's given me more than I could ever give back. And I have memories of sweet Meggie, even if circumstances keep us apart.

Megan's breath caught. She kept reading.

I wonder about her often. What she's doing, who she's become, and whether she's happy. I send cards, but they feel inadequate—what can you say in a birthday card to a girl you haven't seen in years? A girl who probably doesn't remember the visits we had before everything fell apart in her life?

My brother made his choices. I can't fix what he broke or undo the hurt he caused. But I can hope that someday, somehow, Meggie knows she was loved by me. That there was someone who never forgot her, who kept her picture on her desk and talked to it, and who believed she was something special.

Maybe that's foolish. Maybe she's moved on and built a life that doesn't include space for an aunt she barely remembers. But hope isn't logical. It's a choice. And I choose to hope that someday she'll know.

Megan closed the journal, her hands shaking. The tears came harder now, hot and fast and impossible to stop. All these years, she'd thought she was alone. Forgotten. But Phyllis had been here, remembering, hoping, and believing in her even from a distance.

She pulled out her phone, thinking she'd text her mother and ask if she'd known about Phyllis's feelings. But what would she say? Did you know Aunt Phyllis kept my picture on her desk? Did you know she never stopped thinking about me? Why didn't you make an effort to bring me here for visits?

Her mother had a life of her own now. Rick and Florida and a fresh start that didn't include dwelling on the past. Megan couldn't blame her for that. Some things were too painful to hold on to.

The phone buzzed in her hand, making her jump. A text from Kyle.

Hey, Dad and I will be able to paint soon. Could you make time to pick out paint colors in the next day or two? And we need to know what fixtures you want for the kitchen and bathroom—faucets, cabinet hardware, that kind of thing.

Megan stared at the message. Paint colors. Fixtures. Decisions about the space that would become her home.

She had no idea even where to start.

She typed back: *Sure. I'll get right on it.*

The reply came quickly: *Great, if you need help, just text me.*

Megan set the phone down and looked around Phyllis's office. At the journals that held a lifetime of hopes and fears and dreams. At the newspaper clippings that documented years of dedication and success. At the photograph of young Megan holding that giant lollipop, frozen forever in a moment of pure joy.

She should go and pick paint colors and choose fixtures and make the decisions that would transform the apartment into her home. But the truth was, she had no idea what she was doing. No idea what colors were appropriate or what fixtures cost or whether she should be making these choices at all. And she had no idea if there was a store locally where she could shop or if she'd need to drive to a bigger city.

Megan stood, wiping her eyes on her sleeve. She grabbed her phone and walked down the short hallway to Beth's office, knocking on the open door.

Beth looked up from her computer, her expression immediately shifting to concern. "Megan? Are you okay?"

"I'm fine. Just—" Megan gestured vaguely back toward Phyllis's office. "I was reading through some of Phyllis's things. Don't mind me, I'm an emotional person."

"I understand." Beth's voice was gentle. "What can I do?"

Megan held up her phone. "Kyle just texted. He wants me to pick out paint colors and fixtures for the apartment. And I realized I don't know if there's a budget for that. Or if Phyllis had plans for renovations that I should follow. Or—" She stopped, feeling foolish. "I don't know what I'm supposed to do."

Beth gestured to the chair across from her desk. "Sit. Let's talk through it."

Megan sank into the chair gratefully.

"Okay, first question," Beth said, pulling up something on her computer. "Did Phyllis have plans for the apartment? Sort of. She always meant to fix it up—she'd talk about it sometimes, especially after the last tenant moved out. But she was in her fifties, busy with the shop, and I think the project just felt like too much for her, maybe. So she kept putting it off."

"So there's no budget set aside? No specific plan?"

"No budget, no." Beth turned her monitor so Megan could see the spreadsheet displayed. "But that doesn't mean you can't afford to do the renovations. Let me show you how the finances work."

Megan leaned forward, trying to make sense of the columns and numbers.

"This is the business checking account," Beth explained, pointing. "Currently sitting at about forty-two thousand. This covers payroll, utilities, inventory, supplies—all the regular operating expenses. We typically keep it around this level so we always have a cushion for unexpected costs."

"Okay," Megan said slowly.

"Now, the apartment is part of the building, which the business owns. Technically, any improvements to the apartment could be considered a business expense—it's maintaining the property, increasing its value. But more importantly—" Beth pulled up another screen. "Phyllis also had this savings account that she used for larger expenses. Building maintenance, equipment replacement, that kind of thing. It currently has about sixty-three thousand in it."

Megan's eyes widened. "Oh, my goodness... I don't remember that account being mentioned."

"Phyllis was very good about setting aside money for the future. She believed in being prepared. This specific account is in the business's name only." Beth smiled. "The point is, you have funds available for the renovations. This isn't money you're taking from the business's operating budget or from your personal inheritance. This is building maintenance money that's been sitting here waiting to be used. Phyllis always called it her safety net."

"But how much is reasonable to spend?" Megan asked. "I don't want to waste it or—"

"Let me put it this way," Beth interrupted gently. "That apartment will be your home. You need it to be safe, comfortable, and functional. You need appliances that work. You need windows that keep out the cold. You need a space that feels like yours."

Megan nodded, not trusting her voice.

"But beyond that," Beth continued, "you also need to think long term. What if someday you decide you want to buy a house? Or what if your situation changes? A properly renovated apartment could be rented out, providing additional income. It's an investment in the property's value and your future options."

"So I shouldn't cut corners," Megan said.

"Exactly. Do it right the first time." Beth pulled out a calculator. "Let me run some numbers based on what I know needs to be done. New appliances—figure three to four thousand for a good refrigerator, stove, and microwave. Painting the whole apartment plus the supplies, maybe five or six hundred. The one window replacement you already know about, but in my opinion, if I were you, I would replace all the windows eventually. Fixtures—faucets, cabinet hardware, light fixtures—probably another thousand or so if you're not going crazy expensive. Then there are the cabinets themselves."

"The cabinets?" Megan asked.

"The kitchen cabinets are in rough shape, Megan. Mitch mentioned to me yesterday that he thinks you'd be better off replacing them entirely rather than trying to repair what's there. Quality cabinets might run you five to seven thousand installed."

Megan felt her stomach drop. "That's a lot."

"It is," Beth agreed. "But cabinets last decades if you get good ones. And honestly, the kitchen is the heart of any home. You deserve a kitchen that works well and looks nice."

She typed some numbers into the calculator. "So let's say, conservatively—appliances, painting supplies, windows, fixtures, cabinets, plus a little buffer for unexpected issues—you're looking at maybe twelve to fifteen thousand total. And that is a very low estimate."

The numbers made Megan's head spin. Fifteen thousand dollars.

"I know it seems like a lot," Beth said, clearly reading Megan's expression. "But look at it this way—you have sixty-three thousand in that maintenance account. Spending fifteen of it leaves you with almost fifty thousand still available for future needs. And you'll have an apartment that's genuinely livable, not just barely functional."

"You really think I should spend that much?"

Beth's expression was firm but kind. "I think you should stop thinking about what you 'should' do and start thinking about what you actually need. You need a home, Megan. A real one. Not a patched-together space you can tolerate."

The words hit harder than Beth probably intended. Megan had spent her entire adult life in patched-together spaces, tolerating situations until they fell apart. She'd never once asked herself what she actually needed or wanted, only what she could afford or what was available.

"I'm not good at making decisions. What if I pick the wrong paint colors or the wrong cabinets and waste all that money?"

"Then you'll have learned a valuable lesson," Beth said simply. "Megan, there's no such thing as perfect choices. There are just choices. And the only way you learn to make good ones is by making some and seeing how they turn out."

Megan looked down at her hands. "I've never had to do any of this before. I don't even know what's normal or what things should cost or what's too much versus too little."

"That's why you have people to help you." Beth's voice was patient. "Kyle and Mitch know construction and what's reasonable quality-wise. Leslie has an eye for design and could probably help with color choices. And I'm here to help you understand the financial side. You don't have to figure it all out alone."

The kindness in Beth's voice made Megan's throat tight again. She'd cried enough this morning—over Phyllis's journals, over realizing how much her aunt had cared, and over the weight of all these decisions she didn't feel qualified to make. But Beth's steady reassurance made her feel like maybe she could do this after all.

"Kyle asked if I could choose paint colors and fixtures in the next couple of days," Megan said.

"Then let's get you set up to go shopping." Beth rolled her chair back to her desk and opened a drawer. She pulled out a business debit card and handed it across the desk. "This is linked to the maintenance account. Use it for whatever you need for the apartment—paint, fixtures, appliances, and whatever else Mitch recommends. Don't stress about every dollar. Just focus on making good choices that will serve you well."

Megan took the card, staring at it as if it might bite. "You're sure?"

"I'm sure." Beth smiled. "Go shopping, Megan. Pick out paint colors that make you happy. Choose fixtures you'll enjoy using. Make that apartment yours. And really consider having all the windows replaced... there is plenty of money there to cover those costs."

"Okay, I'll ask Mitch if he can get an estimate on good windows, not top of the line, but good solid windows. Beth... what about the staircase outside to the apartment? I really want that fixed; it scares the daylights out of me."

"Mitch called me this morning and filled me in on the staircase; you're fine. There is plenty of money to pay for that, and it is needed.

Those current stairs are unsafe, and you have every right to want them replaced."

Megan stood slowly, the debit card clutched in one hand and her phone in the other. Through Beth's office window, she could see Kay and Linda working in the kitchen, the steady rhythm of the business Phyllis had built, the life that was now somehow hers to continue.

"Beth?" Megan paused in the doorway. "Thank you for being patient with me."

"That's what I'm here for." Beth turned back to her computer, already moving on to the next task on her list. "Now go... have fun picking out stuff that makes you happy. If you need me while you're out, just call."

Megan walked back toward Phyllis's office, intending to grab her jacket. But she stopped in the doorway, looking at the journals still spread across the desk, the newspaper clippings documenting a life of dedication and purpose.

Phyllis had built this place from nothing. Had made decisions—probably terrifying ones—about everything from recipes to renovations to running a business. And somewhere along the way, she'd stopped being afraid and started being brave.

Megan picked up her jacket and slipped the debit card into her purse. And headed out the door.

Chapter 13

Megan stood just inside the doorway of the apartment, taking in the transformation that had happened in a single day. The peeling paint was gone—scraped away to reveal smooth, clean walls that practically begged for fresh color. The water-stained ceiling had been patched.

Kyle stood near the kitchen, work gloves tucked into his back pocket, and a slight sheen of perspiration on his forehead despite the November chill that still permeated the space. Mitch was crouched by the sink cabinet, his toolbox open beside him.

"Wow," Megan said, moving further into the room. "You two have been busy."

"We have," Kyle said, gesturing at the walls. "Dad just fixed the cabinet issue."

Mitch stood, wiping his hands on a rag. "Water damage was worse than I thought once I got in there. Had to replace the entire bottom panel and reinforce the frame. But it's solid now."

Megan approached the kitchen. The cabinets looked old and worn; the hinges were misaligned on most of the doors, and the finish was dull and scratched from decades of use. She opened one door, and it swung crookedly, catching slightly before closing.

"Can I ask you both something?" She looked between Kyle and Mitch. "And I want your honest opinion, not what you think I want to hear."

"Of course," Mitch said.

"If this were your apartment, would you keep these cabinets and try to fix them up? Or would you scrap them and start fresh?"

The two men exchanged glances. Kyle spoke first. "Honestly? I'd tear them out and start over. They're functional right now, but they're at the end of their useful life. You could paint them, replace the hinges, and try to make them work—but you'd probably be dealing with more problems continually."

"Plus," Mitch added, "if you're already doing renovations, this is the time to make the kitchen work the way you want it to. These cabinets were installed in what, the seventies? Eighties? They don't use space efficiently. You could get a lot more storage with modern cabinets, and you'd have options for layouts that make more sense for this space."

Megan nodded slowly, looking around the small kitchen. "What about the bathroom? Same question—if it were yours, would you keep what's there or replace it?"

"Replace," Mitch said without hesitation. "That vanity is old and cheaply made, and there's almost no storage in the bathroom. You'd benefit from a new vanity and maybe a tall storage cabinet. Give yourself room for towels, toiletries, and all the things you need without cluttering the counter."

The decisiveness in both their responses made something ease in Megan's chest. She'd been worried about making the wrong choice, about being wasteful or foolish. But if these men thought replacing everything made sense, then maybe it was the right call.

"Okay," she said. "New cabinets for the kitchen and bathroom. Where would I even find those? Is there somewhere local, or do I need to drive to a bigger city?"

Kyle's expression shifted to something that looked like chagrin. "I'm sorry—I should have thought about this when I texted you earlier. You don't know where anything is in town yet, do you?"

"Not really," Megan admitted. "I know how to get from the candy shop to the resort and back to the shop again. That's about the extent of my navigation skills here."

"Thompson's Hardware," Kyle said. "It's on Cranberry Court, five minutes from here. Chuck Thompson owns it—he's a family friend and has been in business here for decades. He stocks paint, has a good selection of fixtures for kitchens and bathrooms, and what he doesn't have in stock he can usually order and get within a few days."

"Does he have cabinets?" Megan asked.

"He doesn't stock them," Mitch said, "but he's got catalogs and access to vendor websites. You can look through everything and order exactly what you want. He works with several good manufacturers—nothing fancy or overpriced, just solid quality stuff that'll last."

"And I'll need measurements, right?" Megan looked at the kitchen, trying to imagine it with different cabinets, maybe even expanded slightly to use the space better.

"Already on it." Mitch pulled out a measuring tape. "Give me ten minutes and I'll have all the dimensions you need—including some options for expanding the kitchen into that corner space that's currently just wasted. You could fit a decent pantry cabinet there if you wanted."

While Mitch worked, measuring and making notes on a piece of paper, Megan walked through the apartment again. The bedroom with the broken window—which would be replaced soon, along with all the other windows if she followed Beth's suggestion. The second bedroom could be an office or guest room. The bathroom, with its ancient vanity and inadequate storage.

She tried to picture it finished. Walls painted in colors she chose. Fixtures that worked properly and looked nice. Cabinets that actually had enough space for a functioning kitchen and bathroom. A home. Her home.

The thought still felt surreal.

"Got everything," Mitch announced, tearing the page from his pad and handing it to Megan. The measurements were neat and precise, with notes about what each dimension represented. "Take this to Chuck. He'll know exactly what to do with it."

Megan folded the paper and tucked it into her purse. Paint, fixtures, cabinets—things she'd never bought before, decisions she'd never had to make. She could feel the anxiety starting to creep in, the voice that whispered she wasn't qualified to make these choices, that she'd probably mess everything up.

But then she looked at Kyle, who was watching her with that patient, encouraging expression he seemed to always have. And she thought about Phyllis's journals, about how scared her aunt had been when opening the candy shop but how she'd chosen excitement over fear.

She turned to face Kyle, an idea forming. "Are you up for an adventure?"

His response was immediate. "Always."

The quickness of his answer, the way his whole face seemed to brighten at the prospect, sent warmth spreading through her chest. Megan grinned and headed for the door. "Well, Mr. Porter, let's go buy some paint and look at fixtures and cabinets."

Behind her, she heard Mitch chuckle. "Good luck, you two. I'll keep working here. Megan, should I go ahead and tear out all the kitchen cabinets?"

Megan paused at the door, looking back at the worn, outdated kitchen that would soon become something completely new. Something she chose. Something that was hers.

"Yes," she said, and the word came out stronger than she expected. "Absolutely yes. Let's give this apartment a fresh, new look."

The smile that spread across her face felt unfamiliar—confident, excited, and maybe even a little bit brave. She opened the door and stepped onto the exterior landing, the November air cold against her face.

Behind her, she heard Kyle's footsteps, steady and sure as he followed her down the metal stairs. The treads were still slippery with morning frost, but Megan gripped the railing and took each step with deliberate care.

At the bottom, she turned to wait for Kyle, watching him descend. When he reached the bottom, he was smiling.

"So," he said, "ready to go meet Chuck Thompson and make some decisions?"

Megan pulled the folded measurements from her purse, then the debit card, and held them up and smiled. A piece of paper and plastic that represented possibility, choice, and a future she was actively building instead of just letting happen to her.

"Let's go," she said.

Chapter 14

The paint chip display stretched across a ten-foot space in Thompson's Hardware store. Hundreds of color options arranged in gradients from white to cream to beige to tan and other colors Megan couldn't even imagine using to paint the walls of a home. She stood in front of it as if she were facing a firing squad.

Kyle watched her reach for a sample card labeled "Alabaster," study it for five seconds, then put it back and reach for "Ivory Lace" instead. She repeated this process three more times, her brow furrowing deeper with each selection.

They'd been standing in the paint section of Thompson's Hardware for ten minutes, and she hadn't managed to commit to a single color yet.

"You know," Kyle said carefully, "you could take a few samples home. Look at them in the actual space before deciding."

Megan's shoulders relaxed slightly. "I can do that? Just take these cards?"

"That's what they're for." Kyle grabbed a handful of the neutral samples she'd been cycling through and handed them to her. "Take as many as you want. Most people need to see colors in different lights before making a final choice."

"That makes so much more sense than trying to decide here under fluorescent lighting." Megan took the cards and then reached for a few more. "Thank you. I was starting to feel like I was failing some kind of test."

The drive to Thompson's had been easier than Kyle expected. Megan had been quiet at first, staring out the passenger window of his truck as they wound through downtown Mistletoe Falls, but she'd gradually started asking questions. Where was the post office? The library? Did the town have a movie theater?

Kyle had answered each one, acutely aware of how little she knew about the place that was now her home. He'd lived here his entire life except for law school, and even then he'd come back every chance he got. He knew every street, every shortcut, and every business owner by name. The idea of arriving somewhere completely new, with no map and no connections, seemed impossibly lonely.

But Megan was trying. That much was obvious in the way she studied street signs, in how she repeated store names like she was committing them to memory, and in the determined set of her jaw as she faced down the paint chip wall.

Thompson's Hardware occupied a large corner lot on Cranberry Court, its exterior painted a cheerful red with white trim. The building had been there since the 1960s, expanded twice over the decades as Chuck Thompson's father and then Chuck himself built the business into a cornerstone of local commerce. Walking through the front door, Kyle had been hit with the familiar scent of sawdust, motor oil, and the particular mustiness of a well-stocked hardware store.

Chuck had emerged from behind the main counter the moment he saw them, his weathered face breaking into a genuine smile. He was in his early sixties, with silver hair that had retreated from his forehead and the sturdy build of a man who'd spent his life lifting, carrying, and working with his hands.

"Kyle Porter!" Chuck had clasped Kyle's hand in both of his. "Good to see you, son. How're your folks doing?"

"They're great. Busy with the resort, but that's nothing new."

Chuck had turned to Megan then, and Kyle had watched her straighten slightly under the older man's assessment. "And you must be Megan Caldwell. I see a resemblance. I heard you'd inherited Phyllis's place."

"I did." Megan had extended her hand. "It's nice to meet you, Mr. Thompson."

"Chuck, please. Mr. Thompson was my father." He'd shaken her hand warmly, his expression softening. "I was really sorry to hear about Phyllis. She was a good woman and a fine friend. Used to come in here every few months, always had a new project she was working on or something that needed fixing at the shop. Sharp as a tack about construction too—she'd correct me if I tried to sell her the wrong size screw."

Megan's smile had been genuine but tinged with sadness. "I wish I had taken the time to get to know her better."

"She talked about you sometimes," Chuck had continued. "She always hoped you'd find your way back here someday. Guess she found a way to make that happen."

Kyle had seen Megan's eyes glisten and had jumped in before she could get too emotional in the middle of a hardware store. "We're here to pick up supplies for the apartment renovation. Paint, fixtures, and we need to order cabinets."

"Well, you've come to the right place." Chuck had gestured broadly at his store. "Let's get you set up."

Now, twenty minutes later, Kyle stood with an armful of paint supplies while Megan clutched her collection of sample cards like they were lottery tickets.

"How much paint do we actually need?" She asked, looking at the display of gallon cans.

Kyle pulled out his phone and opened the calculator app. "What were the room dimensions Dad measured? The living room, kitchen, two bedrooms, bathroom, and hallway? He wrote them on the back of the page with the kitchen measurements."

Megan dug the paper from her purse and read off the measurements. Kyle did quick calculations, factoring in ceiling height and the fact that they'd need two coats to properly cover the old walls.

"About eight gallons total, maybe nine to be safe for the walls. You'll want primer too, since we're covering up patched areas and old colors. And I'd get 5 gallons of whatever color you want for the ceilings." He looked at her sample cards. "These are all pretty similar—neutral tones. Planning to use the same color throughout?"

"I thought it might make the space feel bigger? And more cohesive?" Megan's voice lifted at the end, turning her statements into questions. "Or is that boring? Should I use different colors in different rooms?"

"No, neutral throughout is smart." Kyle pointed to one of the cards she held. "Especially something warm like this. It'll make the whole apartment feel pulled together, and you can always add color with furniture and decorations later."

"You sound like you know what you're talking about."

"Leslie made me watch about a hundred home renovation shows when we first took over The Christmas Shop. I absorbed more than

I meant to." Kyle selected the paint card labeled "Warm Linen" from Megan's collection. "This one. It's neutral enough to work with anything, but it's got enough warmth that it won't feel cold or institutional."

Megan studied the card, then nodded. "Okay. Warm Linen it is."

"Good choice," Chuck said, appearing from around the corner. "I'll start mixing the paint right now."

"Megan, do you want Chuck to grab the primer we'll need, and maybe you could choose a ceiling paint color now too?"

Megan looked at Chuck and said, "Could you pick out a decent primer for me? And add another 5 gallons of Warm Linen for the ceilings. It just seems easier to me to keep everything one solid color; does that make sense?"

"Makes complete sense to me, Ms. Caldwell. I'm a simple guy myself. I'll mix up 15 gallons of Warm Linen and grab 10 gallons of primer."

They followed Chuck to the paint desk, where he began the mixing process. Kyle gathered rollers, brushes, painter's tape, and drop cloths while they waited, loading everything into a cart. Megan trailed behind him, occasionally picking up something and examining it as if she were trying to understand its purpose through careful study.

"You've done this before," she observed.

"Helped Dad with projects since I was old enough to hold a paintbrush. And Leslie's constantly redecorating something, so I'm usually the one she drags along for supply runs."

"Is that code for 'I'm the one who does the actual work while she supervises'?"

Kyle laughed. "You've met Leslie once, and you already have her figured out."

"She seems like she knows what she wants and isn't afraid to make it happen. I admire that."

The wistfulness in Megan's voice made Kyle look at her more carefully. She was studying a display of paint sundries with more attention than the items warranted, her expression distant.

"You're doing the same thing," Kyle said. "Making things happen. You've been here less than a week, and you're already renovating an apartment and running a business."

"I'm stumbling through renovating an apartment and trying not to ruin a business," Megan corrected. "There's a difference."

"Not from where I'm standing."

She looked up at him then, and the vulnerability in her green eyes hit him square in the chest. She wanted to believe him—that much was obvious. But something held her back, some deep-seated conviction that she wasn't capable or worthy or whatever lie she'd been telling herself for too long.

Kyle wanted to say something, but he chose not to.

The fixtures section of Thompson's Hardware occupied an entire aisle near the back of the store. Faucets, cabinet hardware, light fixtures, and towel bars—everything needed to outfit a kitchen and bathroom was displayed on pegboards and shelves, organized by style and finish.

Megan stopped at the entrance to the aisle and visibly steeled herself. "Okay. Fixtures. How hard can this be?"

"Not hard at all," Kyle assured her. "Just depends on what you like and what your budget allows."

"Beth said I have about fifteen thousand to work with. I've easily spent maybe six or seven hundred on paint and supplies so far, right?"

"About that. So you've got room to choose quality fixtures that'll last." Kyle gestured at the display. "Basic breakdown—you need a kitchen faucet, bathroom faucet, cabinet hardware for all your new cabinets, and probably some light fixtures since the ones currently in the apartment are pretty dated."

Megan pulled out her phone and opened the notes app. "Kitchen faucet, bathroom faucet, cabinet hardware, light fixtures. Got it. Where do we start?"

They started with kitchen faucets, and Kyle quickly realized that Megan's approach to decision-making involved extensive internal debate and a fixation on the cost. She'd pick up a faucet, read the description, check the price, put it back, pick up another one, compare them silently, and repeat the cycle.

"What are you thinking?" Kyle asked after she'd done this five times.

"I don't know what I should be thinking. What's the difference between a pull-down and a pull-out faucet? Why are some two hundred dollars and others four hundred? Is the more expensive one actually better or just fancier looking?" She set down the faucet she was holding and pressed her fingers to her temples. "I've never had to think about faucets before. They were just... there. In every apartment I lived in, they were already installed, and I never questioned them."

Kyle picked up the pull-down model she'd been examining. "Okay. Here's what matters—you want something with good water pressure and a finish that won't corrode. Pull-down means the spray head pulls straight down. Pull-out means it pulls out and can reach further. For a smaller kitchen, pull-downs usually make more sense."

"That helps," Megan said, making a note on her phone.

"As for price—the more expensive ones usually have better internal mechanisms, which means they'll last longer and won't start leaking in a few years. But you don't need top-of-the-line. This one—" Kyle indicated a mid-range pull-down faucet in brushed nickel, "—is a solid quality without being overpriced. It'll last you several years if you treat it right."

Megan studied the faucet, then checked the price tag. "A hundred and eighty dollars. For one faucet. That is insane. "

"For one faucet that you'll use multiple times every single day for the next how many years."

"When you put it that way." She picked it up, turned it over in her hands, and tested the spray head. "Okay. This one."

They moved through the rest of the fixtures with slightly more confidence. Megan selected a brushed-nickel bathroom faucet that matched the kitchen style. She took a few photos of the cabinet hardware that matched and that she liked.

"Figure each cabinet door needs one pull or knob," Kyle explained. "Drawers usually take one pull. Your kitchen's going to have—what did Dad estimate, fifteen cabinets total, including the island he suggested in his drawing if that's what you want? So probably twenty-five to thirty pieces of hardware total. The bathroom will need another six or so."

Megan did the math on her phone, then multiplied by the price per piece. "That adds up fast."

"It does. But again, this is something you'll interact with constantly. Don't cheap out on the things you touch every day."

She selected a simple brushed nickel pull in a classic design—nothing trendy that would look dated in five years, but elegant enough to elevate the space. Kyle approved of the choice, though he didn't say so. She didn't need his approval. She needed to trust her own judgment.

Light fixtures took longer. The apartment needed replacements in the kitchen, bathroom, living room, and both bedrooms. Megan kept gravitating toward the cheapest options, and Kyle kept gently steering her toward the middle range.

"I don't need anything fancy," she insisted, holding up a basic flush-mount ceiling fixture that cost thirty dollars. "This is fine."

"It's fine for a rental property where you don't care about aesthetics," Kyle agreed. "But Megan, this is your home. You're allowed to choose things that are more than just fine."

She set down the cheap fixture and picked up the one he'd been looking at—a simple but attractive brushed nickel design that would complement the fixtures she'd already chosen. "This one's sixty-five dollars. And in reality, the apartment is a rental property. Beth pointed something out to me this morning that I hadn't thought about. I may live there forever, and I may not. What if one day I can afford a home?"

"Still, the apartment will look exponentially better upgrading the light fixtures a little from just basic. Plus, better quality means it won't need replacing in a few years when the cheap one burns out. And remember, this is where you will be living for now... what do you want?"

Megan studied the fixture, then nodded. "Okay. You're right. I need to stop thinking like someone who's just passing through."

The observation hung in the air between them, weighted with meaning. Kyle wanted to ask what she meant—did she see herself staying long term? Was she already planning to leave?

He watched her as she selected the light fixtures she wanted for each of the rooms and placed them in the cart.

"How're we doing over here? Found everything you need?" Chuck asked as he approached.

"I think so," Megan said. "We just need to look at the cabinets."

"Follow me. I've got catalogs in my office."

Chuck's office was a cluttered space behind the main counter, its walls covered with calendars, order forms, and family photographs. He cleared a space on his desk and pulled out three large binders, each one stuffed with laminated pages showing different cabinet styles and configurations.

"Now, before we get too deep into this," Chuck said, settling into his chair while Kyle and Megan remained standing, "let's talk about what you actually need. This is an apartment, right? Not a forever home?"

"Right," Megan confirmed. "At least, I don't think it's forever. I mean, I just got here, so I don't know what forever looks like yet."

Chuck nodded, unfazed by her rambling. "Then here's my recommendation—you don't need top-of-the-line custom cabinets. You need good-quality stock cabinets that look nice, function well, and won't break your budget. Save the fancy stuff if you buy a house someday."

Kyle saw Megan's shoulders drop with relief. "That makes sense."

"Good. Let's talk about the size of the space you need to fill." Chuck unfolded the paper Megan handed him, studying Mitch's neat drawing. "He's suggesting expanding into this corner space, which is smart. Wasted area right now. A small island here—" he pointed "—which would give you extra counter space and storage without making the kitchen feel cramped... makes sense to me."

"An island?" Megan leaned forward to look at the drawing. "Do I really need that?"

"Mitch drew in a small one in his diagram, and yeah, in my opinion it would be a smart addition. Four feet long and two feet deep is what he wrote here, and that makes sense. Put some cabinets underneath for storage and use the top for food prep. It'd make the whole cooking area more functional."

For the next twenty minutes, Chuck walked them through options. He showed them a basic shaker-style cabinet in white that would brighten the kitchen and explained the difference between soft-close hinges and standard ones.

Kyle watched her engagement grow as Chuck talked. She asked questions, offered opinions, and even suggested moving one cabinet to a different wall to make room for a larger pantry. The confidence that had been tentative in the paint aisle was solidifying here, where she could see how her choices would translate into actual function.

"What do you think?" Megan asked Kyle at one point, after Chuck had sketched out a different possible layout. "Does this make sense?"

Kyle studied the drawing. "I think it makes sense. But more importantly, does it make sense to you? You're the one who's going to be cooking in this kitchen."

"I really do like the island idea, but it will add a few hundred dollars to the cost," Megan said. "And I like having the pantry cabinet near the refrigerator—which we still need to buy, but that's another trip. This feels thought-out. Functional."

"Then that's what matters."

Chuck made notes on the configuration Megan approved, then pulled up his vendor website to check pricing and availability. "Okay, for the kitchen—twelve cabinets including the island, plus the hardware you picked out—you're looking at about forty-two hundred dollars. That includes delivery, and if I have time, I'll help Mitch install them at no extra charge."

Megan's eyes widened, but she didn't protest.

"Bathroom's simpler," Chuck continued. "Vanity cabinet and a tall storage unit—another six hundred dollars. So, right around five grand for all the cabinets."

"Wow, that's more than I expected."

"I can get these ordered today," Chuck said. "Lead time's about five days for delivery, then a day or two to install."

"Okay. That works," Megan said, and Kyle heard the slight tremor in her voice. The reality of the timeline, the commitment, the cost—it was all hitting her at once.

They headed to the main checkout counter next. Chuck rang up each item, the register beeping steadily as the total climbed. Paint, supplies, faucets, hardware, light fixtures, and the cabinet order.

Kyle watched the numbers on the screen increase. Twelve hundred. Fifteen hundred. Two thousand. Sixty-six hundred.

Megan had gone very still beside him. Her breathing had changed—shallow and quick, like she was fighting panic. When Kyle glanced at her face, he saw a light sheen of perspiration on her forehead despite the comfortable temperature in the store.

"Your total's sixty thousand six hundred twenty-two dollars and thirty-seven cents," Chuck announced.

Megan pulled the debit card from her purse, but her hand was shaking enough that Kyle noticed. She stared at the card as if it were something foreign, something she wasn't sure she had the right to use.

Kyle stepped closer, letting his presence ground her. He reached out and placed his hand on her arm, the contact gentle but firm. "Hey."

She looked up at him, and he could see the fear in her eyes.

"You're doing great," Kyle said quietly. "This is what building a life looks like. It's supposed to feel big."

Something in her expression shifted. The panic didn't disappear, but it receded enough for her to take a deep breath and nod. She handed the card to Chuck, who ran it through with professional discretion, not commenting on the obvious tension at the moment.

The transaction was approved. Chuck handed back the card along with a receipt longer than Kyle's forearm.

"You're all set," Chuck said. "I'll have my guys help you load everything into your truck. And Megan?" He waited until she looked at him. "Phyllis would be proud of what you're doing. That apartment's been empty for a while now. It's good to see it getting the attention it deserves."

"Thank you," Megan managed. "For all your help."

They loaded the supplies into Kyle's truck with help from Chuck's employees, securing everything with bungee cords to make sure nothing shifted during the drive. Kyle started the engine but didn't immediately put the truck in gear. Instead, he turned to look at Megan, who was staring straight ahead through the windshield.

"You okay?" he asked.

"I just spent over six thousand dollars in under three hours." Her voice was quiet. "That's more money than I paid for my car."

"You spent six thousand dollars investing in your home," Kyle corrected. "There's a difference."

"I suppose... but still that's a lot of money."

"Are you hungry?" Kyle asked, changing the subject. "We could grab lunch if you want. There's a good diner not far from here."

Megan turned to look at him, and her answer came without hesitation. "Yes, I'm starving."

The smile that spread across Kyle's face felt entirely too revealing, but he couldn't help it. He put the truck in gear and pulled out of Thompson's parking lot.

Chapter 15

The North Star Diner sat on the corner like something out of a 1950s postcard, all gleaming chrome and cherry-red trim against white siding that practically glowed in the midday sun.

Megan climbed out of Kyle's truck and took in the details—the vintage neon sign shaped like a star with an arrow pointing down to the entrance, the large picture windows revealing red vinyl booths and a long counter with spinning stools, and the hand-painted lettering on the glass that read "Best Pie in Tennessee Since 1962."

"This place is adorable," she said as Kyle came around to her side. "Does it really have the best pie in Tennessee?"

"According to them," Kyle said with a grin. "But I've never had a bad meal or slice of pie here, so I'm willing to give them the benefit of the doubt on the pie claim."

He held the door open for her, and Megan stepped inside to a wave of warm air that smelled like coffee, bacon grease, and something sweet and cinnamon-heavy. The interior delivered on the exterior's promise—black-and-white checkered floor, red vinyl booths along the windows, chrome-trimmed tables in the center, and a long counter where a few solo diners sat hunched over plates and coffee mugs.

The lunch rush was winding down, leaving the diner pleasantly busy rather than packed. Somewhere in the back, a radio played oldies at a volume just loud enough to create ambiance without overwhelming conversation.

A waitress with auburn hair pulled into a high ponytail approached them, her smile warm and genuine. "Kyle Porter! I haven't seen you in a few weeks. Where've you been hiding?"

"Hi, Donna... working mostly, and staying out of trouble." Kyle said. "Is there a booth available?"

"For you? Always." Donna grabbed two menus from the hostess stand and gestured toward the window booths. "Take your pick."

Kyle let Megan choose, and she slid into a booth near the back corner. The vinyl was smooth and well-maintained, the table surface spotless, and the view through the window showed a slice of downtown Mistletoe Falls.

Kyle settled across from her as Donna set down the menus. "What can I get you folks to drink?"

"Coffee, please," Megan said. After the morning they'd had—the apartment, the shopping, the overwhelming reality of spending over six thousand dollars—she needed caffeine.

"Make that two," Kyle added.

"Coming right up." Donna headed toward the coffee station, leaving them alone with the menus.

Megan opened hers and scanned the options. Classic diner fare—burgers, sandwiches, breakfast served all day, and daily specials written on a small chalkboard propped on the table. Everything sounded good in that uncomplicated, satisfying way that diner food always did.

"So," she said, looking up at Kyle. "What's good here?"

"Honestly? Everything. But their burgers are solid, the patty melt is legendary, and if you want breakfast food, their French toast is ridiculously good." He was studying his menu but glanced up to meet her eyes. "What are you in the mood for?"

Megan considered. She was starving—hadn't eaten since a quick piece of toast at the cabin that morning, and shopping had burned through whatever energy that had provided. "I'm thinking burger... loaded with everything on it and fries. I might regret it later, but right now I don't care."

Kyle's smile widened. "That's the right attitude."

Donna returned with two steaming mugs of coffee, a small pitcher of cream, and a handful of sugar packets. "You two ready to order, or do you need a minute?"

"I think we're ready," Kyle said, looking to Megan for confirmation. She nodded.

"Cheeseburger with fries," Megan said. "Cooked well done, and can I get cheddar instead of American and load it up with everything you normally serve on burgers?"

"Absolutely." Donna scribbled on her pad. "Kyle?"

"Patty melt with onion rings."

"Perfect. I'll get that in for you." Donna collected the menus and disappeared toward the kitchen.

Megan wrapped her hands around the warm coffee mug, grateful for something to do with them. "So. You come here often enough that the waitress knows you by name."

"Small town," Kyle said, adding cream to his coffee. "Everyone knows everyone. But yeah, I come here often. Sometimes with Dad, sometimes with Leslie when she needs to vent about the Christmas Shop drama."

"Christmas Shop drama? I didn't realize a shop focused on Christmas could be dramatic."

"You'd be surprised. Last month we had a customer who wanted to return an ornament because she said it 'didn't match her tree's energy'." He shook his head, but his tone was more amused than annoyed. "Leslie spent twenty minutes explaining our return policy while the woman argued that spiritual compatibility should be grounds for a refund."

Megan laughed, the sound surprising her with its genuineness. "What happened?"

"Leslie eventually gave her store credit just to end the debate. Then spent the rest of the day muttering about 'tree energy' and threatening to put it on a sign: 'No returns based on vibes.'"

"I like your sister," Megan said. "She seems like someone who doesn't take any nonsense but also genuinely cares about people."

"That's a pretty accurate summary." Kyle took a sip of his coffee. "She's been the heart of that shop since we took it over. I handle the business side mostly and some decorating here and there, but Leslie's the one who makes it magical. She remembers customers' names, their kids' names, and how the locals like to decorate their homes for Christmas. She's got a gift for sure."

There was such obvious affection in his voice when he spoke of his sister. She'd spent so many years around people who complained about their families, who couldn't wait to escape their hometowns, and who saw obligation where Kyle clearly saw love.

"You're really close with your family," she observed.

"I am. I know that's not everyone's experience, but I'm a lucky man, and I know it." He paused, seeming to choose his words carefully. "What about you? You mentioned your mom remarried and moved to Florida. Are you two close?"

Megan stirred her coffee, watching the cream swirl into the dark liquid. "Not really. I mean, we're not estranged or anything. We just... exist in parallel, I guess. She has her life with Rick now, and I have mine. We text sometimes and talk on the phone now and then. It's fine."

"Fine," Kyle repeated.

"She worked really hard when I was growing up after the divorce," Megan added, feeling the need to defend her mother even as she acknowledged their distance. "After my dad left, she was on her own raising me and putting herself through nursing school. She did the best she could. But she was definitely a changed person after my dad left. She wasn't the mom I had known before the divorce. And now... I don't blame her for wanting her own happiness at all."

"That doesn't mean you can't wish things were different," Kyle said quietly.

The observation was so accurate, so gently delivered, that Megan had to look away. She focused on the window, watching a couple walk past with shopping bags, their heads bent together in conversation.

"I used to wish things were different," she admitted. "When I was younger, I thought if I were just... better somehow, more worth staying for, my dad wouldn't have left. My mom wouldn't have been so tired all the time or distant from me. Everything would be easier." She forced a laugh that didn't quite land. "Turns out that's not how life works."

"No," Kyle agreed. "But for what it's worth, I don't think any of that was about you not being enough. Sometimes people make choices that have nothing to do with the people they leave behind. Your dad leaving—that was his failure, not yours. And your mom changing after your father left... well, I really don't know what to say about that because I've never experienced a divorce, but I can imagine that it was probably a shock for her. Maybe that's how she coped and survived at the time."

Megan's throat tightened. She'd heard similar sentiments before, from school counselors and well-meaning friends. But hearing it from Kyle, said with such certainty, it hit differently.

"Maybe," she managed.

They sat in comfortable silence for a moment, both sipping their coffee. Then Kyle shifted slightly, his expression lightening. "So, change of subject before we both get too depressed—what did you do in the shop this morning before you came up to the apartment?"

"Wow, where do I even start?" Megan felt herself relax into a safer topic. "I spent the morning in Phyllis's office, going through some of her things. Files, newspaper clippings, and journals."

Kyle's expression shifted to something gentler. "That must have been emotional."

"It was." Megan wrapped her hands around her coffee mug again, the warmth grounding her. "She kept everything. Every article written about the shop from the day it opened until just a couple of years ago. Awards, features in magazines, even a piece about her winning first place at the Tennessee State Fair for her hand-pulled taffy."

"I remember her telling me about that. I was only a teenager when she won first place," Kyle said.

"She documented everything in these journals too, Kyle. I found three of them, and I only read a little bit, but..." Megan paused, her throat tightening at the memory. "She wrote about opening the shop, about how terrified she was that first week. About customers she remembered, recipes she perfected. And she wrote about me."

Kyle was quiet, letting her continue at her own pace.

"She kept my picture on her desk all these years. Talked to it, according to what she wrote. She wondered about me, hoped I was happy, and believed I was something special even though we hadn't seen each other in years." Megan looked up, meeting Kyle's eyes. "I had no idea. I thought I was completely alone after my dad left, that everyone had just moved on and forgotten about me. But she never did."

"She talked about you when she was alive," Kyle said quietly. "Not constantly, but sometimes. Out of the blue, she'd say things like, 'I wonder what Meggie is doing right now' or 'I hope one day Meggie comes to visit me again.' She loved you, Megan. That was always clear."

The simple certainty in his words made Megan's eyes sting. She blinked quickly, focusing on her coffee. "I went to talk to Beth after that, and she could tell I'd been crying. I'm sure she thinks I'm a mess."

"I think she probably thinks you're human," Kyle said. "Which is a good thing to be."

Megan managed a small smile. "I also learned about the business finances this morning. Beth walked me through how Phyllis set aside money for building maintenance. I had no idea how any of it worked, and Beth was so patient in explaining it all."

"Beth's great at that. She's been managing the financial side of Sugar & Spice for years."

"She made me feel like it was okay not to know things. Like learning was expected, not something to be embarrassed about. Everyone here keeps doing that. Treating me like I'm capable of figuring things out instead of assuming I'll fail. It's strange."

"Strange how?"

"Strange, because I'm not used to it. In every job I've had, every place I've lived, there was always this underlying assumption that I was temporary. Replaceable. Someone just passing through until they found someone better. Here, people keep acting like I might actually stay. Like I might actually be able to do this."

Kyle leaned forward slightly, his expression intent. "That's because you can do this. You're already doing it."

"I've been here two days."

"And in those two days, you've learned candy-making basics, made decisions about a major renovation, started building relationships with your staff, and you are clearly thinking seriously about the business. That's not nothing, Megan."

She wanted to argue, to list all the ways she was fumbling through everything. But the steady conviction in Kyle's voice made the protests die before they reached her lips.

"Thank you," she said instead. "For believing that."

"I'm not just being nice. I mean it." He held her gaze for a moment longer, then seemed to realize the intensity and looked down at his coffee. "So, what else did you find in the office? Anything interesting besides the journals?"

"More recipes," Megan said, grateful for the shift to lighter ground. "Some of the cards have notes in the margins—'customers love this one at Thanksgiving,' 'adjust cinnamon and add nutmeg,' things like that. It's like having a conversation with her through recipes."

"Are you going to try making any of them?"

"Eventually. Once I'm competent enough." She grinned.

"Don't second-guess yourself," he said. "Just jump in and try. If you fail... then you fail. Start over and try again."

"Eventually... maybe. Now, change of subject. What about you? Why did you come back here after law school?" Megan asked, genuinely curious. "I mean, you could have gone anywhere with a law degree. Worked at a big firm in Nashville or Atlanta or wherever. Why come back to Mistletoe Falls?"

Kyle was quiet for a moment, his fingers tracing the rim of his coffee mug. "Honestly? I tried to convince myself I wanted a big-city career. Make a ton of money, build a prestigious practice, all of that."

"What changed?"

"I came home for Christmas during my third year of law school." His smile was self-deprecating. "Within two days, I realized I'd been lying to myself. This is where I wanted to be. Where I fit. All that stuff I thought I wanted—the prestige, the money, the impressive title—none of it mattered as much as being somewhere that made me happy. I missed my family, and I knew I didn't want to live far away from them."

Megan felt something twist in her chest. Belonging. What must that feel like, to be so certain of where you fit that you'd give up other opportunities without regret?

"Do you ever wonder if you made the right choice?" she asked.

"No." His answer was immediate and certain. "Not even once. Which probably sounds boring or provincial to someone from a bigger city."

"I'm from Bowling Green, Kentucky," Megan said dryly. "It's not exactly a metropolis. And no, it doesn't sound boring. It sounds... nice. Really nice, actually."

Their eyes met across the table, and something passed between them—understanding, maybe, or recognition. Kyle's expression softened, and Megan found herself noticing details she'd been trying not to notice. The way his hazel eyes caught the light from the window. The small scar near his left eyebrow. The way his hands looked wrapped around his coffee mug—strong, capable hands.

She looked away quickly, her heart beating slightly faster.

Donna appeared then, saving Megan from her own thoughts, with two plates balanced expertly on one arm. "Loaded cheeseburger with fries," she announced, setting Megan's plate down with a flourish. "And a patty melt with onion rings. Can I get you anything else?"

"I think we're good," Kyle said. "Thanks, Donna."

The food looked as good as it smelled—Megan's burger was thick and juicy, the fries golden and perfectly salted, and everything was arranged on the plate like someone actually cared about presentation even in a casual diner. She picked up a fry and bit into it, the satisfying crunch and salt hitting exactly right.

"Oh, that's good," she said, reaching for another.

Kyle had already started on his patty melt, and they ate in comfortable silence for a few minutes. Megan hadn't realized how hungry she was until she had food in front of her. The burger was everything a diner burger should be—messy, flavorful, and unpretentious.

"So," Kyle said after he'd made decent progress on his lunch, "can I ask you something?"

Megan looked up, a fry halfway to her mouth. "Sure."

"Do you think you'll stay? In Mistletoe Falls, I mean. Long term."

Megan set down the fry, buying herself time to formulate an answer.

"I don't know," she said honestly. "Three days ago, I lived in Bowling Green, Kentucky. I was unhappy, living below poverty level and making it but barely. It's difficult to describe, but I was in this endless loop of job after job and couldn't seem to work my way up to making a better income. I was living in survival mode, basically. Now I own a building and a business here. It's a lot to process."

"That's fair."

"But," she continued, surprising herself, "I like it here so far. The town, the people, and the pace of things. For the first time in a really long time, I'm not worried about my job letting me go because of a layoff. I'm not worried about having to live with roommates that drive me crazy. I'm starting to feel a little bit more secure. That has to mean something, right?"

Kyle's smile was genuine and warm. "Yeah. I think it means something."

"Your turn," Megan said, steering toward safer ground. "Besides The Christmas Shop and your law practice, what do you do? Hobbies, interests... any secret talents?"

"Secret talents?" Kyle laughed. "I don't know about that. I help Dad with resort maintenance sometimes—fixing things, general repairs. I read a lot. Crime novels mostly, but I'm not picky. And I ski and hike and go fishing, though not as much as I'd like."

"You ski, hike, and fish? Of course you do. You seem like the type that can just do anything."

"Do you like to ski?"

"I've never tried. Never really had the opportunity."

"You should try it. The resort's beginner slopes are perfect for learning, and—" He stopped himself, looking slightly embarrassed. "Sorry, I'm not trying to push you into activities. That's a bad habit of mine."

"A bad habit?"

"Being overly helpful. Leslie says I have a savior complex."

Megan considered this. "I don't think you have a savior complex. I think you're just... helpful. There's a difference. You haven't tried to solve all my problems or take over my life. You've just been there when I needed someone, which is different."

Something in Kyle's expression shifted. "I appreciate you saying that."

"I mean it." Megan picked up her burger again, took another bite, and then added, "Though I have to say, if you ever do want to teach me to ski or hike and maybe... maybe how to fish, I'm willing to try. Fair warning—I'll probably be terrible at all of them."

"Everyone's terrible at first. That's part of the fun."

They talked their way through the rest of the meal; the conversation flowing easily from one topic to another. Kyle told her about some of the more eccentric Christmas Shop customers—the man who collected only nutcracker ornaments and had over three hundred of them and the woman who bought a new tree topper every year and donated the old one to charity. Megan shared stories about her various jobs—the restaurant where she'd worked as a hostess and dealt with increasingly bizarre customer demands and the retail position where her boss had been convinced the store was haunted.

It was easy. Comfortable. Megan couldn't remember the last time she'd sat across from someone and just... talked. Without having to perform or pretend or worry about saying the wrong thing. Kyle listened as if he were genuinely interested, laughed at her jokes, and shared his own stories with the kind of openness that made her want to be equally honest.

She was reaching for her last fry when she realized she'd been smiling for the better part of an hour. The observation startled her. When was the last time that had happened?

"You want dessert?" Kyle asked as Donna swung by to clear their plates.

Megan pressed a hand to her stomach. "I'm so full."

"We could split a slice of pie," Kyle suggested.

"Sold. Let's do it."

Donna returned with the pie menu, and after some debate, they settled on apple crumb. When it arrived—a generous slice with a golden, buttery crumb topping and a scoop of vanilla ice cream slowly melting on top—Megan understood the hype.

"Oh wow," she said after her first bite. "Okay, they're not lying about the pie here."

"This is good. I've never tried the apple crumb before." Kyle took another bite and nodded in satisfaction.

They worked their way through the slice, trading bites and occasional comments about the perfection of the crust or the way the ice cream balanced the sweetness. Megan found herself watching Kyle's hands again—the way he held his fork and the casual competence in his movements. She caught herself and forced her attention back to the pie.

When they'd finished, Donna dropped the check on the table with a knowing smile. "Y'all take your time."

Kyle reached for the check immediately, but Megan was faster. She grabbed it first, studying the total.

"We should split this," she said.

"Absolutely not." Kyle held out his hand. "I invited you to lunch."

"You invited me to lunch while doing me about seventeen favors this morning. I can at least pay for my own meal."

"Megan." His tone was gentle but firm. "Let me get this. Please."

She studied him for a moment, trying to determine if this was about gender roles or Southern hospitality or something else entirely. His expression was patient and open, waiting for her to make the decision without pushing.

"Fine," she relented, handing over the check. "But I'm taking care of the bill next time."

Kyle's smile was immediate and bright, transforming his whole face. "Next time? I'll hold you to that."

Megan felt her cheeks warm, but she couldn't quite stop herself from smiling back. "You better."

Chapter 16

Megan returned to Sugar & Spice, still feeling the happiness and thrill of having lunch with Kyle. She noticed how the afternoon sunlight slanted through Sugar & Spice's front windows, turning the glass display cases into prisms that threw rainbow patterns across the polished hardwood floor. The shop hummed with activity. A couple browsed the truffle display while Savannah stood behind the counter, wrapping a box of caramels. She finished tying the burgundy ribbon and handed the package to her customer with a bright smile, then looked up as Megan approached.

"Hey! How was your shopping trip?"

"Good." Megan set her purse under the counter. "Really good, actually. We shopped; Kyle helped me a lot while I picked out things for the apartment, and then we went for lunch."

"Good. I'm glad everything went well. Ready to learn about the retail side of things?"

"As ready as I'll ever be."

"Perfect." Savannah gestured to the register. "Let's start with the cash register system. Once you've got this down, everything else is easy."

Megan moved behind the counter, eyeing the touch-screen register that looked far more complicated than the older, basic-style cash registers she'd used at previous jobs. Savannah pulled up a stool beside her.

"Okay, so the register looks intimidating, but it's actually pretty straightforward." Savannah's fingers flew across the screen, demonstrating each function. "Item lookup here, quantities here, and payment processing here. We've got discount codes for regulars—they're all saved in the system. Gift cards process through this menu. And special orders go through this separate screen so we can track them."

Megan watched carefully, nodding at each step, trying to commit the flow to memory. "What if I mess something up?"

"Then you use the void function." Savannah demonstrated. "See? Easy. Mistakes happen. It's completely fine."

The front door chimed, and Megan's stomach tightened as a customer entered—a little girl, maybe six or seven, clutching a small coin purse shaped like a ladybug. Her mother trailed behind, smiling.

"Go ahead," Savannah whispered. "You've got this."

Megan straightened, forcing confidence into her voice. "Hi there. Can I help you find something?"

The little girl approached the counter with the serious concentration of someone on an important mission. She set her ladybug purse down and began extracting coins one at a time, arranging them in careful rows on the counter.

"I want a lollipop," she announced. "But I have to count my money first to make sure I have enough."

"I understand." Megan leaned on the counter, watching the child's meticulous work. "Take your time."

It took three full minutes for the girl to count and recount her change. Then came the even more critical decision of which lollipop flavor to choose. She examined each option in the display case with the gravity of a jeweler assessing diamonds.

"The red one is cherry," Megan explained. "The blue is blue raspberry. Green is sour apple. And the purple one is grape."

"What's your favorite?"

Megan considered this seriously. "Blue raspberry. But cherry is my second favorite."

The girl nodded, processing this information. Finally, after what felt like an eternity, she pointed decisively. "Blue raspberry."

"Excellent choice." Megan retrieved the lollipop and rang it up, showing the girl the register screen. "That's seventy-five cents."

Together, they counted the coins the girl had so carefully arranged. When they reached exactly seventy-five cents, the child's face lit up with pure triumph.

"Perfect," Megan said, dropping the coins into the register drawer one by one so the girl could see where they went. She slipped the lollipop into a small bag and handed it over. "Thank you for shopping at Sugar & Spice."

The girl clutched her prize and beamed. "Thank you!"

As they left, the mother turned back at the door. "That was very kind of you. She's been saving that money for two weeks."

When the door chimed shut, Megan smiled. Savannah was grinning too.

"See? You're a natural. That's exactly what Phyllis would have done—made that little girl feel like her purchase mattered just as much as someone buying five pounds of fudge."

The observation settled into Megan's chest, warm and affirming. Maybe she could do this after all.

The next customer was less charming—a businessman in a hurry, ordering a pound of mixed chocolates for a client meeting. Megan managed the transaction smoothly until she entered the quantity. Somehow her finger slipped, and instead of entering one pound, the register showed seven.

The total on the screen made her stomach drop. "That's... that's not right."

The man raised an eyebrow. "I certainly hope not."

"I'm so sorry." Megan's cheeks burned as she stared at the screen, her mind blank on how to fix it.

"Void function," Savannah murmured, reaching past her to demonstrate. "There. Just ring it up again."

The second time went perfectly. The businessman paid, nodded his thanks, and left without commenting on the mistake. Megan exhaled slowly.

"See? Not the end of the world." Savannah patted her shoulder. "You handled it well. Apologized, fixed it, moved on. That's all anyone can ask."

"I thought I was going to pass out."

"It's fine, really. By the end of the week, you'll be running this register in your sleep."

The afternoon settled into a rhythm. Megan handled transactions while Savannah supervised, offering quiet corrections and encouragement. Between customers, Savannah showed her how to read the sales reports, where certain important packing supplies were stored, and how to handle gift card activations.

Around three o'clock, a woman in her sixties entered the shop. She had silver hair in a neat bun and the comfortable manner of someone who'd been coming here for years. Savannah's face brightened.

"Mrs. Hoffman! Good to see you."

"Hello, Savannah dear." The woman's gaze shifted to Megan, and her expression softened with recognition. "You must be Phyllis's niece. I heard you were in town. I can see the resemblance around the eyes."

Megan's throat tightened. "Yes, ma'am. I'm Megan."

"I'm so sorry for your loss, dear. Phyllis was a wonderful woman." Mrs. Hoffman moved to the counter. "I'll take a pound of the maple fudge, please."

While Savannah retrieved the fudge from the display case, Mrs. Hoffman continued. "Phyllis always remembered I liked maple fudge. She'd set a pound aside for me every Friday. I've been coming here for fifteen years."

"Fridays," Megan repeated, filing that detail away.

"Like clockwork." Mrs. Hoffman smiled at the memory. "Once, about five years ago, I mentioned in passing that my grandson was having a birthday party the next weekend. The next Friday, when I came in for my usual fudge, Phyllis had included an extra half pound with a little note that said, 'For your grandson's birthday.' She'd remembered a casual comment from a week earlier." The woman's eyes glistened. "She had such a good memory, and she had a gift for making people feel special and loved."

Savannah set the wrapped package on the counter, and Megan rang up the purchase with careful attention to getting it right. When Mrs. Hoffman paid, Megan managed to smile past the emotion clogging her throat.

"I'll make sure we continue the Friday maple fudge tradition," she promised.

"I'd like that." Mrs. Hoffman squeezed Megan's hand across the counter. "I enjoyed meeting you, Megan, and hope to see you again."

After she left, Megan stood motionless, staring at the door. The bell's chime seemed to echo longer than usual.

"You okay?" Savannah asked quietly.

"Yeah." Megan turned back to the counter, organizing receipt paper she didn't need to organize. "I just... I didn't realize how much my aunt meant to people. How personal she made everything."

"That's what made this place special. Phyllis didn't just sell candy—she built relationships. Remembered names, asked about grandkids, celebrated milestones with customers." Savannah leaned against the counter. "That's the real legacy you inherited. Not just the recipes or the business."

Megan nodded, not trusting her voice. She understood now why the shop thrived and why customers returned. The candy was excellent, but people came back for how Phyllis had made them feel—noticed, valued, and remembered.

Could she do that? Build those connections, remember those details, and make people feel special?

She wanted to try.

The afternoon wore on. Megan handled customers with growing confidence, making notes mentally about regulars and their preferences. A man who liked dark chocolate truffles. A teenager who always bought candy for her younger siblings every Friday after school. A couple celebrating their anniversary with the same box of caramels they'd shared on their first date.

Each transaction felt like learning a new language—not just the mechanics of the register, but the unspoken vocabulary of care that transformed a simple purchase into something meaningful.

Around four o'clock, during a brief lull, Savannah pulled out her iPad. "Want to see what I do with our online presence?"

"Definitely."

Savannah opened Instagram, and Megan leaned in to watch. The shop's account had over three thousand followers, and the recent posts showed professional-quality photos of hand-pulled taffy, chocolate arrangements, and gift baskets.

"This one did really well." Savannah clicked on a video from two days ago. The clip showed Tonya in the kitchen, pulling taffy with the same hypnotic rhythm Megan had watched yesterday. The caption read, "The art of hand-pulled taffy—a tradition we're proud to continue."

The engagement numbers made Megan's eyes widen. Twenty-five hundred likes. There are eighty-three comments.

"Can I scroll through the comments?" Megan asked.

"Sure."

She read through them, each one a small testament to the shop's reputation. 'Best candy shop in Tennessee!' and 'Can't wait to visit again this Christmas!' and 'Phyllis would be so proud of you all carrying on her legacy.'

That last comment made her chest ache.

"We get orders from all over the country through the website," Savannah explained, switching to show the shop's homepage. "I update it every week with seasonal offerings or special promotions. Online traffic has grown about thirty percent in the last year."

"That's impressive." Megan watched Savannah navigate the site with practiced ease. "You do all this from your laptop and iPad?"

"Yeah. The computer in Phyllis's office is ancient. I tried using it once and gave up after ten minutes." Savannah laughed. "My laptop works fine, though."

Megan nodded. The old desktop was slow and outdated, but it wasn't something that needed immediate attention or replacement. Savannah had found a system that worked. They could revisit it later if needed.

"You've really built up the online presence," Megan said. "This is incredible."

Savannah's cheeks flushed with pleasure. "Thanks. I'm actually hoping to get my master's in business next year—digital marketing focus. Phyllis was really supportive of that and helped me think through how to balance school and work."

"If you need flexibility for classes, just let me know. I want to support that too."

"Really?" Savannah's eyes brightened. "That would be amazing. Thank you."

The front doorbell chimed, interrupting their conversation. A man entered carrying a gift basket, his expression somewhere between frustrated and apologetic.

"Can I help you?" Megan asked.

"I hope so." He set the basket on the counter. "I ordered this two weeks ago for a corporate client. The order form specifically said no dark chocolate—my client has strong preferences. But this basket has dark chocolate truffles in it."

Megan's stomach dropped. She glanced at Savannah, who was already pulling up the order system on the register.

"I'm so sorry," Megan said, keeping her voice calm and professional. "That's absolutely our mistake. Let me fix this for you right away."

"I need it by tomorrow morning. The meeting's at nine."

"Not a problem." Megan scanned through the order details Savannah had pulled up. The notes clearly stated, "No dark chocolate," in capital letters. "I'll have a new basket made correctly this afternoon. Can we deliver it to your office later today? Say, in about an hour?"

The man's frustration eased slightly. "That would work."

"And I'd like to upgrade the basket to our premium selection at no additional charge—as an apology for the error."

"You don't have to do that."

"I want to. We take pride in getting orders right, and we didn't this time. Let me make it right." Megan pulled out a notepad. "What's your office address?"

He provided the details, and Megan wrote them down. "I'll personally make sure this is perfect. One of my employees will deliver the new basket in about an hour. Again, I apologize for the confusion."

"I appreciate your handling this so quickly." The man actually smiled. "Thank you."

After he left, Savannah looked at Megan with undisguised admiration.

"That was really well done. You stayed calm and focused on fixing it instead of making excuses."

"It was our mistake. He deserved a solution, not an argument." Megan made a note to talk to Kay about the basket assembly process and to learn more about it. "I should tell the kitchen about the remake."

"I'll handle that," Savannah offered. "You're doing great out here."

The rest of the afternoon passed smoothly. Megan grew more confident on the register, her interactions with customers more natural. She began to recognize the rhythm of the work—the quiet focus required for transactions, the warmth needed for personal exchanges, and the quick thinking necessary for solving problems.

At quarter to five, the front door chimed again. Megan looked up from rearranging the gift area display and felt her pulse quicken a little when she saw Kyle walking in, folder in hand.

He spotted her immediately, and his smile was warm enough to make her forget she was standing in the middle of a candy shop in work-worn jeans and a Sugar & Spice apron.

"Hey, got a minute?"

"Sure," she said as she moved to the counter. "What's up?"

Kyle set the folder on the counter. "Dad and I intend to start painting in your apartment tomorrow. Thought you might want to see how Warm Linen looks in different light before we commit fully."

He pulled out all the paint sample cards from the hardware store, spreading them across the counter. The afternoon sunlight showed subtle variations Megan hadn't noticed before.

She studied them carefully, comparing the samples to the golden light filling the shop. In this natural illumination, Warm Linen still looked exactly right—neutral enough to work with anything, but with enough warmth that it wouldn't feel cold or institutional.

"Warm Linen is still perfect," she said. "I love it."

Kyle's pleased expression made her want to smile too broadly. "Good. I'm glad. We'll start first thing tomorrow morning. With Dad and me working together, the painting should go pretty quickly."

"I wish I could be there to help."

"What are your plans tomorrow?"

"Morning, I'll probably shadow Savannah some more. Learn more about the retail side." Megan gestured vaguely at the surrounding shop. "Then in the afternoon, when the kitchen isn't so busy, I'm going to try making some candy on my own."

"Wow, good for you. You'll do fine."

"We'll see. My first attempt at fudge was... edible. Not quite as good as what the others make, but it was okay."

Kyle laughed, and the sound was warm and genuine. "Edible's a good thing."

From behind them, Savannah's voice carried with barely concealed amusement. "You should come watch us make candy sometime, Kyle. See the magic happen."

He glanced over, seeming to notice Savannah's presence for the first time. "I'd like that, actually."

Megan turned to him, surprised. "Really?"

"Yeah. I mean, if I wouldn't be in the way."

"You wouldn't be in the way at all."

"Then I'll definitely take you up on that sometime." He gathered the paint samples back into the folder. "Oh, before I forget—are you still wanting to take Hazel tomorrow?"

"Yes, definitely." Guilt pinched at Megan. "I feel bad that she's not with me yet."

"She's fine, but yeah, she should probably get settled with you soon. She's been giving me the royal treatment—very clear about when she wants dinner, when she wants attention, and when she wants me to leave her alone."

Megan smiled at the image of an imperious cat training Kyle. "What if I follow you to your place after the shop closes tomorrow? That way I can get her and all her stuff."

"That works. Shop closes at six on Saturdays, right?"

"Right."

"Perfect. I'll swing by here around six, and you can follow me out to the cabin."

"Thanks for taking care of her all this time."

"She's good company... well, she is now that she's gotten used to me. Though fair warning—she's extremely demanding. I'm not sure if you know what you're signing up for."

"I think I can handle one cat."

"We'll see if you still think that after a week of Hazel running your life."

They smiled at each other, and Megan became aware of the moment stretching slightly too long, of Savannah watching them with undisguised interest, and of the way Kyle's eyes stayed on her face like he was in no hurry to leave.

The last browsing customer approached the register, breaking the spell. Savannah moved smoothly into position. "I've got this one."

Kyle stepped back from the counter. "I should go."

"Thanks for bringing the paint samples by. It was thoughtful."

"See you tomorrow around six?"

"I'll be here."

Their eyes met again—just for a moment, nothing dramatic, but enough to make Megan's pulse quicken. Then Kyle headed for the door, lifting his hand in a casual wave before the bell chimed his exit.

Savannah finished with the customer, sent them on their way with a cheerful goodbye, and turned to Megan with a look of pure delight.

"Sooo... Kyle stopped by to show you paint samples? Paint samples of paint that you've already bought."

Megan felt her face warm. "He was being thoughtful."

"Mm-hmm. Thoughtful. That's one word for it." Savannah's grin was irrepressible. "He also arranged to meet you tomorrow after work and looked at you like you're the most interesting thing he's seen all week."

"Don't start."

"I'm not starting anything. I'm just observing." Savannah pulled out the end-of-day checklist from under the register. "But for the record? Kyle Porter is a catch. And he's clearly interested."

"We're just friends... well, starting to be friends."

"Sure. Friends who shop for paint together, have lunch together, and arrange cat custody exchanges."

Megan tried to summon an argument and found she didn't actually want to make one. The truth was, she liked Kyle. More than liked him, if she was being honest.

But admitting that out loud felt dangerous. Like saying it might jinx it, or worse, might reveal how much she was already starting to hope for something she wasn't sure she deserved.

"So... end of the day routine," she said instead. "Show me what needs to be done."

Savannah let her off the hook, moving into teaching mode. "Okay, so end-of-day is pretty straightforward. First, we close out the register..."

Chapter 17

Linda had warned her that candy-making was equal parts science and art, but Megan was pretty sure she knew little about either, yet she was willing to try.

The kitchen was hers for the afternoon. Kay, Linda, and Tonya had left around one o'clock, trusting Megan to practice what they'd taught her over the past few days. Beth and Savannah were handling the retail area, their voices occasionally drifting through the swinging door along with the cheerful jingle of the shop bell.

Megan stood at the workstation, Phyllis's recipe card for peppermint bark propped against a canister of powdered sugar. The instructions seemed straightforward enough. Melt dark chocolate, spread it on parchment paper, and let it set slightly. Melt white chocolate, add peppermint oil, and pour over the dark chocolate layer. Sprinkle with crushed candy canes. Simple.

She'd watched her employees make various candies over the past few days. She'd seen how the women moved with such practiced confidence, stirring with steady pressure and watching the thermometer with hawklike attention, knowing exactly when to remove the pot from heat. They had made it look effortless, like something anyone could do with a little patience and focus.

Megan was discovering that watching and actually doing were entirely different skills.

The dark chocolate had melted beautifully in the double boiler, smooth and glossy. She'd poured it onto the parchment-lined baking sheet with only minor spillage, spreading it carefully with an offset spatula the way Linda had shown her. So far, so good.

The white chocolate was where things started going wrong.

Megan had turned her attention to cleaning the double boiler she'd used to melt the dark chocolate. When she looked back at the other pot on the stove, the white chocolate had gone from perfectly melted to seized and grainy in what felt like seconds. With panic rising, she'd cranked the heat higher, thinking she could salvage it.

That was her first mistake.

The chocolate didn't smooth out. Instead, it began to scorch, the sweet smell turning acrid. Megan grabbed the pot off the heat and stared at the ruined mess.

"Okay," she said aloud to the empty kitchen. "Okay. It's fine. Start over."

She scraped the burnt chocolate into the trash, trying not to think about the waste, and started fresh with a new batch of white chocolate chips. This time she watched it more carefully, stirring constantly, keeping the heat low.

The chocolate melted. Relief washed through her.

Megan reached for the small bottle of peppermint oil. "Just a few drops," Linda had said. "This stuff is powerful. A little goes a long way."

Megan tilted the bottle over the pot.

The dropper mechanism decided this was the moment to fail. Instead of measured drops, a generous glug of peppermint oil splashed into the white chocolate.

"No, no, no!" Megan jerked the bottle upright, but the damage was done.

The scent hit her immediately—sharp, overwhelming, and medicinal. Her eyes started watering. The menthol burned in her sinuses as if she'd just inhaled an entire tin of breath mints.

She stirred frantically, hoping dilution might help, but the smell only intensified. The white chocolate, which had been smooth moments ago, began to seize again from the excess liquid, turning grainy and stiff.

Megan's vision blurred with tears that had nothing to do with emotion and everything to do with the peppermint vapor filling the kitchen. She grabbed the pot off the heat again, coughing.

This was a disaster. A complete and total disaster.

She should throw it out and start over. That's what a sensible person would do. But something stubborn in her—the same stubborn streak that had driven her to pack her car and leave Kentucky with no real plan—made her think she could still save it.

Megan poured the seized, over-pepperminted white chocolate over the dark chocolate layer anyway. It didn't spread smoothly. It clumped and dragged, creating a lumpy, uneven mess that looked nothing like the elegant bark Linda made every day.

"You can do this," she muttered, using the spatula to try to smooth the surface. "It's just chocolate. It's not brain surgery."

But her eyes were streaming now, and she could barely see what she was doing. The menthol cloud seemed to be growing stronger rather than dissipating. She grabbed the crushed candy canes and sprinkled them over the top with shaking hands.

The result looked like something a child might create during a particularly enthusiastic craft project. Lumpy. Uneven. Definitely not Instagram-worthy.

Megan stepped back, wiping her eyes with her sleeve, and tried to assess the damage objectively. Maybe it would taste better than it looked? Maybe once it set properly, the texture would improve?

She was contemplating this optimistic possibility when she smelled it.

Burning.

Her head whipped back to the stove where the bottom of the double boiler still sat, now bone dry, the remaining water having boiled away completely. Smoke was beginning to curl up from the overheated metal.

"No!" Megan lunged for the stove, grabbing the pot handle without thinking.

The metal was hot, and she felt it immediately. She yelped, dropping the pot back onto the burner with a clatter, and the smoke thickened.

That's when the smoke alarm decided to join the catastrophe.

The shrill beeping cut through the kitchen, loud enough to make Megan's ears ring. She grabbed a kitchen towel and waved it frantically under the detector, trying to clear the smoke, but the alarm kept shrieking.

The swinging door from the retail area burst open, and Beth rushed in, followed immediately by Savannah.

"Wow." Beth's eyes were wide.

"Are you okay?" Savannah was already moving toward the stove, turning off the burner.

"I'm fine!" Megan had to shout over the alarm. "I just—the chocolate—and the peppermint." She gestured helplessly at the disaster zone that was the kitchen.

Savannah's eyes started watering immediately. "Wow. That's a lot of peppermint."

"Too much," Megan admitted, still waving the towel. "Way too much."

The back door flew open, and Kyle appeared in the kitchen, slightly breathless. His old t-shirt had paint spattered across one shoulder, and there was a smudge of "Warm Linen" on his left cheekbone.

"Is everyone—" He stopped, taking in the scene. The smoking pot. The overwhelming peppermint cloud. Megan frantically waved a towel at the smoke detector. The lumpy, uneven peppermint bark on the counter.

For a moment, nobody moved.

Then Kyle started laughing.

Not a polite chuckle or a suppressed snicker. A full, genuine laugh that crinkled the corners of his eyes and made his whole face light up with amusement.

"I'm sorry," he managed between laughs. "I'm sorry, it's not funny—"

"It's a little funny," Beth said, her own laughter breaking through.

"It's very funny," Savannah said, opening the back kitchen door to help clear the smoke. "Megan, did you use the entire bottle of peppermint oil?"

"It was an accident!" Megan protested, but she could feel her own laughter bubbling up despite her mortification. The situation was absurd. Completely, utterly absurd. "The dropper malfunctioned."

Kyle grinned as he grabbed another towel to help wave at the smoke detector.

The alarm finally stopped its piercing shriek, leaving blessed silence broken only by their ragged breathing and residual laughter.

"My eyes are burning," Beth said, wiping at them. "Seriously, Megan. What were you trying to make? Peppermint bark or biological warfare?"

"Peppermint bark," Megan said weakly, gesturing at the lumpy mess. "Obviously, I failed."

Kyle moved closer to inspect the bark, and Megan braced herself for criticism. Instead, he broke off a small piece from the edge—one of the less horrifying sections—and popped it in his mouth.

His expression immediately shifted to something between surprise and alarm. He chewed slowly, his eyes watering.

"That's..." He paused, seeming to search for words. "That's definitely peppermint."

"I can feel my sinuses clearing from here," Savannah said, laughing.

"It's awful, isn't it?" Megan asked, mortification flooding back now that the immediate crisis had passed. "It's completely inedible."

"It's just... enthusiastic," Kyle said, though his voice was slightly strained. "Very enthusiastic peppermint."

"You don't have to be nice about it." Megan grabbed the baking sheet. "I'll throw it out."

"Wait." Beth held up a hand. "Before we dispose of the evidence, can I just say that my first attempt at peppermint bark looked exactly like this?"

"My first batch of fudge crystallized so hard that Kay suggested we use it as doorstops," Savannah offered. "Seriously. She wasn't even joking."

"Linda once told me about the time she accidentally used salt instead of sugar in a batch of caramels," Beth continued. "Phyllis made her taste one, just so she'd remember to always double-check her ingredients."

Megan looked between them, still clutching the baking sheet. "You're just saying that to make me feel better."

"Partly, yes, but we're saying it because it's true as well," Beth said gently. "Nobody masters candy-making immediately. It takes practice. And disasters. Lots and lots of disasters."

Kyle moved to help Megan with cleanup, taking the baking sheet from her hands and dumping the unfortunate peppermint bark into the trash. "For what it's worth, I think your disaster is more impressive than most. The peppermint cloud alone was memorable."

"That's one way to describe it," Megan muttered, but she could feel the tension leaving her shoulders. The kitchen still smelled overwhelmingly of menthol, and her eyes were still watering, but the crushing weight of failure was lifting slightly.

Savannah had already moved to the sink, filling it with hot soapy water for the burnt pot. Beth was wiping down the counters, clearing away the evidence of Megan's spectacular failure.

"You know what this means, though," Kyle said, his tone turning thoughtful as he washed the baking sheet.

"That I should give up candy-making?" Megan suggested.

"No." His smile was warm and encouraging. "It means you need an official taste-tester. Someone brave enough to try your experiments before you unleash them on unsuspecting customers."

"I'm pretty sure that violates some kind of workplace safety regulation."

"I'm volunteering," Kyle said. "I'll even sign a waiver if you want."

Megan studied him, trying to determine if he was serious or just being kind. His hazel eyes held nothing but genuine warmth and a hint of amusement.

"Why would you voluntarily subject yourself to more disasters like this?" she asked.

"Because everyone needs someone willing to taste the burnt chocolate and over-pepperminted bark," Kyle said simply. "And because I have a feeling your successes are going to be worth the failures." He paused, then added with a grin, "Plus, I really like candy."

Beth made a small sound that might have been "aw" before catching herself and turning it into a cough.

Savannah wasn't even trying to hide her smile. "That's so sweet. Kyle volunteers as tribute for Megan's candy experiments."

"Someone has to," Kyle said, not taking his eyes off Megan. "Might as well be me."

The warmth in Megan's chest had nothing to do with the lingering heat from the stove and everything to do with the way Kyle was looking at her—not with pity or judgment, but with something that felt like genuine affection.

"Okay," she said. "The official taste-tester position is yours. But don't say I didn't warn you when you end up in the emergency room with peppermint poisoning."

"I'll take my chances." Kyle finished rinsing the baking sheet and set it in the dish drainer. "Besides, I've survived Leslie's experimental cooking. I can handle whatever you throw at me."

They worked together to finish cleaning the kitchen; the conversation flowing easily between the four of them. Beth shared the story of accidentally using baking soda instead of powdered sugar in a batch of truffles. Savannah recounted the time she'd somehow managed to get caramel on the ceiling. Even Kyle admitted to once setting a kitchen towel on fire while trying to flambé something during a disastrous attempt at impressing a date.

"What happened with the date?" Megan asked, curious despite herself.

"She married someone else," Kyle said cheerfully. "Probably for the best. I'm not much of a flambe guy."

By the time the kitchen was restored to order, the peppermint smell had faded to merely noticeable rather than overwhelming. The burnt pot was soaking in the sink. The counters were clean. The only evidence of Megan's disaster was the lingering menthol tingle in everyone's sinuses and the story they'd all be telling for years.

Beth and Savannah headed back to the retail area, giving Megan and Kyle a moment of privacy that wasn't subtle but was appreciated, nonetheless.

Kyle leaned against the counter, studying Megan with that thoughtful expression she was starting to recognize. "You okay?" he asked quietly.

"I think so." Megan wiped her hands on a kitchen towel, then hung it carefully on its hook. "I really wanted to get it right, you know? To prove to myself that I could actually do this."

"You will," Kyle said with such certainty that Megan almost believed him. "Maybe not today. Maybe not tomorrow. But you will."

"You sound very sure about that."

"I am." He smiled. "You're stubborn enough to figure it out. And you're smart enough to learn from disasters instead of being defeated by them. That's more than half the battle."

Megan wanted to argue, to point out all the ways she was fumbling through everything, but the steady conviction in Kyle's voice made the protests die before they formed. Maybe he was right. Maybe disaster really was part of the learning process rather than evidence of fundamental inadequacy.

"What time are you and your dad planning to finish painting today?" she asked.

Kyle glanced at his watch. "Probably around four. We're making good progress."

"I'll meet you then," Megan said. "Savannah and Beth can close the shop on their own. There's no reason for you to hang around and wait until six when we close, and I'll follow you to your house to pick up Hazel."

"Sounds good. Fair warning, though. Hazel's now decided she owns my couch. She might not want to leave."

"I'll try to sweet-talk her then."

"Bribery. I approve." Kyle pushed off from the counter. "I should get back upstairs before Dad thinks I've abandoned him. But hey, Megan?"

"Yeah?"

"Save your next disaster for when I'm around to witness it from the beginning. Today was good, but I feel like I missed the best parts."

Megan threw the damp kitchen towel at him. He caught it easily, laughing, and disappeared through the back door with a wave.

Chapter 18

Megan followed Kyle's truck up the winding mountain road toward Snowflake Mountain Resort. When his truck slowed and pulled into a driveway, Megan realized they were on Snowflake Mountain Resort property, just on the other side of the ridge from her A-frame cabin. She could see the resort's main lodge through the trees, its windows beginning to glow as dusk approached.

Kyle lived here. Probably a ten-minute walk from where she was staying.

But it was his cabin that made her breath catch.

Megan parked behind Kyle's truck and just stared.

The log cabin rose from the mountainside like something from an architect's dream. Natural wood formed the structure, but this wasn't some rustic hunting lodge. Floor-to-ceiling windows reflected the surrounding forest. A wraparound porch stretched across the front, complete with rocking chairs and a porch swing. The craftsmanship was stunning—every log fitted perfectly, the roofline clean and modern despite the traditional materials.

Kyle walked back to her car, and Megan rolled down her window.

"This is where you live?" The words came out more breathless than she'd intended. "Kyle, this is beautiful."

His pleased smile transformed his face. "Thanks. I had it built about five years ago."

"It's gorgeous."

"Come on, I'll show you inside."

Megan grabbed her purse and followed Kyle up the steps to the front porch. A small stack of firewood sat neatly beside the front door, and a boot scraper had been built into the porch itself.

Kyle unlocked the door and pushed it open. "Hazel? We've got company."

The interior was exactly what Megan expected and yet still surprising. The main space was open concept, with the living area flowing into the kitchen. More floor-to-ceiling windows lined the back wall, offering a view of the mountains that made Megan want to just stand and stare. The furniture was simple but quality—a leather sectional that looked well-loved, a sturdy coffee table that looked handmade, and two reading chairs positioned near the fireplace with a small table beside each.

The home was organized but lived-in, comfortable rather than pristine. Shelves lined one wall, packed with books rather than decorative objects.

"This is incredible," Megan said, turning slowly to take it all in. "It feels like you."

Kyle looked pleased with that assessment. "That's the goal, right? A place that fits who you are."

A loud, imperious meow interrupted the moment.

Hazel appeared from the bedroom hallway like a queen making her entrance. She was a substantial gray cat with luminous green eyes and an expression that suggested she was profoundly unimpressed by this disruption to her day.

"There she is," Kyle said. "Hazel, this is Megan. Megan, meet Hazel, your new roommate."

Hazel sat down in the middle of the living room and stared at Megan with regal assessment.

"Hi, Hazel," Megan said softly, crouching down to the cat's level. "I've heard a lot about you."

Hazel's tail twitched. She stood and walked toward Megan with deliberate steps, each paw placed with precision. When she reached Megan, she stopped and began a thorough sniffing investigation—shoes first, then jeans, then hands.

Megan held perfectly still, barely breathing, while Hazel conducted her inspection. The cat's whiskers tickled against her fingers. Those green eyes studied Megan with an intensity that felt almost human.

Then Hazel began to purr. The sound was surprisingly loud—a rumbling engine of contentment. The cat head-butted Megan's leg, then did it again for emphasis.

"Oh," Megan breathed, charmed despite herself. She reached down and scratched behind Hazel's ears. "Oh, you're sweet, aren't you?"

"Don't let her fool you," Kyle said, but his voice was warm with amusement. "She's a tyrant. Phyllis spoiled her completely."

Hazel responded by flopping onto her side at Megan's feet, exposing her fluffy belly in a display of trust that seemed significant.

"I think she likes you," Kyle observed.

"The feeling's mutual." Megan continued scratching Hazel's ears, and the purring intensified. "You're just a big softie under all that attitude, aren't you?"

Hazel's eyes closed to contented slits.

Megan straightened, and Hazel immediately stood too, winding around her ankles in a figure-eight pattern. When Megan took a step toward the kitchen, the cat followed, staying so close she was nearly a trip hazard.

"Hazel," Kyle said with exasperation. "Give her some space."

Hazel ignored him completely, her attention fixed on Megan.

Megan's stomach chose that moment to growl. Loudly.

Kyle's eyebrows rose. "When's the last time you ate?"

"Um." Megan tried to remember. "I had coffee this morning. And I grabbed a piece of fudge around one."

"Megan."

"Food was the furthest thing from my mind today," she protested.

Kyle shook his head and moved to the refrigerator. "Okay, we're fixing that right now. How do you feel about sandwiches?"

"I feel very positive about sandwiches."

He opened the fridge and surveyed the contents. "I've got deli turkey, roast beef, salami, ham, three kinds of cheese, and pretty much every vegetable known to man because my mother keeps restocking my fridge when I'm not looking. And yes... she spoils me. How do you feel about building your own sandwich?"

Megan felt herself light up at the idea. "Really?"

"Really. Consider this a choose-your-own-adventure sandwich situation." Kyle started pulling items from the fridge.

They spread ingredients across the kitchen counter like a buffet. Lettuce, tomatoes, cucumbers, red onions, pickles, and peppers. Mayo, mustard, oil, and vinegar. Provolone, cheddar, and Swiss. Turkey, roast beef, salami, and ham.

Hazel sat nearby, watching the proceedings with interest, occasionally meowing as if offering commentary.

"What do you think, Hazel?" Megan asked the cat as she considered her options. "Tomatoes or no tomatoes?"

Hazel meowed.

"You're right. Definitely tomatoes." Megan grabbed a couple of slices.

Kyle was trying not to laugh. "Are you actually consulting the cat?"

"She has opinions. It would be rude not to listen." Megan layered turkey and salami on her bread. "Besides, she's clearly the expert here."

"The expert on what? Being demanding?"

"On everything." Megan added cheese, and then more cheese. "Right, Hazel?"

Hazel purred her agreement and rubbed against Megan's leg again.

Kyle shook his head, but his smile was fond. "I'm adding four types of meat. Just so you know. This sandwich is going to be legendary."

"Four? Amateur." Megan grabbed the ham. "I'm going for five."

"There are only four types of meat here."

"Then I'm using ham twice. Boom. Five layers of meat." She stacked the ham on top of her existing layers with a theatrical flourish.

"That's cheating."

"That's innovation."

They built their sandwiches with the intense focus of artists creating masterpieces, each trying to outdo the other with increasingly elaborate additions. Kyle's sandwich grew so tall that Megan questioned whether it would fit in his mouth. Her own creation was threatening to collapse under its own weight.

"I think yours is defying the laws of physics," Kyle observed, eyeing Megan's precarious tower of ingredients.

"It's fine. I have a system."

"Your system appears to be 'add everything and hope for the best.'"

"That's a perfectly valid system." Megan carefully placed the top slice of bread on her sandwich, then had to hold it together with both hands. "See? Structural integrity achieved."

"For now," Kyle said.

They carried their sandwiches to the kitchen table. Hazel immediately jumped onto Megan's lap the moment she sat down, settling with the contentment of a cat who'd found exactly where she was meant to be.

"Hazel, you're going to make it very difficult for her to eat," Kyle pointed out.

Hazel closed her eyes and began purring.

"It's fine," Megan said, adjusting the cat slightly so she could reach her plate. "We're bonding."

Kyle picked up his sandwich, and Megan did the same. The first bite confirmed what she'd suspected—it was completely ridiculous and absolutely delicious.

"Oh wow," she said with a mouthful of sandwich. "This is perfection."

They ate in comfortable silence for a moment, and Megan found herself studying the cabin again. Through the windows, she could see the mountains darkening as evening approached. The space felt lived in but cared for, every detail intentional. The books on the shelves ranged from legal texts to fiction to what looked like carpentry manuals. A framed photograph on one shelf showed Kyle and Leslie as children, standing in front of The Christmas Shop.

"Your parents must be proud," Megan said. "Of you and your home and the life you've made for yourself here."

Kyle glanced around his cabin as if seeing it fresh. "They are. Dad especially loves that I used some of the skills he taught me and added features to the house here and there. He's been hinting around that we should build a workshop."

"Will you?"

"Probably. It's hard to say no when he's already drawing up plans." Kyle smiled.

Megan's sandwich chose that moment to begin its structural collapse. The bottom layer of bread simply gave up. Meat and tomatoes slid sideways, pickle slices made a break for freedom, and the top piece of bread tilted at an alarming angle.

"No, no, no—" Megan tried to rescue it, but the sandwich was determined to self-destruct.

Kyle started laughing as she attempted to catch falling ingredients with increasingly desperate maneuvers. Hazel, startled by the sudden movement, jumped off Megan's lap and retreated to a safe distance.

"This is a disaster." Megan surveyed the wreckage on her plate—a deconstructed sandwich that looked like it had been in a fight.

"Want me to make you a new one?"

"No." Megan picked up her fork with determination. "I'm committed now. I'm eating this sandwich even if it's not technically a sandwich anymore."

She speared a piece of turkey and several vegetables, creating what was essentially a loaded fork. Kyle watched with obvious amusement as she took a bite.

They fell into easy conversation as they finished eating. Kyle asked about her first few days at the shop, and Megan found herself telling stories about the staff—Linda's patient teaching, Kay's no-nonsense efficiency, Tonya's endless energy, Beth's warm encouragement, and Savannah's business savvy.

"They're all so different," Megan said, "but they work together perfectly. Like they each know exactly what their role is, and they trust everyone else to do theirs."

"That's what Phyllis built," Kyle said quietly. "Not just a business, but a team. A family, really."

Megan nodded, understanding settling over her. "I want to be worthy of that. Of what she created."

"You're learning, you're trying, and you care about getting it right. That's everything that matters."

Hazel had returned to Megan's lap, apparently having forgiven the sandwich incident. The cat's purring was a constant rumble of contentment, and Megan found herself absently stroking the soft gray fur.

Through the windows, the mountains had faded to dark silhouettes against a sky turning deep blue. Lights from the resort twinkled through the trees. The cabin felt warm and peaceful, insulated from the rest of the world.

It felt like the kind of place where you could be yourself without pretense. Where mistakes were expected and laughter came easily. Where a collapsed sandwich was just funny rather than another piece of evidence that you were fundamentally inadequate.

It felt, Megan realized, like something she could see herself being part of. Not just the cabin, but the life it represented. The rootedness. The contentment with quality over flash. The sense of belonging somewhere specific, somewhere chosen.

The thought was both comforting and terrifying.

"I should probably get going," Megan said, though she didn't immediately move. "It's getting late, and I don't want to keep you."

"You're not keeping me," Kyle said, but he stood and started clearing plates. "Let me help you get Hazel's stuff into your car."

They loaded the cat carrier, food bowls, litter box, toys, and bags of food and litter into Megan's Honda while Hazel supervised from her perch on the porch railing. The cat's expression suggested she was deeply skeptical of this entire operation.

"She's going to be fine," Kyle assured Megan as she eyed the carrier with concern. "Hazel's adaptable. She just likes to act like she's not."

"What if she hates the cabin? What if she runs away?"

"She won't. Cats are territorial, but they bond with people more than places." He smiled. "She's already decided you're her person. Trust me, she'll settle in fast."

Getting Hazel into the carrier required strategic maneuvering and Kyle's patient assistance, but eventually the cat was secured, though her yowls of protest suggested she was deeply offended by the indignity.

Kyle carried the carrier to Megan's car and settled it in the passenger seat while Megan made sure everything else was secured in the back.

"Thank you," she said, closing the trunk. "For dinner. For the tour. For Hazel. For everything."

"See you tomorrow at the shop?" Kyle asked, hands in his pockets, his expression warm in the porch light.

"Definitely."

"Good." He smiled. "Drive safe. Text me when you get back to the cabin so I know you made it okay."

"It's like a five-minute drive."

"Humor me."

Megan found herself smiling. "Okay. I'll text you."

She climbed into the driver's seat, and Hazel's yowling immediately ceased. The cat peered through the carrier door with an expression that suggested she'd made her point and was now ready to proceed with dignity.

Megan started the car and backed out of the driveway. In her rearview mirror, she could see Kyle standing on his porch, watching. He raised a hand in farewell.

The drive to her cabin was indeed short, the road familiar now. Hazel was quiet during the journey, apparently having accepted her fate.

When Megan pulled up to her A-frame, she sat for a moment in the car, the engine still running.

This was her life now. A candy shop she was learning to run. A staff whom she enjoyed being around. A community that was welcoming her despite her mistakes. A cabin in the mountains—temporary but comfortable. And a cat who'd decided they belonged together.

And Kyle. Kind, patient, funny Kyle, who lived a few minutes away and looked at her like she was capable of anything.

Hazel meowed softly from her carrier, a gentle reminder that there were practical matters to attend to.

"Right," Megan said to the cat. "Let's get you settled in."

She carried the carrier inside, then made several trips for the rest of Hazel's belongings. The cat explored the cabin with regal curiosity once released, sniffing every corner and surface before finally jumping onto the couch and curling into a contented ball.

Megan pulled out her phone and texted Kyle: *Made it back safely. Hazel has claimed the couch as her throne.*

His response came almost immediately: *She has good taste in real estate.*

Megan smiled and typed back: *Thank you again for everything.*

Anytime. Get some rest.

You too.

She set down her phone and looked at Hazel, who was watching her with those luminous green eyes.

"I think we're going to be okay," Megan told her. "You and me, Hazel... we've got this."

Hazel's purr was her only answer, but somehow it was enough.

Chapter 19

Hazel had claimed the center of the kitchen table, her substantial gray body sprawled across Phyllis's recipe cards with the satisfied air of a cat who knew exactly what she was doing.

"Hazel," Megan said with little conviction. "I need those."

The cat opened one eye, assessed Megan's tone, and closed it again. Her purring intensified.

Sunday morning sunlight streamed through the A-frame's windows, turning the cabin into a warm cocoon despite the cold outside. Megan had woken early, made coffee, and settled at the table with Phyllis's recipe box and journals, intending to spend the morning reading through her aunt's notes. She'd made it through exactly three recipes before Hazel had decided the papers and cards required her immediate supervision.

Megan carefully extracted a recipe card from beneath Hazel's front paw. The cat made a small sound of protest but didn't move.

"Peppermint Swirl Fudge," Megan read aloud. Phyllis's handwriting covered both sides of the card—the recipe on the front, extensive notes on the back. *"Made this for the Andrews' anniversary party, 2018. They requested extra peppermint. Note: some people prefer subtle peppermint; others want to feel it. Always ask. Mrs. Andrews said it reminded her of her grandmother's candy. She cried. Good tears."*

Megan traced her finger over the words, imagining Phyllis at the shop counter, carefully boxing up fudge for a customer, taking the time to remember preferences and create something meaningful rather than just transactional.

Every recipe card was like this. Not just instructions, but stories. Connections. Small moments of care that had accumulated into a life's work.

She reached for another card, and Hazel shifted, placing one paw directly on top of it.

"You're not helping," Megan told the cat.

Hazel's purr suggested she disagreed.

Megan scratched behind Hazel's ears, and the cat leaned into the touch with shameless pleasure. In less than twenty-four hours, Hazel had completely settled into the cabin. She'd explored every corner, claimed the couch as her throne and Megan's bed as her sleeping spot, and established a routine that seemed to involve following Megan from room to room with regal persistence.

It was surprisingly comforting having another living creature in the space. The cabin felt less temporary with Hazel in it, more like an actual home rather than just a place to sleep between workdays.

A knock at the door interrupted her reading.

Hazel's head came up immediately, ears swiveling toward the sound. Instead of bolting for the bedroom like most cats would, she simply watched with interest as Megan stood and crossed to the door.

Kyle stood on the small porch, hands in his jacket pockets, his breath visible in the cold morning air.

"Morning," he said with that easy smile that always made something warm settle in her chest. "Hope I'm not interrupting."

"Just reading through recipes." Megan stepped back to let him in. "And being supervised by Hazel, who has very strong opinions about which cards I'm allowed to see."

Kyle laughed and followed her inside. Hazel immediately hopped down from the table and wound around his ankles in a figure-eight pattern, purring loudly.

"Looks like she's settled in," Kyle observed, crouching to scratch the cat's head.

"She's decided this is her kingdom, and I'm her loyal subject." Megan moved back to the table, gathering the scattered recipe cards. "She slept on my pillow last night. Right on top of my head."

"That's Hazel's way of claiming ownership." Kyle straightened, and Hazel continued circling his feet. "She did the same thing to me after a few days. I woke up with her tail sprawled across my face."

"How did you breathe?"

"Carefully."

Megan laughed and gestured to the cards spread across the table. "I've been going through Phyllis's recipes all morning. There are so many of them. Each one has these detailed notes about who she made it for, what they thought, and little adjustments she tried."

Kyle moved closer to look. Megan picked up the peppermint fudge card and handed it to him.

He read it slowly, his expression softening. "She put so much thought into everything. It wasn't just about making good candy—it was about making something that mattered to people."

"Every card is like this. Stories. Connections. She remembered everyone and noted everything."

Megan pulled her coffee mug closer, wrapping her hands around the warmth. Through the window, she could see the mountains in the distance, snow-dusted and beautiful in the morning light.

"What are your plans for today?" Kyle asked, his tone deliberately casual.

"This, mostly." Megan gestured at the recipes. "I was going to spend the day reading through more of these, maybe finish the book I've been reading. Watch a movie later. Nothing exciting."

"How do you feel about tobogganing?"

Megan looked up. "Tobogganing?"

"There's enough snow on the ground now. Perfect conditions." Kyle's eyes held a spark of enthusiasm that made him look younger, more carefree. "What do you say? Want to take a break from all the work and learning? You've had way too much work lately and not enough fun."

"I've never been tobogganing," Megan admitted.

"Even better. First time for everything." He leaned against the counter, clearly warming to the idea. "We can use the resort's toboggan run. Mom and Dad have slopes set up for skiing, tobogganing, and tubing. We can ride the ski lift too if you want—just to see the view."

The idea was appealing. More than appealing. Megan realized she'd been looking forward to a quiet day alone mostly because she didn't have any other options, not because she actually wanted to be alone. Spending the day with Kyle, trying something new, sounded infinitely better than sitting in the cabin reading recipes until her eyes crossed.

"I'd love to," she said, then hesitated. "But I'm not exactly equipped for tobogganing. I have a winter coat, but that's about it. No snow pants, no real gloves. Nothing practical for actually playing in the snow."

"Mom has tons of winter gear at the lodge," Kyle said immediately. "She keeps extras for guests who show up unprepared. Half of the people who come here from warmer climates don't realize how cold it actually gets on the mountain."

"Are you sure she wouldn't mind?"

"She'd be thrilled." Kyle pushed off from the counter. "Come on. Let's go see what she's got."

Megan glanced down at herself—sweatpants and an oversized sweatshirt, her typical lounging-around outfit. "I should probably change first."

"Into what? You're just going to put snow pants over what you're wearing anyway." Kyle was already moving toward the door. "Come on, grab your coat."

It was hard to argue with his logic. Megan grabbed her coat from the hook by the door and pulled on her boots. Hazel watched these preparations with obvious disapproval, clearly recognizing the signs of imminent abandonment.

"I'll be back later," Megan told the cat. "Try not to destroy anything while I'm gone."

Hazel's expression suggested no promises.

Outside, the air was crisp and cold, sharp enough to make Megan's breath catch. The sun was bright against the snow, creating a glare that made her squint. Kyle fell into step beside her as they started up the path toward the main lodge, visible through the trees about a quarter mile away.

"I used to come here all the time as a kid," Kyle said as they walked. "Back before my parents owned the place. The previous owners, the Mathesons, ran it for thirty years. They'd let local kids come tobogganing for free on Sundays."

"That was generous."

"They were good people. When they retired and put the resort up for sale, my parents couldn't resist." He pointed toward the slope visible through the trees. "That's where Leslie broke her arm when we were twelve. Tried to do a jump that was way too ambitious."

"How did your parents react?"

"Dad was impressed by the jump height. Mom was less impressed by the broken bone." He shook his head. "Leslie got grounded for a month, but Dad secretly took her back to the jump once she healed so she could land it properly."

The path curved, and the main lodge came into full view. A massive timber-frame structure with soaring rooflines and enormous windows that reflected the morning sun. Smoke curled from multiple chimneys, and the wraparound deck was dotted with outdoor furniture that looked inviting even in the November cold.

Kyle held the door open, and warmth enveloped them immediately. The interior was exactly what a mountain lodge should be—exposed beams, stone fireplaces, and comfortable seating arranged in conversational groupings. A few guests sat near the fire with coffee mugs, and the scent of something sweet baking drifted from somewhere deeper in the building.

Ann Porter stood behind the front desk, her reading glasses perched on her nose as she worked on something on the computer. She looked up as they entered, and her face lit up with genuine delight.

"Kyle! Megan!" She came around the desk immediately. "What a nice surprise. Are you two joining us for breakfast? We have cinnamon rolls this morning."

"We're going tobogganing," Kyle explained. "Megan needs gear."

"Oh, perfect!" Ann's enthusiasm was immediate and infectious. "Come with me. I've got everything you need."

She led them through a door marked "Staff Only" into a back room that looked like a well-organized sporting goods store. Shelves lined the walls, packed with snow pants, jackets, gloves, hats, and various other winter equipment. Everything was sorted by size and clearly labeled.

"Let's see." Ann pulled out a pair of black snow pants and held them up to Megan for size assessment. "These should work. And you'll want a fleece layer under your coat—it's colder up on the slopes than you'd think." She grabbed a bright blue fleece pullover. "Gloves, definitely. These are waterproof and insulated. And a hat." She selected a soft gray beanie from a shelf. "Can't toboggan without a proper hat."

Kyle was already pulling his own gear from a private locker—snow pants, gloves, and a knit hat. "Leslie and I both just store our things here; it makes it easier," he said, tugging the snow pants on over his jeans.

Within minutes, Megan was completely outfitted. Ann worked with efficient maternal attention, helping Megan and making sure everything fit properly.

"There," Ann said, stepping back to assess her work. "You look ready for adventure. Now go have fun. Stop by when you're done to warm up; there's always coffee and hot cocoa in the lounge area."

"Thanks, Mom," Kyle said, dropping a kiss on her cheek.

"Thank you so much," Megan added, enjoying the casual kindness of this family, who kept helping her without expecting anything in return.

"My pleasure, dear. Truly." Ann shooed them toward the door. "Now go before the good toboggans are all taken."

They stepped back outside. The cold felt less biting with the extra layers, more invigorating than uncomfortable.

Kyle led her around the side of the lodge toward a slope she could now see clearly. Several toboggans were stacked at the top, and the run itself looked thrilling—a long, winding path down the mountain with banked turns that promised speed and excitement.

"Ready?" Kyle asked, a spark of enthusiasm bright in his hazel eyes.

Megan looked at the slope, at the toboggans waiting, and at Kyle's obvious excitement to share this with her.

"Ready," she said, and meant it.

Chapter 20

The toboggan looked heavy as Kyle pulled it from the stack at the top of the run and positioned it at the starting point, the smooth wooden runners gleaming against packed snow.

"Okay," he said, his breath clouding in the cold air. "Basic technique: sit in front, feet on the steering bar. I'll sit behind you and help steer until you get the hang of it."

Megan eyed the slope. From this angle, it looked significantly steeper than it had from the lodge. The run curved down the mountain in a series of banked turns, disappearing around a bend before emerging again farther down. Other toboggans dotted the slope—families laughing, couples racing, and the occasional solo rider showing off.

"That's a long way down," she said.

"It is." Kyle's voice held barely suppressed excitement. "It's also incredibly fun. Trust me?"

Megan looked at him. "Okay," she said.

She settled onto the front of the toboggan, gripping the rope handles on either side. The wood was cold even through her snow pants.

Kyle climbed on behind her, his legs bracketing hers, his arms reaching around to grip the steering mechanisms.

"Ready?" he asked, his voice close to her ear.

"No," Megan said honestly. "But let's do it anyway."

Kyle pushed off.

For one heart-stopping moment, they moved slowly, almost gently. Then gravity took over, and the toboggan picked up speed. Wind hit Megan's face, sharp and cold. The runners hissed against packed snow. They approached the first banked turn, and Kyle leaned into it, the toboggan tilting smoothly.

Megan screamed.

It wasn't a scared scream—though there was definitely fear involved—but something more primal. Pure adrenaline and exhilaration mixed with the sudden realization that they were flying down a mountain on a piece of wood and there was absolutely nothing she could do to stop it.

Behind her, Kyle was laughing.

They hit the straightaway, speed increasing. Snow sprayed up from the runners. The world blurred past—white slope, dark trees, bright sky. Another turn approached, and this time Megan leaned with Kyle, feeling the toboggan respond beneath them.

The fear began transforming into childlike joy.

They rounded the last curve, and the run straightened out. The toboggan gradually slowed as the slope leveled. When they finally glided to a stop at the bottom, Megan sat frozen for a moment, her heart racing, her hands still death-gripping the ropes.

"So?" Kyle asked. "What do you think?"

Megan turned to look at him, and whatever he saw in her face made him grin.

"Again," she said. "I want to go again."

They went down seven more times, each run faster and more confident than the last. By the fourth run, Megan stopped screaming and started laughing. By the sixth, she was steering by herself, Kyle's hands hovering near hers but not quite touching, ready to help if needed but letting her figure it out.

On the walk back up after their eighth run, both of them breathing hard from hauling the toboggan uphill, a couple passed them going down. The man called out, "Didn't know you were seeing anyone, Kyle!"

Kyle raised a hand in acknowledgment but didn't correct the assumption. Megan felt a flutter of awareness—they must look like a couple, spending the day together like this. The thought was both thrilling and interesting.

At the top of the slope, Megan pulled off her hat, fanning herself despite the cold. "I need a break. My legs feel like jelly."

"Ski lift?" Kyle suggested, pointing toward the chairlift visible through the trees. "No physical effort required. Just a ride up to see the view."

Megan followed his gesture and felt her stomach clench slightly. The chairlifts rose high above the mountain, small figures swaying gently as they ascended. "How high does it go?"

"High enough to see forever." Kyle studied her face. "You don't have to if you don't want to. But it's worth it for the view."

Megan thought about the woman she'd been a week ago—the one who never tried anything new, never took risks, and never did anything that might lead to embarrassment. That woman would have said no immediately.

"Let's do it," she said.

The lift operator was a teenager with impressive bedhead and a name tag that read "Mark." He directed them to wait behind the line, then guided them into position as a chair swung around.

"Sit back when the chair hits the back of your legs," he instructed. "Keep your feet up as you lift off."

The chair swooped in behind them and caught Megan behind the knees. She sat heavily, and suddenly they were lifting off the ground, feet dangling, and the mountain dropping away beneath them.

"Oh," Megan said, gripping the safety bar. "Oh, we're really up here."

"Look at the view," Kyle said. "Not down."

Megan forced herself to lift her gaze from the ground receding below. The view stole her breath.

The mountains stretched in every direction, snow-covered peaks against a brilliant blue sky. The resort spread below them like a miniature village—the lodge with its smoking chimneys, the scattered cabins, the network of paths connecting everything. Beyond the resort property, she could see Mistletoe Falls itself in the far distance, the town nestled in the valley, church spires and building rooflines visible even from this distance.

"Wow," Megan breathed.

"Right?" Kyle's voice held quiet satisfaction. "I come up here sometimes just to think. Everything looks different from up here. Smaller. More manageable."

They swayed gently as the lift continued its steady climb. The wind was stronger up here, but not unpleasant. Just cold and clean and sharp.

"A week ago I would never have done this," Megan said suddenly. "Any of this. The tobogganing, the ski lift. A week ago I worked at a copy center, then went home to my cramped apartment and just...

existed. Read or watched television. Went to bed. Got up the next day and did it all over again. I didn't have a life at all. Just work and existence."

Kyle was quiet for a moment. "Pretty big change."

"Yes! Now, I'm flying down mountains and riding ski lifts and learning to make candy and living in a cabin with a cat who thinks she's royalty." Megan laughed, surprised by the emotion suddenly tight in her throat. "Now I feel like I might actually be living."

"I'm glad you took the chance," Kyle said. "Coming here. Staying. Trying things even when they're scary."

Megan turned to look at him. His hazel eyes were warm in the bright sunlight, his expression open and genuine. This close, she could see the individual flecks of green and gold that made up the color. Could see the way his cheeks were flushed from cold and exertion. Could see the small scar near his left eyebrow that she'd noticed before but never asked about.

"Me too," she said.

They looked at each other for a moment that stretched and held. Megan felt her breath catch, awareness blooming between them like something physical. It would be so easy to lean in, to close the small distance separating them, to—

The lift crested the top of the mountain, and the operator called out instructions for disembarking. The moment broke, and they lifted the safety bar, preparing to slide off onto the platform.

As they walked away from the lift, heading back toward the lodge, Megan couldn't stop smiling.

"Coffee?" Kyle asked. "I could use something warm."

"Coffee sounds perfect."

The main lodge's great room was exactly what its name implied—a massive space with soaring ceilings, exposed timber beams, and a central fireplace that rose two stories high. The fire crackled cheerfully, radiating heat that hit them like a wall as they entered from the cold.

A few other guests occupied the seating arranged around the fireplace—a family with two young children playing a board game, an older couple reading newspapers, and a group of twenty-somethings in ski gear comparing phones.

Megan and Kyle claimed a leather couch near the fire. Megan pulled off her gloves and held her hands toward the warmth, sighing with relief.

"I didn't realize how cold I was until right this second," she said.

"You get used to it when you're moving. It's when you stop that you notice. Stay here. I'll get coffee."

He disappeared toward what Megan assumed was a kitchen or service area. She leaned back against the couch cushions, letting the heat seep into her bones. Her legs ached pleasantly from hauling the toboggan up the hill so many times. Her cheeks felt tight from the wind and cold. Her chest felt full of something bright and effervescent that was clearly the feeling of simply being happy.

Kyle returned with two steaming mugs.

Megan accepted hers gratefully, wrapping her hands around it. The first sip was rich and strong, exactly what she needed.

They sat for a few minutes, just warming up and watching the fire. The family nearby burst into laughter over something in their game. The crackling logs sent sparks up the chimney. Outside the massive windows, the afternoon sun painted the snow gold.

"Megan! Kyle!"

Ann appeared from a side hallway, Mitch beside her. Both wore slightly harried but satisfied expressions of people who'd been working hard but enjoying it.

"How was tobogganing?" Ann asked, settling into the chair across from them. Mitch took the matching chair, immediately stretching his legs toward the fire much like Kyle had.

"Amazing. I've never done that before," Megan said enthusiastically. "We went down eight times, and I only screamed on the first few runs."

"That's better than Leslie," Mitch said with a laugh. "She screamed throughout her entire first season. Didn't stop her from going again and again, though."

"We took the ski lift too," Kyle added.

"Beautiful up there, isn't it?" Ann's expression was warm. "I never get tired of seeing the mountains from that angle."

"Not to change the subject, but the cabinets for your apartment, Megan, should arrive Thursday," Mitch said. "I'm thinking we can install them Friday if you want to help, Kyle."

"Sounds like a plan," Kyle confirmed.

Ann turned her attention to Megan. "And how are things at Sugar & Spice? You're managing okay with everything?"

"I think so," Megan said. "The staff has been incredible. Patient with all my questions and willing to teach me everything. I have a good handle on the retail end of the business. I've attempted a few batches of candy, though I actually managed to destroy a batch of peppermint bark yesterday, and everyone who witnessed it was so nice about it."

"Sounds like you're jumping in headfirst, and that's a good thing. That's the best way to learn," Ann said fondly.

"Thanksgiving is next week," Mitch said, glancing at his wife. "We do a big family dinner at our house—Kyle, Leslie, and usually some friends. You should join us, Megan."

The invitation was so casual, so natural, that it took Megan a moment to process what he'd said. Thanksgiving. With Kyle's family. As if it were the most obvious thing in the world that she wouldn't have anywhere else to go—which, to be fair, was accurate.

"I don't want to intrude on your family holiday," Megan started.

"You wouldn't be intruding," Ann said firmly. "We'd love to have you. We always have a good time together and plenty of food."

"Well... thank you. I'd love to come."

"Perfect." Ann beamed. "Kyle can give you the details about timing and everything."

The conversation drifted to other topics—resort bookings picking up as December approached, plans for holiday decorations around the property, and a guest who'd somehow managed to lock themselves out of their cabin while wearing only a bathrobe.

Eventually the talk circled back to Sugar & Spice. Megan found herself describing her various candy-making attempts, the recipe cards she'd been studying, and her growing understanding of how much thought and care Phyllis had put into every batch.

"Kyle mentioned yesterday that he's my official taste-tester now," Megan said, smiling at him. "Though I'm not sure he knew what he was signing up for when he volunteered."

"I'm willing to take my chances," Kyle said. "Somebody has to be brave enough to try your experiments."

"You know," Megan said, the idea forming as she spoke, "you should come join me sometime. Learn to make candy with me. It's only fair—I got to learn to toboggan from you; you should learn candy-making with me."

Kyle hesitated. "I don't want to get in the way. Your staff has work to do, and I'd just be—"

"You wouldn't be in the way," Megan interrupted. "Come on, it'll be fun. You can't live in a Christmas town and not know how to make candy. Besides, the staff likes you. They won't mind."

"Join her sometime, Kyle," Ann said, her eyes twinkling.

Kyle looked between his mother and Megan, clearly recognizing he was outnumbered. "Okay. When?"

"Tomorrow? Or Tuesday?" Megan suggested. "Whatever works with your schedule."

"Tuesday," Kyle decided. "Monday, I need to catch up on work at The Christmas Shop and then help Dad in the apartment."

"Tuesday it is." Megan smiled, pleased that he'd agreed. "Fair warning though—I'm probably going to burn something."

"I'll bring a fire extinguisher."

Mitch and Ann exchanged a look that Megan couldn't quite interpret but that made Kyle shift slightly in his seat.

They talked for another half hour, warm and comfortable by the fire, before Megan finally had to admit she was exhausted and just wanted to go home and relax. Every muscle in her body had started making itself known, and despite the coffee, she could feel herself fading.

"I'm going to head back to the cabin," she said, standing carefully. Her legs protested.

"I'll walk you," Kyle said immediately, standing as well.

They said goodbye to Mitch and Ann and stepped out into the late afternoon cold. The sun was lower now, painting the snow pink and gold. Their breath clouded in the air as they walked.

"I enjoyed today," Kyle said as they followed the path back toward Megan's cabin.

"Me too." Megan smiled at him. "Really. Thank you for pushing me to try something new. I needed this."

"Everyone needs fun now and then. Even responsible candy shop owners."

They reached Megan's cabin too quickly. She stopped at the bottom of the porch steps, suddenly reluctant for the day to end.

"So, Tuesday?" she confirmed. "Morning? Around ten?"

"I'll be there," Kyle promised. "With a fire extinguisher and a strong stomach."

"Perfect." Megan climbed the first step, then turned back. "Kyle?"

"Yeah?"

"Today was one of the best days I've had in a really long time. Maybe ever."

His smile was warm enough to rival the lodge fireplace. "Good. You deserve the best days."

He waited while she climbed the rest of the steps and unlocked the door. She waved before going inside, and he waved back before turning to walk home.

Hazel greeted her at the door with an imperious meow that clearly communicated her displeasure at being abandoned for an entire day.

"I know, I know," Megan said, scooping the cat up. "I'm sorry. I went tobogganing and rode the ski lift, and I just... had a really good day, Hazel."

Hazel's purr suggested forgiveness might be possible if appropriate compensation was provided.

After taking off her coat and boots, Megan carried her to the couch, both of them settling into the cushions. Through the window, she could see lights beginning to twinkle on in other cabins and at the lodge. The mountains were dark silhouettes against a sky turning deep blue.

She thought about Kyle's laugh when she'd screamed on that first run. The way his arms had bracketed hers on the toboggan, solid and reassuring. The moment on the ski lift when they'd looked at each other and something had shifted, deepened, and become impossible to ignore.

The invitation to Thanksgiving. The easy acceptance by his family. Tuesday's candy-making plans.

All of it added up to something that felt like belonging. To having a life that was full and meaningful and connected to other people in ways that mattered.

Hazel shifted in her lap, kneading with her paws, and purring so loudly Megan could feel the vibration against her chest.

"We're going to be okay," Megan told the cat. "I think we're going to be better than okay."

Outside, the first stars were beginning to appear, tiny points of light against the darkening sky. Inside, the cabin was warm and comfortable, filled with the soft sounds of Hazel's purring and the quiet certainty that tomorrow—and all the tomorrows after that—held possibilities she'd never imagined.

Chapter 21

Kyle entered Sugar & Spice through the back door. The candy scents hit him immediately—melting chocolate, rich and dark, mixed with vanilla and something buttery that made his mouth water. When he entered the kitchen area, Linda stood at the far counter stirring a copper pot of caramel, the mixture golden and glossy as it caught the light. Tonya worked taffy on the marble slab near the window, her hands moving in the pull-and-fold pattern. Kay was arranging supplies on the center work table—bowls, whisks, candy thermometers, and several pounds of dark chocolate.

And Megan stood beside Kay, studying a recipe card with intense concentration.

Four faces turned toward him as the kitchen door clicked behind him.

"Sorry I'm late," Kyle said, moving further into the kitchen. "Got caught up talking with Dad and the contractor about the stairs."

Megan's head snapped up, her eyes suddenly bright with interest. "The stairs? That's what all that noise was this morning?"

"You heard it?"

"I was in Phyllis's office going through some old supplier contracts and kept hearing banging and what sounded like metal scraping." She set down the recipe card. "What's going on?"

Kyle couldn't help but smile at her enthusiasm. "They're installing the new stair frame. Thicker metal construction, much sturdier than what was there before. Dad's going to install wood treads once the frame is set."

"When will it be done?"

"Dad thinks he should be able to get them done by the end of the day today."

Megan pressed her hands together, and Kyle recognized the gesture—she did that when she was trying to contain excitement. "So I'll actually have stairs that don't scare the daylights out of me soon?"

"Yep. I believe you will."

"That's amazing. I can't believe how fast this is all happening."

"Well," Kay said, clearing her throat in a way that suggested they should return to the task at hand, "now that Kyle's here, we can get started." She gestured at the supplies spread across the table. "Truffles. One of the finickiest candies we make, but also one of the most impressive when you get them right."

Kyle moved to the sink to wash his hands. "I'm ready to learn."

"You might regret that confidence in about ten minutes," Tonya called from her taffy station. "Truffles can be tricky."

"Encouraging," Kyle said, drying his hands and reaching for one of the clean aprons hanging by the door.

Megan was already wearing hers—a white half-apron with "Sugar & Spice" embroidered across the front in cheerful red letters. Kyle pulled on a matching one, tying it behind his back and feeling slightly ridiculous. He spent most of his professional life in button-downs and khakis or flannel, jeans, and work boots. An apron felt like a costume.

"You look very domestic," Megan said, and there was laughter in her voice.

"I look like I'm about to attempt something I'm completely unqualified for."

"That makes two of us."

Kay began laying out the process. "Truffles are essentially ganache—chocolate and cream—that's chilled, rolled into balls, and then coated in tempered chocolate. Sounds simple. It's not." She pulled the bowl toward her. "The ganache we made this morning has been chilling for three hours. Temperature is critical. Too cold, and it won't roll smoothly. Too warm, and it'll be a mess."

She demonstrated, scooping a small portion of the dark ganache and rolling it between her palms until it formed a rough sphere. "It doesn't need to be perfect at this stage. You'll coat it later, which hides imperfections. But you want them reasonably uniform."

Kyle watched as Kay made three more in quick succession, each one nearly identical.

"Now you try." Kay stepped back, gesturing at the bowl.

Megan went first, scooping ganache with a small spoon and transferring it to her palm. She rolled carefully, tongue between her teeth in concentration. The truffle took shape, slightly lopsided but recognizable.

"Good," Kay said. "Keep going."

Kyle took his turn. The ganache was cold against his skin, firmer than he'd expected but still malleable. He rolled it between his palms the way Kay had demonstrated, trying to apply even pressure. The sphere that resulted looked more like a slightly flattened oval.

"That's... a shape," Megan said.

"It's a truffle," Kyle defended. "An abstract truffle."

"It's a flying saucer."

"You're not helping."

She laughed, and Kyle grinned despite his failed attempt. He tried again, this time managing something closer to round. Still not as neat as Kay's demonstration, but an improvement.

They fell into a rhythm—scooping, rolling, and placing the formed truffles onto parchment-lined trays. Megan's technique improved quickly, her truffles becoming more uniform with each attempt. Kyle's remained stubbornly imperfect, but at least they were spherical.

"How many are we making?" Megan asked after they'd filled one tray.

"Two hundred," Kay said. "We sell them in half-dozen boxes. They're popular gift items. Plus, we always use a few as taste-testing samples for the retail floor."

Megan's eyes widened. "Two hundred?"

"Linda and I already rolled about seventy this morning. So, you two just need to do another hundred and thirty."

"Just," Megan muttered, but she was smiling.

They worked in comfortable quiet for a while, the only sounds being the soft conversation between Linda and Tonya across the kitchen, the rhythmic stirring of caramel, and the occasional scrape of spoon against bowl.

Kyle noticed the changes in Megan as they worked. The way she checked the consistency of the ganache without being prompted. How she adjusted her technique when a truffle came out misshapen instead of getting frustrated. When the ganache started warming too much from the heat of their hands, she was the one who suggested returning it to the refrigerator for fifteen minutes to firm up again.

"Good call," Kay said, taking the bowl. "That's exactly right."

Megan flushed with the praise but smiled, and Kyle saw genuine confidence there. Not the bravado of someone faking it, but real comfort with her growing knowledge.

While they waited for the ganache to chill, Kay began setting up the chocolate tempering station. She melted dark chocolate in a double boiler, explaining the temperature ranges they needed to hit for proper tempering—heating to 115 degrees, cooling to 81, then bringing back up to 88-90 for working temperature.

"Why all the specific numbers?" Kyle asked, watching the thermometer.

"Tempering stabilizes the cocoa butter crystals," Megan said, then looked surprised at her own answer. "Linda taught me that yesterday. Something about Type V crystals being the most stable, and the temperature cycle encourages those to form."

Kay nodded approvingly. "You got it. Properly tempered chocolate has a nice snap when you bite into it and a glossy finish. Skip tempering, and you get dull, streaky chocolate that melts at room temperature."

"Science," Kyle said.

"Delicious science," Megan corrected.

When the ganache had re-chilled, they resumed rolling. Kyle had just finished his fiftieth truffle—he'd been counting—when disaster struck.

Megan reached for the bowl at the same moment Kyle did. Their hands collided, knocking the bowl sideways. The ganache-covered spoon went flying, arcing through the air in what felt like slow motion before landing splat on the front of Kyle's apron.

He looked down at the chocolate smear spreading across the white fabric.

Megan's hand flew to her mouth, but not before a laugh escaped.

"I'm so sorry," she managed between giggles. "I didn't mean to—you just—"

"Attacked me with a spoon?"

"You ran into my hand!"

"I was reaching for the bowl."

"So was I!"

Kyle tried to maintain a serious expression but failed when Megan dissolved into laughter again. He grabbed a towel and wiped at the chocolate, which only spread it further.

"Here, let me—" Megan took the towel from him and dabbed at the stain, still laughing.

Their eyes met, and Kyle felt the moment shift—still light, still playful, but something else underneath. Awareness. Megan must have felt it too because she stepped back, handing him the towel with a suddenly flustered expression.

"You're on truffle-rolling duty," she declared, recovering. "I'll start coating."

Kay had the tempered chocolate ready, the glossy dark mixture at perfect working temperature. She demonstrated the coating technique—dropping a ganache ball into the chocolate, using a fork to roll it until completely covered, then lifting it out and tapping the fork against the bowl's edge to remove excess chocolate before transferring it to a clean parchment sheet.

"The tapping is crucial," Kay said. "Too much chocolate and they'll have feet—those little skirts around the bottom. Not enough, and you'll see ganache through the coating."

Megan tried first. She dropped the truffle into the chocolate, rolled it with the fork, and lifted it out. Chocolate dripped everywhere. She tapped the fork against the bowl's edge like Kay had shown, but somehow managed to splatter tempered chocolate across the counter.

"How did you do that?" Kyle asked.

"Tapping too hard... maybe?" Megan stared at the chocolate spots as if they'd personally offended her.

"You're right, just gentle taps," Kay said mildly. "Gentle. It's all about gentle control."

Megan tried again with the next truffle, this time barely tapping. The result was better—a neat, dark sphere that landed on the parchment without drama.

"There," she said triumphantly.

Kyle handed her another truffle to coat while he continued rolling. They developed an assembly line system—he'd roll, she'd coat, and Kay supervised and offered corrections. When they'd finished twenty, Megan stepped back to survey their work.

"Some of these look professional," she said.

"And some look like they've been through a war," Kyle added, pointing at one particularly lumpy specimen.

"That one's mine," Megan admitted. "I dropped it and had to re-roll."

"It has character."

"It has a problem."

But she was smiling, and Kyle loved that about her—the ability to laugh at her mistakes. He'd watched too many people get discouraged during learning processes, giving up when things didn't come easily. Megan just kept trying, finding humor in the fumbles.

They worked through another batch, then another. The coated truffles covered three parchment sheets, neat rows of glossy chocolate spheres that actually looked professional.

"Last step," Kay said, "is decoration. We can leave them plain, or dust with cocoa powder, or drizzle them with white chocolate, or add a pinch of sea salt and press it in slightly."

"What does Phyllis's recipe card say?" Megan asked, then caught herself. "I mean, what does the standard recipe call for?"

Kay's expression softened. "Phyllis liked variety. Usually, she did a mix—some plain, some with cocoa powder, some with the white chocolate drizzle."

Megan nodded slowly, considering. "Let's do that then." She paused, then added with more confidence, "But maybe we could try something new too? What about crushed peppermint on a few? Christmas is coming, and peppermint feels festive."

Kay exchanged a glance with Linda, who'd abandoned her caramel to watch the truffle-making process.

"I like it," Linda said.

"Then let's do it." Megan began separating the truffles into groups.

Kyle watched her take charge, making the decision without second-guessing herself, and felt something warm settle in his chest. This was what she'd needed to find—not just competence, but authority. The ability to trust her own judgment.

He helped dust truffles with cocoa powder while Megan and Kay worked on the white chocolate drizzle. Tonya, finished with her taffy, crushed peppermint candies for the final variation. The kitchen filled with the sharp-sweet scent of mint.

By the time they finished decorating, Kyle's phone buzzed in his pocket. He pulled it out, glancing at the screen to see a text from his dad:

Need 2 more 2x6 boards for the stair treads. My measurements were off. Can you make a run to Thompson's?

He showed the text to Megan. "Looks like I need to make a supply run."

She leaned over to read it, close enough that he caught the scent of her perfume. "Well, thanks for helping with the truffles. I think we successfully made candy without burning down the kitchen."

"Low bar, but we cleared it. I'll see you later."

Kyle untied his apron and hung it back on the hook by the door. As he was about to leave the kitchen, he had an idea and turned back.

Megan was brushing cocoa powder off her hands, laughing at something Tonya had said. Linda was pouring caramel into molds. Kay was already cleaning up the truffle-making station, everything returning to order.

"Megan?"

She looked up. "Yeah?"

Kyle's heart did something complicated in his chest. "Would you like to go out for dinner with me tonight?"

The kitchen went very still.

Megan blinked. "What?"

"Dinner. Tonight. With me."

A slow smile spread across her face, though her cheeks were turning pink. "Are you asking me out on a date, Kyle Porter?"

He couldn't help grinning. "I believe I am, Ms. Caldwell."

"I accept." Her voice was steady despite the blush now coloring her face and neck. "Now go get that lumber, Mr. Porter, so my stairs can get finished, and I'll see you at—"

"Six," Kyle interrupted. "I'll pick you up at six at your cabin."

He pulled open the door and stepped out before he could see whatever expression Kay, Linda, or Tonya was wearing.

But he heard Megan's giggle and her chatter as she spoke with her employees as the door swung shut behind him. The sound of her laughing carried him all the way to his truck with a spring in his step that hadn't been there that morning.

Kyle climbed into his truck and headed toward Thompson's Hardware, already trying to figure out where he'd take her for dinner.

Somewhere nice. Somewhere that said this mattered, that she mattered, and that he wasn't just being neighborly.

Somewhere that felt like a real first date.

He pulled out his phone at the red light and texted Leslie.

I asked Megan to dinner. Tonight. Help.

The response came back almost immediately.

FINALLY. Where are you taking her?

The Mistletoe Grill???

Perfect. Wear your white henley and your nicer dark jeans. Do NOT talk about apartment repairs. Do NOT talk about work. If you need me, just text.

Kyle laughed and pulled through the intersection.

Chapter 22

The Mistletoe Grill sat just off Highway 441. Kyle pulled into the gravel parking lot as the last traces of sunset painted the mountains behind them in shades of purple and gold.

He cut the engine and glanced at Megan. She was studying the log cabin building with obvious curiosity, taking in the wide front porch decorated with strings of white lights and the large windows that revealed glimpses of activity inside.

"Is this okay?" he asked. "It's not fancy, but the food's good and—"

"It's perfect," Megan said, unbuckling her seatbelt. "I love places like this."

Inside, the Mistletoe Grill was full of rustic charm. Exposed wooden beams crossed the high ceiling, and the walls were decorated with vintage Tennessee memorabilia—old license plates, faded concert posters, and black-and-white photographs of the Smokies. Red-and-white checkered tablecloths covered wooden tables, and the smell of grilled meat and fresh bread made Kyle's stomach growl.

But it was the large wooden dance floor dominating one end of the restaurant that seemed to have caught Megan's attention. A small stage held a band setting up equipment, and already a few early arrivals were claiming tables near the floor.

"They have live music," Megan said, and Kyle caught something in her voice—excitement, maybe, or recognition.

"Yeah, most nights. I hope that's okay? We can request a quieter table if—"

"No, this is great." Her eyes were bright as she scanned the room. "Really great."

The hostess, a young woman with a warm smile, led them to a table for two near one of the large windows.

Kyle held Megan's chair for her, and she smiled as she sat down.

"Very gentlemanly, Mr. Porter."

"I have my moments, Ms. Caldwell."

They shed their coats, draping them over the backs of their chairs, and accepted menus from the hostess. The selection was classic Tennessee fare—burgers, steaks, ribs, catfish, and something called the "Mountain Platter" that promised a little bit of everything.

"I'm starving... as usual," Megan said, studying her menu. "Making truffles all afternoon apparently works up an appetite."

"Same. Though I think I burned more calories laughing at our disasters than actually rolling chocolate."

"Your flying saucer truffles were definitely memorable."

"Says the woman who splattered chocolate across half the kitchen."

Megan grinned. "That was Kay's fault for not warning me properly about the tapping force required."

"Pretty sure Kay showed exactly the right amount of force."

"Details."

Their waitress appeared—a young woman who introduced herself as Jenny and took their drink orders with efficient cheerfulness. When she left, Kyle leaned back in his chair and just looked at Megan for a moment.

She was relaxed. No tension in her shoulders, no nervous fidgeting. Just comfortable, present, and smiling at him across the checkered tablecloth.

"What?" she asked.

"Nothing. Just... you seem happy."

"I am happy. Today was a good day. The truffles, the stairs getting finished, this—" She gestured between them. "All of it."

"The stairs are completely done. Dad texted while I was getting ready this evening. He finished installing all the treads, and they passed the initial inspection."

"So I can use them?"

"Yep, they are ready and just in time for the cabinets to be delivered tomorrow."

"I definitely have to check them out tomorrow." Megan leaned forward, elbows on the table. "Just think. Two weeks ago, I was living in a falling-apart apartment in Bowling Green with four roommates I barely tolerated. Now I have my own place above the candy shop I own in a town that feels like something out of a Christmas movie. Pinch me... is this all real?"

"It's real," Kyle assured her. "Though I get what you mean. Mistletoe Falls can feel a little too good to be true sometimes, and I imagine all these big changes in your life seem... well, different from what you're used to. It's been a big lifestyle change."

Jenny returned with their drinks and took their dinner orders. Megan chose the catfish with sweet potato fries. Kyle went for the ribeye with a loaded baked potato.

When they were alone again, Kyle turned his attention back to Megan. "So tell me, you seem to have led quite an interesting life, but I still don't know much about you. I know you worked at a copy center just before you came here. You said you'd worked a number of different jobs before that... like what?"

"The glamorous careers of Megan Caldwell." She took a sip of her sweet tea. "Let's see. Waitress at a diner in Bowling Green for about a year. Before that, seasonal retail at a department store. Before that, I was a hostess and a waitress at a fun restaurant. Before that, another waitress job at a different place."

"Which restaurant... the fun one? Was it a chain-type restaurant?" Kyle asked.

Something flickered across Megan's face—hesitation, maybe, or memory. "It was a place called The Ranch House. It was... different."

"Different how?"

"Western themed. Country music, line dancing, and waitresses in fun cowgirl uniforms and cowboy boots." She said it casually, but Kyle caught the way she glanced toward the dance floor as she spoke.

"You worked at a place with line dancing?"

"For about eight months. It was actually kind of fun." Megan's smile turned reminiscent. "They required all the waitresses to learn to line dance. We'd perform a few times each night between serving tables. Customers loved it."

Kyle stared at her. "You know how to line dance?"

"I mean, I knew how. It's been a while, so I'm probably rusty—"

"Why didn't you mention this before?"

She shrugged, but he could see the pleasure in her expression at his enthusiasm. "It never came up? It's not exactly a prestigious skill."

"Are you kidding? I can barely manage a regular two-step without tripping over my feet."

"Really?" Megan's eyes sparkled with mischief. "Big, coordinated Kyle Porter can't dance?"

"I didn't say I can't dance. I said I barely manage. There's a difference."

"Sounds like you can't dance to me."

"I can dance," Kyle insisted.

Megan was grinning now, and Kyle realized he'd walked right into whatever she was planning.

Their food arrived before she could press the point, and for a while they focused on eating. The catfish was perfectly crispy; the ribeye was cooked to an ideal medium-well done. They shared bites from each other's plates and argued good-naturedly about whether sweet potato fries were superior to regular fries or if a loaded baked potato was the only correct side for steak.

The conversation flowed easily, moving from food to the candy shop to Kyle's afternoon helping his dad to Megan's afternoon going through more of Phyllis's old business records.

"She kept everything," Megan said. "Every supplier invoice, every employee review, and every customer comment card. There are boxes and boxes of it."

"Sounds overwhelming."

"It is. But it's also kind of amazing? I'm learning so much about how she ran the business, what mattered to her, and how she thought about customer service and quality." Megan paused. "There's this one box of comment cards from the shop's first five years. So many of them mention Phyllis by name. 'Phyllis remembered my daughter's favorite candy.' 'Phyllis made my son feel special on his birthday.' 'Phyllis took the time to help me find the perfect gift.'"

"She was fantastic in the career she chose for herself," Kyle said.

"She was. And I keep thinking about how I want to do that too. Not just run a successful business, but actually matter to people the way she did."

Kyle reached across the table and covered her hand with his. "You already do."

Megan turned her hand palm-up, their fingers threading together naturally. "You're biased."

"Maybe. But I'm also right."

They finished their meals as the band completed its setup. The lead singer—a man in his forties wearing a cowboy hat and a grin—tested the microphone, and the first notes of a fiddle filled the space.

"Folks, welcome to The Mistletoe Grill!" the singer called out. "We're the Smoky Mountain Ramblers, and we're here to get you dancing. Who's ready for some line dancing?"

A cheer went up from several tables, and couples began making their way toward the dance floor.

Kyle noticed Megan's foot start tapping the moment the band launched into their first song—something upbeat with a strong fiddle line. Her attention was fixed on the dancers assembled on the floor, and he could practically see her cataloging the steps.

"You want to dance," he said.

"What? No, I—" She caught herself, then laughed. "Yeah. You know what? I do want to dance. But I don't want to make you—"

"Make me what? Have fun with you?" Kyle stood up and held out his hand. "Come on. Teach me."

"Kyle, I'm serious. If you're not comfortable—"

"Megan." He waited until she looked up at him. "I want to dance with you. Even if I'm terrible at it."

Her smile was brilliant as she stood and took his hand.

The dance floor had filled up with couples and groups, everyone arranging themselves in loose rows facing the same direction. Megan led Kyle to a spot near the back where they'd have room to move.

"Okay," she said, positioning herself beside him. "This one's called the Tush Push. It's pretty basic—grapevine right, grapevine left, step back three times, step forward three times, then the hip bumps."

"Hip bumps?"

"You'll see. Just follow the person in front of you and listen to the beat. Ready?"

Kyle was decidedly not ready, but the music was playing, and Megan was already moving.

She was right about knowing the steps. Her movements were confident, smooth, perfectly timed with the music. She grapevined right—stepping side, behind, side, together—and Kyle tried to follow, managing to get his feet tangled on the "behind" part.

"Cross your right foot behind your left," Megan called over the music, demonstrating without missing a beat. "Then step right, bring your left foot together."

Kyle tried again. This time he managed the grapevine, though his timing was off and he ended up a beat behind everyone else.

"That's it!" Megan encouraged. "Now left. Same thing, opposite direction."

They grapevined left, and Kyle actually got it right. Then came the stepping back—three steps, one beat each. That he could handle.

"Forward three," Megan called, and he stepped forward with her.

Then came the hip bumps.

The entire line of dancers bumped their hips right, then left, then right again, and Kyle froze for a split second before attempting to follow along. His hip bumps were nowhere near as smooth as Megan's or anyone else's on the floor, but he tried.

"There you go!" Megan was laughing, but not at him—with him, sharing the joy of the moment. "You've got it!"

They repeated the sequence as the song continued, and Kyle started getting the hang of it. His movements weren't graceful, and his timing was still slightly off, but he was doing it. Actually, line dancing at the Mistletoe Grill with Megan, who was clearly in her element.

He watched her as they danced, cataloging this new side of her. The confidence in her movements, the unselfconscious smile on her face, the way she moved with natural rhythm, and obvious enjoyment. This wasn't the uncertain woman who'd arrived in Mistletoe Falls or even the confident one who'd suggested peppermint truffles that afternoon.

This was someone completely at ease, joyful, and alive in a way that made Kyle's heart do complicated things in his chest.

The song ended with applause, and the band immediately launched into another. This dance was faster and more complex, and Kyle quickly lost track of the steps.

"Okay, this one's harder," Megan admitted, slightly breathless. "The Electric Slide. Just—watch me and try to follow?"

Kyle tried. He really did. But between the faster tempo and the more intricate footwork, he was hopelessly lost within the first eight counts.

Megan, seeing his struggle, grabbed his hand and pulled him to the side of the dance floor where they could practice without holding up the line.

"Here," she said, positioning herself in front of him. "Forget everyone else. Just watch my feet."

She walked him through it slowly—grapevine right, grapevine left, three steps back, touch, three steps forward, touch, turn a quarter to the right. Then repeat.

"Got it?"

"Maybe?" Kyle attempted the sequence, managing to turn the wrong direction and nearly crash into her.

Megan caught his arms, laughing. "Wrong way! Quarter turn right, not left."

"Right. Right turn. Got it."

They tried again, and this time Kyle made it through the entire sequence without major disasters. His execution was clumsy, and he definitely didn't have the smooth glide that Megan and the other dancers had, but he was getting there.

"You're doing great," Megan said, her hands still on his arms, her face flushed from dancing and laughter. "Seriously. First-time line dancers usually give up after one song."

"I have good motivation to keep trying."

Something shifted in her expression—awareness, pleasure, a spark of something that made Kyle very conscious of how close they were standing, how her hands felt on his arms, how her eyes had gone soft and warm.

The band started another song, slower this time, and several dancers moved into partner position for a two-step.

"Want to try this one?" Megan asked. "It's easier, I promise. Just a basic two-step."

Kyle held out his hand in answer, and Megan stepped into him, one hand on his shoulder, the other clasped in his. He rested his free hand on her waist, and they began moving to the music.

This was easier. Just slow-slow-quick-quick, around the floor with the other couples. Kyle could handle this.

"See?" she said. "You can dance."

"Only because you're a good teacher."

"Or maybe you're a good student."

They danced through the entire song, and Kyle found himself wishing it would last longer. There was something about moving with her like this, about the easy rhythm they'd found together, about the way she fit perfectly in his arms.

When the song ended, the band announced they were taking a short break. Dancers began drifting back toward their tables, and Kyle reluctantly released Megan.

"That was fun," he said.

"Yeah?" She looked pleased. "You didn't hate the line dancing?"

"I didn't hate the line dancing. I think my performance made that obvious."

"You were fine. Better than fine, actually. Most guys refuse to even try."

They made their way back to their table, both slightly breathless and energized. Jenny appeared with their check, and Kyle paid before Megan could offer to split it.

"This was a date," he said when she started to protest. "I asked, I'm paying."

"Old-fashioned."

"Is that a problem?"

"No," Megan said softly. "It's actually really nice."

They gathered their coats and headed for the door. Outside, the temperature had dropped further, their breath visible in the cold night air.

They walked toward Kyle's truck, and Megan stumbled slightly on the uneven gravel.

Kyle reached for her hand instinctively, steadying her, and then just... kept holding it.

Megan's fingers curled around his, her hand small and warm in his larger one.

They walked the rest of the way to the truck like that, hands clasped, neither of them speaking. When they reached the passenger side, Kyle stopped and turned to face her.

"I had a really good time tonight," he said.

"Me too." Megan smiled up at him, and in the glow from the restaurant's lights, her eyes were bright and happy. "Thanks for bringing me here. And for being willing to line dance even though you clearly had no idea what you were doing."

"I had some idea."

"Kyle, you turned the wrong direction multiple times."

"I was distracted by my very attractive teacher."

Megan's smile widened. "Smooth, Mr. Porter."

"I have my moments."

He should open her door. Should let go of her hand and help her into the truck and drive her back to the resort. Should take this slowly, carefully, and not rush things when they were still so new and fragile.

But standing here with Megan, her hand in his, her face tilted up toward his, Kyle didn't want to do any of those things.

He wanted to kiss her.

The realization hit him with startling clarity, and he must have let something show on his face because Megan's expression shifted, her smile softening into something more serious, more aware.

"Come on," he said, his voice rougher than he'd intended. "Let's get you home."

He opened her door, helped her up into the truck, and then walked around to the driver's side.

As he pulled out of the parking lot, Megan's hand found his across the center console, their fingers threading together naturally.

Chapter 23

The front counter of Sugar & Spice looked like a hurricane of organization had swept through and decided to stay. Scheduling charts covered every available surface, overlapping with supplier catalogs and what appeared to be years' worth of Phyllis's handwritten notes. Color-coded sticky notes marked different sections, and Savannah's laptop displayed a detailed spreadsheet that made Megan's eyes cross if she looked at it too long.

"Okay," Savannah said, tapping her pen against a particularly dense chart. "So during the regular season, we keep the display cases stocked with the core items—fudge in six flavors, hand-pulled taffy in twelve, chocolate assortments, caramels, and the specialty items that rotate monthly."

Megan studied the chart, trying to absorb the sheer volume of product. "And this all changes for Christmas?"

"Changes by adding additional offerings to what we normally stock." Savannah pulled out another chart; this one covered in red and green highlighting. "Christmas season officially starts the day after

Thanksgiving and runs through New Year's. We add peppermint bark, candy canes in every flavor imaginable, chocolate Santas, snowmen, reindeer, plus all the pre-made gift boxes and baskets."

"While still making all the regular stuff?"

"Yes, plus we increase quantities because we get way more foot traffic. Tourists, locals buying gifts, and corporate orders for office parties."

Megan felt her stomach do a small flip. "That's... a lot."

"It is. But Phyllis had a system." Savannah spread out several pages of notes, all in Phyllis's neat handwriting. "See? She color-coded everything. Red is for daily essentials that have to be made fresh every morning. Green is for weekly rotations. Blue is for special orders. And she had the supplier deliveries staggered, so we never got overwhelmed with inventory all at once."

Megan leaned closer, studying the intricate planning that had gone into running the shop during its busiest season. Phyllis had thought of everything—staff assignments, backup plans if someone got sick, even notes about which candies sold out fastest and needed extra production runs.

"This is incredible," Megan said quietly. "She really knew what she was doing."

"She did. Years of experience will do that." Savannah pulled up another screen on her laptop. "I took the liberty of creating a digital version of her system. Easier to update and share with everyone. Beth can access it for ordering supplies, Kay can check production schedules, and you can see the whole operation at a glance."

Megan felt a surge of gratitude for Savannah's business instincts. "Wow. I'm glad you did this."

"So what do you think? Should we keep the same schedule Phyllis used, or do you want to make changes?"

It was a real question, Megan realized. Savannah was actually asking for her input, trusting her judgment as the owner.

"I think we keep it," Megan said with more confidence than she felt. "If it worked for Phyllis for years, it'll work for us now. But—" She paused, an idea forming. "What if we added one experimental flavor each week? Something new that we can test before potentially adding to the permanent rotation?"

Savannah's eyes lit up. "I love that. Keep the tradition but leave room for innovation. That's smart."

"My one contribution to Phyllis's perfect system."

"It's a good contribution." Savannah made a note on her laptop. "I'll add a line item for experimental flavors, and we can rotate who gets to develop them. Give everyone a chance to be creative."

They worked through the rest of the schedule, Megan asking questions about quantities and timing, Savannah explaining Phyllis's reasoning for different choices. By the time they finished, Megan had a clearer picture of just how much work went into the Christmas season—and how prepared her staff was to handle it.

"I'll email Beth and let her know the schedule is approved," Savannah said, already typing. "She can cross-reference our current inventory and make sure we have ordered everything we need."

"Perfect." Megan straightened, stretching her back. "How are you so good at this?"

"Business major, remember? Plus, I really like organizing things. It's satisfying when everything lines up properly."

Megan's phone buzzed in her pocket. She pulled it out to see a text from Kyle.

Do you have a few minutes to come up to the apartment? Want to show you something.

Her heart did a small leap. She typed back quickly: *Be right there.*

"I need to run upstairs for a minute," Megan said, grabbing her keys. "Can you handle things down here?"

"Of course. Take your time."

Megan headed through the kitchen, waving at Linda and Tonya, who were working on a batch of pixies, and pushed through the back door into the alley.

The new stairs rose before her, sturdy and solid, with the metal frame gleaming and the wood treads smooth and even. She'd climbed them twice yesterday, marveling at how different they felt from the old rickety ones. No more wobbling with each step, no more fear that the whole structure might collapse beneath her.

She climbed quickly, her hand trailing along the smooth railing. There was something satisfying about this simple upgrade, something that made her future home feel real and accessible rather than a distant dream.

At the top, she opened the door to the apartment and stepped inside.

Then stopped.

The apartment had transformed.

The kitchen cabinets gleamed along the far wall, their warm, soft, white-colored wood just as beautiful as they'd looked in the catalog in the store. The upper cabinets were already installed, creating clean lines and ample storage. Below, the lower cabinets and the island cabinets sat positioned where they would be installed, showing the layout clearly.

But it was more than the cabinets. The light fixtures she'd chosen hung from the ceiling, their brushed nickel finish catching the late afternoon sun streaming through the windows. The walls, painted in the Warm Linen color she'd picked, looked even better than she'd imagined—warm and inviting, making the space feel like a home instead of a construction zone.

Kyle stood near the kitchen area with his father. Both men turned as she entered.

"What do you think?" Kyle asked. "We wanted to check the cabinet layout before we installed everything. Make sure you like where the island is positioned and that you can move around the kitchen comfortably."

Megan walked into the kitchen space slowly. The island was positioned perfectly, leaving plenty of room to move between it and the counter, with space for the bar stools she'd eventually get.

"It's perfect," she said. "The island right there makes sense. I can prep on this side and serve on the other."

Mitch nodded, making a note on his clipboard. "We'll finish installing the cabinets then."

Megan continued through the apartment, taking in all the changes. The living room looked larger with the fresh paint. She moved to the bathroom and found more transformation waiting.

The new vanity was installed, its white cabinet and faux marble top making the small bathroom feel elegant. The tall storage cabinet stood beside it, providing space for towels and toiletries. Above the vanity, the light fixture she'd chosen cast warm light across the space, and in the mirror—

She saw her reflection.

Blond hair slightly messy from a day of work. Green eyes wide with surprise. Face flushed with emotion.

And suddenly, it hit her.

This was her bathroom. In her apartment. Above her candy shop. In a town where people were beginning to know her name and recognize her, and her staff had become friends, and a man who made her heart skip waited in the next room.

Two weeks ago, she'd been a nobody from nowhere, with nothing.

Now she had everything and more.

The tears came without warning, sudden and overwhelming. One moment she was staring at her reflection, and the next her vision was blurring, her breath was hitching, and she was crying.

"Megan?" Kyle's voice, concerned, came from the doorway.

She tried to speak but couldn't get the words out around the sob that escaped instead. She pressed her hand to her mouth, embarrassed and overwhelmed and unable to stop.

Kyle was there instantly, his arms coming around her, pulling her close. "Hey, it's okay. What's wrong? Do you not like something? We can change it."

Megan shook her head against his chest, managing to get out, "No, it's not—I'm sorry, I—"

"Breath," he said gently, one hand smoothing down her back. "It's okay. Whatever it is, it's okay."

She let herself lean into him, let herself feel the solid warmth of his embrace while the emotions crashed over her. It was so much. Everything was so much. The apartment, the business, the staff who trusted her, the town that was becoming home, Kyle himself—all of it together was overwhelming in the best and worst way.

When the tears finally slowed, she pulled back slightly, wiping at her face with embarrassment. "I'm sorry. Gosh, I'm sorry. I don't know where that came from."

"Don't apologize." Kyle's voice was firm but kind. "Talk to me. What's going on?"

"I'm an emotional person," Megan said, the words coming out shaky. "If you haven't noticed. I cry at everything—sad things, happy things, touching commercials about dogs... just everything."

A smile tugged at Kyle's lips. "Noted."

"This is just—" She gestured helplessly around the apartment. "It's so much. All at once. I never imagined I would have—" Her voice broke again. "All of this. A home. A business. People who actually like me. It's hitting me all at once again."

"Are you scared?" Kyle asked.

"No. Yes. Maybe?" Megan laughed wetly. "I'm not sad. I'm not even upset, really. I'm just... grateful. And overwhelmed. And excited. And terrified that I'll somehow mess it all up."

"You won't."

"You don't know that."

"I know you. I've watched you these past two weeks. You're working hard, learning everything you can, and making good decisions. You care about the business and the people. That's what matters."

"I just want to make Phyllis proud," Megan whispered. "She gave me this incredible gift, and I want to be worthy of it."

"You already are."

Megan looked up at him, finding his hazel eyes warm and steady and full of conviction she didn't quite feel herself. But maybe that was okay. Maybe she didn't have to have all the confidence on her own if people like Kyle believed in her.

"Thanks for not thinking I'm completely insane for crying over something that's probably nothing special to you."

"Hey now... you're processing major life changes. That's allowed. You're allowed to feel or say or react however you want. Own it... you deserve it." Kyle's smile was gentle.

They stood there for a moment, and Megan became aware that they were still standing close, that Kyle's hands were still on her arms, and that she could feel the warmth radiating from him.

She stepped back slightly, needing space to breathe and think clearly.

"So," she said, trying for lightness. "The cabinets. They're perfect just the way they are. The lights, the fixtures, all of it is fine."

Kyle's expression shifted, accepting the subject change. "Good. Have you ordered your appliances yet? Do you want to go furniture shopping soon?"

"Beth helped me pick out a stove and a refrigerator online that will fit in the kitchen. She ordered them, and they are supposed to be delivered on Saturday. Let me think about furniture shopping. I need to sit down and figure out just what I need and measure the space so I know what to look for."

"Okay good. Your apartment will be livable soon."

Megan walked back through the apartment, seeing it with fresh eyes now that the emotional storm had passed. The layout was perfect. The paint color was exactly right. The light fixtures cast the kind of warm lighting that made a space feel welcoming.

She stopped at the living room window and looked out over Mistletoe Falls. From here, she could see Mistletoe Lane with its gas lamp lights and decorated storefronts. Beyond that, the mountains rose dark against the late afternoon sky.

This view would be hers. Every morning she could wake up and see this. Come home from work, go upstairs and watch the sunset paint the mountains in shades of gold and purple.

Kyle came to stand beside her.

"It's a good view," he said quietly.

"It's a perfect view." Megan turned to look at him. "I can't thank you enough for all you've done for me. For helping to make this happen so fast. For checking with me before finishing things. For just... caring."

"It's not a hardship, Megan."

"Still, I didn't deserve your kindness, and yet here you are." Megan turned back to look at Mitch and said, "I appreciate everything you've done for me, Mitch. The apartment so far is beautiful. Thank you for all your hard work."

"My pleasure, Megan," he said.

As Kyle returned to his dad's side in the kitchen and began screwing the cabinets in place, securing them to walls and floors, Megan took a moment to envision what this apartment would look like once she moved in. She mentally arranged furniture, decided where to position her bed in the bedroom, and pondered desk options for the spare room that would become her office—solid and sturdy, or sleek and minimal?

When she turned back toward the windows and looked out at the beautiful view of Mistletoe Falls, she sent up a silent thank you to her aunt for making all of this possible.

Chapter 24

The front counter of Sugar & Spice looked like a hurricane of organization had swept through and decided to stay. Scheduling charts covered every available surface, overlapping with supplier catalogs and what appeared to be years' worth of Phyllis's handwritten notes. Color-coded sticky notes marked different sections, and Savannah's laptop displayed a detailed spreadsheet that made Megan's eyes cross if she looked at it too long.

"Okay," Savannah said, tapping her pen against a particularly dense chart. "So during the regular season, we keep the display cases stocked with the core items—fudge in six flavors, hand-pulled taffy in twelve, chocolate assortments, caramels, and the specialty items that rotate monthly."

Megan studied the chart, trying to absorb the sheer volume of product. "And this all changes for Christmas?"

"Changes by adding additional offerings to what we normally stock." Savannah pulled out another chart; this one covered in red and green highlighting. "Christmas season officially starts the day after

Thanksgiving and runs through New Year's. We add peppermint bark, candy canes in every flavor imaginable, chocolate Santas, snowmen, reindeer, plus all the pre-made gift boxes and baskets."

"While still making all the regular stuff?"

"Yes, plus we increase quantities because we get way more foot traffic. Tourists, locals buying gifts, and corporate orders for office parties."

Megan felt her stomach do a small flip. "That's... a lot."

"It is. But Phyllis had a system." Savannah spread out several pages of notes, all in Phyllis's neat handwriting. "See? She color-coded everything. Red is for daily essentials that have to be made fresh every morning. Green is for weekly rotations. Blue is for special orders. And she had the supplier deliveries staggered, so we never got overwhelmed with inventory all at once."

Megan leaned closer, studying the intricate planning that had gone into running the shop during its busiest season. Phyllis had thought of everything—staff assignments, backup plans if someone got sick, even notes about which candies sold out fastest and needed extra production runs.

"This is incredible," Megan said quietly. "She really knew what she was doing."

"She did. Years of experience will do that." Savannah pulled up another screen on her laptop. "I took the liberty of creating a digital version of her system. Easier to update and share with everyone. Beth can access it for ordering supplies, Kay can check production schedules, and you can see the whole operation at a glance."

Megan felt a surge of gratitude for Savannah's business instincts. "Wow. I'm glad you did this."

"So what do you think? Should we keep the same schedule Phyllis used, or do you want to make changes?"

It was a real question, Megan realized. Savannah was actually asking for her input, trusting her judgment as the owner.

"I think we keep it," Megan said with more confidence than she felt. "If it worked for Phyllis for years, it'll work for us now. But—" She paused, an idea forming. "What if we added one experimental flavor each week? Something new that we can test before potentially adding to the permanent rotation?"

Savannah's eyes lit up. "I love that. Keep the tradition but leave room for innovation. That's smart."

"My one contribution to Phyllis's perfect system."

"It's a good contribution." Savannah made a note on her laptop. "I'll add a line item for experimental flavors, and we can rotate who gets to develop them. Give everyone a chance to be creative."

They worked through the rest of the schedule, Megan asking questions about quantities and timing, Savannah explaining Phyllis's reasoning for different choices. By the time they finished, Megan had a clearer picture of just how much work went into the Christmas season—and how prepared her staff was to handle it.

"I'll email Beth and let her know the schedule is approved," Savannah said, already typing. "She can cross-reference our current inventory and make sure we have ordered everything we need."

"Perfect." Megan straightened, stretching her back. "How are you so good at this?"

"Business major, remember? Plus, I really like organizing things. It's satisfying when everything lines up properly."

Megan's phone buzzed in her pocket. She pulled it out to see a text from Kyle.

Do you have a few minutes to come up to the apartment? Want to show you something.

Her heart did a small leap. She typed back quickly: Be right there.

"I need to run upstairs for a minute," Megan said, grabbing her keys. "Can you handle things down here?"

"Of course. Take your time."

Megan headed through the kitchen, waving at Linda and Tonya, who were working on a batch of pixies, and pushed through the back door into the alley.

The new stairs rose before her, sturdy and solid, with the metal frame gleaming and the wood treads smooth and even. She'd climbed them twice yesterday, marveling at how different they felt from the old rickety ones. No more wobbling with each step, no more fear that the whole structure might collapse beneath her.

She climbed quickly, her hand trailing along the smooth railing. There was something satisfying about this simple upgrade, something that made her future home feel real and accessible rather than a distant dream.

At the top, she opened the door to the apartment and stepped inside.

Then stopped.

The apartment had transformed.

The kitchen cabinets gleamed along the far wall, their warm, soft, white-colored wood just as beautiful as they'd looked in the catalog in the store. The upper cabinets were already installed, creating clean lines and ample storage. Below, the lower cabinets and the island cabinets sat positioned where they would be installed, showing the layout clearly.

But it was more than the cabinets. The light fixtures she'd chosen hung from the ceiling, their brushed nickel finish catching the late afternoon sun streaming through the windows. The walls, painted in the Warm Linen color she'd picked, looked even better than she'd imagined—warm and inviting, making the space feel like a home instead of a construction zone.

Kyle stood near the kitchen area with his father. Both men turned as she entered.

"What do you think?" Kyle asked. "We wanted to check the cabinet layout before we installed everything. Make sure you like where the island is positioned and that you can move around the kitchen comfortably."

Megan walked into the kitchen space slowly. The island was positioned perfectly, leaving plenty of room to move between it and the counter, with space for the bar stools she'd eventually get.

"It's perfect," she said. "The island right there makes sense. I can prep on this side and serve on the other."

Mitch nodded, making a note on his clipboard. "We'll finish installing the cabinets then."

Megan continued through the apartment, taking in all the changes. The living room looked larger with the fresh paint. She moved to the bathroom and found more transformation waiting.

The new vanity was installed, its white cabinet and faux marble top making the small bathroom feel elegant. The tall storage cabinet stood beside it, providing space for towels and toiletries. Above the vanity, the light fixture she'd chosen cast warm light across the space, and in the mirror—

She saw her reflection.

Blond hair slightly messy from a day of work. Green eyes wide with surprise. Face flushed with emotion.

And suddenly, it hit her.

This was her bathroom. In her apartment. Above her candy shop. In a town where people were beginning to know her name and recognize her, and her staff had become friends, and a man who made her heart skip waited in the next room.

Two weeks ago, she'd been a nobody from nowhere, with nothing.

Now she had everything and more.

The tears came without warning, sudden and overwhelming. One moment she was staring at her reflection, and the next her vision was blurring, her breath was hitching, and she was crying.

"Megan?" Kyle's voice, concerned, came from the doorway.

She tried to speak but couldn't get the words out around the sob that escaped instead. She pressed her hand to her mouth, embarrassed and overwhelmed and unable to stop.

Kyle was there instantly, his arms coming around her, pulling her close. "Hey, it's okay. What's wrong? Do you not like something? We can change it."

Megan shook her head against his chest, managing to get out, "No, it's not—I'm sorry, I—"

"Breath," he said gently, one hand smoothing down her back. "It's okay. Whatever it is, it's okay."

She let herself lean into him, let herself feel the solid warmth of his embrace while the emotions crashed over her. It was so much. Everything was so much. The apartment, the business, the staff who trusted her, the town that was becoming home, Kyle himself—all of it together was overwhelming in the best and worst way.

When the tears finally slowed, she pulled back slightly, wiping at her face with embarrassment. "I'm sorry. Gosh, I'm sorry. I don't know where that came from."

"Don't apologize." Kyle's voice was firm but kind. "Talk to me. What's going on?"

"I'm an emotional person," Megan said, the words coming out shaky. "If you haven't noticed. I cry at everything—sad things, happy things, touching commercials about dogs... just everything."

A smile tugged at Kyle's lips. "Noted."

"This is just—" She gestured helplessly around the apartment. "It's so much. All at once. I never imagined I would have—" Her voice broke again. "All of this. A home. A business. People who actually like me. It's hitting me all at once again."

"Are you scared?" Kyle asked.

"No. Yes. Maybe?" Megan laughed wetly. "I'm not sad. I'm not even upset, really. I'm just... grateful. And overwhelmed. And excited. And terrified that I'll somehow mess it all up."

"You won't."

"You don't know that."

"I know you. I've watched you these past two weeks. You're working hard, learning everything you can, and making good decisions. You care about the business and the people. That's what matters."

"I just want to make Phyllis proud," Megan whispered. "She gave me this incredible gift, and I want to be worthy of it."

"You already are."

Megan looked up at him, finding his hazel eyes warm and steady and full of conviction she didn't quite feel herself. But maybe that was okay. Maybe she didn't have to have all the confidence on her own if people like Kyle believed in her.

"Thanks for not thinking I'm completely insane for crying over something that's probably nothing special to you."

"Hey now... you're processing major life changes. That's allowed. You're allowed to feel or say or react however you want. Own it... you deserve it." Kyle's smile was gentle.

They stood there for a moment, and Megan became aware that they were still standing close, that Kyle's hands were still on her arms, and that she could feel the warmth radiating from him.

She stepped back slightly, needing space to breathe and think clearly.

"So," she said, trying for lightness. "The cabinets. They're perfect just the way they are. The lights, the fixtures, all of it is fine."

Kyle's expression shifted, accepting the subject change. "Good. Have you ordered your appliances yet? Do you want to go furniture shopping soon?"

"Beth helped me pick out a stove and a refrigerator online that will fit in the kitchen. She ordered them, and they are supposed to be delivered on Saturday. Let me think about furniture shopping. I need to sit down and figure out just what I need and measure the space so I know what to look for."

"Okay good. Your apartment will be livable soon."

Megan walked back through the apartment, seeing it with fresh eyes now that the emotional storm had passed. The layout was perfect. The paint color was exactly right. The light fixtures cast the kind of warm lighting that made a space feel welcoming.

She stopped at the living room window and looked out over Mistletoe Falls. From here, she could see Mistletoe Lane with its gas lamp lights and decorated storefronts. Beyond that, the mountains rose dark against the late afternoon sky.

This view would be hers. Every morning she could wake up and see this. Come home from work, go upstairs and watch the sunset paint the mountains in shades of gold and purple.

Kyle came to stand beside her.

"It's a good view," he said quietly.

"It's a perfect view." Megan turned to look at him. "I can't thank you enough for all you've done for me. For helping to make this happen so fast. For checking with me before finishing things. For just... caring."

"It's not a hardship, Megan."

"Still, I didn't deserve your kindness, and yet here you are." Megan turned back to look at Mitch and said, "I appreciate everything you've done for me, Mitch. The apartment so far is beautiful. Thank you for all your hard work."

"My pleasure, Megan," he said.

As Kyle returned to his dad's side in the kitchen and began screwing the cabinets in place, securing them to walls and floors, Megan took a moment to envision what this apartment would look like once she moved in. She mentally arranged furniture, decided where to position her bed in the bedroom, and pondered desk options for the spare room that would become her office—solid and sturdy, or sleek and minimal?

When she turned back toward the windows and looked out at the beautiful view of Mistletoe Falls, she sent up a silent thank you to her aunt for making all of this possible.

Chapter 25

Megan had never seen so many people gathered in one place for something as simple as turning on Christmas lights, but as she stood in the town square with Kyle's hand warm in hers, she understood why this ceremony mattered—it was less about the lights and more about the community coming together and welcoming in the Christmas season. It was about community members coming together and enjoying a celebration. It was about people coming from miles and miles away to join in the celebration and experience this magical Christmas town.

The town square was packed, every available space filled with bundled families, couples holding hands, and children darting between groups with glow sticks tracing arcs of color through the evening air. The massive Christmas tree stood in the center of the town square beside the Victorian gazebo, dark and waiting, its branches strung with thousands of lights that would soon blaze to life. Businesses ringed the square, their festive window displays glowing warmly, gas lampposts casting pools of golden light onto the sidewalks and Mistletoe Lane, which was blocked off to traffic specifically for this event.

The scent of coffee and hot chocolate hung in the cold air, mixing with the scent of roasted chestnuts from a street vendor's cart. Megan spotted the Sugarplum Bakery's booths placed strategically around the event, with Claire and her staff handing out free hot chocolate, coffee, and sugar cookies to anyone who wanted them.

"This is incredible," Megan said, her breath visible in white puffs.

Kyle squeezed her hand, guiding her through the crowd with ease. "Wait until you see the tree lit up. It's something else."

He led her toward the front, where the crowd was thickest but where they'd have an unobstructed view of the tree. People shifted to make room, several greeting Kyle by name, their curious but friendly gazes landing on Megan.

"Kyle! Over here!"

A tall man with sandy brown hair and a broad smile waved from a few feet away. He wore a heavy canvas jacket and work boots, looking like he'd come straight from outdoor labor.

Kyle steered them over, his hand never leaving Megan's. "Gabe, hey. Megan, this is Gabe Mills. He owns Mistletoe Christmas Tree Farm and serves on the town council with me. Gabe, this is Megan Caldwell."

"The new owner of Sugar & Spice," Gabe said, his handshake firm and warm. "I've heard a lot about you. Phyllis was a good friend and such a kind person to me. I'm really glad you're keeping the shop open."

"Thank you," Megan said. "Did you provide the tree for tonight?"

Gabe's smile widened with pride. "I did. Sixteen-footer. It took six of my guys and the local fire department to get it positioned right, but she's a beauty."

"It's stunning," Megan said, looking up at the massive tree that towered above the crowd.

"Gabe provides the town tree every year," Kyle explained.

"It's a family tradition—we've been doing it for several years now," Gabe said. "And I don't plan on stopping. Listen, you two should come out to the farm sometime. I do wagon rides through the tree fields during December, with hot cider, the whole thing. I have a new gift shop this year and a few other things. Bring the family—" He caught himself, glancing between them with a knowing smile. "Or, you know, whomever."

"We'd like that," Kyle said easily.

"Great! Just give me a call." Gabe glanced over his shoulder as someone called his name. "I'd better go check on something. Good to meet you, Megan. Welcome to Mistletoe Falls."

They chatted for a few more minutes before Gabe was pulled away by someone asking about tree delivery. Kyle continued guiding Megan through the crowd, stopping every few feet to greet someone or be greeted.

"Kyle! There you are!"

A woman about Megan's age approached, her dark curls bouncing beneath a knit hat, her arms full of shopping bags from various stores. Her smile was bright and genuine.

"Emma," Kyle said warmly. "Megan, this is Emma Sullivan. She owns the Once Upon a Time Bookshop, just down from Sugar & Spice. Emma, Megan Caldwell."

"Oh, I'm so glad to finally meet you!" Emma shifted her bags to free a hand for shaking. "I've been meaning to stop by your shop and introduce myself, but we've just been so busy lately, plus I'm helping with the children's Christmas play at the elementary school."

"I haven't made it to your shop yet either," Megan admitted. "But I've walked past—your window displays are beautiful."

"Thank you! I spend far too much time on them, but I love it." Emma's enthusiasm was infectious. "We should get coffee sometime. I'm part of a group of women business owners here in Mistletoe Falls, and we meet once a month. Very informal, just comparing notes and supporting each other. You'd be more than welcome."

"I'd like that," Megan said, meaning it.

"Perfect. I'll text Leslie and have her bring you to the next one." Emma glanced toward the stage, where the mayor was beginning to gather with other town officials. "I'd better find my spot before it gets too crowded. Great to meet you, Megan!"

As Emma disappeared into the crowd, Megan felt Kyle's thumb trace circles on the back of her hand. "Are you enjoying yourself?" he asked.

"I am. This is amazing!"

"Kyle! Hey, man!"

A man in an expensive-looking wool coat approached, his grin wide and teasing. He was about Kyle's height, with dark hair and the kind of easy confidence that suggested he was comfortable anywhere.

"Luke," Kyle said, pulling him into one of those brief masculine hugs that involved more back-slapping than actual embrace. "Didn't think you'd make it."

"And miss the tree lighting? Caroline would never forgive me. She's around here somewhere with the kids." Luke turned his attention to Megan, his expression curious but friendly. "And you must be the famous Megan I've been hearing about."

"Megan, this is Luke Webb," Kyle said. "We grew up together, went to law school together, and somehow he still hasn't learned to be less annoying."

"That's hurtful," Luke said, not looking hurt at all. He offered Megan his hand. "Luke Webb. Attorney at law, Kyle's oldest friend, and the person who knows all his embarrassing secrets."

"Nice to meet you," Megan said, shaking his hand.

"Luke has a practice here in town," Kyle explained. "Family law mostly."

"Someone has to help the good people of Mistletoe Falls navigate their divorces and custody agreements," Luke said. "Though thankfully, we don't get a lot of that here. Small-town life breeds either lifelong happiness or quiet resentment, and this town seems to lean toward the former." His gaze shifted between Kyle and Megan, his smile turning knowing. "So this is the girlfriend Leslie's been telling Caroline about."

The word landed between them—girlfriend—and Megan felt her heart kick against her ribs. She'd known it was coming, had known since their conversation on the porch that they were heading in this direction, but hearing Kyle's friend say it out loud made it real in a way that caught her slightly off-guard.

Kyle's hand tightened slightly on hers. "Yes. This is my girlfriend, Megan."

Luke's grin widened. "Good for you, man. It's about time." He turned to Megan. "He's a good guy. Little uptight sometimes, takes his work too seriously, but overall he is a decent human being."

"I'll keep that in mind," Megan said, finding her voice steadier than she'd expected.

"Luke! There you are!"

A woman with two young children in tow appeared, looking frazzled but happy. Luke made quick introductions—his wife Caroline and their kids, seven and five—before they were swept back into the crowd.

"You okay?" Kyle asked quietly once they were alone again.

"Yeah," Megan said. "Just—girlfriend. It sounds so official when someone else says it."

"Is that okay?"

"Sure." She looked up at him, finding his expression open and slightly uncertain. "The word 'girlfriend' just sounds so big."

"It is big," Kyle agreed. "But good big, right?"

"Yeah. Good big."

Before she could say more, a new voice called Kyle's name. Megan turned to see an older man in an elegant overcoat making his way toward them, people parting naturally to let him through. He had the kind of presence that suggested importance without being overbearing about it.

"Mr. Mayor," Kyle said warmly. "I was hoping we'd run into you."

"Kyle, good to see you." The mayor's handshake was firm; his smile genuine. "And this must be Megan Caldwell. Roger Hayes," he said, offering his hand to Megan. "Mayor of our little town and a longtime admirer of your aunt's confectionery skills."

"It's nice to meet you," Megan said, shaking his hand.

"The pleasure is mine. Phyllis was a treasure—not just her candy, though that was exceptional, but her spirit. She had a way of making everyone feel welcome and loved, whether they were first-time tourists or lifelong residents." His expression grew more serious, though no less kind. "Her passing hit me hard. I miss her."

"Thank you," Megan said, emotion tightening her throat. "That means a lot."

"But I'm delighted to hear that Sugar & Spice is staying in the family and remaining open. That shop is part of Mistletoe Falls' identity. Having you here, continuing Phyllis's legacy—it means a great deal to all of us." He glanced between Megan and Kyle, his expression turning slightly mischievous. "And I hear through the grapevine that you two are keeping company. Kyle's a good man. Former Eagle Scout, current town council member, and never misses a community event."

"Are you campaigning for me?" Kyle asked, his tone dry but amused.

"Just stating facts," the mayor said innocently. "Megan, you're welcome to attend town council meetings. They're open to the public, and we always appreciate input from our business owners."

"I'd like that," Megan said.

"Excellent. Well, I'd better take my place before they start without me. Welcome to Mistletoe Falls, Megan. Truly."

As the mayor walked toward the stage erected near the tree and the gazebo, Megan felt Kyle's arm slide around her waist, pulling her closer against the cold.

"Everyone's been so nice," Megan said. "It's wonderful."

"That's Mistletoe Falls. We're aggressively friendly."

The crowd began to quiet as the mayor stepped up to the microphone. Someone adjusted the sound system, causing brief feedback that made several children cover their ears. Then the mayor's voice rang out clear and strong across the square.

"Good evening, Mistletoe Falls, and welcome to our annual Tree Lighting Ceremony!"

Cheers erupted from the crowd, along with whistles and applause that echoed off the surrounding buildings.

"Welcome, friends, neighbors, and visitors," Mayor Hayes continued, his voice carrying easily through the crisp evening air. "Tonight we gather for more than just the lighting of our community Christmas tree. We celebrate the spirit of collaboration, dedication, and love that makes Mistletoe Falls truly special."

Scattered applause rippled through the crowd, underscored by the warm hum of genuine pride rather than polite formality.

"This year's ceremony represents something extraordinary," the mayor continued, gesturing toward the magnificent Fraser fir that towered above them like a regal sentinel. "Through the partnership between Sugarplum Bakery and Mistletoe Christmas Tree Farm—coordinated by Claire Whitfield and Gabe Mills—and with the help of many dedicated volunteers, we've seen the kind of teamwork that creates lasting holiday memories."

Megan glanced toward where Claire stood near one of the bakery booths, her face glowing with pride as people around her nodded their appreciation.

"What makes Mistletoe Falls special is all of you," the mayor said, his voice warming with emotion. "It's the way we show up for each other. The way we support our local businesses, volunteer for community events, and welcome newcomers with open arms. It's the way we gather together on cold November evenings to celebrate tradition and light and the promise of the season ahead."

Megan felt Kyle's arm tighten around her waist, his warmth seeping through her coat.

"This year, we've welcomed new faces to our community," the mayor continued. "And we've said goodbye to some beloved friends. Phyllis Caldwell, who ran the Sugar & Spice Candy Shop for over forty years, passed away this fall. Many of you knew her. Many of you have childhood memories tied to her peppermint fudge or her chocolate truffles. Phyllis understood what this town is about—she understood that a small act of kindness, a perfectly made piece of candy, or a warm welcome could make someone's day a little brighter."

Megan's eyes stung with unexpected tears, and she felt Kyle's hand squeeze hers gently.

"I'm pleased to report that Sugar & Spice is staying in the family. Phyllis's niece, Megan Caldwell, has moved to Mistletoe Falls and is keeping the shop open. Let's give her a warm welcome."

Applause broke out, and Megan felt hundreds of eyes turn toward her. Her face flushed hot despite the cold air, but Kyle's steady presence beside her kept her grounded. She managed a small wave, overwhelmed by the genuine warmth radiating from the crowd. Several people near them smiled and nodded at her, and a woman she didn't recognize called out, "Welcome home, honey!"

"As we light this beautiful tree tonight—generously donated once again by Gabe Mills and Mistletoe Christmas Tree Farm—let's remember what this season is really about. Connection. Community. Light in the darkness. Hope for the future. Love for each other."

The mayor stepped back from the microphone, and someone near the gazebo began the countdown.

"And now," Mayor Hayes announced with a theatrical flourish, "the moment we've all been waiting for. In ten seconds, our magnificent community Christmas tree will officially welcome the holiday season to Mistletoe Falls!"

The crowd erupted into a unified countdown, children's voices tumbling over one another with giddy excitement while the deeper tones of the adults kept the rhythm steady. Anticipation shimmered in the cold air like static before a storm.

"Ten! Nine! Eight!"

Megan found herself caught up in the energy, her own voice joining the chorus. Kyle's hand tightened on hers.

"Seven! Six! Five!"

The children were practically bouncing now, their excitement contagious.

"Four! Three! Two! One!"

The tree blazed to life.

Thousands of lights—white, red, green, gold, and blue—erupted across the massive evergreen, transforming it from dark branches into a beacon of color and brilliance that seemed to pulse with its own heartbeat. The crowd erupted in cheers and applause, the sound deafening and joyful, reverberating across the square.

In that moment, Kyle turned to her. His hands came up to frame her face, gentle and sure, and he kissed her forehead. The gesture was tender and public and claiming all at once. Then he pulled her close, holding her against his chest, and Megan felt the significance of it wash over her.

"Beautiful," Kyle murmured against her hair.

"It really is," Megan said, her voice catching with emotion.

"I wasn't talking about the tree."

She pulled back enough to look up at him, finding his expression open and warm and completely genuine. The lights from the tree reflected in his eyes, creating patterns of gold and silver. "That was incredibly cheesy and cute."

"I know. Did it work?"

"Yeah," she said softly. "It worked."

The choir began singing "O Come, All Ye Faithful," their voices clear and strong in the cold air. The crowd joined in almost immediately, the familiar words rising from hundreds of throats in a wave of sound that seemed to fill every corner of the square. Kyle sang along, his voice pleasant, and Megan found herself joining in, her voice blending with his and with the surrounding people.

They stood there for three more carols— "Silent Night," "Joy to the World," and "Hark! The Herald Angels Sing"—surrounded by the crowd but somehow feeling separate from it, existing in their own small bubble of warmth and connection. Megan thought about how much her life had changed in just a few short weeks. How she'd gone from feeling alone and stuck in a rut to standing here, part of something bigger than herself, held close by someone who looked at her like she hung the moon.

As the final notes of another Christmas carol faded into the night air and the crowd began to disperse—some heading home, children being carried on tired parents' shoulders, others lingering to chat or visit the vendors still selling roasted chestnuts and kettle corn—Kyle turned to her.

"What would you like to do now? The night's still young."

Megan looked around the square, at the lit storefronts and the people milling about, at her new town celebrating its favorite season. Energy buzzed through her.

"I want to walk around," she said. "See the shops, really experience this. My new home."

Kyle's smile was immediate and genuine, lighting up his whole face. "Sounds good to me."

They crossed Mistletoe Lane, which curved around the town square to the sidewalk in front of a strip of businesses. The brick walkway was slightly uneven in places, worn smooth by decades of foot traffic, and Megan found herself noticing details she'd missed before—the way each gas lamp had been wrapped with evergreen garland, the brass plaques beside each door showing the year the building was constructed, and the way the storefronts seemed to lean slightly toward each other as if sharing secrets.

Some shops had closed for the evening, but their window displays were spectacular—elaborate Christmas scenes with animated figures, twinkling lights woven through carefully arranged merchandise, everything designed to catch the eye and spark wonder. Other businesses remained open, taking advantage of the post-ceremony crowd, their warm interiors spilling golden light onto the sidewalk.

"Let's go in here," Kyle said, guiding her toward a shop with "Pinecone & Ivy Florist" painted in elegant script across the window. A wreath of white roses and silver bells hung on the door.

The shop smelled of evergreen and roses, the warm interior a welcome relief from the cold. Arrangements filled every surface—traditional Christmas centerpieces overflowing with red berries and pine cones, modern minimalist designs featuring white orchids and silver branches, and elaborate wreaths hung on the walls like pieces of art.

"Well... hello, Kyle!" a woman in her early thirties said as she approached, wiping her hands on her apron. She had chestnut brown hair pulled back in a messy bun and the kind of smile that made you feel like you were already friends.

"Heather Bentley," Kyle said. "Heather, this is Megan Caldwell."

"Oh, I'm so glad to finally meet you!" Heather pulled Megan into a quick hug before Megan could prepare for it, the embrace warm and genuine. "I've been meaning to stop by Sugar & Spice, but the flower business has been absolutely insane lately. Everyone wants centerpieces and arrangements and wreaths all at once. I've been busy with numerous weddings and Thanksgiving arrangements for weeks now."

"I can imagine," Megan said, slightly breathless from the unexpected embrace. "Your work is beautiful."

"Thank you! That's sweet of you to say." Heather's enthusiasm was palpable.

"Heather's on the town council too," Kyle explained. "And she provides all the flowers for town events."

"Someone has to make this place beautiful," Heather said with a chuckle. "Listen, Megan, I've been thinking. Phyllis and I talked a few months ago about collaborating—special boxes of chocolates that could be included with flower deliveries for anniversaries, birthdays, that kind of thing. Would you be interested in exploring that?"

"Absolutely," Megan said. "That sounds like a great idea. I can see how that would work really well."

"Perfect! Let's set up a time to meet after the holiday rush calms down. Maybe January?" Heather was already pulling out her phone. "I'll make myself a note to get in touch with you after the first of the year. Oh, this is going to be wonderful. I'm so glad Sugar & Spice is staying open. Phyllis would be so happy."

They chatted for a few more minutes before Heather was called away by a customer asking about poinsettia care and whether they needed special soil. Kyle guided Megan back out onto the sidewalk, his hand warm on the small of her back.

"She's a lot," Kyle said with affection.

"I liked her," Megan said. "She's enthusiastic. I love her energy."

They continued walking, passing the darkened window of a coffee shop called The Cozy Cup, then a sandwich shop with a sign reading "The Pickle Barrel Deli," and then stopping at The Mistletoe Mercantile. The old-fashioned general store was still open, its wooden floors creaking beneath their feet as they entered. Barrels of candy canes and penny candy lined the entryway, and shelves stretched toward the back filled with everything from local honey to handmade soaps to vintage-style toys that looked like they belonged in another era.

"Welcome! Oh, Kyle, hello!" A woman emerged from behind the counter, adjusting her glasses. "And this must be Megan. I see a family resemblance. Megan dear, you are your Aunt Phyllis made over for sure. I'm Natalie Collins. I own this wonderful mess."

"It's not a mess," Megan said, charmed by the organized chaos. "It's perfect. I love it!"

"You're kind to say so." Natalie's smile was warm, the kind that reached her eyes and made her whole face light up. "I knew your aunt well. She used to bring me samples of new candies she was testing and let me give her my opinion. I'd tell her they were all delicious, and she'd tell me I had no discerning palate, and we'd argue about it for twenty minutes before having tea and starting all over again."

Megan smiled. "I love that memory of yours. Thank you for sharing it with me."

"Let me ask you something," Natalie continued, leaning against the counter. "Would you be interested in letting me continue to purchase some of Sugar & Spice's packaged candies at wholesale? I do gift baskets around the major holidays, and Phyllis's candies always worked perfectly. Phyllis and I had this handshake arrangement the past few years, and this year—well, I just didn't have the heart to come over and bother you with this right away, but do you think maybe we could discuss it? I'd like to start planning for Valentine's Day as soon as possible."

"I'd love to," Megan said. "In fact, there's no need to wait. If you'd like to include some of our chocolates in your Christmas baskets, get in touch with Beth at the shop. She can get everything set up for you. I'm still learning the ins and outs of the business, but Beth knows everything."

"Wonderful. Take one of my cards." Natalie produced a business card from seemingly nowhere. "And I'll be sure and contact Beth this coming Monday."

They left The Mistletoe Mercantile with Megan's mind spinning with possibilities. Collaborations with the florist, with the general store, and with Kyle and Leslie's shop—suddenly her business didn't exist in isolation but as part of an interconnected web of local enterprises supporting each other. It was like discovering she'd been given not just a shop but an entire network of people who wanted her to succeed.

"One more stop," Kyle said, guiding her toward a shop just down the lane.

Stitches Quilt Shop had already turned off most of its interior lights, but a woman was visible through the window, straightening displays. Kyle tapped on the glass, and the woman looked up, her expression shifting from concentration to recognition and welcome. She unlocked the door.

"Kyle Porter, if you're here to sell me on another town initiative, I'm telling you right now the answer is no." But her tone was teasing, and her smile genuine.

"Would I do that?" Kyle asked innocently.

"Yes." The woman turned to Megan, her eyes crinkling with warmth. "Laura Ashford."

"Megan Caldwell," Megan said, shaking her hand.

"Caldwell? Ahh, you must be Phyllis's niece I've heard about. Phyllis made candy for my sister's wedding back in September," Laura said. "Hundreds of individually wrapped pieces, each one perfect and tied with a ribbon that matched the wedding colors exactly. That's the kind of woman Phyllis was—she cared about the details and about making things special."

"I wish I had made a better effort to get to know her," Megan said softly, emotion rising in her throat again.

"She was a wonderful woman. Welcome to Mistletoe Falls, honey. I'm glad you're here. I'm glad that the candy shop's staying open, especially because a girl needs her maple fudge fix now and then." Laura winked.

They talked for a few more minutes before Laura gently mentioned she needed to get home. As she locked the door behind them, Megan and Kyle found themselves standing in the quiet street, most of the post-ceremony crowd having thinned out. Only a few couples still strolled the sidewalks, and the vendors were beginning to pack up their carts.

The tree still glowed brilliantly in the square, a beacon of light against the dark sky. The air had grown colder, and Megan's breath came out in larger white clouds now, but she barely noticed.

"Everyone's been so welcoming," she said.

"That's Mistletoe Falls," Kyle said. "We take care of our own. And you're one of us now."

They walked slowly down the sidewalk, passing more darkened shops and a few that remained lit. Megan noticed how all the businesses seemed to complement each other rather than compete, everything designed to encourage people to stroll and explore rather than visit one place and leave.

"It's intentional," Kyle said when she mentioned it. "The business owners all meet quarterly to talk about town events, promotion strategies, and how to support each other. Everyone understands that when one business thrives, we all benefit. When Mistletoe Falls does well as a destination, all the shops see increased traffic."

"That's smart," Megan said. "And kind of beautiful, actually. Co-operation instead of competition."

"Small-town life at its best," Kyle agreed.

They found themselves standing outside Sugar & Spice, and Megan paused to really look at it. Savannah had outdone herself with the window displays—a winter wonderland scene with fake snow that looked almost real, twinkling lights creating the illusion of stars, and carefully arranged boxes of candy that looked both elegant and inviting. The burgundy awnings above had been strung with white lights that twinkled like diamonds, and the shop's sign glowed warm against the building.

"It looks like it belongs here," Kyle said quietly. "Like it's always been part of the landscape."

"It has been," Megan said. "For forty years."

"I mean, with you running it. It looks right."

Megan stared at her shop—her shop, she reminded herself, not just Phyllis's legacy but hers now too—and felt something shift inside her chest. She'd been thinking of herself as a replacement, as Phyllis's niece who was filling in and eventually taking over once her confidence and experience grew.

But standing here, with Kyle's hand warm in hers and the memory of a dozen genuine welcomes still glowing in her mind, she realized she'd been thinking about it all wrong.

She wasn't a replacement. She wasn't just filling in.

She was carving out a space for herself in this town. She was building relationships, making business connections, and becoming someone people recognized and welcomed. She was Kyle's girlfriend. She was the owner of Sugar & Spice. She was becoming part of Mistletoe Falls.

And maybe, just maybe, this was exactly who she was meant to be.

Chapter 26

Megan couldn't remember the last time she'd sat around someone's kitchen table on a Saturday morning, eating breakfast and planning a business venture, but as Leslie refilled her coffee and Kyle reached for another serving, she thought maybe this was what having good friends felt like.

"The hash browns are perfect," Megan said, scraping the last bite from her plate. "What's your secret?"

"Frozen shredded potatoes and absolutely zero shame." Leslie settled back into her chair with her cup of coffee. "My mother makes everything from scratch, and I admire that, but sometimes convenience wins."

"Sometimes?" Kyle raised an eyebrow. "You use boxed brownie mix for your 'famous' brownies."

"They're still famous. Nobody needs to know about the box." Leslie turned to Megan. "Don't let him fool you. He can't cook anything that doesn't involve a grill or a microwave or that doesn't come from a box either."

"I make sandwiches," Kyle protested.

"Assembling ingredients isn't cooking."

"It absolutely is."

Megan smiled, letting their familiar sibling rhythm wash over her. Leslie's apartment was warm and comfortable, morning sunlight streaming through the windows and catching on the Christmas decorations Leslie had scattered throughout the space. Everything here felt intentional and loved, from the throw pillows on the couch to the collection of vintage Christmas books on the shelf.

"Okay, back to business," Leslie said, pulling a notepad closer. "We need to finalize pricing tiers before we can create sample boxes. Three levels—basic, mid-tier, and premium."

"What's the price range again?" Megan asked, reaching for her own notebook. She'd started carrying it everywhere, jotting down ideas and observations as they came to her.

"We talked about twenty-five dollars, mid-tier at forty-five, and premium somewhere between seventy-five and eighty." Leslie tapped her pen against the paper. "Does that still feel right to you? You know your candy costs better than I do."

Megan considered the numbers, mentally calculating ingredient costs, labor, and packaging. Weeks ago, she wouldn't have been able to estimate any of this. Now, after working daily with Kay and Beth, and studying everything on her own, sometimes late into the night, she had a decent grasp of the shop's margins.

"I think that works. The basic box would have simpler candies—chocolate-covered pretzels, candy canes, maybe some fudge. Mid-tier add in truffles and more elaborate chocolates. Premium gets the really special stuff—hand-pulled taffy, custom chocolates, maybe a larger package of fudge."

"Perfect." Leslie made notes. "And from my side, basic gets a few small ornaments and some festive ribbon. Mid-tier adds nicer ornaments, maybe a small decorative item. Premium gets high-end ornaments, a statement piece, and luxury packaging."

Kyle leaned forward, his forearms resting on the table. "What about the themes? You mentioned those on Thanksgiving, Megan, but we didn't nail anything down."

"Traditional Christmas," Megan suggested. "Red and green, classic ornaments, peppermint and chocolate flavors."

"Winter Wonderland," Leslie added. "Silver and white with snowflake ornaments, white chocolate and vanilla flavors."

"Nostalgic Vintage," Kyle said. "That's my vote. Old-fashioned ornaments, retro packaging, and classic candy flavors that remind people of childhood."

"I love that," Megan said. "We could add ribbon candy for that one. It's time-consuming, but it's so visually striking, and people seem to love it."

"Can you make ribbon candy?" Leslie asked, her eyes bright with interest.

"Kay can. I've not attempted it yet." Megan paused, then pushed forward despite the flutter of uncertainty in her chest. "Wait, I have another idea. What if we created special Christmas chocolates exclusively for these boxes? Something you can't buy separately in my store. It would make the boxes feel more special and give people a reason to buy them instead of just putting together their own selection."

Leslie's face lit up. "That's brilliant. What were you thinking?"

"Maybe chocolate bells dusted with edible gold or truffles with Christmas spice flavors—cinnamon, nutmeg, clove. Something festive and different from our regular stock. I'll think about it a bit more and figure it out."

"I can already picture the display," Leslie said. "This is going to be amazing."

Kyle was watching Megan with that expression he sometimes got—like she'd just done something that impressed him, but he didn't want to make a big deal about it. It made her chest feel warm and tight at the same time.

"I need to work on the cross-promotion coupons," he said, pulling out his phone.

"Yes, we cannot forget those," Leslie agreed. "Gets people coming back."

"We need to figure out the timing too," Megan added. "These need to be ready to launch soon, which means we need samples created, photographs taken, and marketing materials finished within the next few days."

"Look at you, thinking like a business owner," Kyle said, and there was genuine pride in his voice that made Megan's face warm.

"I've been learning a lot from Beth," she said, deflecting slightly. "She's well-organized and detailed."

"You're well-organized," Leslie corrected gently. "Give yourself credit."

Megan looked down at her notebook, filled with her own hand writing—neat columns of ideas, cost estimates, and timing notes. Leslie was right. She was organized. When had that happened?

"Should we start putting together sample boxes?" she asked. "I brought supplies in my car."

"Great idea. Let's move to the stockroom in The Christmas Shop," Leslie said, standing and collecting plates. "We can spread out there, and if we need anything from the shop floor, it's right there."

They cleaned up breakfast together—Kyle washing dishes, Leslie drying, and Megan putting things away in the cupboards Leslie directed her toward.

Afterward, they descended the stairs from Leslie's apartment. The November air was sharp and cold, their breath visible in white clouds. Megan's car was parked beside Leslie's SUV in the alley, and she popped the trunk to reveal two large plastic bins packed with supplies.

"You came prepared," Kyle said, reaching for the first bin.

"I had trouble sleeping last night." Megan grabbed the second bin, lighter than Kyle's but still substantial. "I kept thinking about what we'd need for today, so around four this morning I went to the shop and packed everything I could think of."

"Four this morning?"

"Yep. I packed up these supplies and then organized my new office a little more before coming here."

Kyle held the door open for her, and they carried the bins through the back doorway into the stockroom. The space was large and well-organized—metal shelving units lined the walls, packed with inventory, seasonal decorations, and packaging materials. A long worktable dominated the center of the room, its surface already cleared and waiting.

From the front of the shop, Megan could hear the sounds of activity—customers' voices, the cheerful jingle of the bells above the entrance door, and Christmas music playing softly through the sound system.

Leslie was already pulling ornaments from a nearby shelf—delicate glass balls in jewel tones, rustic wooden stars, and elegant silver snowflakes. "Do we still agree that we should start with the mid-tier boxes since those will give us the best sense of balance?"

"I agree," Megan said as she glanced at Kyle, who nodded.

Megan opened her bins and began laying out options: clear cellophane bags of peppermint bark, small boxes of truffles tied with ribbon, candy canes in various flavors, individually wrapped caramels, ribbon, and other decorative items, along with several styles of boxes and baskets they could use as base containers.

"What about these?" She held up a set of square boxes in deep red with gold accents. "They're sturdy and pretty enough for gifting."

"I love those," Leslie said immediately. "Classic but not boring."

They began experimenting with arrangements, placing items in boxes, rearranging, and discussing what felt balanced and what felt cluttered. Kyle had excused himself briefly and returned with his laptop, settling at the end of the worktable where he could watch them while working on promotional materials.

"What do you think about this coupon design?" he asked after about twenty minutes, turning the laptop to show them a mock-up. "I used both logos and created a bordered layout with—"

"Can I see that for a second?" Megan interrupted gently, moving closer to examine the screen.

Kyle slid the laptop toward her, and she studied the design. The Christmas Shop's logo was prominent at the top, with Sugar & Spice mentioned in smaller text at the bottom.

"This is really well-designed," Megan said, choosing her words carefully. "But I wonder if we could adjust it slightly. Right now it feels like Sugar & Spice is secondary to The Christmas Shop, and I think for this collaboration to work well, both businesses should feel equal."

Kyle looked at the screen again, and Megan watched understanding dawn on his face. "You're right. I didn't even realize I was doing that."

"It's subtle," Megan said quickly, not wanting him to feel criticized. "But maybe we could have both logos side by side at the top, same size, and with the same visual weight?"

"Absolutely." Kyle pulled the laptop back and began making adjustments. "Like this?"

The revised design was noticeably more balanced, with both businesses given equal prominence. Megan nodded, relieved he hadn't been defensive about the feedback.

"Much better," Leslie agreed, looking over from where she was arranging ornaments around a selection of candies. "We're partners in this, so it should look that way."

"Sorry," Kyle said, glancing at Megan. "I have a bad habit of just diving in and making decisions without checking first."

"You're efficient," Megan said. "That's not a bad thing. I just want to make sure we're building something that works for both of us and one business doesn't stand out from the other."

"I agree," Kyle said.

They worked through the late morning, falling into a comfortable rhythm. Leslie and Megan assembled sample boxes—the mid-tier was the main focus, then the basic tier and premium versions of all three themes—while Kyle refined promotional materials and checked in periodically for input. The stockroom filled with their creative process: tissue paper rustling, ribbon curling, and the soft thuds of ornaments being placed in boxes.

"I'm thinking we need chocolate bells for the traditional Christmas box," Megan said, making notes. "And the white chocolate snowflakes for Winter Wonderland. For Nostalgic Vintage, definitely the ribbon candy, and maybe some of those old-fashioned chocolate drops Kay makes."

"Can you actually produce all of this in addition to your regular stock?" Leslie asked. "I don't want you feeling overwhelmed."

Megan considered the question seriously.

"I'll need to talk to Kay," she said. "But I think so. The ribbon candy is time-intensive, and we already make it anyway. We could just up the production a little. The chocolate bells and snowflakes are basically molded chocolates with some finishing work. I feel confident enough that I could handle those if need be, and Tonya can handle the finishing details. I'm thinking if I plan production carefully and maybe ask a couple of employees if they'd like extra hours, it's doable."

"You're really getting the hang of this," Leslie said warmly. "The business side, I mean. Knowing what's feasible and what's not."

"Beth's been teaching me a lot about planning and capacity." Megan felt a familiar flutter of pride mixed with disbelief. Was she actually getting good at this?

A knock at the stockroom door interrupted them, and Gracie, one of The Christmas Shop's younger employees, poked her head in. She had glitter in her hair—an occupational hazard—and held a clipboard.

"Leslie? Sorry to interrupt, but we need approval for the window display refresh. Jan wants to photograph it this afternoon for social media, like you requested."

"Be right there," Leslie said, standing and brushing tissue paper scraps from her jeans. "You two okay if I step away for a bit?"

"We're good," Megan assured her. "I might actually need to start packing up soon anyway."

Leslie disappeared into the front of the shop, and suddenly it was just Megan and Kyle in the stockroom, surrounded by assembled gift boxes and scattered supplies.

"Your sister's really good at what she does," Megan said, continuing to arrange items in the premium Winter Wonderland box. "She makes everything look so effortless."

"She works harder than people realize," Kyle said. "Same as you."

Megan glanced up at him. He'd abandoned his laptop and was now helping her, his hands carefully positioning a silver snowflake ornament in the box she was working on. Their fingers brushed as they reached for the same piece of ribbon, and Megan felt that now-familiar spark of awareness.

"I was thinking," Kyle said, not quite meeting her eyes, "my afternoon's open. After you're done here, do you want to head over to Sugar & Spice together? We could experiment with those Christmas chocolates you mentioned. Get a jump on production."

"Kay's working until late tonight," Megan said, the plan forming in her mind. "She could help us figure out the technical stuff. That's actually an excellent idea."

"It's a date then." Kyle's eyes crinkled at the corners when he smiled. "A work date, I mean. Obviously."

"Obviously," Megan echoed, trying not to smile too widely.

They continued working, and Megan found herself relaxing into the moment. This—creating something with her hands, planning for the future, and working alongside someone who treated her as an equal—this was what she'd been missing all those years in Bowling Green. Purpose. Partnership. The sense that what she did mattered.

Leslie returned about twenty minutes later, trailing Jan, who immediately began snapping photos of the sample boxes they'd created.

"These are gorgeous," Jan said, her camera clicking rapidly. "Can I post teasers on social media? Build some anticipation?"

Leslie looked at Megan, deferring to her for the decision. The gesture wasn't lost on Megan—this was a collaboration, and Leslie was treating it as such.

"Let's wait until we have a final product," Megan said. "Maybe give us a few days to finalize everything? That way we can show the actual boxes people will receive, not just samples."

"Smart," Jan agreed. "Creates more accurate expectations. Meanwhile, I'll save the photos I just took and maybe create a video montage or something fun of you all creating the boxes. That could be effective on social media."

They spent another thirty minutes finalizing details and making lists of what still needed to be done. By the time they finished, Megan had pages of notes, a clear production timeline, and a genuine sense of accomplishment.

"I should probably get back out front," Leslie said, checking her phone. "Ada needs help with the ornament personalization station, and we have a birthday party group coming in at two."

Megan began packing her supplies back into the bins, organizing as she went. Kyle immediately moved to help, and together they carried everything back to her car.

"Want to grab lunch before heading to the shop?" Kyle asked as she closed her trunk. "There's that sandwich place on—"

"Actually," Megan interrupted gently, "I packed a lunch. I was thinking I'd eat in my office at Sugar & Spice and spend some quiet time working through logistics before we start experimenting in the kitchen."

She saw something flicker across Kyle's face—disappointment, maybe, or concern—but it was gone so quickly she might have imagined it.

"That's fine," he said. "Should I meet you there in an hour?"

"Perfect." Megan smiled up at him, and his expression softened. "Thanks for making the promotional materials and for being so willing to adjust things. That means a lot to me."

"We're partners," Kyle said simply. "That means listening to each other."

Kyle reached out and squeezed her hand briefly. "See you in an hour," he said.

"See you then."

Megan climbed into her car and watched Kyle walk back toward the shop's rear entrance, his hands in his pockets, his breath fogging in the cold air.

She started the engine and pulled out of the alley, pointing her car toward Sugar & Spice. The morning had been good—really good—but she needed this time alone to process everything. To think through the production schedule, yes, but also to sit with this growing feeling in her chest that felt suspiciously like happiness.

The kind of happiness that scared her because it had so much potential to be lost.

"Focus, Megan. You deserve to be happy. Just take it one thing at a time," she said out loud. "One thing at a time."

Chapter 27

Kyle pushed through the kitchen door carrying three coffees just as Megan was explaining the gift box collaboration to Kay.

"—and that's the basic concept," Megan said, looking up as Kyle entered. "Three price tiers, three themes, and exclusive chocolates that customers can only get in certain boxes."

Kay's eyes had brightened considerably during Megan's explanation, and now she turned her attention to the cups Kyle was distributing. "You're a lifesaver."

"I figured everyone could use some caffeine." Kyle handed Megan her cup—medium with cream, exactly how she liked it—and she felt a small flutter of warmth that he'd remembered without asking.

"So what do you think?" Megan asked Kay, wrapping her hands around the cup's heat. "Is it feasible? Can we produce specialty items for all three themes without disrupting our regular production schedule?"

Kay took a long sip of coffee, her expression thoughtful as she considered the question. "Not only is it feasible, it's brilliant. The cross-promotion alone will drive traffic to both stores, and exclusive items create urgency." She set her cup down on the counter and moved to the supply cabinet, already mentally cataloging ingredients. "For the traditional Christmas boxes, I agree with the chocolate bells dusted with edible gold. For Winter Wonderland—" She paused, her face lighting up with sudden inspiration. "What about white chocolate peppermint bark with light blue swirls and silver sugar crystals? It would be stunning and on theme."

"That's perfect," Megan said, excitement building in her chest. "And for Nostalgic Vintage?"

"Ribbon candy, definitely, just as you suggested. And maybe some of those chocolate drops that look vintage—the ones I make with the old-fashioned molds. We can add edible gold or silver dust to those as well. Plus, we can even shake the candy selection up and make snowflakes, Christmas trees, or just whatever we're in the mood to make. But we need to be certain they stand out as different and special from what we offer in the store. When do we need samples?"

"As soon as possible. We want to launch the boxes within the next few days or so."

"Then let's get started." Kay tied on her apron with quick, efficient movements. "Megan, are you comfortable handling the molded chocolates? The bells, snowflakes, or whatever you have in mind?"

"Yes. I can do those."

"Good." Kay's smile was approving. "Kyle, you're on assistant duty. Follow Megan's lead and try not to break anything." Her tone was teasing but warm.

"I'll do my best," Kyle said, rolling up his sleeves.

They fell into a comfortable rhythm quickly. Kay set up her station for the peppermint bark, measuring white chocolate with the precision of someone who'd done this thousands of times—her movements automatic, no need to consult recipes or measurements. Megan gathered molds from the storage shelf—delicate bell shapes with intricate details and snowflakes with lacy patterns—and began the process of tempering chocolate.

"Temperature is everything," she said, more to herself than to Kyle, but he moved closer to watch. "If it's too hot, the chocolate won't set properly. Too cool, and it won't flow into the molds correctly."

She used the digital thermometer to check the melted chocolate, stirring slowly with a silicone spatula and watching the numbers climb and then carefully fall. The motion was meditative, requiring focus but no longer causing the anxiety it had weeks ago when everything felt overwhelming and uncertain. Her hands were steady now, confident.

"Ninety degrees," she said, checking the display again. "Perfect."

"You've gotten really good at this," Kyle observed, watching her pour chocolate into the bell molds with smooth, even movements that left no air pockets.

"Kay's a good teacher, and I've spent so much of my spare time in this kitchen just practicing." Megan glanced at the older woman, who was spreading melted white chocolate across a parchment-lined sheet pan with a large offset spatula, creating an even layer.

"I believe candy making is in your blood, Megan. You're a good student too," Kay said without looking up from her work. "Being teachable is a skill. Not everyone has it."

Megan felt her face warm with the compliment. She tapped the molds gently against the counter in a rhythmic pattern, releasing any trapped air bubbles that might create imperfections, then used a scraper to remove excess chocolate from the edges with precise strokes. The movements had become almost automatic, her muscle memory taking over.

"Now we wait for them to set," she said, sliding the molds carefully into the refrigerator. "Snowflakes next."

They worked for the better part of an hour, falling into an easy collaboration that felt natural and unforced. Kay drizzled light blue-tinted white chocolate across her peppermint bark in artistic swirls that looked almost too beautiful to eat, then added a generous shower of silver sugar crystals that caught the overhead lights and sparkled like fresh snow. Megan and Kyle produced dozens of chocolate bells and snowflakes, each one emerging from its mold with satisfying perfection—no cracks, no air bubbles, just clean lines and beautiful detail.

"These are going to look amazing in the boxes," Kyle said, examining a finished snowflake with genuine appreciation. The detail was remarkable—every point and curve visible in the dark chocolate, each delicate arm of the snowflake perfectly formed.

"Assuming I don't mess up the gold dust," Megan said, holding up a small container of edible shimmer that caught the light.

"You won't," Kay said with quiet confidence, glancing up from where she was breaking her finished peppermint bark into irregular, rustic-looking pieces. "Just use the fine brush and dust lightly. Less is more with shimmer."

Megan dipped the brush carefully and swept gold across the surface of a bell with light, feathery strokes. The transformation was immediate and dramatic—the chocolate went from simple to elegant with just that touch of shimmer, catching the light with every movement.

"See?" Kay smiled with satisfaction. "You've got this."

They were arranging finished pieces on wax paper, creating an attractive display, when Megan's phone buzzed in her pocket. She wiped chocolate from her fingers with a damp towel and checked the screen. A text from Mitch:

Appliances were delivered, and I just finished installing them. Come see when you get a chance.

Her heart jumped with anticipation. "The appliances are here."

"For the apartment?" Kay asked.

"Yes." Megan looked at the chocolate spread across the counter. "We should go look."

"Absolutely, we should." Kay was already untying her apron.

They cleaned their hands quickly at the sink, scrubbing away chocolate residue, and headed through the stockroom to the back door. The alley was cold and bright, afternoon sun glinting off the metal handrail of the stairs that led up to the apartment. Megan climbed first, her pulse quickening with each step.

The apartment door was propped open with a paint can, and she could hear a high-pitched whine from a machine that Mitch was using. She stepped through the doorway and stopped abruptly, her breath catching.

The transformation was dramatic.

The living room floor gleamed with fresh stain—a warm honey color that made the entire space feel larger and more inviting than she'd imagined possible. The wood grain was visible beneath the finish, creating natural patterns that added character. The new white cabinets lined the walls of the kitchen space, their clean lines a stark contrast to the warped, stained units that had been there before. The island stood proudly in the center, topped with a butcher block countertop that matched the floor perfectly, creating visual continuity.

And the appliances. The stainless-steel refrigerator stood against the far wall, its surface still protected by blue film, looking modern and efficient. The stove gleamed beside it. A microwave sat on the counter, waiting to be mounted above the stove.

"Megan!"

Mitch emerged from one of the bedrooms, wiping his hands on a rag tucked into his belt. Sawdust clung to his flannel shirt and jeans, and there was a streak of dark stain across his forearm like war paint.

"What do you think?" he asked, gesturing around the space with obvious pride in his work.

"It's incredible," Megan said, her voice coming out steadier than she felt. This was real. This was actually happening. Her own apartment. Her own space. "Everything looks amazing, Mitch. Really amazing."

"Still got some work to do." Mitch pointed toward the living room, where new windows leaned against the wall in a neat row, still wrapped in protective plastic with shipping labels visible. "Got two of my guys coming this afternoon to start on the window installation. If everything goes smoothly—no surprises with the frames or any rot I didn't catch—we should have this place finished by the end of next week."

"End of next week," Megan repeated, the timeline suddenly very real and immediate. That was soon. That was hardly any time at all.

"The trim work will go fast once the windows are in," Mitch continued. "Then just final paint touch-ups, and you're good to move in. Probably looking at about five or six days total if the weather cooperates."

Kyle had come up behind Megan, and she felt his presence like warmth at her back, solid and reassuring. "It looks great, Dad."

"Thanks, son. I really appreciate all your help so far." Mitch's gaze moved between them with quiet assessment, something knowing in his expression. "Leslie mentioned you two were working together this afternoon in the kitchen downstairs. Did you get your chocolate work done?"

"For today," Megan said. "We made good progress on samples."

"More than good," Kyle added. "Everything these women have made looks amazing."

Kay had been walking slowly through the space, running her hand along the smooth surface of the new countertop, testing the cabinet doors, and peering into the bedroom where Mitch had been working. Now she stood in the middle of the living room, her expression distant and thoughtful, as if seeing something beyond the present moment.

"You okay, Kay?" Megan asked.

"I lived here once," Kay said. "Did you know that?"

Megan shook her head, surprised by this revelation.

"When my husband, Tim, and I got married—gosh, it feels like that was just yesterday, but it's been decades now—we needed a place to stay while our house was being built. This apartment was empty at the time." Kay's voice held a wistfulness Megan had never heard before, softer and more vulnerable than her usual confident tone. "Phyllis rented it to us for almost nothing. Said she was happy to have the space occupied."

She walked toward a window overlooking Mistletoe Lane, though the view was currently semi-blocked by thick plastic sheeting taped over the frame to try to block out the cold from the old window removal.

"We had dinner here with her every Sunday evening," Kay continued, her voice taking on the quality of someone remembering something precious. "Phyllis would come up those back stairs with a pie or a casserole—she was an excellent cook, not just a candy maker—and we'd sit at that little table that used to be right here." She indicated a spot near where the island now stood. "She'd tell us stories about her travels and the experiences she had, about the town's history, and about her life. Tim loved her chocolate fudge more than anything. She always brought extra just for him, wrapped in wax paper."

Megan felt her chest tighten with emotion, imagining a younger Kay and her husband sitting with Phyllis, sharing meals and stories, and building memories.

"I'm glad it's you getting this place," Kay said, turning back to Megan with a warm smile. "Phyllis would be thrilled to know you're here, making it yours."

"I think she would be happy too," Megan said quietly, her voice thick.

Kay crossed the room and pulled Megan into a side hug, the gesture both maternal and supportive, her arm warm and solid around Megan's shoulders. "Everything's coming together for you. The shop, this apartment, and your life here. I'm delighted to see it."

Megan leaned into the embrace briefly, drawing strength from Kay's steadiness. "It does feel like things are working out."

"Because you're making them work out. You're showing up every day, learning, and trying your best. That matters more than talent or luck. That's what builds a life."

Mitch had returned to the bedroom, the sound of his work resuming. Kyle moved to examine the cabinets more closely, running his hand along the smooth doors, testing the hinges, and giving Megan and Kay their moment together.

Megan looked around the apartment again—at the gleaming floors that reflected the afternoon light, the new cabinets with their promise of organized storage, and the appliances waiting to be used for her first meal here. In a week, this would be ready. In a week, she could move out of the cabin and into her own space. Her permanent space.

The realization should have felt purely exciting. Instead, it felt enormous.

"I need furniture," she said suddenly, the practical concern cutting through the emotion.

Kay laughed, the sound breaking the wistful mood. "Yes, you do. The place will echo without it."

Megan turned to Kyle, who was testing the soft-close mechanism on one of the cabinet doors with an obvious appreciation for the craftsmanship. "You ready for another adventure?"

He looked up, eyebrows raised with interest. "What kind of adventure?"

"The furniture shopping kind. Tomorrow morning. Nine o'clock." Megan felt her confidence building as she spoke. "Pick me up at the cabin and be prepared to help me make important decisions about couches and tables and," she gestured vaguely at the empty space, "all of it."

Kyle's smile was slow and genuine, lighting up his whole face. "I'm in."

"Then it's a date, and lunch is on me this time."

"Deal," Kyle said.

Kay was watching them with an expression Megan couldn't quite read—something knowing and gentle and approving all at once, like she could see something they hadn't fully acknowledged yet.

"Well, let's get back to work," Kay said, breaking the moment. "I need to finish that peppermint bark and get it boxed up before closing."

They descended the stairs together. At the bottom, Kay paused and turned to face Megan directly.

"You deserve this, Megan," she said quietly but firmly. "The apartment, the business, all of it. Don't forget that."

"I'm trying not to," Megan said, and meant it completely.

Kay headed into the shop through the stockroom door, leaving Megan and Kyle standing in the alley.

"You okay?" Kyle asked, studying her face.

"Yeah. I'm better than okay," Megan said, looking up at the apartment, at the space that would soon be hers—truly, permanently hers.

Kyle's hand found hers, their fingers threading together naturally, his palm warm against her cold fingers. "For what it's worth, I think Kay's right. You deserve all of this."

Megan squeezed his hand, letting the warmth of his palm seep into her cold fingers and spread up her arm. "I'm not sure if I deserve all the good that's come my way, but I do appreciate it all. Every bit of it."

They stood there for another moment, hands clasped, the town's late afternoon sounds filtering into their quiet space—distant car engines, a dog barking somewhere down the block, and the gentle sound of Christmas music floating in the air from outdoor speakers at the nearby diner playing "Joy to the World."

Megan smiled, the expression coming easily and genuinely. Life was working. The shop was thriving. The apartment would be ready soon. She had friends, a community, and a purpose. She had Kyle standing beside her, solid and present and choosing to be here, choosing her.

For once, she let herself enjoy the contentment without immediately searching for what could go wrong, without waiting for the other shoe to drop. Things were going well. She was allowed to enjoy that. She was allowed to be happy.

Tomorrow, they'd shop for furniture—picking out pieces that would make the apartment feel like home. Next week, she'd move into her own space. The gift boxes would launch, the holiday season would ramp up even more, and her life would continue building itself into something she'd never imagined possible when she'd driven into Mistletoe Falls just weeks ago.

The thought should have terrified her. Instead, standing here with Kyle's hand in hers and the promise of her own apartment waiting above, it just felt right.

Chapter 28

Kyle pulled into the massive parking lot of Furniture World, and Megan clutched her small notebook like a lifeline, every room dimension of her apartment written in her careful handwriting.

"You ready for this?" Kyle asked, putting the truck in park and turning to look at her.

Megan studied the sprawling building in front of them—easily the size of three warehouses combined, with brightly colored banners advertising everything from bedroom sets to dining room tables flapping in the November breeze. The sheer scale of it was intimidating.

"I think so," she said, opening her door and stepping down from the truck. "I've got measurements and a budget in mind. Let's do this."

They walked across the parking lot, weaving between cars and following painted arrows toward the main entrance. The automatic doors whooshed open as they approached, and a wave of heated air hit them along with the scent of new furniture—fabric, wood polish, leather, and that indefinable smell of newness and possibility.

A salesperson approached immediately—a woman in her forties with shoulder-length brown hair, a warm smile, and a name tag that read "Sharon."

"Good morning! Welcome to Furniture World. What brings you in today?"

"I'm furnishing an apartment," Megan said, already feeling more confident just by stating her purpose. "Living room, small office, bedroom, and I need a set of bar stools for a kitchen island."

"Wonderful! Are you working with a particular budget?"

"I am. Nothing extravagant, but I want quality furniture that'll last."

"Smart approach." Sharon gestured toward the showroom with a welcoming sweep of her arm. "Let's start with the living room and work our way through. I'll show you options at different price points, and you let me know what feels right."

They followed her into a massive space filled with living room displays that seemed to stretch endlessly. Couches, sectionals, chairs, and coffee tables stretched in every direction, arranged in carefully styled vignettes that looked like they belonged in home magazines—complete with throw pillows, decorative lamps, and artfully placed books.

Megan pulled out her notebook, flipping to the first page. "The living room is about fourteen by sixteen feet. I need seating, a coffee table, and maybe an end table or two."

Sharon led them to a section featuring mid-range furniture with price tags that didn't make Megan's stomach clench. "These pieces are popular with first-time furniture buyers—good construction, comfortable, and they'll hold up well. This sectional here," she indicated a soft tan L-shaped couch with clean lines, "is on sale this week. Normally twenty-two hundred, marked down to eighteen."

Megan sat on it, testing the cushions by shifting her weight from side to side. Firm but not hard. The fabric felt durable under her fingers, not the cheap material that would pill after a few months. She checked the tag, verifying the price was just as Sharon had mentioned, and did quick mental math. Eighteen hundred was manageable.

"What about this one?" Kyle had wandered to a different display nearby, pointing to a cream-colored sectional with rolled arms and an array of decorative pillows in shades of blue and gray. The price tag read thirty-four hundred.

"It's beautiful," Megan said honestly, standing and walking over to examine it more closely. The fabric was noticeably softer, almost luxurious to the touch, and the construction more substantial—she could tell just by looking at the frame. "But it's almost double the price."

"It is," Kyle agreed easily. "Just thought I'd point it out."

Megan ran her hand along the rolled arm, appreciating the quality even as she knew it wasn't practical for her budget. "I believe I will stick with the tan one. It fits my budget better, and it's still nice. It'll work perfectly in the space."

"Makes sense," Kyle said. "What about a coffee table?"

They spent the next hour moving through the living room section, Megan carefully evaluating each piece against her budget and measurements. She selected a simple rectangular coffee table in dark wood with a lower shelf for storage and two matching end tables that would flank the sectional. Kyle offered opinions when asked—commenting on sturdiness or suggesting which finish might work better—but didn't push when she chose differently than he might have.

"Office furniture next?" Sharon asked, consulting her tablet and making quick notes about Megan's selections.

"Yes. I have a spare bedroom that's going to be my office." Megan flipped to a new page in her notebook where she'd sketched a rough floor plan. "Ten by twelve feet. I just need a desk and chair for now."

The office section was smaller but well-stocked with everything from elaborate executive desks to simple writing tables. Megan gravitated toward a streamlined desk in warm oak with three drawers on one side and a built-in filing system. It was functional without being boring, and the price was reasonable.

The chair took longer—she tested five different options, rolling back and forth, adjusting heights, and checking lumbar support. Finally, she found one that offered good back support without being overly expensive, upholstered in a dark gray fabric that would hide inevitable wear.

Kyle observed as she made detailed notes about the chair's model number, color, and price, a slight smile playing at his lips.

"What?" Megan asked, noticing his expression.

"Nothing. You're just well-organized about this."

"I would rather not get home and realize I forgot what I bought," she said, closing her notebook. "These are big purchases."

They moved to the kitchen and dining area next, weaving through displays of farmhouse tables and modern dining sets. Megan had decided against a dining table—the apartment's eat-in kitchen was small, and the island would serve for most meals. But she needed bar stools.

"How many?" Sharon asked.

"Three," Megan said decisively. "The island has space for four, but three feels less crowded and gives people room to move around."

The bar stool selection was overwhelming—an entire wall of options. Metal frames, wooden seats, upholstered backs, swivel bases, different heights, various finishes.

Megan climbed onto the first option—a sleek metal stool with a minimalist design and a thin cushion. Too tall. Her feet dangled awkwardly several inches above the footrest.

The second one looked perfect but wobbled alarmingly when she sat down, the base shifting on its support. "That can't be safe."

Kyle tried the third one, a sturdy wooden stool with a cushioned seat in charcoal gray. He sat down and tested its stability. "This one's solid."

Megan tested it herself, appreciating the way Kyle had warmed the seat. The height was perfect, her feet resting comfortably on the metal footrest. The seat was comfortable without being too soft—firm enough to provide support during long meals. And the price—a hundred and twenty each—fit her budget without strain.

"I'll take three of these," she told Sharon.

"Excellent choice." Sharon made notes on her tablet with quick, efficient taps. "Now for the bedroom?"

"Lead the way."

The bedroom section was at the back of the store, and as they walked through it, passing displays of platform beds and canopy frames, Megan's eyes kept catching on different sets. Some were too modern, all sharp lines and minimalist design that felt cold. Others were too ornate, heavy with carvings and decorative details that would overwhelm her space.

Then she saw it.

A sleigh bed in rich cherry wood, with a headboard and footboard that curved in graceful lines that drew the eye. Two matching nightstands flanked the bed, each with three drawers and brushed nickel hardware that caught the overhead lights. A dresser with a large mirror completed the set, the wood grain consistent and beautiful across all pieces.

Megan stopped walking abruptly.

"You okay?" Kyle asked, nearly bumping into her.

"That one," she said, pointing.

They approached the display slowly, and Megan ran her hand along the smooth footboard. The wood was flawless; the finish shone under the light. The craftsmanship was evident in every detail of the bedroom set—the way the dresser drawers slid open effortlessly on ball-bearing glides, the subtle decorative touches on the mirror frame that added elegance without fussiness, and the sturdy construction that promised decades of use.

She looked at the price tag and felt her breath catch in her throat.

Thirty-eight hundred for the complete set.

That was significantly more than she'd planned to spend on the bedroom. More than double her budget for this one room.

"I'll give you two a moment," Sharon said tactfully, reading the situation with professional intuition, and drifting toward another customer examining a four-poster bed.

Megan pulled out her notebook and started calculating with careful precision, her pen moving across the page. The living room furniture, office pieces, and bar stools totaled about four thousand. She'd planned to spend around twelve hundred on the bedroom, bringing her total to just over five thousand—a number that had felt reasonable, manageable. If she bought this set instead, her total would be nearly eight thousand.

"What are you thinking?" Kyle asked quietly, his voice not pushing, just curious.

"I'm thinking it's expensive," Megan said, but she couldn't take her eyes off the bed—the way the wood gleamed, the graceful curves, the promise of waking up to something beautiful every morning. "I'm thinking I should look at something more practical."

Kyle was silent for a moment, standing beside her but giving her space to think. "What do you want to do?"

"I want to buy it," Megan admitted, the words coming out almost reluctantly.

"Then go for it."

"It's expensive."

"This is furniture you'll use every single day for years, Megan." Kyle's voice was gentle but certain. "This is the only thing all day that actually made you stop in your tracks. You're in love with this bedroom set."

Megan looked at her notebook again, at all her careful calculations and conservative choices. She'd been so sensible with everything else. The living room furniture was practical and affordable. The office pieces were functional. The bar stools were simple and sturdy.

"I haven't had a matching bedroom set since I was a little girl," she said quietly, her voice taking on a wistful quality. "Mom and Dad bought me a white set with gold trim when I was eight. I loved it so much—I felt like a princess every time I went to bed."

Kyle moved closer, his presence warm and steady beside her, close enough that their shoulders almost touched. "Then this seems important to you."

"It feels indulgent."

"It sounds to me like you'd be giving yourself something you've wanted for years. Something you deserve."

Megan closed her notebook slowly and looked at the bedroom set again—really looked at it, imagining it in her apartment. In her space above the shop, where she'd wake up every morning and go to sleep every night. This could be the first thing she saw each day and the last thing before she turned out the lights.

"I'm going to buy it," she said, and as soon as the words left her mouth, she felt certainty settle over her like a warm blanket. "I'm going to splurge on this one thing because I love it, and because I can, and because I deserve to have something beautiful."

Kyle's smile was slow and genuine, lighting up his entire face.

Sharon reappeared with perfect timing, as if she'd been watching from a distance. "Have we decided?"

"Yes," Megan said firmly, her voice strong and confident. "I'd like the cherry sleigh bed set—the complete bedroom collection."

"Wonderful choice. It's one of our best pieces—the craftsmanship is exceptional." Sharon made notes on her tablet with obvious approval. "Let me get everything totaled for you, and then we'll schedule delivery."

They followed her to the checkout desk at the front of the store, passing through the showroom they'd spent the morning exploring. Megan watched the total climb on the computer screen—sectional, coffee table, end tables, desk, chair, bar stools, and a bedroom set. Each item appeared with its price, the numbers adding up steadily. The final number appeared: seventy-eight hundred and forty-three dollars, including delivery.

Her hand trembled slightly as she pulled out her debit card, the small piece of plastic suddenly feeling significant and weighty. But she completed the transaction without hesitation, sliding the card through the reader and entering her PIN with steady fingers.

"Delivery will be Friday of next week," Sharon said, handing Megan a printed receipt still warm from the printer. "They'll call the day before to confirm a time window. Usually morning or afternoon."

"Perfect," Megan said, tucking the receipt carefully into her notebook between pages where it wouldn't get bent or lost. "Thank you for all your help today."

"My pleasure. Congratulations on your new furniture."

They walked toward the exit doors and out into the parking lot. The afternoon sun was bright and slightly warmer than the morning had been, making Megan squint as they headed toward Kyle's truck parked several rows away.

"How do you feel?" Kyle asked as they walked.

"Slightly numb and completely excited," Megan admitted with a breathless laugh. "I just spent almost eight thousand dollars in one morning, and I'm happy I don't have to do that again anytime soon."

Kyle laughed, the sound warm and genuine as he pulled his keys from his pocket. He held the passenger door open for Megan, and she climbed into the truck and fastened her seatbelt.

Her stomach growled loudly enough that Kyle heard it.

"Hungry," he said with a grin as he closed her door and walked around to the driver's side.

"Starving, actually." Megan pulled out her phone and opened a restaurant search app as Kyle climbed in and started the engine. "Let's see what's nearby."

She scrolled through the options. Chain restaurants with familiar logos, pizza places advertising lunch specials, and a few cafes. Then one caught her eye: The Old Mill Restaurant. The photos showed a rustic building beside a creek with a water wheel; the menu featured comfort food and home cooking—meatloaf, fried chicken, and cornbread.

"What about this place?" She held up her phone to show Kyle, angling the screen so he could see. "The Old Mill Restaurant. It looks charming."

Kyle's face lit up with recognition. "Oh, I love that place. Haven't been in a while, but their food is excellent. They make everything from scratch. Definitely want to go there."

"Perfect, let's go." Megan set her phone down in the cup holder, satisfied with the choice.

Kyle pulled out of the parking lot and navigated through Pigeon Forge's busy streets with practiced ease. The town was packed with tourists even on a Sunday in late November—families walking between attractions with shopping bags, children pointing excitedly at storefronts, and vehicles filling the streets and every available parking space. The traffic moved slowly but steadily.

At a red light, Kyle reached over and took her hand, threading their fingers together with a naturalness that made Megan's chest warm. The gesture had become familiar, expected, and right.

Megan looked at their joined hands resting on the center console and felt something shift inside her. This morning she'd been nervous about spending money—worrying about choosing the wrong furniture or spending too much. Now, driving through an unfamiliar tourist town with furniture being delivered to her very own apartment next week, she felt different.

She felt like she held the world in her hands.

Not because everything was perfect or because she'd figured everything out. Not because she'd stopped being afraid or stopped doubting herself completely. But because she was making choices—actual choices about her life, her space, her future and she wasn't paralyzed by fear anymore. She had a place that was hers, work that mattered and brought satisfaction, and someone beside her who let her make her own decisions while still being there when she needed support.

The light turned green, and Kyle accelerated smoothly into traffic, his thumb rubbing gentle circles against the back of her hand in a rhythm that felt like a heartbeat.

Megan watched the town pass by her window—shops decorated for Christmas, restaurants with people visible through windows, families walking together, people living their ordinary, extraordinary lives—and let herself sit fully in this moment. Happy. Content. Grateful. Exactly where she wanted to be, with exactly who she wanted beside her.

Chapter 29

Megan walked through The Christmas Shop's stockroom door she had propped open, carrying the third bin of chocolates, as Kyle followed, carrying another.

"There's more?" Leslie asked, laughing as she cleared more space on the large worktable.

"I may have gone a little overboard," Megan said, setting the bin down carefully.

"A little?" Kyle set his bin beside hers and headed back toward the alley door. "Your car looks like a candy warehouse."

By the time they'd brought in all five bins and three enormous shopping bags, the worktable was covered. Megan began unpacking, and Leslie moved closer to examine the contents.

"Megan, these are gorgeous," Leslie said, picking up a cellophane bag tied with red ribbon. Through the clear plastic, chocolate bells dusted with gold shimmered in the overhead lights.

"Thanks. Kay, Linda, Tonya, and I worked really hard on these. We wanted everything to look special."

She arranged items on the table—boxes with clear lids showing chocolate snowflakes, bags of peppermint bark with blue and silver accents, ribbon candy in vintage-style packaging, and butterscotch disks wrapped in gold foil. Each piece had been carefully packaged with ribbons, festive stickers, or decorative tags.

"I stayed at the shop until after midnight last night finishing everything up," Megan said, pulling out more packages. "I wanted to make sure every detail was perfect—the ribbons, the tags, everything."

"These are all incredible," Leslie said, examining a box of snowflakes.

Kyle was studying the package of chocolate bells he held. "These are better than what I've seen in shops in Gatlinburg."

"Stop, you're making me blush," Megan said, but she couldn't hide her smile.

"I'm serious." Kyle set the bell down carefully and met her eyes. "You've really mastered this."

The moment stretched between them, warm and significant, until Leslie cleared her throat.

"Should we start assembling?" She gestured at the supplies she and Kyle had already gathered—decorative boxes in various sizes, tissue paper in various colors, ribbons, and the promotional coupons Kyle had designed. "I'm excited to see how these come together."

Megan pulled out her notebook, where she'd sketched rough layouts for each design.

"For the traditional Christmas," she said, pointing to her drawing, "I'm thinking red boxes as the base, chocolate bells and peppermint bark as the main candy features, then ornaments and whatever else your shop will be contributing."

"Perfect." Leslie was already selecting ornaments from the inventory she'd set aside—classic red and green glass balls, small wooden nutcrackers, and miniature wreaths.

They worked side by side, experimenting with arrangements. Kyle proved surprisingly good at the visual composition, suggesting when to add more tissue paper or filler or adjust an item's placement. Leslie had an instinctive eye for balance, knowing exactly when a box looked too crowded or too sparse.

"Hand me that roll of gold ribbon," Megan said, and Kyle passed it to her, their fingers brushing in the exchange.

She felt the now-familiar spark of awareness but kept her focus on the box she was arranging. The traditional Christmas box was coming together beautifully—tissue paper, a box of chocolate, peppermint bark wrapped in cellophane beside them, three ornaments nestled in carefully, a sprig of artificial holly tucked along the edge, and Kyle's promotional coupon tucked in the corner.

"What do you think?" Megan stepped back so that they could all see.

"I love it," Leslie said immediately. "Festive without being over the top."

Kyle was nodding. "The balance is good. Nothing's fighting for attention."

They created several more traditional Christmas boxes before moving on to Winter Wonderland. These used silver boxes with white tissue paper, white chocolate snowflakes, silver and blue-accented peppermint bark, and Leslie's collection of silver and blue ornaments.

"Remember to tuck the coupon where it's visible but not covering the chocolate," Kyle said, demonstrating on the box he was working on.

"Yes, boss," Megan teased, and he grinned at her.

"Just trying to be helpful."

"You're doing great," she assured him, her hand resting briefly on his arm.

The Nostalgic Vintage boxes proved the most challenging. They required careful color coordination—kraft paper boxes, cream tissue, the vintage-style ribbon candy, butterscotch disks, chocolate snowflakes, and antique-looking ornaments.

"This one needs something," Leslie said, studying the box she'd just assembled.

Megan looked at it, then rummaged through her supplies. "What about these?" She pulled out the small tags she'd made, each stamped with "Handcrafted with Love" in old-fashioned script.

"Perfect." Leslie added the tag, and suddenly the whole box came together.

They worked for nearly three hours, falling into an easy rhythm. Megan would prepare the candy elements, Kyle would arrange the coupons and help with placement, and Leslie would add the ornaments and finishing touches. Between them, they created thirty boxes.

"These are going to sell so fast," Leslie said, stepping back to admire their work.

"Speaking of which," Kyle said, glancing at his watch, "we should probably get photos before we divide everything up."

"Great minds think alike; I just sent Jan a text," Leslie said.

The stockroom door opened, and Jan entered with her camera in hand. She stopped when she saw the table. "Oh, these are beautiful."

"Right?" Leslie moved to give Jan better access to the display.

Jan circled the table, snapping photos from different angles while Megan and Leslie adjusted boxes for the best presentation—turning items to catch the light, creating small groupings, and ensuring variety was visible.

"Can you all stand behind the table?" Jan asked. "I want some shots with the creators."

Afterward, Megan and Leslie joined in, both taking pictures with their phones as well—individual shots of each box type, group photos of all three themes together, and close-ups of the chocolate details. Megan found herself enjoying the process, proud of what they'd created.

"I'll edit the photos I took and send them to both of you in a couple of hours," Jan said, reviewing images on her camera's display. "These are really going to pop on social media."

"Thanks, Jan," Megan said. "Savannah and I will be working on creating and scheduling posts, so the timing will be perfect."

After Jan left, they began dividing inventory. Fifteen boxes would stay at The Christmas Shop, and fifteen would go to Sugar & Spice.

"I have a feeling we will be getting together again soon to make more of these," Leslie said.

"I agree; I don't think either of us will have any problem selling these."

Kyle had been making notes on his phone. "I need to distribute flyers around town—City Hall, the visitors bureau, and community boards. Want to ride with me?"

Megan saw the hope in his expression. Part of her wanted to say yes, to spend the afternoon driving around with him, and to enjoy his company.

But she had work to do.

"I should get back to Sugar & Spice," she said. "I need to price these boxes and get them displayed in the store. And I'm eager to work with Savannah on social media. Leslie and I already discussed launching these simultaneously."

Kyle's expression shifted slightly—not quite disappointment, but close. Then he smiled. "That makes sense. You've got a lot to do this afternoon, I get it."

Megan felt both relieved and slightly guilty for declining. But this was the right call, and she knew it.

"Let me help you load your car up," Kyle said.

They carried boxes out to Megan's car parked in the alley. The gift boxes took up more space than she'd anticipated—they could only fit six boxes carefully arranged in the trunk and a few in the back seat, along with two bins of individual candy packages they hadn't used.

"The rest will have to go in my truck," Kyle said. "I'll follow you over and drop them off before I head out with the flyers."

"You don't have to; I can make two trips."

"I want to," Kyle interrupted gently. "It's on my way anyway."

They loaded the remaining boxes and supplies into Kyle's truck, and Megan climbed into her car. As she pulled out of the alley, she checked her rearview mirror and saw Kyle's truck behind her, following at a comfortable distance.

The drive to Sugar & Spice took less than ten minutes, even with all the tourist traffic that had doubled after Thanksgiving through Mistletoe Falls' downtown area. The town was busy with Wednesday afternoon shoppers—people carrying bags, stopping to peer in windows, and couples walking hand in hand. Christmas decorations sparkled in every storefront, and garland wrapped around streetlights swayed gently in the breeze.

Megan parked in the alley behind Sugar & Spice, and Kyle pulled in beside her. Together, they carried the remaining boxes into the stockroom.

"The boxes turned out even better than I'd imagined," Megan said as they set down the last load.

"They really did." Kyle stood close enough that she could see the flecks of gold in his hazel eyes. "You should be proud."

"I am," she said, and meant it completely.

His hand found hers, their fingers threading together naturally. "I'll see you soon?"

"Soon," she agreed.

He squeezed her hand gently, then headed back outside. Megan followed him to the door and watched as he walked to his truck, climbed in, and pulled out of the lot with a wave.

She stood there for a moment, thinking before heading back inside to start pricing the gift boxes.

Kyle was becoming someone she couldn't imagine her life without.

The realization settled over her quietly, without fanfare or panic. Just a simple truth that felt both significant and completely natural.

She wanted to be with him. Wanted his company, his support, and his presence in her life.

Chapter 30

The delivery truck's backup beeping echoed in the alley below, and Megan stood watching from the landing at the top of the stairs outside her apartment.

The morning air was crisp, carrying the scent of pine from the mountains and coffee from the cafe nearby. She wrapped her arms around herself, watching as the massive truck maneuvered into position. The driver cut the engine, and suddenly the alley fell quiet except for the sounds of downtown Mistletoe Falls coming to life—shop doors opening, cheerful greetings called between business owners, and the gentle background music from outdoor speakers playing "Silver Bells."

Four men climbed out of the extended cab delivery truck. One rolled up the back door to reveal her furniture secured inside.

"Morning!" The driver, a man in his fifties with graying hair and a clipboard, said as he approached the bottom of the stairs. "Megan Caldwell?"

"That's me."

"I'm Frank. We've got quite a haul for you today." He consulted his clipboard, flipping through pages. "Sectional sofa, coffee table, two end tables, bedroom set with four pieces, office desk, office chair, and three bar stools. That sound right?"

"Yes, that's everything."

Frank looked up at the stairs, assessing the narrow width and the steep climb with the practiced eye of someone who'd navigated countless difficult deliveries. "These stairs gonna hold four of us carrying furniture?"

"They're brand new; I sure hope they can handle the weight," Megan said while grinning.

"Well... let's get this show on the road then." Frank said as he turned to his crew.

They moved with efficient coordination born from years of working together, and within minutes the first end table was making its way up the stairs wrapped in a heavy blanket.

Megan held the apartment door open as they maneuvered the table inside.

"Where do you want this, ma'am?" Frank asked.

"Living room, please." She gestured toward the space she'd mentally arranged dozens of times over the past few days.

They set the table down gently, removed the blanket, and disappeared back down the stairs without wasting time.

The second end table followed, then the coffee table—simple, solid, and exactly what she'd chosen. Megan stood in her living room watching the furniture take shape, feeling the space begin to transform from empty potential into actual living space.

"Megan!"

The voice came from outside, and Megan stepped out onto the landing to find Kay, Linda, Beth, Tonya, and Savannah clustered at the bottom of the stairs, all of them holding wrapped packages with bright bows and cheerful paper.

Her heart jumped in her chest, surprise flooding through her. "What's going on? Who's watching the shop?"

"Chelsea and Morgan came in early," Kay called up, referring to the two part-time employees, whom they had hired and trained last week. "We asked them to cover for a bit. We have a surprise for you."

"Come on down!" Beth added, her smile wide and mischievous. "Or we can come up. Actually, we're coming up."

They ascended the stairs in a parade of laughter and wrapped gifts, and Megan found herself pressed back into the apartment as they filed through the door.

"Surprise!" Savannah announced, holding her package high. "We're throwing you a housewarming party."

"What?" Megan's voice came out higher than intended, emotion already tightening her throat. "You planned this for me?"

"Of course we did," Linda said warmly, setting her gift on the coffee table. "You didn't think we'd let you settle into your new apartment without celebrating, did you?"

"I didn't—I mean, I never expected—" Megan pressed her hand to her mouth, blinking rapidly against the sudden sting of tears.

"Now… none of that," Kay said gently, moving to Megan's side and wrapping an arm around her shoulders. "No tears allowed today. This is a celebration."

The delivery men reappeared at that moment, Frank calling from the doorway. "Sectional pieces coming in."

Megan gestured toward the living room.

What followed was controlled chaos that somehow felt perfect.

The women settled themselves throughout the living room—Kay and Linda sitting on the floor with their backs against the wall, Beth perched on one of the end tables, and Tonya and Savannah standing near the newly installed windows—creating a cheerful background hum of conversation as the delivery men worked. They carried in the sectional pieces one at a time, the heavy cushions and sturdy frame requiring two men per section, carefully maneuvering around the women who cheerfully moved out of the way when needed.

"A little to the left," Megan directed as Frank and Mike positioned the main section against the wall.

"Your left or my left?" Frank asked with good-natured patience.

"Your left. No, wait—my left. Sorry, your right."

The women laughed, and even Frank cracked a smile as they adjusted the placement.

The sectional took shape slowly—first the main piece, then the chaise extension, and finally the remaining pieces that connected them. Once assembled, it dominated the living room in the best way, inviting and substantial and exactly what Megan had envisioned.

"That's a beautiful sectional," Beth said, admiring the clean lines and the way the tan fabric complemented the warm honey floors.

"It looks perfect in here," Megan said, running her hand along the back cushion.

"Bar stools next," Frank announced, and the crew disappeared again.

While the men worked, Kay stood and gestured to the wrapped packages on the coffee table. "Should we do gifts now, or wait until they're finished?"

"Now," Tonya urged. "I'm terrible at waiting."

"The suspense is killing me," Savannah added with a grin.

Megan sat on the floor in front of the coffee table, her legs folded beneath her, feeling like a child at her own birthday party.

"This one first," Linda said, handing Megan a rectangular package wrapped in silver paper with a white bow. "From me."

Megan carefully removed the paper, revealing a set of kitchen towels in shades of cream and burgundy with delicate embroidered designs along the edges—a candy cane, a snowflake, and a little Christmas tree.

"Linda, these are gorgeous," Megan said, running her fingers over the embroidery. "Thank you so much."

"Every kitchen needs good towels," Linda said with a warm smile.

"They're perfect."

Beth handed over her gift next—a coffee maker.

The bar stools arrived with a clatter of chair legs and cheerful instructions from Frank about not scratching the floors. Megan watched as they positioned all three stools with careful spacing. The charcoal gray seats looked elegant against the butcher block countertop, and the metal footrests gleamed under the kitchen lights.

"Next gift!" Tonya said, pushing a large package toward Megan as the delivery men headed back down for another load.

This one was wrapped in festive paper with dancing snowmen. Inside, Megan found a beautiful throw blanket in soft cream with a cable-knit texture, the kind that invited curling up on cold evenings.

"For your new couch," Tonya said.

"It's so soft." Megan held it against her cheek, the texture comforting. "Thank you, Tonya."

Savannah's gift came next—a collection of candles in different sizes, all in complementary scents. Vanilla bean, cinnamon spice, and winter pine. Each one had a handwritten label.

"Candles make everything feel homier, you know?" Savannah said.

"I love them," Megan said, already imagining lighting them on quiet evenings, the warm glow and pleasant scents filling her home.

Kay handed her another gift, with a smile on her face. When Megan removed the wrapping, she found a framed photograph—all six of them standing in front of Sugar & Spice's storefront, taken during the shop's holiday photoshoot last week. They were smiling, arms around each other.

"Oh... I love this," Megan's voice cracked.

The tears came then, hot and sudden and unstoppable. Megan pressed the frame to her chest and let them fall, not bothering to hide or apologize for the emotion overwhelming her.

"Oh, honey." Linda moved closer, wrapping Megan in a gentle hug.

"I'm sorry," Megan managed, her voice thick. "I'm just—this is all so much. I can't believe you did all this."

"You're family, honey, and we wanted to make this day extra special for you," Beth said, joining the hug from the other side.

"Bedroom set coming through!" Frank called from the doorway, and the women pulled back, laughing through their own damp eyes as they scattered to make room.

The bed frame came first, the beautiful cherry wood gleaming even wrapped in protective blankets. Frank and his crew assembled it with practiced efficiency—frame, slats, headboard, footboard—while the women watched and offered completely unhelpful commentary that made everyone laugh.

The nightstands followed, one on each side of the bed, their brushed nickel hardware catching the light. Then the dresser with its large mirror, positioned against the opposite wall.

"This is one gorgeous bedroom set," Kay said appreciatively as they looked at the new furniture in Megan's bedroom.

"I fell in love with it the moment I saw it," Megan admitted, running her hand along the smooth footboard. "I splurged on it, but it was worth it."

"Absolutely worth it," Linda agreed.

While the men assembled the office furniture in the spare bedroom, the women moved back out into the living room area and presented two last gifts.

"We all chipped in for these," Kay explained, gesturing to the first box. "Open it."

Inside, Megan found a complete set of stainless-steel cookware. Quality pieces that would last years, the kind she'd never have bought herself but had always wanted.

"This is too much," she protested.

"It's exactly enough," Beth countered. "You can't cook proper meals without good cookware."

The second box held dishes—a full set for eight people in classic ivory with simple blue trim, elegant without being fussy, perfect for everyday use or special occasions.

"We figured you'd be hosting people eventually," Savannah said. "Hint... hint... I'm always up for a friends gathering."

Megan looked at the women surrounding her, at the gifts chosen with such thoughtfulness and care, at the apartment taking shape around them with furniture and warmth and the promise of actual living, and she felt so happy. So overjoyed, these women had thought to make this day special for her.

"I don't know how to thank you all. You all mean so much to me. I've never had something like this done for me before. I can never repay you for welcoming me the way you have, for making me feel like family, for teaching me and supporting me, and just—" Her voice broke completely. "Just loving me."

"Megan." Kay's voice was firm but gentle. "You've already repaid us a hundred times over. You kept the shop going. You honored Phyllis's legacy while making it your own. You showed up every day, willing to learn and work hard and care about what we do. You've enriched each of our lives just by being here. We don't want repayment. We just want you to know you're loved."

"And that you're stuck with us now," Tonya added with a grin. "No take-backs."

"We're your family whether you like it or not," Beth agreed.

"I like it," Megan said through her tears, laughing and crying at once. "I really, really like it. I love it, in fact."

The last piece of furniture—the office chair—arrived with Frank announcing it was their final item. They positioned it behind the desk in her office, adjusted the height, tested the wheels, and declared the delivery complete.

Frank handed Megan his clipboard for a final signature. "Does everything look good to you, ma'am?"

"It's all perfect. Thank you so much."

"Our pleasure. You folks have a great day." Frank and his crew filed out, their footsteps echoing down the stairs until the truck's engine started and pulled away, leaving quiet behind.

The women stayed for another twenty minutes, helping Megan arrange the throw blanket artfully over the sectional, position the framed photo on one of the end tables, and set the candles on the coffee table in a pleasing arrangement. They hung kitchen towels on the oven handle, positioned the coffeemaker on the counter, and generally fussed over details until everything looked intentional rather than just placed.

"We should probably get back," Kay said reluctantly, checking her watch. "It's almost two, and Chelsea and Morgan's shift ends at two-thirty."

"Thank you. For everything. For the whole day. I'll never forget it." Megan said as she walked them to the door, hugging each woman tightly.

"Enjoy your new home, sweet girl." Linda said, squeezing Megan's shoulders.

They descended the stairs in a cheerful parade, calling final congratulations, and then Megan was alone.

She walked around the space, savoring the moment as she walked through each room slowly, trailing her fingers along furniture surfaces, opening drawers just to feel the smooth glide, testing the office chair's swivel, and sitting on the bed to test the mattress support. Everything was real. Everything was hers.

The joy and the fear and the gratitude and the disbelief all tangled together in her chest until she couldn't separate one from the other.

She removed her phone from her back pocket, opened a new group text with Kyle and Leslie, and typed quickly before she could overthink it.

The furniture's all here, and the place looks amazing. Want to come over for pizza at 6 to celebrate? My treat.

The responses came almost immediately.

From Leslie: *YES! So excited to see it all put together!*

From Kyle: *Absolutely. Can't wait to see your place all finished.*

Megan smiled, warmth spreading through her chest. She wanted to share this joy with them, wanted both of them here in this space that was finally, truly hers.

She stood, tucking her phone in her back pocket, walked into the kitchen, and realized she needed groceries and basic supplies.

At the door, Megan paused and looked back at her living room—at the sectional waiting for people to sit on it, at the kitchen ready for meals to be cooked, and at the new windows framing the mountains and the town she'd somehow found her way to. This was home. Hers. Real and permanent and full of possibility.

She locked the door behind her and descended the stairs to the alley, keys jangling in her hand, a smile on her face, and her heart full of more emotions than she had names for.

Chapter 31

Kyle appeared at her door at six sharp, carrying a large wrapped box, with Leslie right behind him balancing two more packages and a bottle of sparkling cider tucked under her arm.

"There's more in the truck," Kyle announced.

"More?" Megan stepped back to let them in. "You guys didn't have to bring anything."

"Of course we did," Leslie said, depositing her packages beside Kyle's and immediately pulling Megan into a hug. "It's a housewarming party. Gifts are mandatory."

Kyle was already heading back down the stairs, and Megan could hear his footsteps echoing in the alley as Leslie looked around the apartment with obvious delight.

"Megan, this is gorgeous! The furniture looks perfect in here."

"Thank you. Come on, I'll give you the full tour."

They moved through the apartment slowly, Leslie exclaiming over each detail—the way the bar stools complemented the island, how the light fixtures cast warm glows in each room, and the beautiful bedroom set that made the space feel elegant.

"This bedroom is stunning," Leslie said, running her hand along the cherry wood footboard. "You really splurged on this, didn't you?"

"I fell in love with it," Megan confessed. "It felt worth it."

"It absolutely was. This is furniture you'll have for decades."

As they left the bedroom, Kyle reappeared carrying another large box and a gift basket covered in cellophane, setting them with the growing collection in the living room.

"I hate to say this, but dinner will be a little late. I just ordered the pizza twenty minutes ago. It won't be here until seven. I meant to order it when I got home from the grocery store, but I was getting everything put away, and it completely slipped my mind," Megan said.

"So we open gifts first!" Leslie declared, clapping her hands together.

They settled in the living room, Megan on the sectional with Leslie beside her, while Kyle claimed one of the bar stools he'd pulled over from the kitchen island, looking relaxed and comfortable in her space.

Leslie handed Megan a rectangular box wrapped in silver paper with a red bow. "This one first."

Megan unwrapped it carefully, revealing a box containing a deep fryer. She looked up at Leslie with surprise and delight.

"You like it," Leslie asked.

"I love it! I've been wanting one of these forever. Thank you."

"You're welcome. Now this one." Leslie stood and retrieved one of the large boxes Kyle had brought up, placing it in front of Megan with obvious excitement. "This one's my favorite."

The box was substantial, and when Megan opened it, she found herself staring at an artificial Christmas tree—a beautiful seven-foot tree with realistic-looking branches and built-in lights.

She felt the oncoming tears immediately.

"Leslie," she managed, her voice barely above a whisper.

"I know you've been so busy with the shop and the apartment that you probably haven't thought about getting a tree yet," Leslie said gently.

Tears spilled over before Megan could stop them. She covered her face with her hands, overwhelmed by the gesture's significance.

"Hey," Leslie said, but her own voice was thick with emotion as she wrapped an arm around Megan's shoulders. "I hope those are happy tears."

"I've never had my own Christmas tree," Megan said, the words coming out broken.

"Well, now you do," Kyle said softly, and when Megan looked up at him through blurred vision, his expression was tender and understanding. "And we'll help you set it up if you want."

Megan nodded, wiping at her eyes and laughing. "I'm sorry. I'm being ridiculous."

"You're not," Leslie assured her.

"Okay," Kyle said, standing and retrieving his gifts as Megan composed herself. "My turn. Maybe I should grab some tissues?"

Megan laughed. "Might not be a bad idea."

He handed her the gift basket first, and Megan pulled off the cellophane wrapping to reveal a beautiful collection of items from Mistletoe Mercantile—candles in bakery scents, luxurious soaps wrapped in elegant paper, lotions that smelled of vanilla and coconut, and a few decorative items that would look perfect on her bathroom counter or bedroom dresser.

"These are beautiful," Megan said, lifting out a bar of soap and inhaling the cranberry-orange scent. "Kyle, this is too much."

"It's exactly enough," he countered. "Natalie helped me pick everything out. She said, that every new home needs things that make it feel special."

"She was right. I love all of it." Megan set the basket aside carefully and accepted the card he held out next.

She removed the card from the envelope. The front had a simple watercolor design of a small house with smoke curling from the chimney and warm light glowing in the windows. Inside, Kyle had written in his neat handwriting:

May your new home be filled with warmth, joy, and all the happiness you deserve. Congratulations on this beautiful beginning. Love, Kyle.

He had also included two gift cards—one from Once Upon a Time Bookshop and one from The Christmas Shop.

"The bookshop one is because every home needs good books," Kyle explained as Megan traced the cards with her finger. "And the Christmas Shop one is for ornaments and whatever else you want to decorate your new tree. Leslie and I want you to come pick out things you love, on us."

"You shouldn't have done all this," Megan said, but her protest was weak, overwhelmed by the thoughtfulness.

"We wanted to," Kyle said simply. "Now, the last one."

He stood and retrieved the final large box, setting it in front of her. Megan began unwrapping the box, and her breath caught before she was even finished.

A television. A really nice television.

"Kyle." She looked up at him, shaking her head. "This is far too much."

He sat back down on the bar stool and leaned forward with his elbows on his knees.

The gesture was so generous, so thoughtful, so completely beyond anything Megan knew how to process, that she didn't think—she just moved. She stood, crossed the distance to where Kyle sat, and kissed him on the cheek with enough enthusiasm that she nearly knocked him off the stool.

"Thank you," she said fiercely, her hands gripping his shoulders for balance. "Thank you so much. For everything. For all of this."

Kyle's hands had come up automatically to steady her, gripping her waist, and his face had gone slightly pink with surprise. "You're welcome," he managed, his voice a little rough. "If I'd known that was the response I'd get, I would have bought you two televisions."

Leslie was laughing so hard she'd doubled over on the couch, and even Megan found herself grinning as she stepped back.

"Sorry," she said. "I got excited."

"Don't apologize," Kyle said, with a crooked smile that made Megan's heart skip. "I like your enthusiasm."

A knock at the door broke the moment, and Megan hurried to answer it, finding the pizza delivery driver with three boxes balanced in his arms.

"Megan Caldwell?"

"That's me." She paid quickly, adding a generous tip to the receipt as she signed it, and carried the boxes to the kitchen island.

"I got supreme, pepperoni, and Margherita," Megan announced. "Let's eat while it's hot."

They settled at the island, Kyle and Megan on two of the bar stools while Leslie claimed the third, and the conversation flowed as easily as breathing. Natural and comfortable and punctuated with laughter.

"So how are the gift box sales going?" Megan asked between bites of supreme pizza.

"Really well. We've sold almost all of them. People love the combination of candy and Christmas items. We should get together on Monday and make more," Leslie suggested. "Maybe expand into the small and larger tiered options now that we know the concept works. If we can get inventory ready, we could push them hard between now and Christmas."

"Monday works for me," Megan agreed. "Morning or afternoon?"

"Morning?" Leslie looked to Kyle for confirmation. "Say ten o'clock? That way we have the whole day if we need it."

"I'm in," Kyle said. "I'll make sure I don't schedule any client meetings."

The conversation drifted naturally to other topics—holiday plans, town gossip that ranged from sweet to hysterical, and updates about various community members.

"So what are your holiday plans?" Leslie asked Megan, reaching for her third slice of pizza. "Christmas is only three weeks away."

Megan paused. "I haven't really thought that far ahead," she admitted. "I've been so focused on getting the apartment ready and managing the shop's holiday rush. I imagine I'll watch Christmas movies or something. Maybe work on some new ideas I have for the candy shop."

"Absolutely not," Leslie said firmly. "You're spending Christmas with us. With our family."

"Oh, I couldn't—"

"Yes, you could," Kyle interjected gently. "We spend Christmas Eve at our parents' house—the whole family, tons of food, gift exchange, the works. Christmas Day is usually more flexible. Sometimes we do things with friends, sometimes we gather at Mom and Dad's house again, and sometimes we just find something fun to do together. I'd really like you to spend Christmas with us."

"I don't want to intrude on family time," Megan said, though the invitation warmed her from the inside out.

"Come on, Megan, you're not intruding," Leslie assured her. "Mom and Dad would be thrilled to have you, and I want you to spend Christmas with us."

"Think about it," Kyle said when Megan didn't immediately respond. "No pressure. But the invitation stands."

They finished the pizza over simple conversation, and by the time they'd cleaned up, it was nearly nine o'clock.

"I should get going," Leslie said reluctantly, gathering her purse from where she'd dropped it by the door. "Early morning tomorrow. I need to check inventory before we open and probably place a few orders."

"When are you planning to move in completely?" Kyle asked.

"Tomorrow," she said.

"I'll help," Kyle offered immediately. "What time should I be at the cabin? Eight? Nine? Whenever works for you."

Megan opened her mouth to accept—the automatic response, the expected response—but something made her pause.

"Actually," she said slowly, touching his arm with gentle firmness, "I think I want to do this by myself."

Kyle's expression shifted—surprise first, then something that looked like hurt before he schooled his features into acceptance. "Oh. Okay. Are you sure? I don't mind helping, and it would go faster with two people."

"I'm sure." Megan kept her hand on his arm, maintaining the connection while establishing her boundary. "It's not that I don't appreciate the offer. I really do. But I want to do this alone, you know?

Moving my things, getting Hazel settled in her new space, and just spending the day enjoying the apartment at my own pace. Plus, I really don't have that much to move anyway—everything fits in my car."

"I understand," Kyle said, but his smile was tight, not quite reaching his eyes. "If you change your mind, just text me. I'll be around."

"I completely get it," Leslie said, her voice warm with understanding. "There's something special about doing these milestone moments yourself, claiming them for your own memories."

"Thanks," Megan said, relief flooding through her at Leslie's support. She squeezed Kyle's arm once before dropping her hand. "I promise I'll text you when I'm all settled in."

"Looking forward to it." Kyle's voice was genuine despite the lingering disappointment visible in the set of his shoulders.

They made their way to the door, Leslie hugging Megan tightly and whispering, "Good for you" against her ear before pulling back. Kyle's hug was briefer and more careful, and Megan felt the slight tension in his frame even as he smiled down at her.

"The offer stands; if you want help, just text me," he said.

"Thanks for everything. For all the gifts. For being here. For just—everything."

"Anytime," Kyle said, and then they were gone, footsteps echoing down the stairs until his truck started in the alley and pulled away.

Megan closed the door and turned to survey her apartment.

The sectional sat invitingly in the living room, with the throw blanket artfully draped across one arm. The framed photo of her work family graced the end table. The Christmas tree box leaned against the wall, waiting to be assembled and decorated. Kyle's gift basket sat on the coffee table, the candles and soaps promising future moments of simple luxury. The television sat waiting to be unpacked and mounted.

Everything spoke of care and thoughtfulness and belonging.

She walked to the kitchen island and ran her hand along the smooth butcher block surface, thinking about how she'd just turned down Kyle's help. How his face had shown that flash of hurt before he'd hidden it. How Leslie had understood immediately while Kyle had seemed as if he needed an explanation.

It had been the right choice. She knew it with bone-deep certainty. Not because Kyle was wrong to offer or because she didn't value his support. But because this move was hers to claim. She wanted to remember every detail. She wanted to carry each box up the stairs herself. Wanted to decide where Hazel's things would go without input or help or someone else's pace.

She wanted to do it alone because she could. Because she was capable. Because choosing to do something independently didn't mean rejecting the person who offered help—it meant honoring her own needs.

Megan moved to the living room window and looked out at Mistletoe Lane below, mostly quiet now with just a few cars passing and lights glowing from the shops that stayed open late. The mountains rose dark beyond the town, and stars twinkled brightly in the clear December sky.

Tomorrow she'd pack her car with her boxes, her cat, and her few belongings. She'd drive from the cabin to the apartment—her apartment—and carry everything up the stairs one trip at a time. She'd set up Hazel's litter box and food bowls. She'd hang her clothes in the closet and arrange her toiletries in the bathroom. She'd do all of it at her own pace, in her own way, creating her own memories of this transition.

And it would be perfect because it would be hers.

The thought settled over her like a warm blanket, equal parts comfort and conviction. She'd made the right choice. Even if Kyle didn't fully understand. Even though it had created the first small moment of tension between them.

Some things were worth claiming for yourself, even when someone you cared about wanted to help.

This was one of them.

Chapter 32

Megan loaded the last box into her car and looked back at the cabin that had been her temporary home, knowing that when she drove away this time, it would be for good.

The A-frame stood quiet in the morning light, its windows reflecting the pale December sun and the mountains rising beyond. Smoke curled from the chimney of the cabin next door, but hers was cold and dark now, already belonging to the past. She'd stripped the bed after waking up for the last time this morning, washed the sheets, and remade it. She'd cleaned the kitchen spotless and made sure every surface was exactly as she'd found it weeks ago.

She quickly made a last sweep of the cabin—checking drawers, looking under furniture, and making sure she hadn't forgotten anything. The space felt different already, impersonal without her few belongings scattered about. As if she'd never been here at all.

She placed the key on the kitchen counter with a note for Ann:

Thank you for the refuge when I needed it most. Your kindness meant more than you'll ever know. - Megan

It wasn't enough. Words could never be enough to express what this cabin had represented—the bridge between her old life and her new one, the safe space where she'd begun to believe things could be different. But it was what she had, and it was honest.

She grabbed the cat carrier, Hazel already inside, and closed the door behind her with careful finality and walked to her car without looking back again. Some transitions deserved to be marked, acknowledged, and then released.

The drive from Snowflake Mountain Resort to downtown Mistletoe Falls took fifteen minutes, winding through mountain roads that had become familiar over the past weeks. She'd made this drive dozens of times now, but this time felt different. Final.

She thought about Bowling Green as she drove, about the cramped apartment she'd shared. About the copy center job where she'd been passed over for a promotion she deserved. About the eviction notice that had felt like the end of the world.

That had been one month ago.

Four weeks.

Thirty days that had transformed her entire existence.

Now she owned a business, had genuine friends, had a beautiful apartment, and had somehow found herself falling for a man who looked at her like she hung the moon.

The thought settled in her chest with weight and warmth.

Found herself what?

Falling for Kyle Porter. Maybe already fallen.

She wasn't ready to call it love yet. Saying that word out loud made it too real, too permanent, too vulnerable.

Megan's hands tightened on the steering wheel as she navigated the turn onto Mistletoe Lane, her heart beating faster with the acknowledgment of what she'd been trying not to name.

Downtown was quiet this early on a Saturday morning, with most shops not yet open, the streets still peaceful before the weekend tourist rush began. She pulled into the alley behind Sugar & Spice and parked, then sat for a moment, looking up at her apartment windows.

Home.

Hazel meowed again, more insistent this time.

"All right, you demanding creature. Let's get you inside."

She carried the cat carrier up first, unlocking the apartment and releasing Hazel into the space before the cat could work herself into a full panic. Hazel emerged cautiously, low to the ground, tail twitching as she surveyed her new territory with obvious suspicion.

"It's bigger than the cabin," Megan told her, crouching down. "You'll have more room to claim. More windows to sit in. I think you're going to like it here."

Hazel responded with a skeptical meow before slinking toward the bedroom, her body language screaming distrust of the sudden change in landscape.

Megan returned to her car and began the process of bringing up her belongings. Seven boxes. Two suitcases. A bag of toiletries. Hazel's litter box, food bowls, and supplies. A small stack of books.

Everything she owned from her past life fit in her car with room to spare.

The realization should have felt depressing, but instead it felt liberating. Starting fresh meant she could be intentional about what she surrounded herself with, what she kept, and what she released.

She took her time with each trip, refusing to rush. This was her move, her pace, her choice.

The unpacking went slowly by design. She arranged her clothes in the closet by color, hung towels in the bathroom, and positioned toiletries on the bathroom counter with careful attention to what she actually used daily versus what could go in drawers or in the cabinet. She set up her office with her laptop that Beth had approved the purchase of as a business expense and centered it on the desk. She arranged a container of pens and highlighters, her small collection of notebooks stacked neatly, and placed the recipe box nearby.

Back in the bedroom, she made the bed with sheets and the matching comforter she'd ordered online, a soft pale pink. The sleigh bed looked elegant and inviting, the cherry wood gleaming in the afternoon light streaming through the windows.

Hazel had claimed one of the bedroom's sunny windowsills, having apparently decided this spot provided adequate surveillance of the alley below while also offering optimal napping potential.

"Good choice," Megan told her, running her hand along the cat's back.

Next, she moved into the kitchen, organizing her cabinets with her new dinnerware and the new cookware set her staff had given her. She filled the coffeemaker with water and grounds, testing it just to make sure it worked—the rich smell of brewing coffee filling the apartment and making it feel more like home.

Throughout the unpacking and organizing, her mind kept returning to Thanksgiving. To sitting on the Porters' porch with Kyle, wrapped in a quilt against the November cold, talking about the future.

"I want what my parents have. A partner—someone I can build a life with, someone who knows me completely and still chooses me every day."

His voice had been so certain. So clear about what he wanted.

"The thing is, I'm ready for it. Like, now. I've been ready for a while, actually. I just needed to find the right person."

Now.

Ready now.

Marriage, kids, his entire future mapped out.

Megan sat on her new sectional, pulling the throw blanket over her lap, and let herself think about what that meant. What she wanted.

Did she want a life with Kyle?

The question should have been easy to answer, but it twisted in her chest. Yes—of course, yes. But also...

She pressed her hands to her face.

Why couldn't she just be sure?

She thought about her past relationships—the handful of boyfriends she'd had over the years. None had felt like this. None had made her imagine futures or feel that bone-deep pull. Those relationships had been fine, pleasant even, but ultimately forgettable.

This was different.

What she felt for Kyle was profound and consuming and unlike anything she'd experienced before. When he walked into a room, her whole body oriented toward him like a plant toward sunlight. When he smiled at her, she felt it in her chest. When he touched her hand, electricity sparked along her skin.

This was real. This mattered.

So why did the speed of it scare her?

Megan pulled her knees up to her chest, wrapping her arms around them, trying to understand the fear that wouldn't let go.

It wasn't that she didn't trust Kyle. He'd been nothing but steady, kind, consistent. He showed up. He stayed. He kept his promises.

It wasn't that she didn't want what he wanted—marriage, family, a life together.

She did want those things.

Didn't she?

But when he'd said "now"—when he'd talked about being ready NOW, right now, ready to move forward immediately—something in her chest had seized up. Like she couldn't breathe. Like she was supposed to feel the same certainty but didn't.

Four weeks ago, she hadn't known Kyle Porter existed. Now he was talking about forever, and she was supposed to—what? Match his pace? Feel equally ready? Know with the same certainty?

She loved being with him. She loved how he made her feel. But did that mean she was ready for forever?

How did people know? How did they become so certain so fast?

And if she wasn't as sure as he was, did that mean something was wrong with her—or wrong with them?

Maybe she just needed... what? Time? But time for what? To do what? To become what?

The questions circled in her mind without answers, each one leading to another until she felt dizzy with thinking.

She'd spent her whole life waiting for things to feel right.

Good things in Megan's life had always come with an expiration date she couldn't see until it was too late.

Kyle seemed so sure about everything. About her. About them. About their future.

Why couldn't she be that sure too?

Hazel jumped onto the couch beside her, circling twice before curling into a tight ball against Megan's hip. Her purring started immediately, a deep rumble of contentment.

"You like it here?" Megan asked, running her hand along the cat's spine.

Hazel's purr intensified, and her eyes drifted closed.

"Me too," Megan said softly. "I really like it here."

The afternoon sun slanted through the windows, painting golden rectangles across the honey-colored floors. Her apartment smelled of fresh coffee and vanilla candles from Kyle's gift basket. The sectional was comfortable beneath her, the throw blanket soft and warm, and everything around her spoke of home and permanence and belonging.

She'd done this. Built this life, one choice at a time. Accepted Phyllis's gift and drove to an unknown town and learned a new skill and made genuine friends and created something real.

All by herself.

Well, with help. With so much help and support and kindness from people who showed up when she needed them. But ultimately, the choices had been hers. The courage had been hers. The work had been hers.

She was stronger than she'd given herself credit for. Capable of more than she'd imagined.

So why did Kyle's certainty make her feel uncertain about herself?

Her phone buzzed on the coffee table, and Megan reached for it, her heart doing something complicated when she saw Kyle's name.

Hey. Just wanted to check that you got settled in okay. Hope the move went smoothly.

Warmth spread through her chest—affection, gratitude, something deeper she wasn't ready to examine too closely. She typed her response with a smile that felt both genuine and fragile.

All moved in! Hazel's claimed her favorite spot. Thanks for checking in.

The reply came quickly.

Glad to hear it. Enjoy your new home. Let's go out for dinner soon to celebrate.

Dinner. They'd have dinner. Maybe she could talk to him then. Maybe she could figure out how to say what she was feeling without pushing him away or making him think she didn't—

Didn't what? Care about him? Want to be with him?

She did. She did care. She did want to be with him.

But his "ready now" echoed in her mind, and her own uncertainty echoed louder.

Sounds good. Thanks again for everything.
Anytime. Enjoy your day, Megan.
You too.

She set the phone down and sat with Hazel purring against her hip, the apartment peaceful around her, and tried to let herself just BE here. In this moment. In this home. With these feelings she couldn't quite name yet.

Kyle had texted. They'd make plans for dinner. Everything was fine.

So why did her chest feel tight?

Why did "fine" feel like it wasn't quite enough and also too much all at once?

She was falling for him—maybe had already fallen. She knew that much. But his readiness, his certainty, his NOWNESS... it made her feel like she was supposed to match his pace, and she didn't know if she could.

Or if she should.

Hazel stretched, kneading with her paws against Megan's leg, then settled back into sleep with a contented sigh.

Megan envied the cat's contentment. She wanted to feel that settled. That sure.

Maybe after dinner. Maybe after they talked. Maybe after she figured out how to say what she needed without making everything fall apart.

Maybe then she'd feel more certain.

She leaned back against the couch cushions, Hazel warm and purring against her hip, the apartment quiet and beautiful around her.

This was hers. This life. This home. This journey.

And Kyle was part of it all.

She just wished she knew how to be sure about what that meant.

Chapter 33

"I need to talk to you about something."

The words came out quieter than Megan intended, barely audible over the gentle din of conversation and clinking silverware that filled The Fireside Diner. She'd been rehearsing variations of this opening all day—bolder versions, softer versions, versions that didn't make her sound like she was about to break up with him—but now that the moment had arrived, her voice had abandoned any pretense of confidence.

Kyle looked up from his burger, concern flickering across his face. "Okay. What's going on?"

They sat in a booth near the back of the restaurant. The diner hummed with its comfortable rhythm—the hiss of the grill, Pete Morgan's booming laugh from the kitchen, and the jukebox playing something soft and nostalgic. Everything felt normal. Safe.

Except Megan's heart was hammering against her ribs like it was trying to escape.

"It's not bad," she said quickly, seeing Kyle's expression shift toward alarm. "Or—I don't know. Maybe it is. I can't tell anymore."

Kyle set down his burger and wiped his hands on his napkin, giving her his full attention. The care in that simple gesture—the way he always stopped everything to really listen—made her chest ache.

"Take your time," he said.

Megan pushed a fry through the ketchup on her plate, watching the red streak it left behind. "Remember Thanksgiving? On your porch, when we were talking about the future?"

"Yeah." Kyle's voice carried a note of confusion.

Megan abandoned the fry and looked up at him. "You said you were ready. Ready now. For all of it—marriage, kids, the whole thing."

"I did." Kyle nodded slowly, clearly trying to understand where this was going. "And I meant it."

"I know you did. That's the problem." Megan exhaled, frustrated with her inability to articulate this clearly. "Not a problem, exactly. Shoot, I'm saying this all wrong."

She pressed her palms flat against the table, feeling the coolness of the laminate through her skin, grounding herself. Kyle waited, patient as always, but she could see the tension gathering in his shoulders.

"When you said that," Megan continued, "about being ready right now, it made everything feel—permanent. In a way, I wasn't prepared for."

"But isn't that good?" Kyle asked, genuine confusion coloring his tone. "I thought we both wanted the same things."

"We do. I do." Megan fought the urge to fidget. "But wanting something and being ready for it aren't always the same thing. And when you said you were ready now, it felt like—like you were waiting for me to catch up to where you already are. Like there was this timeline I didn't know about, and I was already behind."

Kyle's brow furrowed. "I wasn't trying to pressure you."

"I know that. Logically, I know that." Megan's voice dropped lower. "But there's this part of me that heard 'ready now' and immediately started panicking because what if I can't get there as fast as you need me to? What if I'm not ready when you are and you decide I'm not worth waiting for?"

"Megan—"

"Let me finish. Please." She needed to get this out before courage failed her entirely. "I haven't told you everything about my dad. About when he left."

Kyle went very still, his hands flat on the table between them.

"I was thirteen," Megan said. "And everything was fine. Or it seemed fine to me, anyway. We'd just gone camping the weekend before—me, him, and Mom. We'd made s'mores, and he'd taught me how to skip rocks on the lake, and I remember thinking everything was perfect." Her throat tightened. "Four days later, I came home from school, and he was packing. There were no obvious signs he'd just had an argument with Mom; he wasn't crying, angry, frustrated, or anything like that. He just seemed like he was doing the most normal thing in the world, packing his clothes and talking to me as if he didn't have a care in the world. Just methodically putting his stuff in boxes like he was moving offices."

The diner's ambient noise seemed to fade into the background, leaving only her voice and Kyle's focused attention.

"I asked him what he was doing, and he said he was leaving. Moving to California. Starting over. Just like that—like he was telling me he was going to the grocery store." Megan's hands curled into fists against the table. "I asked him why. He just rambled on about how he needed a change. I asked him if Mom and I were moving to California as well. He changed the subject and started talking so fast, saying things like, 'I'm not meant to be a father,' and I distinctly remember him saying, 'I don't love your mother.' I asked if I could come visit, and he said maybe someday when he got settled. But he never got settled. Or maybe he did, and I just wasn't part of that settlement."

"Megan." Kyle's voice was rough with emotion.

"The worst part was how normal everything had been right before. If there'd been fights or tension between my parents, maybe I would've seen it coming. But there was nothing. One day I had a dad who loved me, and the next day I didn't. And I've spent fifteen years trying to figure out what I did wrong, what I could've done differently to make him stay."

"I'm sure you didn't do anything wrong."

"I know that now. Mostly." Megan's eyes burned, but she refused to let tears fall in the middle of The Fireside Diner. "But when you talk about being ready now, about wanting all these permanent things right away, it makes me feel like if I'm not ready at the same speed you are, you'll just—leave. Find someone who can keep up with your timeline."

Understanding dawned on Kyle's face, followed immediately by something that looked like regret. "I never meant it that way."

"I know you didn't." Megan finally met his eyes fully. "But I need you to understand that when everything's been temporary your whole life, permanent feels terrifying to me. Even when it's what you want."

Kyle reached across the table, palm up, and after a moment's hesitation, Megan placed her hand in his. His fingers closed around hers, warm and steady.

"Tell me about your mom," he said quietly.

The question surprised her. "What?"

"You said before that your dad left and your mom changed. Tell me about that."

Megan looked down at their joined hands. "Before the divorce, Mom was—she was fun. She'd dance around the kitchen while making dinner, and she'd read me stories with different voices for all the characters. She smiled a lot. Laughed a lot." The memory felt distant, like something she'd watched in a movie rather than lived. "After Dad left, it was like someone flipped a switch. She stopped smiling. Stopped laughing. She worked constantly—two jobs while going to nursing school—and when she was home, she was just exhausted. Barely there."

"Which I imagine, as a teenager, left you feeling very lonely and confused."

"It did." The simple acknowledgment made something crack open in Megan's chest. "I was a latchkey kid, as I told you before. I basically raised myself. My mom wasn't a mother at all for a good portion of my childhood; she was more of a friend at times, and other times she felt like a person who existed to put a roof over my head and make sure I was fed and clothed. And then when I was twenty-three, she met Rick at the hospital. They dated for three months before getting married, and suddenly she was—different again. Happy, but in a way that didn't include me anymore. Like she'd been waiting all those years to become someone else and finally got permission."

"She calls me maybe once a month now, if that. Our conversations are five minutes long: — How's work? How's the weather? Okay, love you, bye." Megan's voice remained steady, but her grip on Kyle's hand tightened. "When I told her about inheriting the shop, she said, 'That's nice, honey,' like I'd told her I bought new shoes. When I told her I was seeing someone, she didn't even ask your name."

"The thing is," Megan continued, "I don't think she's trying to be hurtful. I think she's just—done. Done being the person who raised me, done being the person Dad left, done with that whole chapter of her life. And I'm part of that chapter." She looked up at Kyle. "So I learned that people can love you and still leave. Or they can stay but leave in other ways. And I learned that forever doesn't actually mean forever."

Kyle's jaw worked for a moment before he spoke. "That's what I did wrong. I told you I was ready forever without understanding that forever is the word that scares you most."

"It's not your fault—"

"Let me finish. I've been thinking about what I want for so long that when I finally found you, I just—jumped straight to the end. Like I could skip all the scary parts and go directly to the security of knowing we're building something permanent. But you can't skip those parts. And you shouldn't have to pretend they're not scared just because I'm certain."

Megan's vision blurred slightly. "I'm not trying to hold us back."

"I know that. But I think I've been pushing us forward without checking if you were ready to run that fast." Kyle's thumb traced small circles on the back of her hand. "I got so caught up in being ready myself, I didn't ask what you needed. I just assumed that declaring my certainty would make you feel secure. Instead, I made you feel pressured."

"You didn't mean to."

"That doesn't make it better." Kyle leaned forward slightly. "Here's what I need you to know: I am certain about us. That hasn't changed. But I'm not going anywhere just because you need more time to feel that same certainty. This isn't a race you're losing. It's a journey we're taking together, and together means at a pace that works for both of us."

The tightness in Megan's chest began to ease, just slightly. "What if I can't ever get to where you are? What if I'm always going to be a little bit afraid?"

"Then you'll be a little bit afraid, and I'll be right there with you anyway." Kyle's expression was serious, but his eyes were warm. "Fear doesn't disqualify you from being loved, Megan. It just means you've been hurt before. And I'm not going to hurt you the same way."

"You can't promise that."

"I can promise that, and I'll try my hardest not to. And I can promise that if I do hurt you, it won't be because I left or stopped caring. It'll be because I'm human and I make mistakes, and we'll work through it together."

Megan's throat felt tight. "I need you to stop making declarations about the future like they're already decided. It makes me feel like I don't get a say, like I'm just supposed to go along with whatever timeline you've already established."

"Okay. What do you need instead?"

"Questions. Not statements." Megan tried to organize her thoughts. "Like instead of 'I want kids,' maybe 'Do you think you'd want kids someday?' Instead of 'I'm ready now,' maybe 'Where are you at with all of this?'"

"I can do that." Kyle squeezed her hand. "And you need to tell me when I'm pushing too hard. I can't read your mind, as much as I sometimes wish I could."

"I'm not good at that yet. Telling people when they're hurting me."

"Then we'll practice." Kyle's smile was small but genuine. "Start with something easy. Is there anything about right now—this conversation, this moment—that's not working for you?"

Megan glanced around The Fireside Diner, suddenly aware again of their surroundings. "Maybe talking about my deepest childhood trauma in a restaurant wasn't my best plan."

Kyle's laugh was soft and relieved. "Fair point. You want to get out of here?"

"Yeah." Megan realized she'd barely touched her food. "Yeah, I do."

Kyle signaled for the check, and within minutes they were outside, the December night crisp and cold against their faces. Christmas lights twinkled along every storefront, casting colored shadows across the sidewalk. Megan pulled her coat tighter and fell into step beside Kyle as they headed in the direction of her apartment.

They walked in silence for a while, but it wasn't uncomfortable. If anything, the quiet felt cleaner than it had in days—like she'd been carrying something heavy and finally set it down.

"Can I ask you something?" Kyle said as they passed Once Upon a Time Bookshop, its windows displaying a cozy reading nook decorated with evergreen garland.

"Sure."

"When did you know you needed to have this conversation? Was it just building up since Thanksgiving, or was there a specific moment?"

Megan thought about it. "It's been building. Every time someone introduced me as your girlfriend or asked when we were making things official or just—assumed we were on this fast track to forever. It felt like the whole town had this expectation, and I was terrified I'd disappoint everyone."

"Including me."

"Especially you." Megan's breath came out in visible puffs. "Because you're the one I actually care about disappointing."

Kyle stopped walking, and after a few steps Megan turned back to face him. They stood in the middle of the sidewalk, Christmas lights reflecting in his hazel eyes.

"You couldn't disappoint me," Kyle said. "Not by being honest about what you need."

"Even if what I need is slower than what you want?"

"Even then." Kyle stepped closer, closing the distance between them. "I'd rather have you at a pace that feels right to you than lose you by pushing too hard."

Megan's heart did something complicated in her chest—part relief, part longing, part terror. "I'm trying to believe that."

Kyle's hand came up to brush a strand of hair away from her face, his touch gentle. "And I'm trying to show you it's true. We'll figure out the rest as we go."

They started walking again, and Megan found herself gravitating closer to his side. She reached for his hand, and his fingers laced through hers without hesitation.

When they reached the alley behind Sugar & Spice, Kyle walked her to the base of the new stairs—so much sturdier than the old rickety ones that had scared her weeks ago. At the top of the stairs, outside her apartment door, Megan turned to face him. The porch light cast a warm glow across both of them, and the cold air made their breath mingle in the space between.

"Thanks," Megan said. "For listening. For understanding. For not making me feel crazy for being scared."

"You're not crazy." Kyle's hands rested lightly on her waist, his touch careful. "You're just careful with your heart. Which makes sense, considering."

Megan placed her hands on his chest, feeling the steady thump of his heartbeat through his coat. Everything in her wanted to close the remaining distance, to kiss him and let that speak for all the things she still couldn't quite articulate. Kyle's gaze dropped to her mouth, and she knew he was thinking the same thing.

But then he stepped back, just slightly, his hands sliding away from her waist. "I'm gonna go."

Megan blinked, caught off guard. "You don't have to—"

"I know." Kyle's smile was crooked, a little rueful. "But I think after the conversation we just had, I shouldn't rush anything. Even the good stuff."

The gesture—his willingness to pull back, to respect the very pace they'd just agreed to establish—made Megan's chest ache in an entirely different way. It would've been so easy for him to kiss her, and part of her desperately wanted him to. But the fact that he didn't, that he chose restraint over impulse, somehow mattered more.

"Okay," she said softly.

"I'll see you tomorrow?" Kyle was already backing toward the stairs, as if he didn't leave now he might not leave at all.

"Tomorrow."

Megan watched him descend the stairs, listened to his footsteps fade into the alley, and then let herself into the apartment where Hazel waited with her usual imperious demands for attention.

She picked up the cat and carried her to the couch, settling into the corner where she'd sat just days ago, feeling overwhelmed by her own happiness.

Kyle had listened to her. Really listened. And instead of getting defensive or hurt, he'd adjusted. He'd understood.

Megan buried her face in Hazel's soft fur, feeling the cat's purr rumble against her chest. Outside, the town twinkled with its perpetual Christmas magic, and somewhere in the distance, she could hear carolers practicing for the weekend's festivities.

Everything was the same as it had been a few hours ago. The apartment, the town, the cat in her arms.

But something fundamental had shifted between her and Kyle—a new understanding, a better foundation. They'd had their first real difficult conversation and come out the other side closer instead of fractured.

Chapter 34

The maple fudge was reaching the perfect temperature when the phone rang.

Megan glanced up from the copper pot she was stirring, careful not to lose focus on the candy thermometer's steady climb. Two hundred thirty-four degrees. Almost there. Around her, the kitchen hummed with its usual Thursday morning rhythm.

"I'll get it," Kay said, wiping her hands on her apron as she crossed to the wall-mounted phone near the office door.

Megan's arm ached slightly from the constant stirring, but her technique remained steady. Weeks ago, she would've been second-guessing every movement, terrified of burning the batch. Now, the motion felt natural and effortless.

"Sugar & Spice," Kay answered cheerfully. A pause. "Hey, Leslie. Yeah, she's right here." Kay held out the phone toward Megan. "Leslie wants to talk to you."

"Can you watch this fudge?" Megan asked Linda, already moving toward the phone.

"Got it, honey. Go on."

Megan accepted the phone from Kay, tucking it between her shoulder and ear. "Hey, what's up?"

"Good morning to you too," Leslie said, her voice bright with the particular energy that usually meant she was planning something. "Quick question—what are you doing Saturday afternoon?"

"Um, working? The usual?" Megan leaned against the wall.

"Listen... I'm doing a Pictures with Santa event at The Christmas Shop on Saturday. Two to five. We've got a professional photographer coming, ornament personalization included in the package, the whole thing. And I was thinking—what if we collaborated?"

Megan straightened slightly. "Collaborated how?"

"Every family that books a session gets a complimentary candy bag from Sugar & Spice. Good for you—more visibility and introducing families to your shop who might not have been in yet. Good for me—adds value to the package, makes it feel more special. Win-win."

The idea sparked something in Megan's chest—that particular combination of excitement and opportunity recognition that she was learning meant good business instinct. "How many families are we talking about?"

"I've got fifteen slots booked so far, and I'm expecting walk-ins. Figure twenty-five bags of candy to be safe?"

Megan mentally ran through their current inventory. They had plenty of individually wrapped candies already packaged and the gift bags they'd been assembling for the holiday rush. Twenty-five bags were completely doable, especially with nearly two full days to prepare. "Yeah, I can do that. Actually, that sounds really fun."

"Excellent!" Leslie's enthusiasm was infectious. "Can you come around one on Saturday? That gives us time to set up before the first appointment."

"Absolutely." Megan was already making mental notes—red and green organza bags, a mix of candy canes, chocolate truffles, maybe some of Linda's maple fudge cut into small pieces. If she had time, she could even whip up a few specialty candies. "This is a great idea, Les."

"I have my moments. Okay, I've got to run—a shipment just arrived, and Reuben's giving me the look that means he needs signatures. See you Saturday!"

The line went dead before Megan could respond. She hung up the phone, turning back to find three pairs of curious eyes watching her.

"What was that about?" Tonya asked.

"We're doing a collaboration with The Christmas Shop on Saturday." Megan crossed back to her fudge. "Pictures with Santa event. We're providing candy bags for all the families."

"How many?" Kay asked.

"Fifteen for sure, but I'll make up twenty-five, to be safe. I was thinking of a mix of our bestsellers and a few fun things the kids would enjoy. I figure we can—"

A loud mechanical groan cut through the kitchen, followed by an ominous clicking sound that made everyone freeze. The noise came from the large industrial stove where Kay had been melting chocolate for a batch of truffles.

"That's not good," Linda said, stating the obvious as the clicking grew louder, then stopped abruptly.

Kay reached for the temperature dial, twisting it. Nothing happened. No heat indicator light, no sound, nothing. "It's dead."

"What?" Megan joined her at the stove. She tried the dial herself—still nothing. Checked the circuit breaker panel near the door—everything looked fine. "How is it just dead?"

"These stoves are ten years old," Kay said, her tone matter-of-fact. "We've been lucky so far and have never had any problems."

"But we're in the middle of the Christmas season." Megan heard the edge in her own voice and tried to moderate it. "We've got standing orders, regular inventory to maintain—"

"We've still got one working stove," Linda pointed out calmly, gesturing to the other industrial range across the kitchen. "It's not ideal, but we can make it work."

Kay was already in motion, transferring her chocolate pot to the working stove. "We all just work together and do what we can and adjust as needed."

"I'll have Beth call a repairman." Linda was moving toward the office before Megan could respond. "Maybe they can come today."

Megan watched her team adapt in real time, reorganizing their workspace without panic, already problem-solving the production schedule in their heads. This was what decades of experience looked like—the ability to pivot without losing momentum.

"Okay." Megan took a breath, grounding herself in their calm competence. "So we prioritize what absolutely needs to be done today, and we adjust the rest of the schedule around one stove."

"Yep, that's exactly what we need to do." Kay was already checking their production list, her finger running down the page. "Gift box chocolates are a priority—we're getting low on inventory, and those sell fastest this time of year. Another priority is peppermint bark and peppermint fudge."

The morning reorganized itself into a new rhythm. Slower, requiring more coordination, but functional. Megan fell into the work alongside her team, the kitchen filling with the familiar scents of vanilla, chocolate, and peppermint that meant Sugar & Spice was doing what it did best.

Linda returned from the office minutes later, her expression apologetic. "The repairman can't come until next Tuesday at the earliest. He's backed up with emergency calls."

"Of course he is." Megan's laugh was short but not entirely humorless. "Okay. We work with what we have. Four more days, we can handle that."

"That's the spirit," Linda said.

Megan lost herself in the meditative process of cutting fudge into uniform pieces, arranging them on wax paper, and checking temperatures for Kay, who was now managing three different processes on the single working stove with the skill of someone who'd been doing this for decades.

By eleven, they'd found their groove. Production was slower, yes, but steady. They were going to be fine.

And then Kay's cell phone rang.

The sound cut through the kitchen's ambient noise—a cheerful ringtone that normally wouldn't have warranted attention. But something about the way Kay's expression shifted when she looked at the screen made Megan's hands still on the fudge she was cutting.

"It's my daughter Livie," Kay said, already moving toward the swinging kitchen doors. "I'll be right back."

She disappeared through the doorway, and candy production continued despite her absence. Megan exchanged glances with Linda and Tonya, all of them curious but not saying anything.

When Kay reappeared minutes later, she was untying her apron, her movements quick and purposeful. "I have to go. Livie's in premature labor—she's only thirty-two weeks with the twins. They've got her on bed rest at Vanderbilt, but she's terrified and alone. Her husband is out of town on business. I need to go to Nashville—I have to go now."

"Of course." Megan's response was immediate, automatic. "Don't even think twice. Go. Be with her."

"But—"

"Go. No buts." Megan crossed to Kay, taking her hands firmly. "Your daughter needs you. Do you need anything? Gas money, or—"

"No, no." Kay was shaking her head, already moving to grab her purse and coat. "I'm sorry, I hate leaving you like this—"

"Kay." Megan waited until the older woman met her eyes. "Go. Everything here will still be here when you get back. Your family comes first. Always."

Kay's eyes filled with tears, but she nodded. Within seconds, she was gone, the back door swinging shut behind her with a finality that seemed to echo through the suddenly too-quiet kitchen.

Megan stood in the middle of the room, aware of Linda and Tonya watching her with careful expressions. The reality of the situation settled over her like cold water.

One working stove.

No Kay.

Peak holiday season.

Standing orders to fill.

And twenty-five candy bags for Saturday's event.

The overwhelm hit fast—a tightness in her chest, a fluttering panic that made her vision narrow slightly. This was too much.

But then she looked at Linda and Tonya, both waiting for her to either fall apart or take charge, and her perspective shifted. These women had worked here for years. They knew their jobs. Everything that had happened this morning couldn't be changed. They all just needed to focus on what could be done with what they had.

"Okay." Megan's voice came out steadier than she felt. "Savannah's out front and is scheduled to work all day, right?"

"Yep," Tonya confirmed.

"Good. We might need to have Beth skip office work for a few days and come help us in the kitchen. I need to figure out who can cover what. Linda, do you know Kay's usual schedule? What she handles daily?"

"Sure do." Linda set down her spatula, giving Megan her full attention. "Most of it, anyway."

"Can you take over her normal tasks temporarily?"

"Absolutely."

"Tonya, you're comfortable with production scheduling... well, rescheduling, right?"

"Born comfortable." Tonya's grin was quick. "I can keep us on track for what needs to be made and when."

"Perfect." Megan was thinking out loud now, organizing the chaos into manageable pieces. "I'll fill in wherever I'm needed, and I'll have Beth call both the new hires and ask them how many more hours they'd like to work."

"What about the Santa event bags?" Linda asked.

"We make what we have on hand work. Originally I thought maybe I'd make up a few cute candies to include, but that idea is long gone. No time for that now." Megan surprised herself with how certain she sounded. "We've got candies already packaged or ready to use. Tomorrow, I'll set aside an hour and assemble the bags. The event's not until Saturday afternoon—I have time."

She looked between Linda and Tonya, seeing their expressions shift from concern to something that looked like respect.

"You've got this," Linda said simply.

Did she? Megan wasn't entirely sure. But she was going to try.

The rest of the day unfolded in a blur of adaptation and crisis management. They worked through lunch—sandwiches from The Pickle

Barrel that Savannah ran to get, eaten in shifts so production never fully stopped. The single working stove became a carefully choreographed dance of timing and temperature, everyone hyper-aware of not wasting a single minute of heat.

By four o'clock, when Megan finally emerged from the kitchen, she felt like she'd run a marathon. Her feet ached, her back protested, she had chocolate under her fingernails, and she was fairly certain she had sugar in places sugar had no business being.

Savannah looked up from the register, where she was helping a customer select gift boxes, taking in Megan's appearance with barely concealed amusement.

"Rough day?"

"You could say that." Megan leaned against the counter, grateful for something solid to hold her upright. "How's it been out here?"

"Steady but manageable. Morgan's killing it with the upsells. That girl could sell ice to Eskimos. I'm glad we hired her." Savannah finished ringing up the sale, wrapped the boxes in festive paper, and sent the customer on their way with a warm smile before turning back to Megan. "How's everything in the kitchen?"

"By sheer force of will and determination, we're making it work." Megan filled her in on the redistributed responsibilities, the adjusted production schedule, and the Santa event commitment that now felt slightly insane but still doable.

"You're doing good," Savannah said when she'd finished. "Better than good, actually. You're a born leader."

The observation landed somewhere deep in Megan's chest. Leading. Was that what this was?

Her phone buzzed in her apron pocket, and she pulled it out to find a text from Kyle.

Kyle: *Hey, gorgeous. Want me to bring dinner over tonight? I'm thinking Chinese, if that's okay with you.*

The endearment made her smile despite her exhaustion. She typed back quickly.

Megan: *Yes, please. After today, takeout and a quiet dinner sound perfect. What time?*

Kyle: *6:30 okay? I'll bring my tools as well and mount your television for you.*

Megan: *Perfect. Thank you.*

Megan slipped her phone back into her pocket and looked around the shop. Customers were browsing the penny candy jars, selecting items with the careful deliberation of people who took their sweets seriously. Morgan and Savannah moved between customers with easy confidence, their voices warm and welcoming. In the kitchen, she could hear Linda humming while she worked; the sound carried through the swinging door along with the scent of cooling peppermint bark.

Everything was different from what it had been this morning. Equipment broken, Kay gone for who knows how long, responsibilities shifted and expanded. But the shop was still standing. Still functioning. Still making candy and serving customers and being exactly what Phyllis had built it to be.

And Megan had kept it that way.

The thought should've been triumphant. Instead, it left her with a hollow, aching awareness of just how much could go wrong. How fragile this all was. How quickly everything could collapse if she made one wrong decision, pushed too hard, or failed to keep all the pieces in motion.

She'd handled today's crisis without falling apart.

But what happened when the next crisis hit, and the one after that? How many emergencies could she navigate before her luck ran out?

With a smile on her face that didn't quite reach the worry in her chest, Megan pushed away from the counter, heading back toward the kitchen where work still waited.

Right now, she'd survived.

Tomorrow, she'd have to do it all over again.

Chapter 35

The shower had been running for fifteen minutes. Megan stood under the hot spray, letting it pummel her shoulders and wash away the physical evidence of the day, but it couldn't quite wash away the bone-deep tiredness that had settled into her muscles.

When she finally emerged, wrapped in her softest towel with her hair dripping down her back, the apartment felt unnaturally quiet. Hazel sat on the bathroom counter, watching her with judgmental green eyes that seemed to say, 'You still smell like peppermint candy.'

"Yeah, well, you smell like cat food," Megan told her, which earned an imperious tail flick before Hazel jumped down and stalked toward the kitchen.

Megan pulled on leggings and an oversized sweater—the kind of soft, shapeless comfort that felt like a hug—and padded barefoot into the living room. The apartment still carried a new-home smell, a combination of fresh paint and possibility. She'd lived here less than a week, and already it felt more like hers than any place she'd ever rented before.

Her phone buzzed on the kitchen counter.

Kyle: *On my way now. Hope you're hungry.*

Megan: *Yep. You're a lifesaver.*

Kyle: *Just a guy with takeout hoping to put a smile on your face. See you in 10.*

Megan set down her phone and looked around the apartment with fresh eyes, suddenly seeing it the way Kyle would when he walked through the door. Lived-in but tidy. The kitchen was clean. Nothing needed immediate attention.

A knock on the door came ten minutes later, and Megan opened it to find Kyle standing there with two large paper bags that smelled like heaven and salvation. He wore jeans and a dark green henley that made his eyes look more startlingly green, and his hair was mussed as if he'd been running his hand through it.

"Hi," she said and was surprised by how much warmth flooded through her at the sight of him.

"Hi yourself." Kyle's smile was soft as he took her in—the damp hair, the oversized sweater, the bare feet. "You look comfortable and cute."

"I look exhausted." Megan stepped back to let him in. "But comfortable and cute works too."

Kyle set the bags on her kitchen island, then turned to pull her into a hug before she could overthink it. His arms came around her firmly, one hand cradling the back of her head, and Megan let herself sink into it with a sigh that came from somewhere deep.

"Rough day?" he murmured against her hair.

"That's putting it mildly." Her voice was muffled against his chest, but she didn't pull away. Not yet. "Thanks for coming."

"Wouldn't want to be anywhere else." Kyle pressed a kiss to the top of her head before stepping back. "Come on. Let's get some food in you, and you can tell me how your day went. Wanna eat here in the kitchen or on the couch?"

"Couch most definitely."

They worked together to set up their meal, Kyle pulling out containers and arranging everything on the coffee table while Megan grabbed plates and silverware. Hazel appeared from wherever she'd been sulking, immediately rubbing against Kyle's legs with shameless affection.

"Traitor," Megan told the cat.

"She knows quality attention when she sees it." Kyle bent to scratch behind Hazel's ears, earning a rumbling purr. "Don't you, Your Majesty?"

They settled on the couch after filling their plates, with the food spread across the coffee table within easy reach. Kyle had brought enough food to feed an army—egg rolls, sesame chicken, lo mein, fried rice, and crab Rangoon—like he'd anticipated her being too tired to know what she wanted and had simply ordered everything.

He wasn't wrong.

Megan took her first bite of sesame chicken and made an involuntary sound of pleasure that made Kyle grin.

"Good?"

"So good. I didn't realize just how hungry I was until now."

Kyle speared a piece of chicken with his fork. "Leslie mentioned you're going to be at the Pictures with Santa event on Saturday?"

"Yeah." Megan felt a flutter of excitement beneath the exhaustion. "She called this morning and asked if I wanted to provide candy bags for all the families coming. It's a great marketing opportunity, and honestly, it sounds fun. Kids and Santa and Christmas magic and all that."

"It'll be good." Kyle's expression was warm and genuine. "I'm glad you'll be there. Leslie's been planning this for weeks, and having your candy as part of it makes the whole package more special."

"You're not worried about me stealing your thunder?" Megan teased lightly.

"Never." Kyle reached for an egg roll. "Besides, I think this is a beautiful continuation of the partnership between our businesses. Leslie's already imagining a permanent Sugar & Spice candy corner in the shop—maybe a small display of your gift boxes and seasonal candies."

"Really?"

"Really. She's been waiting for the right moment to bring it up." Kyle glanced at her, his expression pleased. "I think you two are going to end up being really close friends."

"I hope so." Megan took another bite, then set down her fork. "So, Leslie told you about the event, but did she mention the rest of the day I had? I called her for moral support this afternoon."

"She said something went wrong with one of your stoves, but she didn't really go into detail. What happened?"

Megan leaned back against the couch, her plate balanced on her knees. "One of the two industrial ranges in the kitchen just died, right in the middle of production. No warning, just—dead."

Kyle winced. "Ouch. Can it be repaired?"

"Eventually... at least I hope so. The repairman can't come until Tuesday." She picked up an egg roll, turning it over in her hands. "So we spent the rest of the day working with one functioning stove."

"That must've been stressful."

"It was. But we figured it out." Megan heard the note of pride in her own voice. "Linda, Tonya, Kay—they just adapted. No panic, no drama. Just problem-solving and getting it done."

"Good team."

"The best." Megan took a bite of the egg roll, chewing slowly. "And then Kay got a call from her daughter. Livie—she's thirty-two weeks pregnant with twins, and she went into premature labor. They've got her on bed rest at Vanderbilt, and her husband's out of town, so Kay had to leave immediately."

Kyle set down his fork, his expression shifting to concern. "Is Livie okay?"

"For now. Bed rest, monitoring, all that. But I imagine Kay will be gone for a while." Megan met his eyes. "So in the span of a few hours today, I went from a full staff with two working stoves to being down my general manager and one working stove in the middle of peak holiday season."

"And you have twenty-five candy bags to prepare for Saturday."

"And that." Megan's laugh was short. "Though honestly, that's the least complicated part. The bags are totally doable—I've got plenty of inventory I can use, and I can put the bags together tomorrow. It's everything else that felt overwhelming."

"But you handled it."

"Yeah. I did. I had this moment after Kay left where I just—froze. Standing in the middle of the kitchen with Linda and Tonya watching me. I could feel the panic starting. Like, this is too much. I can't do this; I'm going to fail and prove everyone right that I never should've tried to run this business."

"But then I looked at them—at Linda and Tonya—and I realized they weren't panicking. They were just waiting for directions. And I thought, okay, we can't change what happened. The stove is broken, and Kay is gone, and none of that is anyone's fault. So what can we actually control? What decisions can I make right now that will help?"

"What'd you do?"

"Redistributed responsibilities. Asked Linda to take over Kay's daily tasks. Had Tonya handle production rescheduling. Told Beth to call our new part-time hires and see if they want more hours. Adjusted Beth's office work schedule and moved her into the kitchen to help for a few hours a day. Decided the Santa event bags would use existing inventory instead of making anything special like I had hoped." Megan ticked off each decision on her fingers. "I just—made choices. Solved problems. Led."

The word felt strange in her mouth, too big and important for what she'd actually done. But Kyle was looking at her with admiration.

"That's really impressive, Megan."

"I don't know about impressive. More like survival instinct." She picked at her lo mein. "But it was like I got a crash course in business management and decision-making all in one day. And the weird thing is—we're going to be okay. Production will be slower until the stove is fixed, and we'll all be working harder to cover for Kay, but we can handle it."

"You can handle it," Kyle corrected gently. "You're the one making the decisions."

"With a lot of help from people who actually know what they're doing."

"That's called delegating. It's what good leaders do." Kyle reached over and squeezed her knee. "You should be proud of yourself."

Megan looked down at his hand on her leg, that casual touch that somehow steadied something loose inside her. "I think I am. Exhausted, definitely. A little terrified about tomorrow. But also—proud. Yeah... I guess I am a bit proud."

"Good." Kyle picked up his fork again, taking a bite of fried rice. "So, business crisis managed, candy bags planned, and you survived your first major challenge as an owner. What else happened today?"

The question was so normal, so genuinely interested, that Megan found herself smiling. "Honestly? Not much else. Just constant production, problem-solving on the fly, Beth making miracle schedule adjustments, and Savannah and Morgan holding down the front counter like champions. Oh, and I think I cut about five hundred pieces of fudge. My arm's going to hate me tomorrow."

"I'll remember that when we mount your television later."

"Speaking of which—" Megan glanced at the television box against the wall. "Are you sure you're up for that tonight? You've been working all day too."

"I'm sure." Kyle polished off the last of his chicken. "Besides, you need a TV. What else are you going to watch while eating ice cream at midnight and avoiding sleep?"

"I don't eat ice cream at midnight."

"Yet." Kyle's grin was quick. "Give it time. This place is going to corrupt you into all kinds of comfortable habits."

The way he said it—like he planned to be around to witness her developing those habits—made Megan's chest do that complicated fluttering thing again. She focused on her food, trying to ignore the warmth spreading through her.

They finished eating, and when they were done, Kyle gathered the empty containers while Megan rinsed their plates and left them in the sink to wash later. The domesticity of it struck her suddenly—this wasn't a date or a special occasion. This was just Thursday night takeout and tired conversation and cleanup. This was normal. Easy.

Real.

Kyle retrieved his toolbox from his truck while Megan opened the television box and decided where on the wall it should go. When he returned, he was all business—measuring, marking, and checking for studs with a small device that beeped at strategic intervals.

"Can you hold this level while I mark the second mount?" he asked, and Megan stepped up beside him, pressing the long metal tool against the wall where he indicated.

They worked together with easy coordination—Kyle drilling pilot holes while Megan held the mount steady, trading off between holding and marking and checking measurements. He explained what he was doing as he went, his voice patient and clear, and Megan found herself genuinely interested in the mechanics of mounting a television properly.

"You're good at this," she observed as he secured the second mount.

"Lots of practice mounting things at the resort and at the shop. Leslie's constantly rearranging displays, which means I'm constantly remounting shelves." Kyle tightened the final screw and stepped back to check his work. "Okay, this is the tricky part. We need to lift the TV together and hook it onto the mounts. You ready?"

"Ready."

They maneuvered the television out of its box—heavier than it looked and awkward to grip—and lifted it together. There was a tense moment where Megan was sure she was going to drop it, but then Kyle made a small adjustment, and the television clicked into place on the mounts with a satisfying sound.

"There." Kyle stepped back, hands on his hips, admiring their work. "How's that look?"

Megan moved to sit on the couch, checking the angle from the best viewing position. "Perfect, actually. Good height, centered on the wall. Yeah, that's really good."

"Excellent." Kyle gathered his tools, returning them to his toolbox with the kind of organized precision that made her smile. "Want to test it out?"

They spent the next ten minutes connecting cables and navigating menus, Kyle patient with technology while Megan figured out which remote controlled what. Finally, they had streaming services loaded and ready, and Megan found herself sinking into the couch with a sigh of relief.

Kyle settled beside her. "So, what are we watching?"

"I don't know if I have the brain capacity for watching anything." Megan tipped her head back against the cushions. "I might just fall asleep right here."

"That's allowed. You had a really hard day."

"Yeah." Megan turned her head to look at him, finding his expression gentle. "Thanks for being here. For dinner and the TV and just—this."

"Anytime." Kyle reached over and tucked a strand of hair behind her ear, his fingers lingering briefly on her cheek. "I like being here. With you. Even on hard days. Especially on hard days."

"Kyle—"

"I just wanted you to know. You don't have to handle everything alone anymore. I'm here. For whatever you need."

Megan searched his face, seeing nothing but sincerity there. No expectations, no pressure. Just genuine care and the steady presence he'd shown her since the day she'd driven into Mistletoe Falls with everything she owned packed in her car.

"I know," she said softly. "And I'm trying to get better at accepting help without feeling like I'm failing somehow."

"You're doing great." Kyle's smile was warm. "Better than great. You're building something real here, Megan. A business, a home, a life. And today, when everything went wrong, you didn't run. You didn't panic. You led. That's not nothing."

The praise made her chest tight with emotion. She didn't quite know what to do with. She wanted to deflect, to make a joke, to minimize what she'd done. But the look in Kyle's eyes stopped her.

He meant it. Every word.

"Stay a little longer?" she heard herself ask. "We don't have to watch anything. I just—I'm not ready for you to go yet."

Kyle's expression softened further, something tender crossing his features. "Yeah. I can stay."

They settled onto the couch together, Megan tucking her feet under her and leaning slightly into Kyle's side. He wrapped an arm around her shoulders, and she let herself relax into his solid warmth, feeling the events of the day loosen their grip on her muscles.

Hazel jumped up onto the couch, circled twice before settling into Megan's lap with a contented purr. The apartment was quiet except for the cat's rumbling and their steady breathing, the new television casting a soft glow across the room.

This was nice. More than nice. It was exactly what she needed—not grand gestures or dramatic declarations, just Kyle's presence and the comfort of being together.

But even as Megan let herself sink into the moment, feeling safe and cared for and maybe even cherished, a small voice in the back of her mind whispered the question she couldn't quite silence:

How long until something goes wrong?

She'd survived today's crisis. She'd made decisions and led her team and kept the business running despite equipment failure and staff emergencies.

But what about tomorrow? And the day after that? What about the moment when the crisis became too much, when her luck ran out?

Kyle's arm tightened slightly around her shoulders, like he could sense the tension creeping back into her body. His thumb traced idle patterns on her upper arm, a gesture of comfort and reassurance.

It should've been enough to quiet her fears.

It almost was.

But Megan had learned long ago that "comfort" was just another word for "temporary," and temporary never lasted.

Chapter 36

The last little girl clutched her candy bag like treasure, her eyes still wide with wonder from meeting Santa.

"Say thank you to Miss Megan for the candy," her mother prompted gently, one hand on her daughter's shoulder while juggling a personalized ornament and a photo package in the other.

"Thank you!" The girl beamed up at Megan, gap-toothed and adorable in a red velvet dress. "The candy is my favorite!"

"You're very welcome, sweetheart." Megan crouched down to the child's level, her smile genuine. "Merry Christmas."

She watched them leave through The Christmas Shop's front door; the bell jingling cheerfully as they stepped out into the early evening darkness. Through the window, she could see snow falling—light, lazy flakes that caught the glow of the streetlights and made Mistletoe Falls look like a snow globe come to life.

"That's the last one," Leslie announced from behind the register, already pulling the day's receipts to count. She looked tired but pleased, her hair escaping its ponytail in wisps around her face. "Kyle, can you lock up?"

"On it." Kyle crossed to the front door, flipping the deadbolt with a satisfying click before turning the sign from OPEN to CLOSED. He caught Megan's eye and grinned. "Successful day, wouldn't you say?"

"Very successful." Megan said. The red and green organza bags she'd prepared yesterday were all gone. "Better than I expected, actually."

"The candy bags were a huge hit." Leslie didn't look up from her counting, but her voice was warm. "I had three people ask if we'd be carrying your products permanently. Which, for the record, we should absolutely talk about."

"I'd like that." Megan felt a flutter of excitement beneath the bone-deep tiredness. It had been a long day—arriving at one to set up, working straight through with barely a break. Her feet ached, and she'd smiled so much her cheeks felt sore. But it was the good kind of tired, the kind that came from doing something meaningful and watching it succeed.

A small flicker of guilt twisted in her stomach. While she'd been here playing Santa's helper, her employees had been at Sugar & Spice, probably working their fingers to the bone. She'd texted Linda twice during brief lulls to check in, and both times she'd been assured everything was fine, but still—

"Stop it," Kyle said quietly, appearing beside her.

Megan blinked. "Stop what?"

"Whatever guilty spiral you just went into." He nodded toward her hands, and she realized she'd been twisting her fingers together. "I can see it on your face too."

"I was just thinking about Linda and Tonya and the rest of my staff. They've been handling everything alone all afternoon."

"And you've been here building business relationships and getting Sugar & Spice's name in front of new customers and building your community presence." Kyle's voice was gentle but firm. "That's not shirking responsibility. That's smart business management."

"He's right," Leslie called from the register. "You can't be in production every single day, Megan. Part of owning a business is knowing when to delegate and when to focus on growth opportunities. Today was growth."

Megan knew they were right. Intellectually, she understood that. But there was still a small voice in her head that whispered she should've been working harder and should've been there.

"Hey." Kyle's hand found hers, warm and steady. "You did good today. Really good. Your staff is capable, and you trusted them to handle things. That's what good leaders do."

She squeezed his hand. "Thanks."

"Anytime." Kyle glanced toward the back corner where they'd set up the Santa area—a red velvet chair on a raised platform, surrounded by wrapped presents (empty boxes, beautifully decorated), a Christmas tree sparkling with lights, and a backdrop painted to look like the North Pole. "Come on. Let's get this cleaned up and let Leslie finish closing, and we can all go home."

They worked together, Kyle dismantling the platform while Megan gathered the prop presents into neat stacks, both of them moving around each other and working together.

"Stack the boxes in the storage room," Leslie instructed, not looking up from her paperwork. "We'll reuse them next year."

"Next year?" Megan said. "You're already planning next year's event?"

"Always." Leslie's grin was quick. "That's how you stay ahead in retail. Plus, now that I know this collaboration works, I'm already thinking about a Valentine's event. Maybe chocolate-themed? You could do special truffles or something."

The casual way Leslie included her in future plans made Megan's throat tight. Like it was a given. Like Sugar & Spice would still be thriving.

She pushed the thought away and focused on the task at hand.

Kyle had broken down the platform into manageable sections and was carrying them toward the storage room. Megan followed with an armload of wrapped boxes, weaving through displays of ornaments and garland that looked even more magical now that the overhead lights were dimmed and only the Christmas lights illuminated the store.

"In here," Kyle said, nudging open the door with his shoulder.

They made several trips, clearing the Santa corner and then adjusting displays to fill the space until it looked like any other part of the store—just another carefully curated display of Christmas magic. Leslie finished her counting and disappeared into her office to complete the day's closing procedures, leaving Megan and Kyle alone in the softly lit shop.

"That's everything," Megan said, surveying their work. "I think we're done."

"Almost." Kyle turned to face her, his expression shifting into something playful. "There's one more thing."

"What's that?"

Kyle held out his hand. "Dance with me?"

Megan looked at his outstretched hand, then around the empty shop. "There's no music."

"Don't need music." Kyle's smile was soft, almost shy. "Just you."

Her heart did a complicated flutter in her chest. "Kyle—"

"Humor me." His hand remained extended, patient. Waiting for her to decide.

Megan placed her hand in his, and Kyle pulled her close with a gentle confidence that made her breath catch. His right hand settled at her waist while his left cradled her hand against his chest. They stood that way for a moment in the dim store, surrounded by twinkling lights and the scent of pine and cinnamon, and then Kyle began to sway.

It wasn't really dancing—just a gentle rocking, back and forth, turning in slow circles between displays of nutcrackers and snow globes. But it felt like dancing. It felt like magic.

"This is silly," Megan said, but she was smiling.

"This is perfect," Kyle corrected. His thumb traced small circles on her waist, and Megan found herself relaxing into his embrace, her free hand coming to rest on his shoulder.

They moved through the store like that, Kyle leading her in lazy circles past the Evergreen Lane section with its rustic cabin decor, past the Snow & Sparkle display where silver ornaments caught the light and threw tiny rainbows across the floor, and past the Letters to Santa corner with its red mailbox and child-sized writing desk.

"You know what I realized today?" Kyle's voice was quiet and intimate in the hushed store.

"What?"

"I really like working with you." His hazel eyes met hers, serious despite the gentle smile on his lips. "Not just being around you, though I like that too. But actually working together. Watching you with those families today, seeing how you lit up when the kids got excited about the candy—it just felt right."

Megan's chest tightened. "It did feel right."

"Yeah." Kyle spun her slowly, her back brushing against a display of glass icicles that chimed softly. "I keep thinking about the future—about us. About what it could look like if we keep doing this. Building things together. Supporting each other's businesses. Just—being partners in all of it."

The word partners landed somewhere deep in Megan's heart. Not just romantic partners, though there was certainly that. But true partners—equals building something meaningful side by side.

"I'd like that," she heard herself say. "The future part. With you."

Kyle's expression shifted into something tender and fierce all at once. He stopped moving, just held her there in the middle of The Christmas Shop with Christmas lights casting colored shadows across his face.

"Megan—" His voice was rough with emotion.

She didn't let him finish. She rose up on her toes and kissed him.

For a moment, Kyle went perfectly still, surprised. Then his arms tightened around her waist, and he was kissing her back with a sweetness that made her knees weak. His lips were soft and careful, like he was handling something precious. One hand came up to cradle her face, his thumb brushing her cheekbone with infinite gentleness.

The kiss was everything: unhurried, deliberate, and full of promise. Megan's hands slid up to link behind his neck, and Kyle made a small sound low in his throat that sent warmth flooding through her entire body.

When they finally pulled apart, both slightly breathless, Kyle rested his forehead against hers, his smile soft and wondering.

"Ms. Caldwell," he said, his tone somewhere between teasing and reverent, "I'm madly and deeply in love with you."

She smiled, letting herself feel the weight of what he'd said. "Mr. Porter," she said, her voice steadier than she expected, "you're making me fall for you more and more every day."

It wasn't "I love you"—not yet, not quite—but it was honest. It was what she could give him right now, and judging by the way Kyle's face lit up like she'd given him the world, it was enough.

He kissed her again, slower this time, like they had all the time in the world. Like there was nowhere else he'd rather be than right here, holding her in a Christmas shop after hours while snow fell outside and the future waited somewhere just out of reach.

When they finally broke apart, Leslie's voice called from the office, "Are you two done making out in my store, or do I need to stay back here longer?"

Megan felt her face flush hot, but Kyle just laughed—easy and unashamed. "We're done!" he called back. Then, quieter, to Megan: "For now."

The promise in those words made her shiver.

Leslie emerged from the office, took one look at them—still standing close, Megan's hands on Kyle's chest, his arms around her waist—and grinned. "Finally. I wondered how long it would take you two."

"We're not that obvious," Kyle protested.

"You're absolutely that obvious." Leslie grabbed her coat from the hook behind the register. "I'm heading out. Kyle, lock up when you're done." She winked. "And try not to knock over any displays."

The door closed behind her with a soft jingle, leaving Megan and Kyle alone again in the quiet store.

"We should probably go," Megan said, but she didn't move away from him.

"Probably." Kyle's arms stayed firmly around her waist. "In a minute."

They stood that way, just holding each other in the soft glow of Christmas lights, and Megan felt something settle in her chest—something warm and terrifying and wonderful all at once.

She'd kissed Kyle Porter. She'd told him she was falling for him. And the world hadn't ended.

In fact, standing here in his arms, surrounded by twinkling lights and the promise of tomorrow, the world felt like it might actually be just beginning.

But even as she let herself sink into the moment, feeling happier than she could remember being in years, a tiny voice in the back of her mind whispered the question she couldn't quite silence:

What happens when he realizes I'm not enough?

Kyle's arms tightened around her, like he could sense the shadow crossing her heart. His lips pressed against her temple, warm and reassuring.

"Hey," he murmured. "Where'd you go?"

Megan forced herself back to the present, to the solid warmth of him holding her. "Nowhere. I'm right here."

Chapter 37

"Higher on the left," Megan called from her position on the sectional, tilting her head to get a better angle. "No, wait—lower. Actually, maybe it was perfect where you had it."

Kyle, balanced precariously on the step stool with a delicate glass snowflake dangling from his fingers, shot her an amused look over his shoulder. "You're killing me here."

"I'm sorry!" Megan laughed, pulling the cream throw blanket more snugly around her shoulders. "I just want it to be perfect."

"It's already perfect." Kyle adjusted the ornament one more time. The glass snowflake caught the afternoon light overhead, casting tiny prismatic rainbows across the wall.

He was right. The seven-foot artificial tree stood in the corner near the windows, its pre-lit branches already glowing softly even in daylight. They'd been decorating for over an hour now, and the tree was slowly transforming into something magical—traditional red, green, and gold ornaments mixed with the abundance of glass icicles and snowflakes Megan had fallen in love with at Mistletoe Mercantile that morning.

Hazel sat on the arm of the sectional, her tail swishing with obvious interest as Kyle climbed down from the step stool. The moment his feet hit the floor, she launched herself at a strand of beads draped over a nearby box, batting at it with determined paws.

"No ma'am." Megan scooped up the cat, who protested with an indignant meow. "Those are not toys."

"She's been remarkably patient," Kyle observed, reaching over to scratch behind Hazel's ears. The cat's protest immediately transformed into a rumbling purr. "I expected more chaos."

"Give her time. The day's not over yet."

Kyle grabbed another ornament from the box at his feet—a classic red ball with gold scrollwork. He held it up for Megan's inspection. "Where's this one going?"

"Middle section, right side. Fill in the gap near the green one."

They'd developed a rhythm over the past hour. Kyle handled the higher branches while Megan directed placement from her spot on the couch, occasionally getting up to adjust lower ornaments or add ribbon. It was surprisingly easy working together like this. No disagreements about style, no tension over where things should go. Just natural collaboration that felt as comfortable as breathing.

The morning had been equally effortless. They'd started at The Christmas Shop, where Megan had used the generous gift card Leslie and Kyle had given her as a housewarming present. She'd wandered the themed rooms with Kyle trailing behind, filling two baskets with ornaments that caught her eye—traditional styles mostly, with a few whimsical pieces that made her smile. A wooden nutcracker. A brass angel with delicate wings. A collection of miniature wrapped presents to tuck among the branches.

From there they'd hit Mistletoe Mercantile, where Natalie had shown them her extensive collection of glass decorations. Megan had gone slightly overboard—she could admit that now, looking at the three large bags still waiting to be unpacked—but the icicles and snowflakes had been impossible to resist.

They'd grabbed lunch at The Pickle Barrel, sharing a sandwich and splitting a bowl of tomato bisque, then stopped at Pinecone & Ivy where Heather had helped them select a wreath for her door.

"I think we bought out half the town," Kyle had joked as they'd loaded everything into his truck.

"We absolutely did not," Megan had protested, but she'd been laughing too, giddy with the pleasure.

Now, watching Kyle hang ornaments, she felt that same giddiness mixed with something deeper. Something that made her chest feel too full and her throat tight with emotion she couldn't quite name.

"What are you thinking about?" Kyle asked, glancing over at her. "You've got that look."

"What look?"

"The one where you're somewhere else entirely." He stepped back from the tree, surveying their progress. "Everything okay?"

"Yeah." Megan set Hazel down gently, the cat immediately stalking toward a box of ornaments with predatory focus. "Just thinking about how nice today has been."

"It has been nice." Kyle moved to sit beside her on the sectional, his weight settling into the cushions with familiar ease. "I like doing this kind of stuff with you."

"Decorating?"

"All of it. Shopping, decorating, just—spending time together doing ordinary things." He reached for another ornament, turning the red globe between his fingers. "It's easy. You're easy to be with."

Megan felt warmth bloom in her chest. "You're easy to be with too."

"Good thing, considering how much time we spend together. I was thinking earlier, while we were at The Christmas Shop—we have similar tastes in pretty much everything. Traditional style, classic colors. Even our decorating philosophies match."

"Our decorating philosophies?" Megan couldn't help smiling. "That's very serious language for hanging ornaments."

"I'm a serious man." But his eyes were dancing. "I'm just saying, it's nice. Finding someone whose aesthetic sensibilities align with yours. Makes everything simpler."

"Simpler," Megan echoed, testing the word.

Kyle stood, stretching his arms above his head until his shoulders popped. "Ready to tackle the garland?"

They worked together to drape the burgundy and gold garland around the tree, Kyle feeding it to Megan as she wove it through branches, creating depth and texture among the ornaments. Hazel watched from her perch on the sectional arm, her tail twitching with barely contained excitement.

"I think she's plotting something," Megan said, eyeing the cat suspiciously.

"She's definitely plotting something," Kyle agreed. "The question is what."

As if on cue, Hazel launched herself at the lowest branch of the tree, a glass icicle ornament swinging wildly from the impact. Kyle lunged forward, steadying the tree while Megan extracted the cat from the branches.

"You are a menace," Megan informed Hazel, who looked entirely unrepentant.

"Maybe we should put her in the bedroom until we're done," Kyle suggested.

"Probably wise."

Megan carried Hazel down the hall, depositing her gently on the bed with a stern look that the cat completely ignored. By the time she returned to the living room, Kyle had secured the garland and was sorting through the remaining ornaments.

"We're almost done," he said. "Just the strings of beads and the tree topper left."

They added the beads next, golden strands that caught the tree's pre-lit glow and reflected it back in warm honey tones. Megan stepped back periodically to check the overall effect, adjusting placement until everything felt balanced and intentional.

"Now, the tree topper," Kyle said, as he grabbed the last bag from The Christmas Shop.

Inside were three possibilities: a traditional star, an elegant gold finial, and a beautiful angel with gossamer wings and a porcelain face.

"The angel," Megan said immediately. "Definitely the angel."

Kyle climbed back onto the step stool. Megan watched as he positioned it atop the tree, adjusting until it sat perfectly centered. When he stepped down, they both stood back to take in the full effect.

The tree was stunning. The glass icicles and snowflakes caught the light from every angle, creating a winter wonderland effect. The burgundy, hunter green, and gold accents added richness and warmth. And the angel presided over it all with serene grace.

"It's perfect," Megan whispered.

"It really is." Kyle's arm slipped around her shoulders, pulling her against his side. "This is our first tree."

The words hung in the air between them. Not "your first tree" or "the tree." Our first tree. Like it was the beginning of a tradition rather than a single afternoon's project.

Megan leaned into his warmth, letting herself enjoy the solid presence of him. The way he made everything feel possible. The way being with him was the easiest thing in the world.

"I should probably clean up this mess," she said.

"We should clean up the mess," Kyle corrected. "I helped make it."

They worked together to break down boxes, organize leftover ornaments, and return the step stool to the closet. Kyle tied up the garbage bag while Megan retrieved Hazel from the bedroom, the cat immediately racing to investigate the tree with obvious fascination.

"She's going to knock something off the minute we're not looking," Megan predicted.

"Definitely." Kyle checked his watch, and something shifted in his expression. "I should probably get going. I've got some errands to run and work to finish for a client meeting tomorrow morning."

Megan tried to ignore the small pang of disappointment. She knew he had responsibilities. They both did. But after such a perfect day, it was hard to watch it end.

"Thanks for today," she said, walking him to the door. "For shopping with me and helping decorate and just—all of it."

"I had a really good time," Kyle said and pulled her into a hug.

"Me too."

He pulled back just enough to look at her, his hazel eyes warm in the apartment's soft lighting. Then he was kissing her—gentle and sweet and perfect. Megan's hands came up to rest against his chest, feeling his heartbeat steady beneath her palms.

When they broke apart, Kyle's smile was soft. "I'll see you tomorrow?"

"Coffee before work?"

"It's a date."

He moved toward the door, then paused with his hand on the knob. "Text me if you need anything tonight. Even if it's just to talk or if Hazel destroys your tree."

"I will." Megan leaned against the doorframe, watching him. "Text me when you get home? So I know you made it safely?"

Kyle's expression shifted into something tender. "Megan, it's a fifteen-minute drive to my cabin."

"I know. But still."

"I'll text," he promised. "But don't worry about me, okay? I'm fine."

"I'll try not to worry."

He kissed her once more, quickly and lightly, then headed down the stairs. Megan listened to his footsteps fade, then the sound of his truck starting in the alley below. She stood in the doorway until the engine noise disappeared, then stepped back inside and closed the door.

The apartment felt different suddenly. Quieter. Emptier. Not in a bad way—just noticeable. The space that had felt so full of energy and laughter and Kyle's presence now held only her and Hazel and the soft glow of the Christmas tree.

Megan moved through the apartment, turning off all the lights except the tree. Then she settled onto the sectional in the darkened room, pulling the throw blanket around herself. The tree lights cast everything in warm, multicolored shadows. Red and gold and green and white, all blending together into something magical.

Hazel jumped up beside her, curling into a small ball against her thigh with a contented purr.

It had been an amazing day. Shopping together, laughing together, creating something beautiful together. The easy way Kyle fit into her life, into her space, into every moment. The casual comments about shared tastes and traditions. The kiss goodbye that felt like a promise of more perfect days to come.

And that was the problem.

Not a problem, exactly. But something that made Megan's chest feel tight and her breath catch. Because sitting here in the glow of their tree—and yes, it felt like their tree now, even though it stood in her apartment and they'd only known each other for a matter of weeks—she understood something with bone-deep certainty.

She was falling completely, irrevocably in love with Kyle Porter.

Not the easy, comfortable fondness of early dating. Not the pleasant attraction or the enjoyment of shared time. This was something bigger. Something that lived in the center of her chest and radiated outward until her whole body hummed with it.

She loved the way he made her laugh. The way he showed up for her without being asked. The way he treated her employees with respect and her dreams with seriousness. The way he kissed her like she was precious. The way he looked at her like she was exactly where he wanted to be.

She loved decorating trees with him and sharing sandwiches with him and just existing beside him. She loved his terrible jokes and his competence and the way he remembered things she mentioned in passing. She loved that he brought her coffee out of the blue at the shop while she was working and had mounted her television like it was nothing and never made her feel like accepting help meant she was weak.

The certainty of it should have felt good. Liberating, even. Instead, it felt a bit terrifying.

The old fears stirred in her chest, familiar and insidious.

You don't deserve this.

It won't last.

You'll ruin it.

Something will go wrong.

Megan closed her eyes, feeling Hazel's steady purr against her leg. She recognized these thoughts for what they were—the same pattern she'd been running with since she was thirteen years old. The same automatic assumption that happiness was temporary and love was a trap.

But this time, she didn't let the thoughts spiral. She acknowledged them, felt them, and then consciously chose to set them aside.

This life she was building wasn't the unstable foundation of her childhood. The people in Mistletoe Falls—Leslie and her staff and the entire community—they'd proven over and over that they weren't going anywhere. That they wanted her here. That belonging wasn't something she had to earn or maintain through perfect behavior.

And Kyle had been nothing but steady. Nothing but present. Nothing but genuine in his care for her.

The fear wasn't about him. It was about her. About whether she could let herself have this without waiting for it to end.

Her phone buzzed against the coffee table, and she reached for it with one hand.

Kyle: *Home safe. Thanks again for a perfect day. Sleep well.*

Megan smiled, typing back quickly.

Megan: *Glad you're home. Today was perfect. Goodnight.*

She set the phone down and looked at the tree again. At the angel presiding over their combined choices, traditional and beautiful and exactly right. At the ornaments they'd hung together, the garland they'd woven through branches, and the care they'd taken to create something meaningful.

Hazel shifted against her leg, stretching before settling back into sleep. Megan yawned, suddenly aware of how much energy the day had taken. Her eyes felt heavy, her body pleasantly tired from the physical work of decorating and the emotional weight of processing everything she felt.

She gave the tree one last long look, memorizing this moment. The quiet contentment. The soft glow.

Then she got up, reached for the outlet and switched off the Christmas tree lights, plunging the room into darkness.

Time for bed. Time to let this perfect day end so tomorrow could begin.

Chapter 38

"I think you're supposed to dice those, not massacre them," Kyle said, peering over Megan's shoulder at the cutting board where she'd been reducing an onion to progressively smaller pieces.

"I'm dicing," Megan protested, though she had to admit the pieces were getting somewhat microscopic. "Very finely dicing."

"That's not dicing. That's pulverizing." Kyle reached around her to steal a piece of bell pepper from her prep bowl, popping it into his mouth with a grin. "At this rate, we're going to be eating onion paste."

"Then maybe you should do the onions," Megan suggested, bumping him with her hip to move him out of her space.

"No way. I've seen what happens when I cry while cooking. Very undignified." He returned to the stove where a pot of water was just starting to boil. "How's that recipe looking, anyway? Still think it's easy?"

Megan glanced at her phone propped against the backsplash, the recipe for chicken piccata displayed on the screen. "I said it sounded easy. Past tense. Present tense, I'm having regrets."

"Too late now. We're committed." Kyle added salt to the boiling water, then moved to check the chicken breasts he'd been pounding thin between sheets of plastic wrap. "Though I have to say, your definition of 'easy weeknight dinner' is significantly more ambitious than mine."

"Your definition involves sandwiches."

"Efficient sandwiches," Kyle corrected. "There's an art to it."

They'd been cooking together for the past half hour. Kyle's cabin felt warm and inviting, with the stone fireplace crackling cheerfully in the living room beyond the kitchen. Through the windows, Megan could see fresh snow falling in big, fat flakes drifting down through the early evening darkness.

After dinner, they'd planned to decorate Kyle's Christmas tree—a real spruce he'd cut from the woods behind his house that now stood bare and waiting in the corner of his living room. But first, they had to successfully execute this recipe that had looked much simpler in the photos.

"Okay, the onions are done," Megan announced, scraping the admittedly very finely minced pieces into a bowl. "What's next?"

"Flour the chicken, and then we'll pan-fry it." Kyle handed her a shallow dish with seasoned flour. "The recipe said to coat it evenly but not too thick."

Megan worked the chicken pieces through the flour while Kyle heated olive oil in a large skillet.

"So," Kyle said as the first chicken breast hit the pan with a satisfying sizzle, "Christmas Eve at my parents' place. You're still coming, right?"

"Of course." Megan had been looking forward to it since the invitation had been extended. "I wouldn't miss it."

"Good. Mom's already planning enough food to feed an army... as usual." He flipped the chicken; the golden-brown crust was perfect. "You don't have to bring anything if you don't want to. She always makes way too much."

"I want to bring something," Megan said. "Maybe I could bring a dessert? Or an appetizer?"

"Whatever you want. Just don't stress about it." Kyle transferred the first batch of chicken to a plate, then added more pieces to the pan. "Mom will be thrilled you're coming. She's been asking about you constantly."

"She has?"

"Oh yeah. Wants to know all about the shop, how you're settling in, whether you like Mistletoe Falls." Kyle's smile was warm. "She's already adopted you, I think. That's kind of her thing—she sees someone new in town and immediately wants to make them feel welcome."

"That's sweet."

"That's Mom." He gestured toward the sauce ingredients. "Can you start the sauce while I finish the chicken?"

Megan followed the recipe's instructions, melting butter in another pan before adding the pulverized onions and garlic. The kitchen filled with savory aromas that made her stomach growl. Kyle had opened the bottle of white wine earlier, and she added the required amount to the pan, watching it bubble and reduce.

"So after Christmas," Kyle said, his attention on the chicken, "things slow down a lot in town. Tourist traffic drops pretty significantly until we hit the Valentine's season, and even that's nothing compared to Christmas."

"What do people do?" Megan asked, adding chicken broth and lemon juice to her pan. "When it's not the busy season?"

"All the local stuff that gets pushed aside during the holidays. Hiking when the weather's nice, ice skating at the pond, movie nights at the library." Kyle plated the last of the chicken. "Actually, I was thinking—there's this great hiking trail up to Crystal Falls. It's a moderate climb, maybe two hours round trip, and the waterfall is incredible to see even in winter. We should go sometime in January when you have a day off."

"That sounds nice." Megan stirred the sauce, watching it thicken slightly.

"And I almost forgot, but there's the Winter Carnival in January—it's a whole weekend thing with ice sculptures and sledding competitions and food vendors. Leslie and I usually run a booth for The Christmas Shop, but it's actually pretty fun. You'd like it."

"I'm sure I would."

"Oh... back to February—I was thinking, maybe around Valentine's Day, we could take a long weekend and drive down to Florida. Visit your mom." He said it casually, adding capers to the sauce while Megan stirred. "I'd like to meet her and her husband... it'd be nice to get away from the cold for a few days. Feel some sunshine."

Megan's hand stilled on the wooden spoon. "Florida?"

"Yeah. I mean, only if you want to. No pressure." Kyle returned the chicken to the pan, coating each piece in the sauce. "Just thought it might be nice. Meet your mom. Plus, beach weather in February sounds pretty good right about now."

"I—yeah, maybe." Megan resumed stirring, though the sauce no longer needed it.

"And then in May, for your birthday, we could plan something special. Maybe a trip somewhere you've always wanted to go. Have you ever been to Asheville? Great city, amazing food scene. Or we could head up to Gatlinburg if you want to stay closer." Kyle was clearly warming to his topic, his voice animated. "Whatever you want. It's your birthday—you should get to choose."

"Kyle—"

"Oh, and in August, my parents' 35th wedding anniversary." He wasn't looking at her now, focused on arranging the chicken on a serving platter. "Leslie and I want to plan something really special for them. Maybe a surprise party, or we were thinking about booking a vacation package—one of those all-inclusive resort things. They've never taken a real vacation together, just the two of them. Well, the four of us, actually. Five, with you."

Megan set down the spoon carefully, her hands beginning to tremble. "Five?"

"Yeah. You'd come with us—" Kyle finally looked up from the chicken, his expression shifting as he caught sight of her face. "What's wrong?"

"You're planning our entire year."

"I'm just—we were talking about what happens after Christmas, and I was just thinking out loud about fun things we could do together." Kyle's brow furrowed, confusion clear in his voice. "I didn't mean—"

"Florida in February. A birthday trip in May. A family vacation in August." Megan's voice sounded strange to her own ears—high and tight and wrong. "You've got the next eight months mapped out."

"Megan, I was just making suggestions. Ideas we could talk about." Kyle set down the platter, giving her his full attention. "I wasn't deciding anything."

"You're assuming I'll be there for all of it." The words came out sharper than she had intended. "You're just—you're assuming."

"I thought—" Kyle's confusion was morphing into something that looked like hurt. "I thought that's what people in relationships do—make plans together."

"We've been dating for just over a month!"

"Yes... we have." His voice was quiet. "And I'm in love with you, Megan. I've told you that. So yeah, I'm thinking about the future because I see you in it."

The certainty in his words should have been comforting. Instead, it felt like a weight pressing down on her chest, making it hard to breathe.

"I can't—" Megan stepped back from the stove, her hands clenching into fists at her sides. "You can't just plan everything like it's already decided."

"I'm not planning everything. I'm sharing ideas about things we might want to do together." Kyle's voice was measured and patient, which somehow made it worse. "If you don't want to do any of those things, we don't have to. I was just thinking out loud."

"You're thinking eight months ahead!" The panic was rising now, unstoppable. "Meeting my mother, birthday trips, anniversary parties—"

"Because I care about you! Because I want to share those things with you!" Kyle's patience was starting to crack. "Why is that a problem?"

"Because!" The word burst out of her too loud, too raw. "Because I'm certain about you too, okay? I'm so certain it terrifies me."

Kyle went very still. "What?"

"I'm certain." Megan's throat was tight, her eyes burning. "I'm certain in a way that I haven't been certain about anything in my entire life, and it scares me to death because everyone I've ever been certain about has left."

"Megan—"

"My father. My mother, in a different way. Every person I've ever counted on to stay has found a reason to leave." The words were pouring out now, unstoppable. "And you're standing here making plans like it's a given that I'll be around in August, like there's no possibility that this won't work out, and I can't—I can't let myself believe that. I can't let myself be that certain because when it ends, it'll destroy me."

"When it ends?" Kyle's voice was sharp now. "Not if—when?"

"Yes, when!" Megan could feel tears threatening, hot and unwelcome. "Because it always ends. People leave. They always leave."

"I'm not your father, Megan."

"I know that!"

"Do you?" Kyle moved toward her, his expression a mixture of hurt and frustration. "Because it sounds like you're already planning our breakup. Like you're just waiting for me to prove that you're right about not deserving good things."

"That's not fair."

"None of this is fair!" Kyle's voice rose for the first time. "I've been nothing but honest with you. I've shown up, I've supported you, I've been patient while you work through your fears. But you're holding my feelings against me like it's a crime that I love you and want a future with you."

"You want too much too fast!"

"I want what I want! I can't help that I'm ready for this, that I know what I want and you're it." Kyle's hands went up in a gesture of helplessness. "I'm not trying to pressure you. I was just talking about fun things we could do together. That's what people do when they're happy—they make plans. They look forward to things."

"Well, maybe I'm not ready for that." Megan's voice cracked. "Maybe I need you to slow down and stop planning our whole life together before I've even figured out how to be in a relationship without constantly waiting for it to end."

"I can't slow down my feelings, Megan. That's not how this works."

"Then maybe this doesn't work!"

The words hung in the air between them, sharp and terrible. Kyle flinched as if she'd struck him, his expression going carefully blank.

"Is that what you want?" His voice was quiet now, controlled. "Do you want to end this?"

"I don't—" Megan pressed her hands to her face, the tears finally spilling over. "I don't know what I want. I just know that standing here listening to you plan the next eight months of our lives made me feel like I can't breathe."

"Because you're terrified of being happy." Kyle's words were gentle but unyielding. "Because you're so convinced you don't deserve this that you're looking for reasons to sabotage it."

"That's not—"

"It is." He took a step toward her, then seemed to think better of it. "You said it yourself—you're certain about me. But instead of letting yourself be happy about that, you're panicking because certainty means vulnerability. It means having something real to lose."

"You don't understand."

"I understand perfectly." Kyle's eyes held hers, sad and frustrated and still somehow full of love. "I understand that you're so afraid of being left that you're willing to leave first. To protect yourself from a pain that hasn't even happened yet."

Megan couldn't argue with that because he was right. She was armoring herself against a future hurt by creating one now.

But knowing it didn't make the fear go away. It didn't make her chest feel less tight or her breathing any easier or the panic any less overwhelming.

"I should go," she said, her voice barely audible.

"Megan, don't—"

"I need to go. I'm sorry. I just—I can't do this right now." She was already moving toward where she'd left her coat by the door, her movements jerky and uncoordinated.

"We haven't even eaten dinner. Just—stay. Please. We can talk about this."

"I can't." Megan shrugged into her coat with fumbling fingers, not looking at him. If she looked at him, she'd break completely. "I'm sorry. I'm sorry I ruined dinner, and I'm sorry I'm such a mess, and I'm sorry I can't be what you need."

"You are what I need." Kyle's voice was raw with emotion. "You're exactly what I need. If you'd just let yourself believe that—"

"I have to go."

She was out the door before he could respond, the cold December air hitting her face like a slap. Her car was parked beside his truck, already accumulating a thin layer of snow. She brushed off the windshield with shaking hands, aware of Kyle standing in the doorway backlit by the warm light of his cabin.

He didn't call after her. He didn't try to stop her. Just stood there watching as she climbed into her car and started the engine, her breath coming in short, panicked gasps that fogged the windows.

The drive back to her apartment was a blur of dark roads and falling snow and tears that wouldn't stop coming. She'd done it. She'd taken the perfect evening and the perfect relationship and blown it apart because she couldn't handle her own certainty.

Kyle had been right about everything. She was sabotaging this. She was running away from happiness because the vulnerability of loving him felt more dangerous than the loneliness of being alone.

But being right didn't make him wrong for planning their future like it was inevitable. Didn't make her wrong for needing more time before she could look eight months ahead and see them still together without panic clutching at her throat.

She pulled into the alley behind her building; the stairs leading up to her apartment looked steep and unwelcoming in the darkness. Inside, her Christmas tree would be lit and beautiful. Her apartment would be warm and comfortable and hers.

And she would be completely, utterly alone.

Megan turned off the engine and sat in the darkness, the snow accumulating on her windshield, blocking out the world. Her phone buzzed in her pocket—probably Kyle—but she couldn't bring herself to look at it.

Chapter 39

Megan stood on the landing outside Leslie's apartment, her hand raised to knock, wondering if this was a terrible idea. It was 8:30 on a Friday night. Leslie could have plans. She could have company. She could be relaxing after a long week.

Before she could second-guess herself into leaving, she knocked.

Footsteps approached, then the door swung open to reveal Leslie in comfortable clothes—leggings and an oversized sweater, her hair pulled back in a messy bun. Her expression shifted from surprise to concern in an instant.

"Megan? What's wrong?"

"I'm sorry to just show up like this." Megan's voice cracked on the last word. "I should have called first. I can go—"

"Don't you dare." Leslie reached out and pulled her inside, closing the door firmly behind them. "Come in. Sit. Do you want coffee? Wine? Both?"

"Wine, please," she managed.

Leslie guided her to the plush sofa, then disappeared into the kitchen. Megan heard the sound of a cork being pulled, glasses clinking, and then Leslie was back with two generous pours of red wine.

"Okay." Leslie settled beside her on the couch, turning to face her fully. "Tell me what's going on."

"You don't know?"

"Know what?" Leslie's confusion seemed genuine. "Megan, I haven't seen you in a week. Wait... did something happen between you and my brother? He's been acting weird for the past couple of days. He's been holed up in his office instead of helping on the floor, barely says two words when I ask him anything, and yesterday he snapped at Gracie for humming. Kyle never snaps at anyone, especially not Gracie."

So he hadn't told Leslie. He hadn't confided in his sister about what had happened. Megan didn't know if that made things better or worse.

"We had a fight," Megan mumbled. "A bad one."

"When?"

"Wednesday night. At his cabin." Megan took a large gulp of wine. "We were making dinner together, and it was perfect—everything was perfect—and then I ruined it."

"I seriously doubt you ruined anything. But start from the beginning. What happened?"

So Megan told her. About cooking together and their easy banter. About the conversation shifting to post-holiday plans, Kyle's suggestions starting small and building to major future commitments. Florida in February. Her birthday in May. His parents' anniversary in August.

"And I just—I panicked," Megan said, the words tumbling out faster now. "He was planning our entire year like it was a given that we'd still be together, and I couldn't breathe. I accused him of moving too fast, of assuming too much, and he didn't understand why that was a problem."

Leslie was quiet for a moment, her expression thoughtful. "What did he say?"

"That he loves me. That he sees me in his future, and he was just sharing ideas about things we could do together." Megan's throat felt tight. "That I was holding his feelings against him as if it were a crime that he wants a future with me."

"Was he wrong?"

The question was so direct that Megan nearly choked on her wine. "What?"

"Was he wrong?" Leslie repeated, her voice kind but unflinching. "Because from where I'm sitting, it sounds like Kyle was being honest about his feelings and making normal relationship suggestions about things you could do together. And you panicked."

"He was planning eight months ahead!"

"He was thinking about fun trips you could take together." Leslie set down her wine glass. "Megan, those weren't commitments. They were ideas. Possibilities. The kind of things people talk about when they're happy and want to share experiences."

"But—"

"And honestly?" Leslie leaned forward slightly. "My brother has been in love with you since about three days after you arrived in Mistletoe Falls. He can't help that he knows what he wants. That's just who Kyle is—when he's certain about something, he's all in."

"That's the problem," Megan whispered. "He's so certain."

"No." Leslie's voice was firm now. "That's not the problem. The problem is that you're just as certain as he is, and that terrifies you."

Megan opened her mouth to deny it, but Leslie held up a hand.

"I've watched you two together, Megan. I've seen the way you look at him. The way your whole face lights up when he walks into a room. The way you lean into him without even realizing it. You're not afraid he's moving too fast. You're afraid because you want everything he described."

"I don't—"

"Yes, you do." Leslie's tone was gentle but absolutely certain. "You want the Florida trip and the birthday celebration and the family vacation. You want to be part of our family and build traditions with Kyle and have a future together. But wanting those things means being vulnerable. It means trusting that this is real and lasting, and that scares you more than anything."

Megan felt tears building behind her eyes. "You don't understand."

"Then help me understand." Leslie shifted closer, her expression open and patient. "Talk to me. What are you really afraid of?"

"People leave." The words burst out raw and desperate. "My father left without looking back. My mother chose her new husband over me. Every person I've ever counted on to stay has found a reason to leave, and Kyle—" Her voice broke. "Kyle is so steady and present and certain, and I keep waiting for him to realize I'm not worth it. That I'm too damaged or too difficult or too much work."

"Has he given you any sign that's true?"

"No, but—"

"Has he done a single thing that suggests he's going to leave?"

"No."

"Has he been anything other than completely consistent in his actions and feelings toward you?"

"No!" Megan's hands clenched around her wine glass. "That's what makes it worse! He's perfect. He shows up and supports me and loves me and doesn't ask for anything in return, and I don't know how to trust that. I don't know how to believe that someone that good won't eventually realize I'm not worth the effort."

Leslie was quiet for a long moment, her eyes searching Megan's face. When she spoke, her voice was soft but steady.

"You know what I see when I look at you and Kyle together?"

"What?"

"Two people who are completely in love with each other. Two people who fit together in a way that makes everyone around them smile. Two people who could have something really beautiful if one of them would stop trying so hard to protect herself from happiness."

"Leslie—"

"My brother isn't your father, Megan. He's not your mother. He's not any of the people who've hurt you before." Leslie reached out and took Megan's hand, squeezing firmly. "Kyle is the most loyal, steady, dependable person I know. When he commits to something—or someone—he doesn't back out. He doesn't change his mind. He doesn't leave."

"You can't know that for sure."

"Yes, I can. Because I've watched him my entire life. I've seen him take care of our family business and build his law practice and show up for every single person in this town who needs help. I've seen him weather hard things and boring things and frustrating things without quitting. And I've never—not once—seen him as happy as he is with you."

The tears were falling now, hot trails down Megan's cheeks. "Then why am I so scared?"

"Because you're in love." Leslie's voice was achingly gentle. "Real, deep, committed love. The kind that requires trust and vulnerability and risk. And that's terrifying when you've been hurt before."

"I don't know how to do this," Megan whispered. "I don't know how to let myself be this certain without constantly waiting for something to go wrong."

"You do it by choosing courage over fear. Every single day. Every single moment that the fear tells you to run, you choose to stay instead." Leslie squeezed her hand again. "You do it by trusting your own feelings as much as you trust his. By believing that what you feel for Kyle is real and worth fighting for."

"What if I'm wrong? What if I trust him completely and it still falls apart?"

"Then you'll survive. You've survived worse." Leslie's expression was fierce now. "But Megan, what if you're right? What if you let yourself be certain and choose vulnerability and build a life with Kyle, and it's everything you've ever wanted? What if the risk is worth it?"

Megan closed her eyes, Leslie's words settling over her like a weight. Or maybe not a weight. Maybe more like an anchor. Something solid to hold on to while the current of her fear tried to pull her under.

She wanted the future Kyle had described. Wanted it with a bone-deep certainty that made her breath catch. She wanted to visit her mother with him by her side. Wanted to celebrate birthdays and anniversaries and ordinary Tuesdays. Wanted to decorate Christmas trees and cook dinner together and build traditions that were theirs.

She wanted him. All of him. The certainty and the commitment, and the way he looked at her like she was exactly where he wanted to be.

And she'd been using "you're moving too fast" as a shield to protect herself.

"I messed up," Megan said, opening her eyes to meet Leslie's gaze. "I messed up so badly."

"Yes, you did." Leslie's honesty was somehow comforting. "You hurt him. He's been miserable these past two days, and now I understand why."

"I haven't answered his texts."

Leslie's expression softened. "Here's the thing about my brother—he's patient. He'll wait for you to figure out what you need. But Megan, he can't fight your fears for you. You have to choose to trust him. Choose to trust yourself. Choose to believe that you deserve this and that it's real and that sometimes good things actually do last."

"What if I don't know how?"

"Then you learn. You practice. You start by apologizing and being honest about what you're actually afraid of. And then you keep choosing courage even when it's hard." Leslie picked up her wine glass again, taking a small sip. "Love isn't about never being scared. It's about being scared and doing it anyway."

Megan sat with that for a moment.

She'd been so focused on protecting herself from potential hurt that she'd created actual hurt. She'd pushed away the best thing in her life because the vulnerability of loving him felt more dangerous than the safety of being alone.

But alone wasn't safe. Alone was just lonely.

And Kyle—steady, patient, certain Kyle—deserved better than her fear. He deserved the version of her that could choose courage over fear.

"I need to talk to him."

"Yes, you do." Leslie smiled, warm and encouraging. "But maybe not tonight. It's late. Give yourself tomorrow to sit with everything we've talked about. Let it settle. Then go to him."

"What if he doesn't forgive me?"

"He will." Leslie's certainty was absolute. "He loves you, Megan."

Megan nodded, wiping at her damp cheeks with the back of her hand. She felt wrung out and raw and also somehow lighter than she'd felt in days.

"Thanks for listening," she said quietly. "For not judging me. For helping me see what I was really doing."

"That's what friends are for." Leslie pulled her into a hug, warm and solid and reassuring. "And Megan? You're not too damaged or too difficult or too much work. You're exactly right. For Kyle, for this town, for the life you're building. You just have to start believing that."

Megan held onto Leslie for a long moment, drawing strength from her certainty and her kindness. When she finally pulled back, she felt something she hadn't felt in two days.

She felt ready.

Not ready to have all her fears magically disappear. Not ready to suddenly become someone who didn't struggle with trust and vulnerability. But ready to try. Ready to choose courage. Ready to fight for the relationship she wanted instead of sabotaging it out of fear.

They talked for another hour—easier conversation now, Leslie sharing funny stories about holiday shoppers and Megan admitting how much she'd missed Kyle's spontaneous coffee deliveries and replying to his text messages. When Megan finally left, the night air was crisp and cold, but the snow had stopped, leaving the world quiet and pristine.

She drove back to her apartment slowly, Leslie's words echoing in her mind.

Choose courage over fear.

Trust your own feelings.

Believe that you deserve this.

Chapter 40

Kyle stared at the bowl of cereal in front of him, the milk having long since turned the cornflakes into a soggy, unappetizing mess. He'd poured it twenty minutes ago—or maybe thirty—and had managed maybe three bites before his mind wandered back to Wednesday night. To Megan's face when she'd accused him of planning their entire year without asking her. To the hurt in her voice when she'd said she couldn't breathe.

He pushed the bowl away with more force than necessary; the spoon clattering against the ceramic.

Three days. It had been three days since she'd walked out of his cabin, and he still didn't understand exactly what he'd done wrong. He'd replayed the conversation a hundred times, analyzing every word, every suggestion he'd made. Florida. Her birthday. His parents' anniversary. None of it had been demands or expectations—just ideas. Things they could do together.

His phone sat on the counter where he'd left it after checking it for the dozenth time that morning. Still no text from Megan. She'd responded to exactly one message in three days—a single word "okay" when he'd asked if she'd made it home safely Wednesday night. Everything else had gone unanswered.

Kyle stood and carried his bowl to the sink, dumping the ruined cereal down the disposal. Through the kitchen window, he could see fresh snow blanketing the mountains, the morning sun making everything look clean and pristine. It was the kind of perfect winter day that usually made him grateful to live here. Today, it just made him feel hollow.

A knock at the door pulled him from his thoughts. He checked the time—8:47 AM.

When he opened the door, his father stood on the porch holding a toolbox and wearing work clothes.

"Mornin'," Mitch said. "Got a plumbing issue in one of the A-frames. Thought you might be free to help."

"Yeah, I'm free."

"Good. Grab your coat."

They walked in silence down the snow-packed path toward the resort's rental cabins, their boots crunching in rhythm.

They reached the A-frame in question, and Mitch led them inside to the small bathroom where water had apparently been leaking from the toilet's base. Kyle knelt to examine the connection while his father retrieved tools from the box.

"Wax ring's shot," Kyle said after a moment. "Needs replacing."

"That's what I figured." Mitch handed him a wrench. "You want to shut off the water valve, or should I?"

"I'll do it."

They worked together with the easy coordination of people who'd done this dozens of times before. Kyle shut off the water, flushed to empty the tank, then began disconnecting the supply line. His father held the bowl steady while Kyle removed the bolts anchoring it to the floor.

It wasn't until they'd lifted the toilet and set it aside, revealing the old wax ring beneath, that Mitch finally spoke.

"So. You going to tell me what's wrong, or are we going to pretend you're fine?"

Kyle scraped at the old wax with a putty knife, not looking up. "What makes you think something's wrong?"

"Your mother mentioned she hasn't seen you in a couple of days. And you dumped a soggy bowl of cereal down the drain." Mitch's tone was matter-of-fact.

"You were watching me while I ate breakfast?"

"I looked through your kitchen window when you didn't answer the door right away. Saw you staring at that bowl like it held the answers to life's mysteries." Mitch settled onto the floor beside him, handing over a new wax ring. "Want to talk about it?"

Kyle positioned the new ring carefully, buying himself a moment. Then, because keeping it in wasn't working and because his father had always been someone he could trust with the hard things in life, he started talking.

He explained the dinner at his cabin. The easy cooking, the plans to decorate his tree. How the conversation had naturally shifted to future possibilities—trips they could take, things they could do together. How Megan had grown quieter and quieter before finally exploding with accusations about him planning their entire year without asking her.

"And I wasn't planning," Kyle said, his frustration bleeding into his voice. "I was just—I was excited. I was thinking out loud about fun things we could do together because I love her dad... and I see her in my future, and I thought she felt the same way."

"Did you ask if she felt the same way?"

The question was gentle but pointed. Kyle sat back on his heels, considering.

"Not in those exact words. But she knows how I feel. I've told her I love her. I've been completely honest about wanting a future with her."

"That's not what I asked." Mitch's voice remained patient. "Did you ask how she felt about those specific plans? Or did you assume because you wanted those things, she must want them too?"

Kyle opened his mouth to defend himself, then closed it. He thought back to Wednesday night. To him, talking about Florida and birthdays and anniversary parties while Megan grew increasingly quiet. Had he asked what she wanted? Or had he just kept building this vision of their future without checking if she was building it with him?

"I thought I was sharing," he said quietly. "Not deciding. They were only ideas."

"Maybe you were. But son, there's a difference between sharing an idea and planning a year's worth of trips without pausing to gauge someone's reaction." Mitch's expression was kind but honest. "Especially someone who might need more time to process what a future together actually means."

"But I didn't think—" Kyle stopped, trying to organize his thoughts. "She's the one. I know she is. And I thought—I thought she knew that too. I thought we were on the same page."

"Maybe you are. But you're reading that page at different speeds." Mitch reached for the toilet bowl, and together they lifted it back into position. "Let me tell you something about your mother."

Kyle held the bowl steady while his father aligned it over the new wax ring. "What about Mom?"

"When I asked her to marry me, she said no."

That got Kyle's full attention. "What?"

"Said no. Told me she needed more time." Mitch's voice was calm, matter-of-fact. "Took her two years to finally say yes."

"Two years?"

"Two years." Mitch began securing the bolts, his movements practiced and sure. "Her parents had just gone through this awful, ugly divorce. I mean truly devastating—the kind where lawyers get rich and everyone else gets destroyed. She'd watched her mother fall apart and her father become someone she barely recognized, and the whole thing made her terrified of marriage."

Kyle processed this information, trying to reconcile it with the strong, confident woman his mother was now. "I didn't know all that."

"It's not something we talk about much. But son, it taught me something important." Mitch looked up from his work, his expression serious. "My timeline wasn't her timeline. I was ready to get married, ready to build a life together, ready for all of it. But she needed time to believe that love could last. That marriage didn't have to end the way her parents' marriage had ended. And the most loving thing I could do wasn't to convince her or pressure her or prove how ready I was. It was to be patient. To be present. To let her work through her fears at her own pace."

"But you waited two years?"

"I would've waited longer if that's what she needed." Mitch's voice was firm. "Because I loved her, and love isn't just about being ready yourself. It's about understanding that the person you love might need different things at different times. That your certainty doesn't automatically become their certainty just because you share it."

Kyle sat back against the bathroom wall, his father's words settling over him. "You think I pushed too hard."

"I think you're excited about your future with Megan, and that's good. That's how it should be." Mitch reconnected the supply line, testing the connection. "But son, women process things differently than we men do. We see something we want, we make a plan, we move forward. Pretty straightforward. But women—they need to examine things from every angle. They need to think through not just what they want but what it means and whether they can trust it and whether they deserve it."

"That's not fair. Of course Megan deserves—"

"I know she does. You know she does. But does she know she does?" Mitch's question hung in the air between them. "Because from what you've told me about her childhood, she's spent most of her life believing she doesn't deserve good things. Her father left. Her mother chose someone else and left. She's been conditioned to expect abandonment."

Kyle felt something twist in his chest. "I'm not going to leave her."

"I know that. But she doesn't. Not bone-deep, not yet." Mitch stood, brushing off his jeans. "And you planning a year's worth of trips without pausing to check if she's ready for that level of commitment—that probably felt overwhelming. Not because she doesn't want those things, but because wanting them means being vulnerable. It means trusting that you won't do what everyone else in her life has done. Kyle... I imagine you scared the dickens out of the poor woman.

"

"So what am I supposed to do?" Kyle heard the frustration in his own voice. "Just not talk about the future? Pretend I don't know what I want?"

"No. You be honest about what you want while also being patient. You let her know you're all in while also giving her space to get there at her own pace." Mitch turned on the water valve, checking for leaks. "You do what I did with your mother—you prove through your actions that you're not going anywhere. That her fears don't scare you off. That you're willing to wait as long as it takes for her to trust what you're building together... and most importantly trust herself."

Kyle watched his father work, the words sinking in slowly.

"You're a lot like me, son." Mitch smiled slightly. "You see what you want, and you go after it. You make decisions quickly and stick with them. Megan's more like your mother was—she needs time to trust her own feelings. Time to believe good things can last. And that's not a weakness. It's just a different way of moving through the world."

"Son, here's my advice. Be present and be patient. You show up and support Megan and prove through your consistency that your love isn't conditional on her matching your timeline." Mitch tested the toilet flush, nodding with satisfaction when everything worked properly. "And son? That waiting? That patience? That's not passive. That's one of the most active, loving things you can do—giving someone the time and space to choose you freely, without pressure."

Kyle stood, helping his father gather the tools. He thought about Wednesday night. About Megan's panic when he'd mentioned Florida and birthday trips and anniversary celebrations. About how she'd accused him of planning without asking, when really what she'd been saying was I'm scared of how much I want this.

He'd heard the accusation but missed the fear underneath it. Missed that her panic wasn't about his timeline—it was about her own certainty and the vulnerability it required.

"I really messed up, didn't I?" he said quietly.

"You had a fight. It happens." Mitch clapped him on the shoulder. "The question is what you do next. Do you push harder to convince her you're right? Or do you step back and let her come to you when she's ready? That girl loves you, Kyle. Anyone with eyes can see it. She just needs to learn to trust it. To trust herself. And that's work she has to do—you can't do it for her."

They walked back to Kyle's cabin together, the morning sun climbing higher and warming the air slightly. Kyle felt something loosening in his chest—not resolution exactly, but understanding. His father was right. He'd been so focused on his own certainty, his own readiness, his own timeline, that he'd missed what Megan actually needed from him.

Not more declarations of love. Not more plans for the future. Just patience. Presence. Proof that he wasn't going anywhere regardless of how long it took her to believe in them.

At Kyle's cabin, Mitch paused before heading back to his truck. "You know what your mother told me when she finally said yes to marrying me?"

"What?"

"She said waiting those two years was hard and miserable at times for her, but she learned a lot about herself while standing her ground. She learned to believe that she deserved to be loved the way I loved her." Mitch's expression softened. "Megan might need the same thing. Time to believe she deserves you. Time to trust that what she feels is real and lasting. And the best thing you can do is give her that time."

Kyle nodded. "Thanks, Dad."

"Anytime." Mitch headed toward his truck, then paused and turned back. "You know what? Why don't come and work with me on that fence repair your mother's been after me about? Keep your hands busy, keep your mind occupied. Things have a way of working themselves out, son. No sense driving yourself crazy thinking in circles when you could be doing something productive."

Kyle looked at his father—at the man who'd waited two years for the woman he loved, who'd learned patience not as passive waiting but as active love—and felt grateful beyond words.

"Yeah," he said. "Let's do that."

Chapter 41

Megan's hands gripped the steering wheel so tightly her knuckles had gone white. She'd been sitting in Kyle's driveway for three minutes now, the engine off, her heart hammering against her ribs like it was trying to escape her chest.

Through the windshield, she could see his cabin—solid logs and wide porch, smoke curling from the chimney into the cold December morning. His truck sat in its usual spot, which meant he was home. Which meant she couldn't use his absence as an excuse to drive away and try again later.

She'd spent all of yesterday alone in her apartment, thinking through everything Leslie had said. Examining her fears from every angle. Recognizing patterns she'd been running since she was thirteen years old. And she'd come to one unavoidable conclusion: she owed Kyle an apology. A real one. Not deflecting blame or making excuses, but taking full responsibility for the hurt she'd caused.

She climbed out of the car before she could second-guess herself again. The morning air was sharp and cold, her breath fogging in white clouds as she walked up the porch steps. Her hand trembled slightly as she raised it to knock.

Three raps. Then, there was nothing but the sound of her own heartbeat in her ears.

Footsteps approached from inside. The door swung open.

Kyle stood there in jeans and a flannel shirt, his hair slightly mussed like he'd been running his hands through it. His expression shifted from surprise to something that looked like hope, carefully guarded but unmistakable.

"Megan."

"Hi. Can I come in?"

He stepped back immediately, gesturing her inside. "Of course."

The cabin was warm; the fireplace crackling cheerfully in the living room beyond the entryway.

Kyle closed the door and turned to face her, his hands sliding into his pockets. Waiting.

Megan took a breath and dove in before she could lose her nerve.

"I was wrong."

Kyle's expression shifted slightly. "Megan—"

"Please. Let me say this." She clasped her hands together to keep them from shaking. "I've been thinking for the past few days about what happened Wednesday night, and I was wrong. Not about needing time—that part was true. But I was wrong about the reason I needed it."

"What do you mean?"

"I told you I was scared because you were planning our future too fast. I accused you of moving too quickly, of assuming too much, of not including me in decisions." Megan forced herself to meet his eyes. "But that wasn't the real problem. The real problem was that I was terrified of my own certainty about you."

Kyle went very still. "Your certainty?"

"I'm in love with you. I'm so completely bone-deep certain about you that it scares me more than anything I've ever felt. And when you started talking about Florida and birthday trips and family vacations, it wasn't your planning that panicked me. It was realizing I wanted all of it. Every single thing you described. I wanted it so much it made me feel vulnerable in a way I didn't know how to handle."

"Megan—"

"I've been using your pace as an excuse." She needed to get all of this out, needed him to understand. "Telling myself you were moving too fast when really I was just scared of admitting how ready I was to move with you. Because being that certain means being that vulnerable. It means having something real to lose. And I've spent most of my life protecting myself from exactly that kind of loss."

Kyle took a step toward her, his expression softening.

"I sabotaged us," Megan continued, the words tumbling out faster now. "I picked a fight over something that wasn't really the problem because the real problem—loving you this much—felt too scary to face. And I hurt you in the process, and I'm so sorry. I'm so sorry I made you feel like your feelings were wrong or too much or something to apologize for when really they were exactly right."

"Megan, stop." Kyle's voice was gentle but firm. He closed the distance between them, his hands coming up to cup her face. "Breathe."

She did, dragging in air that felt too thin.

"I talked to my dad yesterday," Kyle said quietly. "He helped me understand a few things about myself and what you might be going through."

Megan let out a nervous laugh. "I reached out to your sister to talk. She's the only person I felt would listen to me without judging me."

"You talked to Leslie?" Surprise flickered across Kyle's face.

"I showed up at her apartment at 8:30 pm Friday night, looking like a disaster, and she let me in and listened to me fall apart." Megan managed a shaky smile. "She's a good sister. And a good friend."

"She is." Kyle's thumbs brushed her cheekbones, the touch achingly tender. "What did she tell you?"

"That I was afraid of my own certainty. That I wanted everything you described, but the vulnerability scared me more than the loneliness of being alone. That love requires risk, and I needed to stop protecting myself from happiness." Megan covered his hands with hers. "She was right. About all of it."

"My dad said something similar to me. That my timeline wasn't necessarily yours. That the most loving thing I could do was be patient while you worked through your fears at your own pace." Kyle's expression was open and honest in a way that made Megan's chest ache. "I wasn't trying to pressure you Wednesday night. I was just excited about our future, and I got carried away thinking out loud without checking if you were ready for that conversation."

"I know you weren't pressuring me. I know that now." Megan held his gaze. "You were sharing your feelings honestly, and I panicked because I felt the same way and didn't know how to trust it."

"So, what do we do?" Kyle asked quietly. "How do we move forward from here?"

"I need you to be patient with me. I need time to learn how to trust my own instincts without constantly waiting for something to go wrong. I need to practice believing I deserve this—deserve you—without sabotaging it when things get too good. I need you to call me out when I start spiraling."

"I can do that." Kyle's response was immediate, certain.

"And I need to be honest about what I'm actually feeling instead of deflecting or making excuses." Megan took a shaky breath. "Like right now, being honest means telling you that I love you. That I want the Florida trip even though that scares me to death, and I'm not sure if Mom will welcome us or act like I'm just some random person she used to know. I want a birthday celebration in May to celebrate me... a big one because I've always wanted a gigantic birthday party with fun and laughter and people I love just coming together and celebrating. I want that family vacation to celebrate your parents' anniversary... you, me, Leslie, and your mom and dad and I vote for a cruise. I want you to know that I'm just as certain as you are about us. That I'm all in, even though being all in terrifies me."

Kyle's expression shifted into something that looked like wonder. "You're all in?"

"Completely." Megan felt tears building but didn't try to stop them. "No more negative thinking. No more waiting for the other shoe to drop. No more protecting myself from happiness because I'm scared it won't last. I want this. I want you. I want the future we can build together."

"Megan." Her name came out rough with emotion. Then Kyle was kissing her—urgent and sweet and full of relief and love and promise. His arms came around her, pulling her close, and Megan melted into him with a small sound that might have been a laugh or a sob or both.

When they finally broke apart, both slightly breathless, Kyle rested his forehead against hers.

"I love you," he said. "I'm so in love with you it's ridiculous."

"I love you too." Saying it felt like freedom. Like choosing courage over fear. "And I'm sorry I made you doubt that. I'm sorry I let my fear hurt you."

"We're okay." Kyle's hands slid down to link with hers. "We're going to be okay. Better than okay."

"Yep." Megan squeezed his hands, feeling certainty settle in her chest beside the fear. Not replacing it—she'd probably always have that fear, at least a little. But making room for something stronger. Something worth fighting for. "I need to communicate better. I need to talk through things with you instead of letting them build up."

Kyle pulled back slightly to look at her properly. "No more assumptions on my part about what you're ready for. I'll ask instead of just planning."

"And no more deflecting on my part when I'm scared. I'll tell you the real reason instead of picking fights over surface issues."

"Deal." Kyle's smile was soft and genuine and full of love. "So. What do you need right now? Space? Time? Do you want to talk more, or—"

"I want to be with you." Megan heard the certainty in her own voice and felt proud of it. "I want to spend today together, doing normal things."

"I'd like that too." Kyle kissed her again, quick and light.

Megan felt something warm bloom in her chest—part joy, part amusement, part wonder that they could be here after everything. That they could go from fighting to reconciling to making Sunday plans like this was exactly where they were supposed to be.

"So, Mr. Porter." She let a teasing note enter her voice. "What are your plans for today?"

Kyle's smile widened, his hazel eyes crinkling at the corners. "Well, Ms. Caldwell, what are you thinking?"

"I'm thinking we should take a hike." Megan rose up on her toes to kiss him once more, sweet and certain. "I remember someone mentioning Crystal Falls?"

"Best idea I've heard all week." Kyle wrapped his arms around her waist, lifting her slightly off the ground in a hug that made her laugh.

When he set her down, his expression was tender and serious. "Thank you for coming here. For being brave enough to have this conversation. For choosing us."

"Thank you for being patient with me." Megan touched his face, memorizing this moment. "For loving me even when I'm scared. For not giving up on me."

"Never." Kyle's voice was firm. "I'm not going anywhere, Megan. Not now, not ever. You're stuck with me."

"Good." She meant it completely. "Because I'm not going anywhere either."

They stood there for another moment, wrapped in each other's arms, the fire crackling behind them and the promise of a hike to a frozen waterfall waiting ahead. Outside, snow was falling, big flakes drifting past the windows like a benediction.

Megan thought about the girl who'd driven into Mistletoe Falls weeks ago with everything she owned packed in her car. That girl had been running from her old life, desperate and afraid and convinced good things weren't meant for people like her.

She wasn't that girl anymore.

She was someone who owned a business and had friends and a community. Someone who'd learned to make candy and trust herself and take up space without apologizing. Someone who was learning, slowly but surely, that love didn't have to mean loss. That certainty didn't require a safety net. That sometimes the bravest thing was letting yourself be happy.

Kyle pulled back and grinned. "I should probably change into hiking clothes. And grab water bottles. I'll grab the emergency kit just in case. Don't forget to grab your phone. Do you need hiking boots? Mom might have an extra pair up at the lodge. Oh, and the trail can be slippery this time of year, so we'll need to be careful on the—"

"Kyle."

"Yeah?"

"You're planning again."

He stopped mid-thought, then laughed—a real, genuine sound that made Megan's heart feel too full for her chest. "You're right. I'm a work in progress."

"We both are." Megan laced her fingers through his. "But we'll figure it out together."

"Together," Kyle agreed, and the word felt like a promise.

Chapter 42

"Megan, these truffles are absolutely incredible." Ann said as she reached for her third one, holding it up to admire the perfect chocolate coating before popping it in her mouth with an expression of pure bliss. "You made these yourself?"

"I did. Kay and Linda have been teaching me, but this batch was all me. Start to finish. They're not perfect, but they'll do."

"She's being modest," Kyle interjected from his spot beside her on the Porters' oversized sectional. "She's been perfecting her technique for weeks. These are professional quality."

"They really are." Mitch selected a dark chocolate truffle from the beautiful tray Megan had brought. "I might have to hide the rest of these before your mother eats them all."

"You absolutely will not," Ann protested, though she was laughing. "It's Christmas Eve. Calories don't count."

"That's what you always say... even when it's not a holiday," Leslie pointed out from her position curled up in the oversized armchair, already working on her second truffle.

"Hush," Ann said with a grin.

Megan watched the easy teasing between them, warmth blooming in her chest. This was what a family looked like. Not perfect, not without its quirks and dynamics, but full of love and laughter and the kind of comfort that came from truly belonging.

The evening had unfolded like a dream she'd never dared to have. Dinner had been a feast—Ann's famous prime rib with all the traditional sides, followed by three different desserts. The Porter family Christmas tree dominated one corner of the great room, its branches heavy with ornaments that clearly held decades of memories. Presents had been opened amid much laughter and a few happy tears.

Ann and Mitch had given her a beautiful wooden recipe box already filled with recipe cards that Ann had taken the time to fill out with Porter family recipes. Along with a framed photo of the entire family taken at Thanksgiving. Leslie's gift had been a stunning ornament personalized with "Megan's First Christmas in Mistletoe Falls 2024" that had made Megan cry happy tears and a beautiful cashmere sweater.

Kyle's official gift had been a gorgeous leather-bound journal with her initials embossed on the cover. "For writing down your candy experiments," he'd said. "Or whatever else you want to remember."

Now, sitting in the cozy warmth of the Porters' living room with Christmas music playing softly and the tree lights twinkling, Megan felt a contentment so complete it was almost overwhelming.

"Megan?" Kyle's voice pulled her from her thoughts. "Want to step outside for a minute? Get some fresh air?"

"In December?" Leslie raised an eyebrow. "It's like twenty degrees out there."

"I'll turn on the porch heaters." Kyle was already standing, offering Megan his hand. "Just for a few minutes."

Something in his expression made Megan's heart skip. "Okay."

She followed him through the house to the back door that led onto the covered porch overlooking the mountains. Kyle flipped the switch for the porch heaters, and within moments, the space was filling with warmth despite the cold night air.

The view was breathtaking. The Smoky Mountains rose dark against a sky absolutely packed with stars, the kind of brilliant display only visible far from city lights. Fresh snow covered everything, pristine and untouched, glowing faintly in the starlight.

"It's beautiful out here," Megan said, moving to stand at the railing.

"It is." Kyle moved beside her. "I wanted to talk to you. Away from everyone else for a minute."

Megan turned to look at him, her heart beating faster. "Okay."

"This past month and a half has been—" Kyle paused, seeming to search for words. "It's been the best time of my life. Since the day you drove into Mistletoe Falls, everything has felt different. Better. More complete. Like I was waiting for you without even knowing it."

"Kyle—"

"Let me finish." His smile was gentle. "I know we've had our stumbles. I know you're still learning to trust this. To trust us. And I want you to know that I understand that, and I'm okay with it. I'll wait as long as you need. I'll be patient while you work through your fears because I know—I know—that what we have is worth it."

Megan's throat felt tight. "I know that too."

"Good." Kyle reached into his pocket, and Megan's breath caught as he pulled out a small velvet box. "Because I have something for you."

He opened the box, and even in the dim porch light, the ring inside sparkled. It was gorgeous—a simple, elegant design with a round diamond set in what looked like rose gold, with smaller stones set into the band. Classic but unique. Traditional but special. Perfect.

"Kyle." Her voice came out barely above a whisper.

"Before you panic," he said quickly, "this can be whatever you want it to be. If you want to consider it a promise ring—a symbol of my commitment while you take more time—that's okay. If you want to call it an engagement ring, that's okay too. There's no pressure, no timeline, no expectations. Just—this is me telling you that I'm certain. That I want to spend my life with you. However that looks, whatever pace feels right to you."

Megan stared at the ring.

She looked up from the ring to Kyle's face. His expression was open, hopeful, and patient. Ready to wait as long as she needed. Ready to give her whatever time, whatever space, and whatever processing she required.

And she realized with perfect clarity that she didn't need any of it.

"Engagement ring," she said.

Kyle's eyes widened. "What?"

"Engagement ring." Megan's voice was stronger now, certain. "I choose engagement ring."

"Megan, are you—are you sure? We can—"

"I'm sure." She felt tears building, but they were happy tears, joyful tears. "I'm completely sure. I don't need more time to know that I want to spend my life with you. I love you, and I want to marry you."

Kyle's expression shifted from surprise to wonder to pure joy. Then he was moving, dropping to one knee on the porch while still holding the ring box.

"Then I'm going to do this properly." His voice was thick with emotion. "Megan Caldwell, I love you more than I knew it was possible to love someone. You've made my life fuller and richer and better in ways I didn't even know I was missing. You're brilliant and kind and brave and absolutely perfect. Will you marry me?"

"Yes." The word came out on a sob-laugh. "Yes, of course yes."

Kyle pulled the ring from the box with slightly shaking hands and slid it onto her finger. It fit almost perfectly; the diamond catching the porch light and throwing sparkles across both of them. Then he was standing and pulling her into his arms, kissing her with a sweetness that made her knees weak.

When they finally broke apart, both slightly breathless and definitely crying, Kyle rested his forehead against hers.

"I can't believe you said yes," he whispered.

Megan laughed, the sound watery but genuine. "You asked, and I said yes."

"We should probably go tell my family." Kyle pulled back to look at her properly, his smile so wide it had to hurt. "They're going to lose their minds."

"Your mom is going to cry."

"She will." Kyle kissed her again, quick and joyful. "Ready?"

Megan looked down at her hand, at the ring that represented everything she'd been too afraid to want and was now brave enough to claim. Then she looked at Kyle—steady, patient, and loving Kyle.

"Ready," she said.

They walked back inside hand in hand, the warmth of the house enveloping them immediately. In the great room, Ann and Mitch were still on the sectional, while Leslie had claimed another truffle and was flipping through a coffee-table book about Christmas traditions.

Megan walked straight to the center of the room and held out her left hand.

For a moment, there was absolute silence. Then Ann gasped, her hand flying to her mouth.

"Is that—" She couldn't seem to finish the sentence.

"She said yes," Kyle announced, his voice full of joy and pride. "She said yes!"

Ann was up and moving before anyone else could react, pulling Megan into a fierce hug. "Oh, sweetheart! Oh, this is wonderful! This is—Mitch, they're engaged!"

"I can see that, honey." But Mitch was grinning as he stood to clap Kyle on the shoulder. "Congratulations, son."

Leslie set down her truffle and walked over to examine the ring more closely. "It's beautiful. Good choice, Kyle." Then she looked at Megan with a knowing smile. "Though I have to ask—did my brother give you his whole speech about how this could be a promise ring if you weren't ready and you could take all the time you need?"

"He did," Megan confirmed, laughing through happy tears.

"Of course he did." Leslie pulled her brother into a hug. "You're such a dork. A sweet, romantic dork, but still a dork. And by the way in the future... when you're in your office practicing a big speech... close your door next time. I and half the town heard you fumbling through figuring out how to ask Megan to marry you."

Kyle laughed. "Sorry... but hey, I was trying to be respectful and figure out what to say to her and make sure she knew I wasn't trying to rush anything!"

"And I love you for it," Megan said, squeezing his hand.

Ann was crying openly now, and Mitch had his arm around her shoulders while also looking suspiciously damp-eyed himself. Leslie was grinning like she'd won some kind of bet, and Kyle—Kyle was looking at Megan like she'd hung the moon and stars.

"We need champagne," Ann declared, wiping at her eyes. "This calls for champagne. Mitch, where did we put the good bottle?"

"I'll get it," Mitch said, already heading toward the kitchen.

"And we need to take pictures," Ann continued. "Oh, and call people! Do you want to call your mother, Megan? We should—"

"Mom," Kyle interrupted gently. "Maybe give us a minute just to enjoy this?"

"Right. Yes. Of course." But Ann was still beaming, still radiating joy so complete it was almost tangible.

Leslie sidled up to Megan while Kyle was accepting congratulations from his father. "So. You chose engagement ring immediately, huh?"

"I did."

"No hesitation?"

"None." Megan looked at her ring again, at the way it caught the Christmas tree lights and sparkled.

"Good for you." Leslie's voice was warm, genuine. "Welcome to the family, Megan."

"Thank you." Megan pulled her into a hug. "For everything. For being my friend."

"That's what sisters are for," Leslie said against her shoulder.

Sisters. The word settled into Megan's chest alongside all the other impossibly good things that had happened tonight. Family. Belonging. Love. Forever.

Kyle appeared at her side, slipping his arm around her waist. "You okay?"

"Better than okay." Megan leaned into him, feeling his solid warmth against her side. "I'm engaged to the man I love, I'm surrounded by my found family, and I'm wearing the most beautiful ring I've ever seen. I'm pretty sure this is the best Christmas Eve of my entire life."

"Mine too." Kyle kissed her temple. "And it's only going to get better from here."

Mitch returned with champagne and glasses; Ann was already planning an engagement party, and Leslie was teasing Kyle. The

Christmas tree twinkled in the corner, carols played softly from the speakers, and outside the windows, snow was falling.

Megan looked around at this family that had become hers, at this man who loved her enough to give her all the time she needed while being brave enough to ask for forever anyway, at this life she'd built from nothing but determination and inherited candy recipes and the decision to stay instead of run.

She'd driven into Mistletoe Falls weeks ago with everything she owned packed in boxes, expecting nothing more than a fresh start and maybe a chance to finally figure out who she was supposed to be.

Instead, she'd found home.

She'd found love.

She'd found herself.

And standing in the warm glow of the Porter family's Christmas Eve celebration, wearing an engagement ring and surrounded by laughter and joy and unconditional acceptance, Megan made one more choice.

She chose to believe that this was real.

She chose to trust that it would last.

She chose finally and completely to let herself be happy.

Leave A Review

If you enjoyed this book, please consider leaving an honest review on Amazon

Visit Our Website:

www.tarabaisden.com

Visit Our Amazon Author Page HERE

Find Us On Social Media:

Facebook

Facebook Author Page

Instagram

Also by Tara Baisden

<u>Laurel Ridge Series</u>

#1. Season of Hope

#2. Finding Grace

#3. His Perfect Plan

#4. Love Redeemed

#5 Snowbound Blessings

#6 Sheltered Hearts

#7 Restoring Faith

#8 Love Rekindled

#9 Where She Belongs

#10 Shelter in His Arms

#11 Where Love Stands

#12 The Pieces We Mend

#13 Where Love Grows

#14 Where Hearts Heal

#15 Harvest of the Heart

#16 Heart of the Season

#17 Season of Forgiveness

#18 Threads of Grace

Riverbend Valley Series

#1 A Cowboy's Second Chance

#2 Wanderlust & Wild Horses

#3 Heartstrings on the Horizon

#4 Runaway in Riverbend Valley

#5 Mended Hearts

#6 Healing Hearts

#7 Home to Lost Creek

Mistletoe Falls Series

#1 Whisk Me Under the Mistletoe

#2 Once Upon a Christmas

#3 The Mistletoe Express

#4 Candy Canes & Sweet Dreams

#5 Wrapped Up in Christmas

#6 Jingle All the Way Home

About The Author

Tara Baisden writes the kind of sweet, wholesome romances that feel cozy, comforting, and full of heart. She's the author of the beloved *Laurel Ridge* and *Riverbend Valley* inspirational series, as well as the *Mistletoe Falls* series, where Christmas magic and small-town charm are always on the menu.

A proud West Virginian, Tara makes her home on a peaceful stretch of mountain land where deer wander past her windows, the garden never quite weeds itself, and her pets supervise her writing schedule with great dedication. When she's not dreaming up stories of love, faith, and second chances, you'll likely find her quilting, digging in the dirt (sometimes successfully), hiking in the mountains, or curled up with a good book.

Family means everything to Tara, and some of her favorite moments are spent on the porch with loved ones—sharing stories, laughter, and maybe a slice of pie (because every good gathering needs pie). She also loves exploring the rich history of her home state and can't resist stopping at any bookstore she comes across.

Tara's readers often say her characters feel like family and her fictional towns like places they'd love to visit. Through every story, she hopes to inspire faith, celebrate love, and remind readers of the beauty found in life's simple joys.

You can connect with Tara at www.tarabaisden.com or follow her on social media for new releases, behind-the-scenes peeks, and the occasional glimpse of country life.

About Mistletoe Falls

Welcome to the fictional town of Mistletoe Falls, Tennessee!

Where Christmas Magic Lives Year-Round

*H*igh *in the Tennessee mountains, where winter lingers longer and Christmas spirit fills the air year-round, lies a town that feels almost too perfect to be real and looks like it stepped straight out of a holiday postcard.*

The winding mountain road to Mistletoe Falls tells you this isn't just any destination. Scenic Route 265 climbs higher into the Smoky Mountains with each breathtaking curve, past ancient trees heavy with snow that arch over the road like nature's own cathedral. But it's the final approach that steals your breath—crossing the enchanting Snowbell Covered Bridge, draped in evergreen garland and twinkling lights, as it spans the crystal waters of Mistletoe Creek below.

Beyond the bridge, the Welcome Pavilion greets every arrival with a hand-carved wooden sign: *"Welcome to Mistletoe Falls—Home of the Christmas Spirit."* The cheerful red pavilion, complete with candy cane striping and an archway of year-round twinkle lights, promises that something wonderful awaits just around the bend.

Mistletoe Falls (population 6,200) nestles in a perfect valley where the musical sound of cascading waterfalls mingles with church bells and children's laughter. The town spreads gracefully along Mistletoe Creek, whose series of waterfalls create the melodic backdrop to daily life.

This is Tennessee's beloved Christmas Town—because Christmas simply lives here. From the gas lamp streetlights wrapped in evergreen garland to the horse-drawn carriages clip-clopping down brick streets, every detail whispers of simpler times and sweeter moments.

The town square draws everyone like a magnet, centered around a Victorian gazebo where carols drift through the air and community life unfolds. Ancient oak trees frame the square, their branches creating natural shelter for the wooden benches below—each dedicated to a beloved neighbor who helped shape this special place. Thousands of lights transform the square into pure magic.

Mistletoe Lane curves gently around the town square before branching into charming side streets lined with century-old brick buildings. Each storefront tells a story through hand-carved details and cheerful striped awnings in hunter green, burgundy, and cream. Wide brick sidewalks invite leisurely strolls, while cozy benches appear just when you need them most.

The architecture whispers of careful love—original stonework preserved alongside modern conveniences, ensuring comfort while honoring the past. Three-story buildings house everything from the town bakery to the bookshop, with apartments above where business owners live.

From November through February, Mistletoe Falls transforms into a living snow globe. The special mountain microclimate ensures gentle snowfall that blankets everything in pristine white, while temperatures hover between 15 and 45 degrees—perfect for outdoor adventures and cozy indoor moments.

The partially frozen waterfalls become nature's chandeliers, catching winter light like thousands of diamonds. Snow-covered trails wind through frosted forests where the only sounds are your footsteps and the distant laughter from the town below. Long winter evenings mean crackling fireplaces, hot cider, and the kind of conversations that matter.

The Mistletoe Lodge stands as the town's crown jewel—a century-old mountain lodge with wraparound porches and stone fireplaces where love stories begin over morning coffee and evening wine. Its guest rooms blend historic charm with modern comfort, creating the perfect retreat for visitors who never quite want to leave.

The Snowbell Covered Bridge serves as more than transportation; it's where proposals happen and first kisses are shared, sheltered from mountain weather while framing perfect views of the approaching town.

The Mistletoe Christmas Tree Farm spreads across rolling hills on the town's outskirts, where families create memories among rows of Fraser firs and the air smells like pine and possibility.

What makes Mistletoe Falls magical isn't just its picture-perfect setting—it's the people who call it home. Three generations often work side by side in family businesses, while newcomers quickly discover they're not visitors but neighbors-in-waiting.

Local business owners coordinate holiday decorations and community events with the kind of collaboration that creates the seamless magic visitors remember long after they've returned home. This isn't performed charm—it's the real thing, preserved and protected by people who understand what they have.

In Mistletoe Falls, Christmas isn't a season—it's a way of life. The town square's gazebo hosts summer concerts alongside winter caroling. Local shops maintain touches of holiday magic through every season, because visitors quickly learn that any time is the right time to discover this special place.

The waterfalls provide cooling mists in summer and ice sculptures in winter. Mountain trails offer wildflower walks in spring and dramatic vistas in fall. But somehow, every season here feels like it's building toward December's grand celebration.

9 781966 093398